The 500

Matthew
Quirk

The 500

headline

First published in Great Britain in 2012 by
HEADLINE PUBLISHING GROUP

1

Cataloguing in Publication Data is available from the British Library

Hardback ISBN 978 0 7553 8740 3
Trade paperback ISBN 978 0 7553 8741 0

Typeset in Palatino by Avon DataSet Ltd,
Bidford-on-Avon, Warwickshire

Printed and bound by CPI Group (UK) Ltd, Croydon, CR0 4YY

Headline's policy is to use papers that are natural, renewable and
recyclable products and made from wood grown in sustainable forests.
The logging and manufacturing processes are expected to conform
to the environmental regulations of the country of origin.

HEADLINE PUBLISHING GROUP
An Hachette UK Company
338 Euston Road
London NW1 3BH

www.headline.co.uk
www.hachette.co.uk

For Heather

Prologue

Miroslav and Aleksandar filled the front seats of the Range Rover across the street. They wore their customary diplomatic uniforms – dark Brionis tailored close – but the two Serbs looked angrier than usual. Aleksandar lifted his right hand high enough to flash me a glint of his Sig Sauer. A master of subtlety, that Alex. I wasn't particularly worried about the two bruisers sitting up front, however. The worst thing they could do was kill me, and right now that looked like one of my better options.

The rear window rolled down and there was Rado, glaring. He preferred to make his threats with a dinner napkin. He lifted one up and dabbed gently at the corners of his mouth. They called him the King of Hearts because, well, he ate people's hearts. The way I heard it was that he'd read an article in the *Economist* about some nineteen-year-old Liberian warlord with a taste for human flesh. Rado decided that sort of flagrant evil would give his criminal brand the edge it needed in a crowded global marketplace, so he picked up the habit.

I wasn't even all that worried about him tucking into my heart. That's usually fatal and, like I said, would greatly simplify my dilemma. The problem was that he knew about Annie. And my getting another loved one killed because of my mistakes was one of the things that made Rado's fork look like the easy out.

I nodded to Rado and started up the street. It was a beautiful May morning in the nation's capital, with a sky like blue porcelain. The blood that had soaked through my shirt was drying, stiff and scratchy. My left foot dragged on the asphalt. My knee had swollen to the size of a rugby ball. I tried to concentrate on the knee to keep my mind off the injury to my chest, because if I thought about that – not the pain so much as the sheer creepiness of it – I was sure I would pass out.

As I approached, the office looked as classy as ever: a three-story Federal mansion set back in the woods of Kalorama, among the embassies and chanceries. It was home to the Davies Group, Washington, DC's most respected strategic consulting and government affairs firm, where I guess technically I may have still been employed. I fished my keys from my pocket and waved them in front of a gray pad beside the door lock. No go.

But Davies was expecting me. I looked up at the closed-circuit camera. The lock buzzed.

Inside the foyer, I greeted the head of security and noted the baby Glock he'd pulled from its holster and was holding tight near his thigh. Then I turned to Marcus, my boss, and nodded by way of hello. He stood on the other side of the metal detector, waved me through, then frisked me neck to ankle. He was checking for weapons, and for wires. Marcus had made a nice long career with those hands, killing.

'Strip,' Marcus said. I obliged, shirt and pants. Even Marcus winced when he saw the skin of my chest, puckering around the staples. He took a quick look inside my drawers, then seemed satisfied I wasn't bugged. I suited back up.

'Envelope,' he said, and gestured to the manila one I was carrying.

'Not until we have a deal,' I said. The envelope was the

only thing keeping me alive, so I was a little reluctant to let it go. 'This will go wide if I disappear.'

Marcus nodded. That kind of insurance was standard industry practice. He'd taught me so himself. He led me upstairs to Davies's office and stood guard by the door as I stepped inside.

There, standing by the windows, looking out over downtown DC, was the one thing I was worried about, the option that seemed much worse than getting carved up by Rado: it was Davies, who turned to me with a grandfather's smile.

'It's good to see you, Mike. I'm glad you decided to come back to us.'

He wanted a deal. He wanted to feel like he owned me again. And that's what I was afraid of more than anything else, that I would say yes.

'I don't know how things got this bad,' he said. 'Your father . . . I'm sorry.'

Dead, as of last night. Marcus's handiwork.

'I want you to know we didn't have anything to do with that.'

I said nothing.

'You might want to ask your Serbian friends about it. We can protect you, Mike; we can protect the people you love.' He told me to sit down at the far end of the conference table, and he moved a little closer. 'Just say it and all this is over. Come back to us, Mike. It only takes one word: yes.'

And that was the weird thing about all his games, all the torture. At the end of the day he really thought he was doing me a favor. He wanted me back, thought of me as a son, a younger version of himself. He had to corrupt me, to own me, or else everything he believed, his whole sordid world, was a lie.

My dad chose to die instead of playing ball with Davies. Die proud rather than live corrupted. He got out. It was so neat and clean. But I didn't have that luxury. My death would be only the beginning of the pain. I had no good options. That's why I was here, about to shake hands with the devil.

I placed the envelope on the table. Inside it was the only thing Henry was afraid of: evidence of a mostly forgotten murder. His only mistake. The one bit of carelessness in Davies's long career. It was a piece of himself he'd lost fifty years before, and he wanted it back.

'This is the only real trust, Mike. When two people know each other's secrets. When they have each other cornered. Mutually assured destruction. Anything else is bullshit sentimentality. I'm proud of you. It's the same play I made when I was starting out.'

Henry always told me that every man has his price. He'd found mine. If I said yes, I'd have my life back – the house, the money, the friends, the respectable facade I'd always wanted. If I said no, it was all over, for me, for Annie.

'Name your price, Mike. You can have it. Anyone who's anyone has made a deal like this on the way up. It's how the game is played. What do you say?'

It was an old bargain. Swap your soul for all the kingdoms of the world and their glory. There would be haggling over details, of course. I wasn't going to sell myself on the cheap, but that was quickly squared away.

'I will give you this evidence,' I said, tapping my finger on the envelope, 'and guarantee that you will never have to worry about it again. In exchange, Rado goes away. The police leave me alone. I get my life back. And I become a full partner.'

'And from now on, you're mine,' Henry said. 'A full partner in the wet work too. When we find Rado, you'll slit his throat.'

I nodded.

'Then we're agreed,' Henry said. The devil held his hand out.

I shook it, and handed over my soul with the envelope.

But that was bullshit, another gamble. Die in infamy, honor intact, or live in glory, corrupted. I chose neither. There was nothing in the envelope. I was trying to barter empty-handed with the devil, so I really had only one choice: to beat him at his own game.

Chapter One

I was late. I checked myself out in one of the giant gilt mirrors they had hanging everywhere. There were dark circles under my eyes from lack of sleep and a fresh patch of carpet burn on my forehead. Otherwise I looked like every other upwardly mobile grade-grubber streaming through Langdell Hall.

The seminar was called Politics and Strategy. I ducked inside. It was application only – sixteen spots – and had the reputation of being a launching pad for future leaders in finance, diplomacy, military, and government. Every year Harvard tapped a few mid- to late-career heavies from DC and New York and brought them up to lead the seminar. The class was essentially a chance for the wannabe big-deal professional students – and there was no shortage of them around campus – to show off their 'big think' skills, hoping establishment dons would tap them and start them off on glittering careers. I looked around the table: hotshots from the law school, econ, philosophy, even a couple MD/PhDs. Ego poured through the room like central air.

It was my third year at the law school – I was doing a joint law and politics degree – and I had no idea how I'd managed to finagle my way into HLS or the seminar. That'd been pretty typical of the past ten years of my life, though, so I shrugged it off. Maybe it was all just a long series of clerical errors. My usual attitude was the fewer questions asked, the better.

Jacket, button-down, khakis: I mostly managed to look the part, if a little worn and frayed. We were in the thick of the conversation. The subject was World War I. And Professor Davies stared at us expectantly, sweating the answer out of us like an inquisitor.

'So,' Davies said. 'Gavrilo Princip steps forward and pistol-whips a bystander with his little Browning 1910. He shoots the archduke in the jugular and then shoots his wife through the stomach as she shields the archduke with her body. He just so happens to trigger the Great War in the process. The question is: Why?'

He glowered around the table. 'Don't regurgitate what you read. Think.'

I watched the others squirm. Davies definitely qualified as a heavy. The other students in class had studied his career with jealous obsession. I knew less, but enough. He was an old Washington hand. Going back forty years, he knew everyone who mattered, the two layers of people below those who mattered, and, most important, where all the bodies were buried. He'd worked for Lyndon Johnson, jumped ship to Nixon, then put out his own shingle as a fixer. He now ran a high-end strategic consulting firm called the Davies Group, which always made me think of the Kinks (that should tell you a bit about how fit I am for cutthroat DC career climbing). Davies had influence and could trade on that for anything he wanted, including, as one of the guys in class pointed out, a mansion in McLean, a place in Tuscany, and a ten-thousand-acre ranch on the central California coast. He'd been guest-teaching the seminar for a few weeks now. My classmates were practically vibrating with anxiety; I'd never seen them so eager to impress. That led me to believe that in the various orbits of official Washington, Davies had pull like the sun.

Davies's usual teaching method was to sit placidly and put a good face on his boredom, like he was listening to a bunch of second-graders spout dinosaur trivia. He wasn't an especially large man, maybe five ten, five eleven, but he sort of . . . loomed. His pull, it was almost like you could see it spread out through a room. People stopped talking, all eyes turned to him, and soon enough he had everyone lined up around him like filings around a magnet.

But his voice: that was the odd thing. You'd expect it to boom out, but he always spoke softly. There was a scar on his neck, right between where his jawline met his ear. It was the source of some speculation, whether an old injury had something to do with his quiet tone, but no one knew what had happened. It didn't matter much, since most rooms went silent when he opened his mouth. In class, though, his students were desperate to be heard, to be noticed by the master. Everyone had his answers to Davies's questions marshaled. There's an art to seminar: when to let others blabber, when to cut in. It's like boxing or . . . I guess fencing or squash or one of those other Ivy League pastimes.

The guy who always went first and never had a point to make began talking about the Young Bosnia movement until Davies's stare put the fear in him. The kid trailed off, mumbling. A feeding frenzy ensued as everyone smelled weakness and started barking over one another, spouting off about Greater Serbia versus the Southern Slavs, Bosnian versus Bosniak, irredentist Serbs and the Triple Entente and the two-power standard.

I was in awe. It wasn't just the facts they'd assembled (and some of these guys seemed to know literally everything; I'd never managed to push them out of their depths). It was their manner. You could see the entitlement in every move; it was like they'd grown up toddling around the study as their fathers swirled single-malts and debated the fate of nations, like they'd spent the last twenty-five years boning up on diplomatic history just to kill time until their dads grew tired of running the world and let them take the wheel. They were just so . . . so goddamn *respectable*. I usually loved to watch them, loved the little toehold I'd managed to gain in this world, loved to think that I could finally pass for one of them.

But not today. I was having trouble. I couldn't keep up with the give-and-take, the points and parries, let alone outdo them. On my good days I had a chance. But every time I tried to think about century-old Balkan micropolitics, I only saw a number, big and red and flashing. It was written in my notebook: *$83,359*, circled and underlined, and followed by a few other numbers: 43-23-65.

I hadn't slept the night before. After work – I tended bar at a yuppie place called Barley – I went over to Kendra's. I figured taking her up on her come-fuck-me look at the bar would do me more good than the ninety minutes of sleep I might have gotten before I had to wake up and read twelve hundred pages of densely written IR theory. She had black hair you could drown in, and a shape that invited lewd thoughts. But the principal appeal may have been that girls named Kendra who worked for tips and didn't look you in the eye in bed were the exact opposite of everything I told myself I wanted.

I headed out from Kendra's and got home around seven that morning. I knew something was up when I saw a few of my T-shirts on the stoop and my dad's ratty old Barcalounger lying on its side on the sidewalk. The front door to my apartment had been forced, and not well. It looked like a mean black bear had done it. Gone: my bed, and most of the furniture, the lamps and small kitchen appliances. The rest of my stuff was scattered everywhere.

People were going through my shit on the sidewalk like it was the giveaway at the end of a yard sale. I shooed them off and gathered up what was left. The Barcalounger was safe: it weighed as much as a hatchback and would require some serious forethought and a couple of guys to haul it off.

As I straightened up inside the apartment, I noticed that Crenshaw Collection Services hadn't seen the value of Thucydides' *History of the Peloponnesian War* or the five-inch-thick stack of reading material that had to be finished before seminar in two hours. They had left me a little love note on the kitchen table: *Furnishings taken as partial payment. Outstanding balance: $83,359.* Outstanding. Spectacular, even. I knew enough law by then to recognize at a glance about seventeen fatal flaws in Crenshaw's approach to debt collection, but they were as ruthless as bedbugs and I'd been too slammed trying to pay for school to sue them to a pulp. But that day would come.

Your parents' debts are supposed to die with them, settled out of the estate. Not mine. The eighty-three grand was the balance due for my mother's stomach cancer treatment. She was gone now. And if I may share one piece of advice, it's this: if your mother is dying, don't ever pay her bills with your own checkbook.

Because some unsavory creditors, folks like Crenshaw, will take that as a pretext to come after you once she's dead. You've tacitly assumed the debts, they'll say. It's not exactly legal. But it's not the kind of thing you know to look out for when you're sixteen and the radiology bills start coming in and you're trying to keep your mom alive by working overtime at Milwaukee Frozen Custard and your dad's doing a twenty-four-year bid at the Allenwood Federal Correctional Complex.

I'd been through this sort of hassle too often to even waste time with anger. I'd do what I always did. The more all that stuff from the past tried to drag me down, the more I'd work my ass off to rise above it. And that meant putting a wall around this little disaster, meant plowing through as much work as I could before class so I wouldn't sound like a moron in Davies's seminar. I took my reading out to the sidewalk, then righted the recliner. I kicked back and dug into some Churchill essays as traffic cruised by.

By the time I made it to seminar, however, I'd crashed. My punchy up-all-night post-lay energy was gone, as was the jolt of enthusiasm I'd had to spite Crenshaw by nailing class. To get to seminar, I had to swipe my ID at the entrance to Langdell Hall. I joined the long queue of students swiping and hitting the turnstiles and hustling to class. But my card made the LED flash red, not green. The metal bar locked and bent my knees back. My upper half continued forward in one of those agonizingly slow falls where you realize what's happening and can't do a thing about it for the ten minutes it seems to take to eat shit headfirst onto a thin layer of carpet over cement.

The cute undergrad behind the circulation desk was nice enough to explain that I might want to check with the Student Receivables Office about unpaid tuition or fees. Then she treated herself to a little pump of hand sanitizer. Crenshaw must have gone after my bank accounts and screwed up my tuition payment, and Harvard was just as serious about getting paid as Crenshaw. I had to circle around the back of Langdell and sneak in behind a guy going out for a smoke by the shipping dock.

In class, I guess my fugue state was now pretty obvious. It felt like Davies was looking right at me. Then I felt it coming. I fought it with every muscle in my body but sometimes there's nothing you can do. I had to yawn. And this one was big, lion big. There was no hiding it behind my hand.

Davies fixed me with a dagger look sharpened over God knows how many face-offs – he used to stare down labor bosses and KGB agents.

'Are we boring you, Mr Ford?' he asked.

'No, sir.' An awful weightless feeling grew in my stomach. 'I apologize.'

'Then why don't you share your thoughts on the assassination?'

The others tried to hide their delight: one less grade-grubber to climb over. The particular thoughts distracting me went like this: *Can't shake Crenshaw until I have a law degree and a decent job and can't get either until I shake Crenshaw, which leaves me with the eighty-three grand due Crenshaw and one hundred sixty due Harvard and no way to pay it back.* Everything I'd worked my ass off for ten years to earn, all the respectability filling that room, was about to slip from my hands, and be gone for good. And at the root of it all: my father, the convict, who first got tangled up with Crenshaw, who left me the man of the house at twelve, who should have done the world a favor and kicked instead of my mom. I pictured him, pictured his smirk, and as much as I tried not to, all I could think about was . . .

'Revenge,' I said.

Davies brought the earpiece of his glasses up to his lips. He was waiting for me to go on.

'I mean Princip is dirt-poor, right? He has six siblings die, and his parents have to give him away because they can't feed him. And he thinks the whole reason he can't get ahead in life is that the Austrians have had their foot on his family's neck since he was born. He's scrawny; the guerrillas laughed him out of the room when he tried to join up. He was just a nobody trying to make a splash. The other assassins lost their nerve, but he . . . he was, well, pissed off like no one else. He had something to prove. Twenty-three years of resentment. So he'd do what he had to do to make his name, even if it meant killing. Especially if it meant killing. The more dangerous the target the better.'

My peers looked away in distaste. I didn't talk much in seminar, and when I did I tried to use polished, high-sounding Harvard English like everyone else, not the regular-Mike tone I had just slipped into. I waited for Davies to tear me up. I sounded like a street kid, not a young establishment comer.

'Not bad,' he said. He thought for a moment, then looked around the room.

'Grand strategy, world war. You are all getting caught up in abstractions. Never lose sight of the fact that at the end of the day it comes down to men. Someone has to pull the trigger. If you want to lead nations, you have to start by understanding a single man, his wants and fears, the secrets he won't admit to and may not even be aware of himself. Those are the levers that move the world. Every man has a price. And once you find it, you own him, body and soul.'

After class, I was in a rush to clean myself up and attend to the disaster back in my apartment. A hand on my shoulder stopped me. I half expected it to be Crenshaw, ready to humiliate me in front of the good people of Harvard.

That might've been preferable; it was Davies, with that dagger stare and whisper voice. 'I would like to talk to you,' he said. 'Ten forty-five, my office?'

'Terrific,' I said, my best attempt at calm. Maybe he'd saved the chewing-out for a private conference. Classy.

I needed food and sleep, but coffee would cover both for a while. I didn't have time to go back to my apartment, and without really thinking about it, I walked over to Barley, the bar where I worked. The only thing filling my head was that number, *$83,359*, and the endless pathetic arithmetic of how I'd never be able to pay it off.

The bar was a pretentious box with too many windows. The only one in there was Oz, the manager, who bartended a few shifts a week. It wasn't until I leaned against the oak bar and took the first bitter sip of coffee that I caught myself. I hadn't come for caffeine. I cycled the numbers in my head: 46-79-35, 43-23-65, and so on. They were combinations for a Sentry safe.

Oz, who was also the owner's son-in-law, was skimming. And not just here and there, the usual retail 'shrinkage'. He was robbing the place. I'd been watching him up his game for a while, no sale-ing drinks and pocketing the money, comping his regulars half their tabs and never punching a thing into the register. Fishing that large a volume of stolen money from the cash drawer every night must have been a little difficult, since he had to do it while we were waiting around to be tipped out. So I was certain, dead certain, that this ass-hole was now keeping it in the safe. I could just tell. Probably because his act was basically a clumsy version of what I'd be doing if I were him and hadn't sworn off grifting a long time ago. The academic term is *alert opportunism*. It means that if you have the eyes of a criminal, you see the world differently, as nothing more than a collection of unwatched candy jars. I was starting to worry about myself, because now that I needed money, badly, it was all jumping out at me again: unlocked cars, open doors, loose purses, cheap locks, dark entries.

As much as I tried, I couldn't forget my apprenticeship, my ill-gotten expertise. I couldn't ignore all those invitations to stray. People seem to think thieves have to pick locks and shinny up drainpipes and charm widows. Usually, though, they just have to keep their eyes open. The money is more or less left sitting out by honest folks who can't quite believe people like me are walking around. The hidden key, the unlocked garage, the anniversary-date PIN code. It's there for the taking. And that's the funny thing: the straighter I became, the easier it was to be crooked. It was like people were constantly upping the temptations to keep testing me after all these years clean. As a harmless-looking grad student in a button-down, I could probably have walked out of Cambridge Savings and Trust with a trash bag full of hundreds and a revolver in my belt while the guard held the door and told me to have a nice weekend.

Alert opportunism. That's how I picked up that Oz was day-locking the safe, so he only had to dial in the last number to open it. It's how I knew that that number was 65. It's how I recalled that Sentry safes came from the manufacturer preset with only a handful of codes – called tryouts – and so if Oz's code ended in 65, it was almost certain that someone along the line had been too lazy to change the original factory combo from 43-23-65. It's how I noted that Oz was barely able to calculate a tip, let alone keep his skim straight, and that his drinking had gone from bad to worse: at 10:30 a.m. he was already halfway through a five-second pour of Jameson in a mug with a splash of coffee on top. And even if he did notice something missing, who would he tell? No honor among thieves, right?

Oz had the cash drawers on the bar now. He took them into the office. I heard the safe open and shut. He came back out and said, 'I'm going to grab some cigarettes. Can you keep an eye on the place?'

Opportunity knocked. I nodded.

I took my coffee, stepped into the office, and tried the handle on the safe. It was open. Jesus. He was practically begging me. Scanning the contents, I counted about forty-eight thousand dollars in bank bundles and maybe another ten grand or so in cash just piled up. Oz was way behind on the deposits.

There were two plays: I could nibble away at his skim and keep Crenshaw off my back long enough to get my degree. Or I could just rip off the Band-Aid, come in before dawn and clean it out. The bar's back door was like Fort Knox, but the front you could pry open with a Wonderbar in a minute and a half – typical. No one would get hurt. As long as there are signs of forced entry, insurance pays out. I checked the top drawers of the desk, then the corkboard, and sure enough, there it was, tacked to the wall in Oz's third-grader handwriting: *43-23-65* – the combination. Begging me.

I needed to pay Harvard at least, that week. Or else no degree. All that work, gone. The blood was pumping. A thrill coursed through me. It felt good. Really good. I'd missed it. Ten years I'd been clean, the upstanding go-getter. I hadn't strayed, hadn't lifted so much as a malted-milk ball from the grocery-store candy bins.

Standing in front of that open safe felt good. It felt way too good. It was in my blood. And I knew that shit would destroy me – like it did my dad, like it did my family – if I gave it the slightest chance. I looked over my button-down shirt, my loafers, Thucydides staring up from the cover of my book.

'Fuck me,' I muttered. Who was I kidding? I was too damn respectable to be crooked. And somehow still too crooked to be respectable. I swallowed the last of my coffee, then looked down at the empty mug. I'd chosen honest a long time ago, to survive, and I was going to stick with it even if it killed me.

I clanked the safe door shut.

* * *

I had pictured Davies's office like a World War II film set: a map room with man-size globes and him shoving around armies on table maps with a croupier's rake. Instead, Harvard had put him in a spare office in Littauer Hall, all Office Depot cherry veneer and no windows.

Sitting across from him, I felt an eerie bit of déjà vu. He seemed to grow as he looked me over, and I remembered, from a long time ago, what it was like to be standing dead center in the courtroom with a judge staring down.

'I have to catch the shuttle back to DC in a few minutes,' Davies said. 'But I wanted to talk to you. You were a summer associate at Damrosch and Cox?'

'Yes, sir.'

'You're planning to work with them after you graduate?'

'No,' I said.

That's pretty unusual. All the real work in law school is in the first year and a half, when you're gunning for a summer associateship at a firm. Then they wine and dine and overpay you to do nothing in order to make up for the seven years of hell they're going to make you pay as an actual associate. Once you're in for the summer, you're more or less guaranteed a job after you graduate unless you're a major fuckup. Damrosch and Cox didn't invite me back.

'Why not?' Davies asked.

'Tough economy,' I said. 'And I know I'm not the typical candidate.'

Davies pulled out a few sheets of paper and looked them over. My résumé. He must have pulled it from the Office of Career Services.

'Your manager at Damrosch and Cox said you were excellent, a force of nature.'

'That's very kind of him.'

Davies squared the papers and put them down on his desk.

'Damrosch and Cox are a couple white-shoe fucking snobs,' he said.

That was my working theory for why they didn't hire me too, but it took me a second to process it coming from Davies. His firm had a rep that could easily out-white-shoe-fucking-snob the best of them.

'You join the navy at nineteen, when most of your chums in seminar here probably went to get drunk in Europe during their gap year. Top noncommissioned officer. A year at Pensacola Junior College, then you transfer to Florida State and graduate first in your class in two years. Damn near perfect LSATs. Now a joint degree from the Kennedy School and Harvard Law. And' – he checked another paper – 'you're doing the four-year degree in three. How are you paying for it?'

'Loans.'

'About a hundred and fifty thousand dollars?'

'Give or take. And I tend bar.'

Davies seemed to check the circles under my eyes. 'How many hours a week?'

'Forty, fifty.'

'On top of class.' He shook his head. 'I'll ask you this, because you did a decent job figuring out what moved Princip. What lit the fire under you?'

So apparently this was a job interview. I tried to think of the usual platitudes about my work ethic, summon my inner grade-grubber, but I really didn't know how to play this one. Davies made it easy.

'I'd prefer it if you didn't bullshit me,' he said. 'I called you in here because, based on what you said in class, you actually seem to know something about the real world, what drives men. What's driving you?'

He'd find out sooner or later, so I figured I might as well

get it over with. It was expunged from the record, but I could never really erase it. People, like the partners at Damrosch and Cox, always managed to find out. It's like they could smell it on me.

'I got into some trouble when I was young,' I said. 'The judge gave me an easy choice: join up or go to prison. The navy straightened me out, and the discipline took. I liked the routine, the drive, and I put that into school.'

He lifted the files off the desk, dropped them in his attaché, then stood up. 'Good,' he said. 'I like to know who I'm working with.'

I looked at him, puzzled by the 'working with' bit. Usually when people caught a hint of who I really was, they showed me the door ('tough economy' or 'not our kind of man'). Not Davies.

'You'll come work for me,' he said. 'We'll start you at two hundred a year. Thirty percent bonus based on performance.'

'Yes.' I heard myself say it before I even had a chance to think.

That night, I slept on a wheezing air mattress in my empty apartment. I had to get up every couple hours to pump it back up. Dawn was a long time coming, and at some point, I remember, I realized that when Davies said I was coming to DC, he'd been telling me, not asking.

Chapter Two

The Mahogany Box wasn't a coffin, but after I'd been trapped inside it for four hours, it started to feel distinctly tomblike. I found it hard to rest. That may have had something to do with the fact that most people in similar situations were lying on their backs, and dead. After a while, however, I learned that if I leaned my head forward and wedged it in a corner, I could catch a few winks.

The story of how I found myself in that box is a bit complicated. The short version is that I was stalking a guy named Ray Gould because I was in love – with a girl named Annie Clark in particular, and with my new job in general.

I'd been at the Davies Group for almost four months. The firm was a strange place, opaque by design. If you asked, they told you they did government affairs and strategic consulting. Usually that's a euphemism for lobbying.

Picture a lobbyist and you probably call to mind the bought-and-paid-for, tasseled-loafer-wearing scum who funnel corporate and special-interest bribes to politicians, take generous skims for themselves, and ultimately make the world safe for lung cancer and poisoned rivers. There are plenty of those guys. But the go-go days of the 1970s and 1980s, when payoffs and vice flourished, are long gone. Now most lobbyists spend their days clicking through PowerPoint slides about obscure policies while bored junior congressional staff check their BlackBerrys under the table.

Those guys are the rabble. Comparing them to the folks at the Davies Group is like comparing Zales to Tiffany and Cartier. Davies is among a handful of strategic consulting firms that do very little formal lobbying. These outfits are run by Washington heavies – ex-House Speakers, ex-secretaries of state, ex-national security advisers – and they exert a far more powerful and lucrative influence through the Beltway's back channels. They're not registered as lobbyists. They don't do volume. They don't advertise. They have *relationships*. They're discreet. And they're very, very expensive. If you really need something done in Washington, and you have the money, and you know the people you have to know to even *get* a referral to a top firm, that's where you go.

The Davies Group is at the peak of that cozy little world. It occupies a mansion in Kalorama, set among the trees and old European embassies, far from K Street downtown, where most lobbyists duke it out.

During those first days in DC, I started to realize that the Davies Group thought of itself less as a business and more as a secret society or shadow government. People I was used to seeing on the front page of the *Post*, or in history books, for God's sake, would be strolling up and down the hallways or cursing at jammed laser printers.

Davies, like the other principals, spent his days doing essentially the same work he had done while in government. He marshaled decades of bureaucratic mastery: knowing exactly which string to tug, which functionary to pressure. It was a miracle how he made this sluggish, awkward, all-powerful yet barely functioning apparatus – the federal government – come alive and turn his whims into realities.

Once he'd had to answer to voters and donors and political parties. Now he answered to only himself. He was offered far more business than he could ever take and so had the luxury of taking only those clients whose cases fit with his own agenda.

None of this was said outright, of course. You had to pick up all the routines and rituals by keeping your eyes open and asking the right questions. The Davies Group was old-school. Most consulting firms still keep a little gentlemanly patina – the suits, the library, the hardwood trim. But any gentility has long ago been squeezed out by the number crunchers. Everyone measures his life by cells on a spreadsheet: hours billed. You have to hit your numbers. From day one, you're on the hamster wheel. At Davies it was different. There were no orientations, no quotas or guidelines. There were only a half dozen or so new hires. Some years there were none.

They gave each new initiate an office, a secretary, and a paycheck for forty-six hundred dollars every other week. Beyond that it was up to you. You had to find the work. The principals and partners inhabited the third floor – to me it looked like a wing of Versailles – and the senior associates the second. We were the junior associates, new fish, and we were parked on the first floor with all the admin, HR, and research folks. Junior associate was basically probation. You had six months, maybe a year, to prove your worth to the company, or you were gone. No one taught you how to do it. You had to hustle your way past every associate's door to learn the rules of the game, but you could never seem pushy. Tact and discretion were the cardinal virtues at Davies Group.

You'd scrounge for any little project at first, and typically they'd have you do research on a mark – sorry, that's the old Mike's lingo – on a 'decision-maker' the firm wanted to influence. That meant you had to find out everything there was to know in the world, public and private, about your mark, and narrow it down to only the things that mattered for the case at hand *and nothing more*. That went into a memo, one page maximum. The partners called it 'boiling the sea'. And what mattered? We junior associates had no idea, but we knew we had damned sure better get it right.

That was the worst part. The partners and associates knew that if they let you squirm, you would only work harder, desperate for a pat on the head. So they never said exactly what was right or wrong. A partner would just tent his fingers in front of his lips and say, 'Why don't you have another go?' then slide back across the desk the product of your endless nights and weekends at the office, always wanting more. If you were lucky, you would receive the rarest of gifts, a 'not bad' – the equivalent of a panting orgasm at the Davies Group. And if you pulled the wrong grains of salt from the sea? You were gone. Sink or swim.

I was going to swim. I'd been hazed pretty hard starting out in the navy, and if staring at a computer was the worst they had for me, I was going to be fine. If I was awake (which I was for eighteen or nineteen hours a day), I was working.

The money was enough to keep Crenshaw off my back, and even with me saving 20 per cent (I was still convinced that any day the rug would be pulled out) there was more left than I knew how to spend. I had to get used to going out for dinner without coupons and having an apartment decent enough to invite people over without shame.

Money wasn't the only draw. In my short time at Davies, I started getting perks I hadn't even known existed, things I wouldn't even have known to want. They had sent movers up to Cambridge to pack up my old place. Young guys, they were nice enough not to laugh at my picked-over apartment. It took them a half hour to convince me I shouldn't help. All I had to do was pack a bag for myself and drive my fifteen-year-old

Jeep Cherokee down to DC. The shocks were gone, so it lurched on the leaf springs like a seesaw anytime I went over fifty-five. Davies put me up in the firm's corporate apartment on Connecticut Ave., a nine-hundred-square-foot one-bedroom with a den, a balcony, a doorman, and a concierge.

'Take as long as you want to find a place,' Davies told me the first day. 'We'll set you up with a real estate agent, but if you're focused on working instead of going to open houses, that's fine with us.'

Even if I hadn't been trying to save money, there was nothing I needed to buy. The firm had a car service, and most days my coworkers and I ended up eating catered breakfast, lunch, and dinner at the office.

My first week, I met my assistant, Christina, a petite Hungarian. She was so tiny, neat, and efficient that I half suspected she was a robot. She kept catching me as I tried to run my own errands. I'd ask where the post office was, or the dry cleaner's. She would extend her hand, looking a little put out that I'd try to do some task myself, then take what I was holding and do whatever chore I needed done.

'Sorry for the tough love, Mr Ford. Don't think of it as a luxury. Think of it as Davies making sure he keeps you on task and gets his money's worth out of you.'

That made it a little easier. The fifty annoying errands you have to do when you move – standing in line at the DMV, waiting for the cable guy – they just got done. And it kept up after that, all life's little hassles gone. That's when I started to understand. I'd always needed money to survive, for bare necessities month to month. I never really stopped to think about what it really brought, those countless graces that people wrap up in the word *comfortable*.

All that made me feel a bit uncomfortable, soft even. I liked to think of myself as hungry, driven. But when you have twelve interviews and fourteen hundred pages of documents to plow through a day, two weekly reports that can make or break you, and partners ready to drop by any time for a 'little check-in' that could be your last, you don't really have time to worry about going soft. I started to realize that Christina was right: some pad thai ordered in to the conference room and a Town Car home was a small price for Davies to pay to keep each employee humming along and billing out at two or three hundred bucks an hour, seventy hours a week.

I needed the money, and I liked the perks, but that's not what pulled me out of bed every morning at 5:45. It was the ritual of shined shoes and a crisp shirt. It was crossing off eight tasks before 9:00 a.m. It was the soles of my Johnston & Murphy's cracking across the marble floor of the Davies Group foyer and echoing back from the oak panels. It was walking through the halls and seeing wise men do work that mattered, seeing Henry Davies and an ex-CIA director in the courtyard laughing like old roommates and realizing that if I kept busting my ass, I might one day belong in their company. It was the same thing that had been driving me ever since a judge gave me a choice: the need to find something larger than myself to be a part of, some honest work to lose myself in; anything to hold off the criminal in my blood.

I was going to do everything it took to make it at Davies, to make that respectable world stick. And that's how I found myself sealed up in the mahogany box.

Those first few months were like pledging a fraternity. Nobody said how exactly, but you knew you were being scrutinized at every step. Every so often someone would disappear and you had the feeling that in some clubby chamber at Davies Group the night before, ballots had been cast in secret, and black marks scratched beside the name of the unfit.

That was the chatter among the junior associates, at least. I thought it was a little much. But the piece of it I did buy was that your first real assignment was do-or-die. In the government affairs business, when you're needling some politician or bureaucrat to give you what your client wants, there comes a moment called the ask. No matter how byzantine the issue, it ultimately comes down to one question: Will he give you what you need? Yes or no.

A partner does the actual ask. He is the august face of the company. The real work, however, is all left to the associate. And when you get your first case, you own it. If the mark says yes, you're golden. No: you're gone.

William Marcus gave me my first real case. He had the office next to Davies on the third floor. It was the executive corridor. An oak-paneled boardroom ran along one side. On the other there were six or seven suites, each as big as my apartment, all looking down over the District from this hilltop perch in Kalorama. Walking that hall made my hair stand on end. I would flash back to drills and forward march with thirty-inch steps, head, eyes, and body at attention.

The men on that hall had literally run the free world, and they daily, without a second thought, made or crushed the careers of dozens of strivers like me. Most of the principals at the firm had bios as long as your arm; that's what the clients paid for. But Marcus's background was a mystery. As far as I knew, I was the only junior associate he was keeping an eye on. It was either a very good or a very bad thing, and given the caliber of the talent I was up against, I figured the latter.

Marcus was in his late forties, maybe a little older; it was hard to tell. I took him for a triathlete or, given his build, maybe one of those white-collar guys who spend four nights a week trading leather at the boxing gym. He had reddish-brown hair trimmed short, a strong jaw, and drawn cheeks.

He always seemed to be in a good mood, which cut down the intimidation factor a bit, but only until he had you alone in his office. Then the smiles and easy manner disappeared.

He put me on to my first ask. A giant multinational based in Germany (which I probably shouldn't name outright, so I'll just call it what we called it around the office: the Kaiser) had finagled a tax-and-tariff loophole and was using it to lowball American companies and drive them out of business. It was a typically complex international tax case, but in the end it came down to this: overseas companies that sell services to Americans pay way less in taxes and tariffs than companies that ship actual goods to the United States. The Kaiser people sure looked like they were selling goods to the United States. They claimed, however, that they were just offering a service, connecting American customers to overseas vendors and manufacturers, and so they should have to pay only the cheap tax on services. We're just a middleman, the Kaiser would argue, who never actually takes possession of the goods. But once you looked at their supply chain, it was clear they were selling goods just like everybody else and simply dodging the higher taxes.

Still awake? Bravo. The folks who were getting driven out of business had hired the Davies Group. They wanted us to close the loophole and level the playing field. That meant getting some bureaucrat in the bowels of Washington to sign a piece of paper that said the Kaiser was offering goods, not services.

One little word. And for that, the Davies Group was getting at least fifteen million dollars, which, rumor had it among the junior associates, was the minimum required to attract the firm's attention.

Marcus laid the case out for me, with a few more details but not many: my first ask. He didn't even tell me what he wanted me to give back to him – the product, as it was known around the office. My ass was now officially on the line and I had zero clue what I was doing.

I'd been out of my depth for the last ten years, though, and it had worked out surprisingly well, so I figured I'd just keep doing what I always did: hustle. A hundred and fifty hours of work and ten days later, after talking with every expert who would answer a plea for help and reading every legal code and journal article that even vaguely touched on the issue, I distilled the case against the Kaiser into ten pages, then five, then one. I boiled the sea. Eight bullet points. Each one alone was potent enough to annihilate the Kaiser. It was the memo equivalent of uncut heroin, and I was proud and sleep-deprived enough to pass it along to Marcus thinking it would blow him away.

He skimmed it for thirty seconds, grumbled a little, and said, 'This is all fucked up. You can't know the why until you know the who. These things always turn on one man. Don't waste my time until you find the fulcrum.'

I wanted marching orders. I got Confucius. So I dug back in. Among my junior-associate peers hustling for a spot at Davies Group were the secretary of defense's son, a guy who at thirty years old had already been deputy campaign manager on a successful presidential bid, and two Rhodes scholars, one of them a former CIA director's grandson. The job came down to knowing Washington, and the issues, sure, but more important, knowing the deep anthropology of the place, the personalities, the loves and hates, the hidden nodes where power massed, who had pull on who, who owed who chits. It was stuff that takes a lifetime of connections, of being immersed in the DC elite, to learn. The other guys had it. I didn't. But that wasn't going to stop me. Because I had learned a few things along the way too. What I did have was will, in spades.

So I got out of the office, away from LexisNexis and the endless Googling, to actually talk to some human beings (to many of my youngish peers, this was an art as mysterious as levitation or snake charming). I was working on the premise that official Washington, however peculiar, could ultimately be understood as a neighborhood like any other.

About six different government offices had a say in the decision on whether the Kaiser could hang on to the loophole. But the final stop turned out to be a typical example of Washington bureaucracy: a sub-body of something called the Interim Interagency Working Group on Manufacturing at the Commerce Department.

It took about a week to crack the working group. Everything was a little harder because Marcus had told me that for now there shouldn't be any obvious signs we were working the case. I had to talk to about four or five junior staffers until I found a chatterbox, big ego, who knew nothing that mattered to me. He did, however, turn me on to a paralegal who moonlighted for fun as a bartender at Stetson's – a U Street bar that the Clinton White House staffers used to frequent, though by now it had gone to seed. She was a redhead with a nice tomboyish thing going, as amiable as you could want, though she snored like a chain saw and had a habit of 'forgetting' things at my apartment.

She laid it all out. There were two figureheads who would sign off on it, but in the end, the real decision came down to three people on the working group. Two were typical agency staffers, human paperweights; they didn't matter. The third – a guy named Ray Gould – was the actual decision-maker, the one who was keeping the Kaiser's loophole open. Gould was a deputy assistant secretary (that is, under the assistant secretary under the undersecretary who was under the deputy under the actual secretary of commerce. Having fun?).

I found myself saying these org-chart tongue twisters in all seriousness. If I needed something to keep me from thinking the whole thing was a ridiculous bit of policy trivia, I would just remember that nailing it meant fifteen million minimum to my boss and, more important, would save me from spending the rest of my life wiping down a bar and hiding from Crenshaw.

Besides, I was starting to really enjoy myself. The characters were less interesting and the money was better, but otherwise this wasn't all that dissimilar from the hustles I knew growing up. That had me equal parts excited and worried.

I had my fulcrum. Marcus didn't seem pleased with me, exactly, when I brought him Gould's name, but at least he seemed a little less angry. He told me to start from scratch on making the case to close the tariff loophole. I had to tailor it all to a single goal: change Gould's mind. I read Gould's theses from college and graduate school. I found out what newspapers and journals he subscribed to, the charities he donated to, every decision he'd ever made that there was a record or memory of. I started zeroing in, fine-tuning every argument against the Kaiser's loophole so it would appeal to Gould's particular habits and beliefs. I boiled down the arguments over and over until I'd trimmed them to a single page. The previous memo had been uncut heroin. This was a designer drug. Gould would have to give us the decision we wanted.

'You'd better hope so,' Marcus said.

Even with all the reading and interviews, I couldn't get a sense of the guy, of what made him tick, until I saw him in person. In profiling Gould, I may have gone a little overboard. I knew where his kids went to school, what car he drove, where he went on his anniversary dinner, his usual lunch spots. They were mostly high-end: Central Michel Richard, the Prime Rib, the Palm, but every other Thursday he would go to Five Guys, a burger place.

The week after I turned in my new report on Gould, Marcus called me upstairs, then led me into Davies's suite. Davies gestured for Marcus to wait outside. This was the master-of-the-universe office I had imagined back at Harvard, except of course Davies had better taste than my imagination did. Books ran from floor to ceiling on three walls. They'd been read too; they weren't just leather-bound props. Everything was kitted out in mahogany. And the ego wall – mandatory for Washington: snapshots of grip-and-grins with anyone influential you've ever met – was like nothing I'd ever seen. He had shots with world leaders going back decades, and they weren't the usual two-guys-in-suits-at-a-fund-raiser variety. There he was, younger than I was, bowling with Nixon; there fishing in a little skiff with Jimmy Carter; and there skiing with . . .

'Is that the pope?' I blurted it out before I could stop myself.

Davies stood behind his desk. He didn't look happy. 'Gould hasn't budged,' he said.

They'd given my memo – the arguments tailored specifically to Gould – to the trade group fighting the Kaiser, and the group had made the case to Gould's working group. Davies had people inside Commerce who would know if Gould was starting to come around. He hadn't given an inch.

'I'll do more,' I said.

He lifted up the memo I had put together. 'This is perfect,' he said, then let me hang for a minute. His tone didn't make it sound like a compliment.

'I already have a hundred and twenty guys downstairs who can give me perfect. I don't need another. Do you know what this contract is worth?'

'No.'

'We've worked out arrangements with every single industry and trade group affected. Forty-seven million.'

I felt the blood drain from my face. He looked me over for a few seconds.

'We can't bill by the hour here, Mike. If we win, we get the forty-seven. If we lose, we get nothing. We won't lose.'

He walked a little closer and stared me down. 'I took a risk with you, Mike. I hired you for the same reason others wouldn't, because you're not the usual candidate. I fear I may have made a mistake bringing you here. Prove I didn't. Show me what you have to offer that the others don't. Give me more than perfect. Surprise me.'

It's easier to have nothing all along than to get your hands on something and lose it. And all the time at Davies Group, I'd thought of the money and privileges as a mistake soon to be rectified. I didn't dare think I could really have it; I didn't dare think of it as my life. But eventually you find something you really want. Something you need. Then you're fucked. You can never let that life go.

What I wanted wasn't anything fancy. For me, the moment I found it came around August of that first year at Davies, three months after I'd moved to the District. I was strolling through Mount Pleasant, a ten-minute walk from the office. The neighborhood had one main drag, with an eighty-year-old bakery and a hardware store that'd been there for decades. It was where the Italians, then the Greeks, and then the Latinos found their first foothold in DC, and it felt like a little village. Off the main street of shops, the area was wooded, and to me it seemed like the suburbs. The houses were small, and I saw one for rent, a two-bedroom with a porch and a backyard where you could look down into the woods of Rock Creek Park, a band of streams and forest that cuts DC in half north to south. While walking past the house one night, I saw a whole family of deer, just standing there, calm, unafraid, looking back at me.

That's all it took. I hadn't had a backyard since I was a kid. My dad had had some steady money coming in – I didn't know where from back then. We had finally moved out of the apartment complex in Arlington where I'd grown up – it sort of looked like a motel, and I remember it always smelled like cooking gas – out to a place in Manassas, just a small ranch house. And I know this is a little corny, but I remember we had a swing set there, all rusty aluminum tubes that would open your palm right up if you grabbed the wrong spot. We didn't live there for long, but I remember summer nights when my parents and a couple of their friends would be sitting around a fire pit, laughing and drinking beer. I would stay on that swing all evening, pumping my legs like a locomotive, and I'd go so high up, up with the bar, looking out over the trees, that I'd be weightless, and the chains would go slack, and I would've sworn I could just take off flying into the night.

Then they sent my dad up, for burglary, and it was back to where we belonged: the gas-smell motel.

After I finished work at Davies, ten or eleven o'clock at night, sometimes even later, I would walk through that neighborhood and picture myself in that backyard with a little fire going, a couple of lawn chairs, a nice girl. It felt like starting over, like making things right again.

The thought of losing it all lit a fire beneath me. After my meeting with Davies in his suite, it was a week before I went back to Marcus's office. I laid down two more files. One profiled Gould's mentor at the Department of the Interior, where he'd worked for nine years before joining Commerce. The second focused on the best man at Gould's wedding, a roommate from law school who was now in private practice. He was still Gould's go-to for advice; they had dinner every other week or so, one of Gould's few social outlets.

'And?' Marcus said.

'These guys are easier' – I caught myself before I said *marks* – 'influentials. If you look at their decision-making, you can see they're likely to be sympathetic to our arguments. I've tailored the arguments against the loophole to appeal to each man. The first already has a relationship with Davies Group. If we can't influence Gould, we can influence those around him. If we change their minds, we can change Gould's without his ever knowing it was our words in his ear.'

Marcus was silent. I knew what was coming. I had given him more than he wanted on Gould. I had done everything but case the poor bastard's house, and I was thinking about doing that the next night. Marcus shifted in his chair. I hunkered down for a reaming-out.

Instead, Marcus smiled. 'Who taught you that?'

That would be my dad's old friend Cartwright. In his younger days, he'd used a similar technique to charm lonely women hitting their late thirties out of their savings.

'Just sort of came to me,' I said.

'It's a variation of a technique we call grass-topping,' Marcus said. 'You slowly, subtly lobby everyone close to the decision-maker – wife, chief fund-raisers, grown kids even – until he comes around.'

'Grass-topping?'

'That's where we make it look like we have broad bottom-up support – from the grass roots – but we're faking it. You don't need to waste time with the roots when the legislator can see only the tops.'

'Do you want me to take a stab at the next step? Actually influencing the people around Gould?'

'No,' Marcus said. 'I'll put a few people on it.'

I caught something in his voice, something I didn't like.

'We're running out of time, aren't we?' I asked.

Marcus paused. He never said much, and always thought carefully before he spoke. But I could see he didn't want to bullshit me, saw maybe even a glimmer of respect.

'Yes.'

The next week one of the Rhodes scholars washed out. He was a nice enough guy, with the swept-back blond waves and entitled air of a true prep. Someone told me, and I could believe it, that the guy didn't even own a pair of jeans. I could have resented him, I guess – every privilege had just been handed to him – but he had a sense of humor about himself and I had to like him.

He was a gunner like me, the first in our group to have an ask. But the decision-maker didn't come around. And that was it. Rhodes tried to play it off like he'd decided to move on to greener pastures, but he had this hitch in his voice as he was making his good-byes, like he'd been crying. It was hard to watch. I guess the kid had never failed at anything. He'd done everything he could. The case just hadn't gone his way.

I hadn't quite believed that these multimillion-dollar contracts were riding on a bunch of junior-associate twits with no idea what they were doing. But by all appearances, they were. I guess you could say it wasn't fair. Maybe they give you an unwinnable case; there's only so much you can do and then it's out of your hands. But it's hard for me to get worked up about things being unfair. That's life, the only way I've ever known it. You could cover up your head and moan about it, but my approach was just to make sure I won, no matter what. I'd been going for a long time on fumes, on some abstract dream of the good life. Now I was close. I could smell and taste it. The more real the dream became, the more intolerable I found the idea of losing it.

Case in point: Annie Clark, senior associate at Davies Group. I'd never had much trouble talking to women, never really even given it much thought. But around this particular woman, the usual one-thing-leads-to-another ease abandoned me. From the first moment I saw her, on the second floor, all manner of corny nonsense crowded my brain.

Every time she and I talked (and we worked together fairly often), I found myself thinking that she had everything that I'd ever been drawn to in a woman – black curls, innocent face, and sly blue eyes – and some things I hadn't even known to look for. After observing her all day as she ran circles around all the smug boys in meetings and fielded phone calls in three or four different languages, I'd be walking out of the building with her and all I'd want was to blurt out what I was thinking: that she was what I'd been looking for, that she embodied the life I wanted but had never had. It was crazy.

I began to wonder if she was maybe *too* perfect, haughty and spoiled and impossible to reach.

The first time we pulled an all-nighter at work – she and I and two other junior associates – she ran the show. We all sat at a conference table, and, deep in thought, she pushed her rolling chair back, about to set us straight on another fine point of the influence game.

Instead, she tipped over, slowly but surely, disappeared behind the edge of the table, and fell backward onto the carpet. I half expected her to wail or come back up in a rage. Instead I heard her laugh for the first time. And hearing her lie there and crack up – free, easy, unself-conscious and unconcerned about anyone or anything – instantly cut through my bullshit sour-grapes attitude. Every time I heard her laugh, I knew this was a woman who didn't have time for pretense, who just took life as it came and enjoyed the hell out of it.

That laugh put me on dangerous ground. Whenever I ran into her I wanted to throw the memo I'd spent the last month working on out the window, drop to one knee, and ask her to run away and spend the rest of her life with me.

That probably would have been a better approach than what I ultimately did do. I was in the break room after a meeting, trying to discuss my Annie Clark strategy with the remaining Rhodes scholar without sounding like a smitten moron (and mostly failing). Unfortunately, Annie Clark herself was there, unseen, behind a pillar eight feet away, as the Rhodes scholar, a guy named Tuck I'd grown friendly with, gave me a not-unwise piece of advice about office romance:

'Don't shit where you eat, man.'

'Charming,' Annie said, coming out from behind the pillar; she raised her bottle and pointed to the watercooler. 'Do you mind?'

So I was a few runs down with regard to Annie Clark. But as I said: will in spades. I just needed a rally. And when I started picturing her beside me on a gentle July night in the backyard at the house up in Mount Pleasant I dreamed of buying, I resolved to hang on to this decent life I'd won even if it took my last breath. I was going to nail Gould.

The next time I saw Marcus – he was sipping coffee and reading in the dining room – after a few preliminaries, I asked him straight out.

'When's the ask?'

'Has somebody been telling tales out of school?' he responded. The whole ordeal of surviving the first year at Davies was supposed to be a black box. Inquiring about what was inside was a little bold, but I think all the partners knew that we junior associates had started to piece together some clues about our fates.

'Three days,' he said. 'Davies is going to pay Gould a visit. We've slowly been working on his confidants.'

'And if it doesn't work? If he doesn't change his mind about the loophole?'

'You've done everything you can, Mike. And I hope, for your sake, he says yes.'

I left it there. I could read it in Marcus's face. Business is business.

I wasn't about to sit around and count on hope and crossed fingers. Henry had tapped me because he thought I knew something about what made people tick. He'd said every man has a price, a lever you can use to force him to do your will. I had three days to find Gould's.

I stepped back from the politics and policy research, the reams of Commerce Department reports, all the official Washington bullshit I thought I had to know to do my job. Instead I just thought about Gould, this dumpy bureaucrat living out in Bethesda, about what he wanted and what he feared.

Watching him the last few weeks, I'd noticed a few things that had stuck out, dumb stuff that I hadn't thought was worth mentioning to the bosses because I wasn't a hundred percent sure what it meant. Gould's house was modest for Bethesda, and he had a five-year-old Saab 9-5. But the guy was a clotheshorse – went shopping at J. Press or Brooks Brothers or Thomas Pink two or three times a week. He dressed like a high-society heel in a Billy Wilder movie: tweed everywhere and whales dancing on suspenders and contrasting-color bow tie. He was a foodie too and posted on an online forum called DonRockwell.com under the name LafiteForAKing, mostly bitching about waiters who didn't know their place. Every week he dropped at least a few hundred bucks on lunch; he had a regular table at Central and favored the lobster burger.

But then, every other Thursday, like clockwork, this gourmet goes to Five Guys, which is a greasy slice-of-heaven burger joint. It started in DC, though now it's all over the East Coast. He would always order regular fries and the little cheeseburger – just one patty – and leave with a doggie bag. I'm the last person on earth to begrudge someone a heart-stopper on a bun every now and then. But something wasn't right. The leftovers suggested a superhuman restraint that I knew Mr Gould did not have. And with the amount of money he was dropping on food and clothes, it didn't add up. So I was suspicious. But mostly I was desperate, and maybe just swinging at shadows; anything to save myself.

By now I was one day away from Davies's meeting with Gould: the ask. There was nothing for me to do but follow Gould and hope I caught a Hail Mary. I found him on the way out of his office, heading for Five Guys. Right on schedule. I'd like to think it was my uncanny, Columbo-like powers of detection – picking up on the nervous edge to his walk, the way he stared down at the table the whole time, the fact that his take-out bag was the only one I'd ever seen from Five Guys not stained half translucent with grease. Maybe it was just desperation and luck. Or maybe the honest life was starting to feel like too much pressure, and I just wanted to say fuck it and get myself caught doing something dumb. Whatever the reason, I had to find out what was in the brown bag Gould was carrying.

He went straight from lunch to his club – the Metropolitan Club, a massive brick building a block away from the White House. It was founded during the Civil War, and, with a few exceptions, every president since Lincoln has been a member.

It's the social center of the Treasury–Pentagon–Big Business set. The more liberal-arts-type folks – journalists, academics, writers – tended to cluster around the Cosmos Club in Dupont Circle. Membership in the Met was an indisputable marker that you were a somebody. Since I was a nobody, I had to improvise.

Gould walked straight through the entryway, past the reception desk, and turned left toward a sitting room. I tried to follow him. Four stewards, squat South Asians, stood at attention near reception. They stopped me like a brick wall. 'May I help you, sir?' said one.

It took me a second to realize how *in place* I actually looked. My assistant had sent an Italian tailor to my office my second week of work. She told me not to take it personally, but I'd need a couple proper suits. I'd never actually met an Italian tailor (I thought they'd somehow all been converted to Korean dry cleaners sometime in the 1970s), but there he was, measuring my ass. At the final fitting, he actually said, 'This is-ah nice-ah suit.' So I looked the Met Club part. That gave me a half second to improvise with the Gurkhas.

I scanned the plaques and photos on the wall beside the desk as discreetly as I could, looking for an appropriate titan of industry and government. Breckinridge Cassidy seemed old enough (the plaque said *1931–*) that the odds were he wouldn't be around the club. I just hoped he was still around at all; maybe the club just hadn't had time to note his expiration date on the plaque.

I checked my watch and did my best to look entitled.

'Breckinridge Cassidy,' I said. 'Is he already here?'

'Admiral Cassidy hasn't arrived yet, sir.'

'Very well. We're on for drinks. I'll wait in the library.'

I strode inside . . . and nothing, no frog-march out, no heave-ho by the collar and waistband. I was in. Fortunately,

Cassidy was alive. Unfortunately, he was a fucking admiral and it sounded like he might actually show up any second. I took a spot in the library and noticed one of the stewards glancing at me every minute or so. The club had an open atrium with a beautiful double staircase. Everything about the place – the bas-relief wall decorations, the forty-foot Corinthian columns, the quiet servants at every door – made one thing perfectly clear: this was power's home.

I thought I saw Gould on one of the mezzanines, then I glanced back at the reception desk. The steward wasn't looking at me but was pointing my way and conversing with a very confused and formidable-looking Admiral Cassidy.

Time to go.

On the second floor, I caught sight of the back of Gould's head and followed him down a set of stairs. From the faint chlorine smell and shriek of sneakers on hardwood, I knew I was heading to some sort of gym. Then I saw the sign. Squash, of course. The official pastime of DC heavies. I trailed him into the locker room.

You can only loiter fully dressed around a bunch of half-naked world leaders for so long before you raise a few eyebrows. So I stripped down, grabbed a towel, and found a nice spot in the sauna between the chairman of the Joint Chiefs and a guy I didn't recognize but who turned out to be the CFO of ExxonMobil, very chatty.

I didn't see Gould pass by through the sauna windows, so I took my leave and headed for the changing rooms. The lockers were all mahogany with little brass plaques indicating their owners. I found Ray Gould's. It was directly opposite Henry Davies's. Using a lock at a place like the Met Club seemed a little silly – what, was someone going to swap out your Cartier for his Rolex? – and yet Gould had a Sargent and Greenleaf padlock. It's the hardware the DOD uses to lock up its secrets, and Gould apparently needed to secure his uneaten French fries.

It never seems obvious when you cross the line. Was it when I began trailing Gould? When I lied to the steward? When I slipped into one of the guest lockers in the back corner of the locker room? Or when I stayed there for hours, until I heard the last guest clear his throat, saw the lights die through my little ventilation slits, and heard the door slam shut and lock, echoing through the tiled halls?

Wherever the line was, I was certain it was now way behind me. And this was no high-school smash-and-grab. I imagined that the trilateral-commission types who frequented the place wouldn't take kindly to my trespass. But for some reason I didn't have the same visceral need to get the fuck out of there, to keep on the honest path, that I'd had back when I opened up the safe in the office at Barley. There was something about being behind Henry's shield of respectability, about having legitimate ends for my sketchy means. I'd forced my way into this club, but if I played my cards right I could turn that trespass into a real admission to this world.

Or maybe, trapped in a mahogany box with five or six hours to think, I'd managed to talk myself into believing anything.

By 11:30 p.m., I figured I was safe. I stepped out. There was no chance of breaking the Sargent and Greenleaf, not without liquid nitrogen. Trapped in the basement, I'd had plenty of time to consider other approaches. Gould's locker shared a back panel with the locker behind it, which was empty. Whoever built the place had been more concerned about varnish and fluting than security. It was simply a matter of backing out about thirty-six wood screws, which was easier said than done because, after a careful search, I concluded that I'd have to do the whole thing with the tip of a key.

Five hours. My fingertips red and swollen from the work. My nerves shot from bolting back to the safety of the guest locker every time I heard that old building creak or saw a glimmer of light near the locker-room entrance. I knew these old run-the-world types liked to wake up early. At Davies Group, they were always suggesting six a.m. breakfasts (you know, after squash). When the gray-blue of predawn started showing through a basement window, I started to sweat. When I heard the rattle and clank of the stewards' arrival, my heart rate revved up like a hummingbird's. Blood welled around my cuticles from working the screws. I could hear voices upstairs when I yanked the last fastener out and pulled back the panel.

There was a jock and an old squash duffel in Gould's locker. In the duffel there were twelve brown bags: $120,000 total, in neat stacks of cash. No wonder I couldn't sway him.

Never return to the scene of a crime. It's good advice. But unfortunately, by the time I extricated myself from the Met Club and arrived at work, I really had no other choice.

I asked Marcus where the Gould-Davies meeting was taking place.

'The Metropolitan Club,' he said. I felt nauseated.

'Lunch?'

'Breakfast,' he said, and glanced at the time on the phone on his desk. 'About now, probably.'

So, still reeking of nervous sweat after my long night of B and E, I found myself strolling up to Seventeenth and H Street Northwest, with the Secret Service glaring down from the tops of the high-rises around the White House. Closed-circuit cameras kept watch on every corner. And there was the police officer examining the broken window latch in the rear of the Metropolitan Club, where I had made my escape two hours before. There were a half a dozen cops in the lobby and, of course, the same steward from yesterday.

He gave me a not-so-friendly look. I told him I was there to see Henry Davies and took a seat in the library. He kept his eyes fixed on me as he went back to talk to the cops. I could see into the dining room from where I sat. It was the size of a football field, so it took me a while to catch sight of Davies, who was sitting at a table across from Gould, spreading jam on a croissant.

What could I do? Walk into the middle of the Met Club, publicly accuse Gould of taking bribes, then politely explain to the gathered dignitaries, Davies, and various thick-necked representatives of the Metro Police that I'd come across my circumstantial evidence by stalking the guy and breaking into and out of these hallowed halls? Davies had me the most worried. He'd offered me decency and I'd repaid him with crime. Just another con man. It was in my blood. Any shot I had at an honest life was a gross mistake, soon to be corrected.

I tried to follow his and Gould's conversation from their gestures and watched it segue from chitchat to substance, as Davies moved a little closer, over the table. I was watching for the ask. The yes-or-no that would decide my fate. I saw Davies lean in farther, then sit back. Then nothing. Gould looked pensive. Neither spoke. Was that it?

I was watching so intently that it took me a while to notice that two of the cops were now staring at me. When I looked back at the table I saw Gould make a pained expression and raise his hands. It was clear enough. He was saying no. Just like that, the decent life slipped away.

So what the hell did I have to lose?

Three cops were now having an earnest discussion, their eyes fixed on me. I fished out my cell phone and called the

Metropolitan Club. A moment later the phone started ringing at the reception desk. I told them I was the assistant to Gould's boss, and that the call was urgent. Then I watched the steward make his way across the checker tiles to interrupt Davies and Gould's meeting.

As Gould walked out of the dining room, I walked in, fast, past the cops. One broke away and stayed between me and the exit. As I approached his table, Davies seemed oddly unsurprised to see me there.

I leaned over and whispered, 'Gould is on the take,' then showed him a picture I had shot with my phone: the money stacked in the duffel. Davies didn't ask any questions. His demeanor didn't change.

'Go,' he whispered. A police officer saw to that. He gripped my arm in a very persuasive come-along hold and steered me back toward the library, where the other police and the steward were waiting.

'Were you on the premises here yesterday, son?' a plain-clothes detective, presumably running the show, asked me.

'Yes.'

'Why don't you wait right here with us.'

The cops asked the steward for Admiral Cassidy's number. More patrol cars pulled up outside, lights flashing. Two officers flanked me. I was fucked. My mind flashed forward through every step – handcuffs, squad car, the holding cell with the center-stage toilet and the crowd of DC's funkiest lowlifes, the interviews, the shitty coffee, the worthless public defender, the arraignment: that judge looking down at me like the one ten years before had. But this time there were no second chances. They'd finally recognize me for what I was, a hustler in a suit I didn't pay for. I couldn't even see around the wall of blue polyester cop uniform to find out what happened between Davies and Gould.

'Can I help you gentlemen?' It was Davies, standing behind me. The steward withered under his stare. The cops backed off a few inches.

'You know this man?' one asked.

'Of course,' Davies said. 'He is an associate at my firm. One of my best.'

'And he is an acquaintance of Admiral Cassidy?'

'I had hoped to introduce them yesterday, but I was held up at the office. I was thinking of putting this gentleman up for membership here at the Met. Anup, this is Michael Ford.'

'Pleased to meet you,' the steward said. I could see he was bristling behind his practiced smile.

'Likewise,' I said.

'Now, what is this all about?' Davies asked.

'Just a misunderstanding, sir,' the steward replied.

'Then you gentlemen will excuse us?'

'Of course,' the detective said.

Davies's manner was obliging, but he clearly commanded the scene. I finally had a chance to look into the dining room. Gould still sat at the table, staring down at his coffee like it would tell him the future. He looked sucker-punched.

'It'd probably be best for you to leave,' Davies whispered to me. He had this sphinxy look I couldn't peg. I still wasn't sure if my cat-burglar act had saved the day or detonated my career. Maybe he'd fobbed off the cops so he could mete out the punishment himself. Just before I left, he told me, 'Be in my office at three.'

His suite was at the end of the seemingly endless executive corridor. I knew I was being a little dramatic, but I couldn't shake the image I'd seen in a dozen movies of the final stroll down death row. He kept me waiting in a little hallway outside his office until 3:20. I'd been up for roughly thirty-four hours; fatigue weighed down my body like a dentist's lead blanket. Finally, I saw Davies striding up the hallway. He walked straight into his office and beckoned me in behind him. I stood as he stopped beside his desk.

He pinned me for a while with that same inscrutable look then took something out of his pocket and held it up between his thumb and index finger. It was a wood screw, and it looked awfully familiar. I'd twisted in enough to secure the locker's back panel, and I'd covered the empty holes with the wood trim. I guess I'd forgotten one.

'Play any squash recently, Ford?'

I'd keep my mouth shut until I could see where this was going. Davies stood twisting the screw slowly between his thumb and finger, then he tossed it up in the air. I snatched it a foot in front of my chest.

'Gould said yes,' Davies said.

'And the police?'

Davies waved it away. 'And don't worry about the admiral. He's getting a little soft, introduces himself to his own reflection.'

'I apologize for—'

'Forget about it. Your exploits may have been a little bit more cowboy than I'd have chosen, but the important thing is we got to yes. Fifty-eight million dollars.'

'Fifty-eight?'

He nodded. 'I signed on a few more parties this week.'

'And what happens to Gould? Do you go to the inspector general at Commerce, the police?'

Davies shook his head. 'Ninety-nine percent of these cases get buried. If he had a bunch of body parts in there, it would be a different story, but the sad fact is a hundred-twenty-grand sweetener is nickel-and-dime stuff in this town. Though I'm glad you caught it.'

'So how did you bring him around? Just threaten to out him? Is it like . . .' I tried to find a nice word for it.

'Blackmail?' Davies said.

'No, sir, I didn't mean to suggest—'

'You haven't hurt my feelings,' Davies said, laughing a bit. '*Blackmail* is a little too crude a term to describe the work we perform. Though it would be a refreshingly direct alternative. Picture it. You show a guy a photo of himself ass-end up in a motel with some pross, and say, "Campaign finance reform now, or it's curtains for you." '

Davies considered that for a moment. 'It has a certain straightforward appeal, I'll admit. But no. Gould is a smart guy. You need only say you've heard he may have gotten in over his head. You say you might be able to help him avoid any unpleasantness. Usually you don't even have to say that much. Suddenly he's all ears, suddenly so agreeable. People don't acquire power by being dim, at least not when it comes to their own self-interest.

'It's win-win,' Davies went on. 'Typically the guy knocks off whatever the hell he was up to faster and more certainly than any ethics investigation could ever have gotten him to. Meanwhile we advance the policies we believe in. We make the best of their bad behavior.'

I stood by the window, considering that little wood screw between my still-raw fingertips.

'You were thrown into the hardball pretty suddenly, Mike. You never see it in the papers. But that's how things are done. I think you're cut out for it.'

It didn't feel right. Maybe it was that strange reluctance you get when you're offered something you've wanted so badly for so long: you're scared to take it once it's yours. Or maybe I just wanted things black and white. I wanted that decent life without a shred of gray. And now I'd found out that what I was running toward was tangled up with what I was running from.

'There's something you should know, sir. Full disclosure. About that trouble—'

'I know everything I need to know about you, Mike. I hired you – well, not because of it, but because of the good you can do with it.'

He stuck his hand out. 'Are you still on board?'

I could see the capital's skyline through the window behind him. The kingdoms of the world and all their glory.

'Yes, sir,' I said. We shook.

'Good,' he said. 'Now call me Henry. The way you say *sir* makes me feel like a goddamn drill instructor. And tell the real estate agent you'll take that place on Ingleside Terrace.'

The house in Mount Pleasant. 'I may hold off for now, find somewhere with a little lower rent, sock away some more savings.'

'Rent?' Davies said. 'No. If you like it, buy it. Understand this, Mike. You never have to worry about money again.'

'Well, I do have some past debts, school loans. Maybe now isn't—'

He slid a folder across the desk. 'The civil case against Crenshaw Collection Services. Ready to file. The criminal complaint will be set by Wednesday. We're going to tear their spines out.'

He led me to a pair of French doors before I could even register what was happening.

'Now, Marcus will be your mentor, but I thought I'd introduce you to the rest of the gang.'

He opened the doors into a conference room that put the Met Club to shame. The principals – a gallery of the weightiest heavies of them all – were waiting for me.

'Everyone, I'm pleased to present Michael Ford, our newest senior associate.'

They applauded, then passed me around, shaking my hand and clapping my shoulder. I'd been at Davies for four months – May through August. Someone told me it was the shortest time to promotion in the history of the Davies Group.

Davies raised his hand, and the room quieted. 'Now let's get out of here,' he said in his half whisper. 'I'll see you all at Brasserie Beck in half an hour. We have the back room.'

The principals made their last congratulations as they ambled out. Davies walked me down to the second floor to a beautiful office, as cozy as an Oxford library.

'We'll move you up here on Monday.'

He caught me measuring the distance, not more than fifty feet, to Annie Clark's door. He gave me the faintest smile but didn't say a word. The guy really did know his levers.

'What do you want, Mike? Name it.'

I blanked. I had everything I'd been gunning for. A decent life, a good job, respect. And more, something I never thought possible. Going after Gould had thrilled me in a way I'd missed for years, ever since I'd given up hustling. And Davies was happy with it, the honest work and the not-so-honest habits I could never shake. I could be the man I wanted and not have to hide where I'd come from.

'I'm happy, sir. Really. This is all too much.'

'Anything,' he urged me. This wasn't some inspirational exercise, I realized. He was serious. I was silent for a minute, daring to take him at his word.

'I don't know if this is the right . . .' I trailed off. He probably thought I was calculating a doable ask: a Benz SLK350, a private bathroom. But the only thing I could think of to ask for was trickier than that, because I'd been covering it up for so long, and because, to tell a hard truth, some part of me didn't even want it.

'My father,' I said. 'He . . .' I trailed off.

'I know about your father.'

'He has a parole hearing coming up. He has sixteen years in, and eight left. Can you help get him out?'

'I'll do everything I can, Mike. Everything.'

Chapter Three

In the weeks after my promotion, I kept being assigned to cases that Annie Clark was also working on. I began to wonder if Henry Davies was somehow behind our being thrown together so often, though it was never exactly seven minutes in heaven.

We were both now senior associates, but she was very clearly the boss on every project. She'd already been at the firm for four years, and rumor had it she was on track to be the first female partner. She clocked a lot of one-on-one time with Henry, the ultimate sign of clout around the office.

Davies Group had a macho, competitive streak that reminded me of those Harvard Law seminar rooms. Annie could more than hold her own against the boys. She did it with poise, a dry humor, and a toughness that, coming from a woman so graceful, was especially lethal. The downside, for my purposes, was that she wasn't someone you could just flirt with. She scared the shit out of most guys.

Working the kind of hours we worked, we developed a rapport and grew to be good friends around the office. Every so often, sitting at the end of an empty conference room at eleven at night, going over the final revisions on a report for a client, I would pick up on a shared vibe: a warmth from her that made it seem like the most natural thing for me to slide closer to her, to touch her arm, her shoulder, stare into her eyes. I got the strangest feeling that she was watching, testing me, to see how bold I really was.

I could easily have been deluding myself, however. I had a serious crush going. And it seemed a uniquely bad idea, now that I'd clawed my way into the good life here at Davies, to make a pass at a woman who, while not quite my boss, was definitely a higher-up and close to Davies himself. And I certainly wasn't going to pull anything in the circumstances we usually found ourselves: sweating a tight deadline surrounded by colleagues.

My schemer's mind was always revving red, contriving ways to throw us together, but she caught me first. Davies Group had a gym in the basement. You opened an unassuming door in a back corner by the parking garage and then found yourself in a twelve-thousand-square-foot fitness utopia: rows of gleaming new equipment, flat-screen TVs, and workout clothes with the Davies Group logo carefully folded and waiting for you.

Around midnight or one a.m., after the cleaning folks had left and the whole building was empty, when you're still working and starting to get the crazies from staring too long at a computer, that gym was heaven.

I was down there one night, and with sixteen hours of bottled-up energy to burn off, I guess I was going a little overboard, doing rounds of treadmill sprints, pull-ups, push-ups, and thrusters, sweating and panting and blasting my iPod. In the course of trying not to retch or let the weights fall on my head, I perhaps forgot myself. In my entire time at Davies, I think I'd seen one other person in there that late. I mean, what kind of maniac uses the office gym at one in the morning?

Excuses, excuses for the inexcusable. A certain song, let's say 'Respect' by Aretha Franklin, came on shuffle on my iPod, and I may have been belting it out at the top of my lungs. And maybe dancing a little between sets. I'll blame the endorphins.

Regardless, just as I was hitting my crescendo during the chorus, I did a little half turn and found Annie, faking innocence, on the elliptical eight feet away. This was the second time she'd sneaked up on me. I stopped dead in the middle of the 'sock it to me's.

She performed a very polite golf clap.

'Oh boy,' I said.

She walked toward me and looked at the screen of my iPod. 'Aretha, huh? I didn't quite peg you for that.'

I raised my eyebrows. 'That?'

'Soulful.'

'Ouch.'

'Not like that,' she protested. 'I mean, it's not exactly a sound track I had imagined when I saw you down here, doing . . . what was that thing on the ground?'

It was called a burpee, though I wasn't about to say that to Annie. 'Nothing,' I said. 'I happen to have a lot of soul.'

'I could tell. Snazzy moves.'

'Thanks.' Deep breath. No time like the present. 'Hey, why don't we get together outside of work. What are you up to this weekend?'

She frowned. 'I'm busy.'

Damage-control time. 'That's cool. We should hang out sometime, though.'

'I'd really like that,' she said, and she draped her towel around her neck. 'Actually, do you like hiking?'

If she had asked if I were into metal detecting, I'd have said yes. 'Oh yeah.'

'Some friends of mine and I are heading out to the country on Saturday, if you're free.'

And that's how I found myself scrambling hands and feet over granite boulders in Shenandoah National Park, with Annie chugging along ahead of me in hiking boots and knee-high wool socks that gave her a distinctly Swiss vibe. Somehow, when I'd pictured her off the clock, I had conjured up scenes of her as a high-society dame in a period drama, waltzing. So imagine my surprise when Annie Clark – blue blood in her veins, Yale on her résumé – led me to a swimming hole in moonshine country.

Her friends said that the water would be too cold for swimming, but she shrugged and looked at me. I didn't care if it was the North Sea. We headed down, just the two of us.

A cascade dropped forty feet through a gorge surrounded by old-growth forest. It was early September, still hot, but the water was ice-cold. Annie took off her shoes and socks and long-sleeved shirt and dropped in first. Seeing her glide through the clear water and then lie out on the bank in her sports bra and hiking shorts, patches of sunlight moving across her smooth skin as the wind moved the branches overhead – to this day that memory stops my heart. I stripped down to my shorts and jumped in. If she were a Siren, I'd have gladly drowned trying to get to her. I didn't think she'd actually call me out on that, though.

'You want to go under the falls?' she asked.

'Sure,' I said. I managed to restrain my first answer: Yes, God, yes.

'It can be a little scary,' she said.

'I think I'll be okay.' I mean, really, what could this sheltered little pixie have in store that could possibly scare me?

She walked up to a rock face formed by two massive boulders – each thirty feet tall – wedged together. 'In here,' she said, and pointed at something between them that wasn't even a crevice; it was maybe a crack. Inside, it was pitch-black.

She wedged herself in and inched into the darkness. I followed. Eight feet in, we were totally blind. There was no space. You could feel your breath bouncing back off the wall in front of you, and hear, distinctly, the sound of rushing water ahead.

'Watch your step here,' Annie said, a disembodied voice in the blackness. I brushed against her hand, and she took mine and led me around a sharp corner. We were in a pocket deep in the side of the mountain. Water dripped from overhead, ran down my face.

'And then into this pool.' The floor fell away. We dropped into ice-cold water up to my belly button. The roof of the cavern sloped down, and the pool got deeper until there was about a foot of headroom above the surface of the water. It was getting a little claustrophobic and drown-y even for me, and I'd spent my fair share of time in windowless ship holds and had gotten suffocated by the best of them at the navy's Recruit Training Command, Great Lakes.

I was starting to wonder just how brass Annie's balls were when that sweet voice informed me: 'Okay, now we're going to duck under and sort of swim through this little underwater tunnel. It's about twelve feet, and then the current will take you the rest of the way and spit you out in this cave under the waterfall.'

'Uhh . . . okay.' Except not okay. I'm not too proud to admit that sounded pretty fucking scary.

'You trust me?'

'Less and less.'

She laughed. 'Just hold your breath and don't fight the current. Ready? Go!'

I heard her inhale, then saw her drop under the surface. I dove down and slipped underwater along the smooth rock walls. I fought back panic. The tunnel was maybe two feet wide, too narrow to use my arms, and completely full of water. There was no way to come up for air. I could only move ahead by kicking. The current picked up, and a second later a wall of water plowed into me from the side and dragged me out into a larger stream. The sunlight hit me like a camera flash after so long in the dark. I shot out of a chute ten feet in the air and landed in a pool in a little open cavern behind the deafening curtain of the main waterfall.

We both came up panting, eyes wide. I was so wired and glad to be alive I grabbed her in a bear hug. 'Holy shit!' I said.

'Right?'

I probably said *holy shit* a few more times and then realized I was in a grotto with Annie. We were both feeling punchy from our near-death dunk. Of course it was too soon to try anything; overeager, I could have ruined the good thing I had going with my dream girl. But come on. A grotto. Under a waterfall. What else could I do?

We looked each other in the eyes. Nothing from her – not a quick look away, but neither that gauzy smooch-me look. No guts, no glory. I got a little closer, a little closer, and . . . still nothing. No lean in, no lean back. A hundred per cent poker face. Stand your ground, man. I closed the distance by 50 per cent, 70, 90, 95 . . . When you are on a very clear descent path to a kiss, maybe not at the very beginning of it, but certainly when your faces are two inches apart and closing, you expect that any halfway decent young woman will give you at least a little sign to tell you if you're home free or blowing your chance.

Nothing. I've never seen anything like it. She didn't react.

I was between the trenches, totally exposed, stranded in no-man's-land. I wasn't going to park one on Miss Annie Clark without getting a welcome sign, however tiny.

So I stopped, an inch away from bliss. This was high stakes:

dream girl, see her at work every day, and so on. I pulled back. She was still staring. Still the poker face.

'It's hard not to kiss you in a place like this.'

'I'd have kissed you back,' she said. 'I guess I was just curious to see how far you'd go.'

I thought about this for a second, then ran my fingers through her hair above her ear, cupped her nape gently, and gave her the kind of leading-man, swelling-strings, knee-weakening kiss they just don't make anymore.

When she dropped me off at my house later that night, I asked when I could see her again.

'We'll see,' she said, and blew me a kiss. 'I try not to shit where I eat.'

I was reeling, still a little shocked that I had broken through with Annie so quickly and trying to square that badass girl from the mountains with the Washington sophisticate I knew from work.

The whole romance had happened, and kept happening, so naturally.

There were a few formal dates in the beginning where I tried to impress her with highbrow delights – tasting menus, wine bars, after-hours drinks at the Phillips Collection – but I was surprised by how quickly we fell into the habits of a contented couple. If we didn't have to work, we could hang out the entire weekend at my place: walking through the neighborhood, spending half the day sitting outside a café, or just reading on the porch. We didn't want to be apart. I watched happily as she colonized my bathroom, one item at a time – first a toothbrush, then a shampoo bottle – slowly staking her claim. My place was bigger than hers, and closer to work. There was no reason for her to go back to her one-bedroom in Glover Park. Like the apartments of most DC workaholics, it was sparsely furnished, with packed boxes hidden in the closets.

One night about three months after that first kiss, she came over straight from work with a bundle of dry cleaning she'd had done near our office. We had a late dinner. I was sitting up on the couch, and she was lying down across it, her legs up on the arm, and her head on my thigh as I stroked her hair. She put her book down and looked over to her outfits hanging in plastic on the doorknob of my front-hall closet.

'Would you mind if I left those here? It would probably be easier than running home at midnight all the time.'

I looked at them thoughtfully. My strategy in the early days of the relationship was to not scare her off by blurting out 'Marry me' whenever she looked me in the eye. I hoped we'd just grow closer and closer, more and more comfortable together, until I had nabbed her without getting into any of the tricky business of relationship talks. It had paid off so far. This was one of those moments when I had to consciously hold my tongue. The truth was, even that early on, I'd have loved for her to just move in.

'I don't want to crowd you or anything like that,' she said.

'Please do,' I said. 'You're the best thing that ever happened to me.' I leaned over and kissed her. She ran her hand through my hair and gave me a long, melting look that indicated the party would be moving to the bedroom.

But then her phone rang. It was on the table, next to me.

'Turn that off,' she said.

I looked at the screen. 'It's Henry Davies.'

She sat up. 'Do you mind?' she asked, and then tried to play it off casually. 'Just in case it's important. I'm doing the ask on the head of the SEC tomorrow.'

'Go for it,' I said, then silently cursed the phone.

She answered and, after a moment, stepped onto the porch to take the call. She was out in the cold for about five minutes.

'Sorry about that,' she said when she came back. She stood behind the couch, leaned over, pressed her cheek against mine, then kissed my neck.

'What do you and Henry talk about all the time?' I asked. We were falling in love, sure, but we both still worked at Davies Group, and that meant a certain amount of jockeying for position, of searching out leverage. We just couldn't help it.

'That's above your pay grade.' She gave me a troublemaker's smile. 'Now,' she said, and ran her hand across my chest. 'Shall we?'

I let the matter drop, then led her by the hand upstairs.

The job, Annie: I had everything I'd ever wanted. It all seemed too easy. Because, of course, it was.

Chapter Four

Welcome to the district, where the fun never starts. I can't count the number of times during my first year in DC that some starched collar at some stick-up-its-butt schmooze-fest told me, 'If you want a friend in Washington, get a dog,' then wheezed laughter. Supposedly the quote came from Truman. Whenever I heard it, I was made aware of two things: First, that social niceties were so lacking in DC that their absence had perversely become a point of pride. Second, that the guy I was talking to thought it was funny to announce that he would shaft me if I gave him half a chance.

Well, at least they're honest. It's easy to make friends in the capital, but hard to make good ones, since the place is packed with barely distinguishable transient twenty-somethings who all work in the same industry – politics – where the essential skills are glad-handing and faked charm. Tuck, the Rhodes scholar who worked with me at Davies, stood out from the parade of acquaintances I acquired in DC.

He was the scion of a Georgetown public-service dynasty: grandfather a former CIA director, father a higher-up at State. He was also on a fast track at Davies Group, yet, maybe because he was born into it, he seemed less obsessed with politics and power than the rest of our peers. We worked a couple projects together and late at night would blow off steam by taking a short break and throwing a football around on the Davies Group lawn. One night, around midnight, he overshot a pass straight into the compound that housed the Syrian embassy. I have some experience in getting over fences, so it wasn't a big problem. He and I clambered over. Only in Kalorama can you enter the territory of a hostile nation to fetch your ball. We'd only just grabbed it when a flash of light shot out from behind a garage. I gave Tuck a boost and then vaulted over the wall just in time.

After that, we started hanging out more outside of work. He knew everyone – rumor had it he was sleeping with the VP's daughter – and introduced me around.

When I first got to town, I'd thought parties were, well, parties. The kind where, if you got the right people and a certain groove going, magic things happen: people start dancing, there's smooching on fire escapes, everyone's still talking around a fire when the sun comes up – you know, fun. But even the twenty-somethings in DC party like married fifty-year-olds, all networking. Tuck was house-sitting for his parents one weekend and invited me over for a barbecue. It was a big Georgetown spread, with a pool in the back, and there were a lot of people there. We began drinking early in the afternoon, and I can't remember if he or I started talking about a dip, but I stripped down to my shorts and dove in. I recall it being a fantastic idea in midair, and refreshing enough a second later. But when I came up for air, soggy and solo in the deep end under the moonlight, I saw no other bathers, only a scandalized crew that included about half the National Security Council's Europe staff. I got the message: never enjoy yourself at a party.

I kept that insight in mind as I headed to this night's cocktail party. The host was a publisher, a well-connected fellow named Chip. That was way up there in the fierce competition for WASPiest names I'd heard at Harvard or DC. (Tuck was actually Everett Tucker Straus IV. The general method in preppy nomenclature is to start with something unbearably stuffy, like Winthrop, and then shorten it to something ridiculous, like Winnie.)

Whenever I arrived at the front door of a place like Chip's – near the US Naval Observatory and the British embassy, another monster Georgetown estate – I had a twinge of that old feeling of being out of place, an interloper. When I rang the bell, I could almost believe that I was a teenage hood again, checking to see if anybody was home, listening for dogs, and clutching a handful of shattered spark-plug ceramic. (These are called ninja rocks in the trade. Even though they feel as light as peanuts, if you toss them at a window, something about the hardness of the ceramic will shatter the glass as surely as a heaved cinder block, but as quietly as drizzling rain. Magic.)

Those days were long gone, of course. When the Filipina nanny opened the door, I looked down to see not my old burgling duds – canvas painter's paints and a hoodie – but my gray Canali with a blue pinstripe and a nice straight gig line.

You might think that given a calendar full of starched-collar nights, of counting drinks and watching what I say, I'd be bored stiff. And at first I was, but eventually I learned that there was a far different kind of fun happening at these quiet salons. Beneath the surface, the passed hors d'oeuvres and polite laughter, the real game is pinpointing weaknesses, extracting promises, gathering intel, avoiding commitments, planting doubts, and sowing rivalries. The well-behaved chatter is a full-contact sport. It comes down to who's a matador and who's a bull. It's a game I was mastering, day by day. Not quite as fun as a moonlight dip, but it had its charms.

A collection of Washington dons and socialites can be a

little intimidating at first, but as I moved farther into the party, I started to see a few familiar faces, and soon enough I was chatting and cracking jokes, fully in the mix. It was now April; I'd been in DC for eleven months, and in that time the Davies Group had opened a lot of doors. This rarefied world was now my scene.

In fact, the present company offered a not-bad recap of my short and mostly happy rise at Davies Group. Here, for instance, among a clutch of youngish ladies, was Senator Michael Roebling, announcing with a modesty that was almost convincing: 'When you see the look in those children's eyes, that's "thank you" enough.'

That would be the Heartland Kids Fund, which we'd helped Roebling set up. There are dozens of ways to buy politicians legally – soft money to a PAC, bundling hard money . . . I could go on for hours. Yet those weren't quite enough for Roebling. Most of that money had to go to campaign expenses, a term you can interpret liberally, but not liberally enough for the good senator's appetites.

When he couldn't get enough personal kitty from legal graft, we offered him some advice and guidance in organizing his little nonprofit, which did, well, a little bit of feel-good everything: summer camps for the delinquents, Disneyland trips for the ailing, petting zoos for the simple-minded, you name it. Donations to a nonprofit are unlimited, exempt from all the reporting hassles that have made fund-raising such a drag over the past decade. And, since the board and staff of Heartland Kids were stocked with Roebling pals, the senator was free to spend however much of the money on the kids his conscience required and leave the rest for the feedbag: cushy jobs for the in-laws, retreat centers near his favorite fly-fishing spots, all-expenses-paid trips, and so forth. His conscience, it turned out, didn't require much.

It's perhaps not the proudest thing I've ever done in my life, but at the very least the kids (and Davies Group, and me) got their cut of the lucre the senator was determined to get his hands on anyway. The Davies Group steered him toward making some good policy at the same time. I had learned that was the way it worked in DC. You couldn't get anything done if you were a choirboy.

Now Roebling pulled out a photo of a little kid in a wheelchair. The senator, a true humanitarian, was getting choked up. A young woman comforted him. He put his arm around her shoulders. I had to excuse myself before I threw up.

And so on it went, around the room: this one needed to get a son out of a felony marijuana possession (Winnie Jr had been following Phish); that one just wanted a membership in Pine Valley; she had to get her dimwit kid into St Albans; and this poor stooped-over bastard had more wife than he could handle and sold out his principles on an immigration bill in exchange for help in getting Celine Dion to sing at the missus's fiftieth birthday party.

Those were the fun ones, the good anecdotes. More often it was simply a grind of finding out who – legislators, regulators, big-time CEOs, special interest groups, foreign governments – needed what favor and who could get it done for what price. Half the time we didn't even have to search out the influentials. They came to Davies, knowing that we discreetly worked out deals between groups that could never admit they were cheek by jowl. The Davies Group was like a massive trading floor, connecting Washington's wants and needs and taking a small percentage for its services.

After a while, all the wheeling and dealing and naked self-interest can make you a little cynical about this town, make you feel like you need a long, hot bath. So I was glad when I looked across the room and saw a handsome man in his midfifties with his coat and hat in his hand, looking less than at ease among the chattering classes.

It was Malcolm Haskins, an associate justice on the Supreme Court and a crucial swing vote on close decisions. He was a very rare sight on the DC social circuit. He looked as unassuming as a high-school science teacher. He avoided the Georgetown cocktail-party scene and was so scrupulous about his impartiality that he wouldn't so much as eat a crab cake at a sponsored reception.

Seeing him was a nice pick-me-up. The logrolling we did at Davies was an inevitable part of politics; it's all there in the Federalist Papers. But even though I was immersed in all the deal-cutting, I liked knowing that there were men and institutions that stood apart and incorruptible.

I examined a piece of modern art on the wall – a woman with four boobs, as far as I could tell – as I waited for the line at the bar to subside. A kinky brown mop of a dog materialized and started yapping and jumping all over me.

It's not that I hate dogs, it's just that we don't have the best history. I can fool all of the people some of the time, and some of the people all of the time, but somehow dogs always sniff me out as a home intruder at heart.

A tight-faced woman walked over, grabbed the beast's collar, and flashed me an apologetic look.

At the same time I felt a stealthy presence beside me. It was Marcus, very much enjoying the show as the dog continued its conniptions.

'Is that a Labradoodle?' he asked.

'Schnoodle,' the woman said.

Marcus smiled. 'Adorable.'

She pulled the dog, still all snapping teeth, away to another room.

'Smart dog,' Marcus said.

'What can I do for you, boss?'

'On your eight o'clock,' Marcus said. I peered over and saw Congressman Eric Walker of Mississippi, who at thirty-two was the youngest member of the House of Representatives.

Bummer. Marcus had invited me to this shindig, but he hadn't told me I'd be working. I had been wondering why he'd asked me, since these folks were a few rungs above me on the social ladder. Now it made sense.

'You thought I brought you here because of your glittering personality?'

'I thought maybe you missed me.' I glanced back at Walker. 'Don't worry. I'm on it.'

I made my way to the sunroom, where the bar was set up, and planted myself in Walker's vicinity without being too obvious about it. With chagrin, instead of Maker's Mark, I ordered a tonic and lime, the official drink of keeping your wits about you while others wash theirs away.

Speaking of: I felt a palm pound on my back, took my drink, and turned to find Walker and a practiced handshake. *The bull enters the arena.*

'How's it going?' I asked.

'Can't complain.'

'And if you could, who'd listen, right?' I said.

'Amen to that.'

We clinked glasses.

Toro!

I'd been hanging out with Walker for a few months now. He had a medium-stakes poker game and on weekends he liked to pick off the fund-raising tarts of Georgetown.

As he and I caught up, I noticed Marcus passing through an entryway on the other side of the sunroom, taking us in through his peripheral vision. Marcus was shepherding me along in the business, and he had played Yenta to my growing friendship with the representative from Mississippi. Walker was all manners around most Washingtonians, but Marcus had watched him long enough to know he liked to loosen up around the younger guys. That's how I got tapped.

Walker was a comer, and he was on track to join the 500 – a little piece of slang they used around Davies Group. I usually heard it only when somebody slipped up, because officially it didn't exist. It wasn't too hard for me to figure out: it was a list of the five hundred people inside the Beltway with real power, the select who ran Washington and, by extension, the country. The Davies Group wanted to be damn sure it was chummy with every one of them. I'd been rising at the company, getting more risks, more responsibilities, more leash. Walker was my next assignment.

And what exactly was the job? Well, when you got right down to it, the work I did for Marcus was a confidence game.

He had brought me into his office a few days after I made senior associate. 'Don't let it go to your head,' he said.

'I won't,' I replied. 'Fortune favors fools, and I got damn lucky catching Gould.'

He looked relieved. 'Then I can skip the part where I convince you of that. We're in the business of changing men's minds. How do you figure we do it?'

'Stumble across piles of dirty money in gym lockers?'

'When appropriate. But for the most part it's a grind.'

And so began my long education in the trade. Actually, it was more of a refresher. My dad used to run cons. He went to prison when I was twelve, so what I got from him directly was very little: overheard snippets of conversation before he closed a door, glimpses of forged papers before he chased me out of the room with his hand cocked back to hit me, though he never really unloaded.

Crime runs in families, but I've never met anyone who intended to pass it down. As my mother told me, everything shady my father did he did so that I would have legitimate opportunities, would never be tempted to follow in his footsteps. But vice sticks around, permeates a place, like years of cigarette smoke. As well-intentioned as he may have been, as much as he tried to hide the seamy side of his life from us, my older brother, Jack, and I absorbed everything. And once he was gone, there was nothing to hold us back.

Your average adolescent boy is up to enough criminal mischief that it would have been hard to tell we were bound for something other than garden-variety pyromania, shoplifting, and sneaking into construction sites and our own high school after hours. Our crew was a set of boys, mostly children of my father's friends, who were always trying to one-up each other. If Smiles, age fifteen, took his father's Lincoln out for a joyride, then Luis would take his neighbor's BMW. You can see how things might get very hairy very quickly. And by the time I was sixteen, and my brother and his friends were around twenty-one, there was really no question that the hard core of them were moving deeper into crime and would never go straight. Community college or what, managing the deli at Food Lion? No. They had the cars and girlfriends and drug habits and gambling thirsts that called for fast and easy money, no union dues or payroll tax.

At first I tried to stay out of all this, since I didn't have the maniac impulse shared by the rest of the boys (although when they dared me to do anything, jumping off roofs and so on, I wouldn't back down. I was more afraid of losing face than breaking my neck). In the back of my mind I always thought of disappointing my father. I tagged along when they would let me, mostly keeping my head down. When singled out and pressed, I would join any mission (we called them missions, like we were the A-Team and not a bunch of hoods). For most of my teens, though, I was more geek than crook. My main criminal passion was taking apart and reassembling locks and dead-bolts. It was fun, done more for curiosity than profit, and not unlike the science labs I was really getting into in school.

With my father off in prison, my brother got more and more into cons and grifts. Maybe it was a way of connecting with my dad. I loved hustles too, loved the logic of them, the neat mechanisms of a well-laid con, like a loaded spring behind the bail of a mousetrap. But Jack had the boldness I lacked, and that was a necessity for shaking people down. My father had it too. It's the willingness to make a scene, to stand in the middle of a restaurant screaming and acting indignant and cheated when the indignities and cheats are all your own doing. When my brother allowed me to come along on one of these cons, I'd hide my shaking hands and, desperate to impress him, play the part, shouting to the whole restaurant that I'd given the guy a fifty and I could prove it.

I was a typical younger brother; I would have done anything Jack asked me to. After my mother got sick, any compunction about stealing went out the window. There was no question that we would do what we had to to pay those bills. And one night, when I was nineteen, and the best lock pick by far that he or his friends knew, he asked me to pull a little job for him. I said yes. It wrecked my life so profoundly that only now, ten years later, was I finally getting it back on track.

The more Marcus taught me, the more I realized my new line of work was very much in keeping with the family business.

Here at Davies, instead of *casing*, we 'assessed' our subjects.

The *hook* became 'development', the *roper* and the *shill* became 'access agents', the *take* became the 'ask', and *cooling the mark* and the *blow-off* became 'termination'.

I must say, the lingo sucked. Instead of the *Jamaican switch*, the *rag*, and the old *pig in a poke*, we had the '501(c)(3)s', 'PACs', and 'affiliated committees'.

But despite all the old-fashioned grifter jargon I liked to collect as a kid, the fact was I knew shit about the real core of both businesses, which was gaining men's trust and getting them to do what you wanted. My father always tried to keep me out of it. I guess he thought if he was crooked enough, he could afford to keep me clean. That made me an eager student as Marcus taught me the straight world's version of everything my father kept from me.

If there was one thing to learn about *human-asset recruitment* – the jargon Marcus occasionally let drop for what we were doing – it was this: MICE. That stands for *money*, *ideology*, *compromise/coercion*, and *ego*. For our purposes, those were the only reasons anyone did anything. It was the foundation for everything Marcus was walking me through, the finer points of all of Henry's talk about levers and owning men.

Marcus put it up on the whiteboard in his office and asked me if it made sense. I looked it over for a minute or two, shrugged, and said I'd give it a try.

'Let's say there's a guy named, I don't know, Henry, who wants to control some sap named Mike.' I walked back and forth in front of the board. 'Money, that's easy: Mike grew up without two nickels to rub together and is now drowning in debt. Ideology: poor Mike still buys that Horatio Alger American-dream bullshit that the meritocracy will always reward hard work and brains. Ego: Mike's blue-collar faux humility is just a cover for his conviction that he's the smartest guy around. On top of that he's got a monster chip on his shoulder about his incarcerated father and seedy past holding him back from the good life he deserves. In short, Mike is a sitting fucking duck.'

Marcus was laughing by this point. 'You forgot one,' he said.

'Compromise and coercion. What do you have on me, Marcus?'

He played it coy, said nothing, and wiped the board. 'Moving on to the McCain-Feingold Campaign Finance Reform Act of 2002 . . .'

It turned out he had plenty.

MICE: those four points became my bible.

Money's straightforward, and, though we can quibble about life philosophies, it can get most people pretty much anything they want as far as achievement and status are concerned. Ideology is getting people to believe in what you want. It'd be nice to think that it was the real trump card (and Americans always have thought that, Marcus explained), but mostly it comes into play in the negative. You can't get somebody to do something if he can't rationalize it to himself. The villain in every movie has to think he's the hero.

Compromise and coercion are getting the goods on someone. Americans as a rule try to avoid these approaches because they violate some basic notions of fair play (the Yankees think they can win everybody over with money and ideology), but it was bread-and-butter to the Chinese and Russians.

Ego is playing on someone's beliefs that he's somehow been shafted by life, that he's smarter than everyone else, or more hardworking, or more honest, and so he deserves a better job, more money, more respect, a better-looking spouse, whatever – beliefs that I imagine are held by about 99.99 per cent of the population.

Now, you may have noticed, like I did, that a lot of this theory – about Chinese and Russians, access agents and terminations – sounded a little hard core for government affairs work. I'd thought lobbying was more about wrangling loopholes over steaks. In fact, I was getting a distinct vibe about William Marcus, the man with no past.

I decided to confirm it one day. Marcus was out in back of the office smoking, which I should have taken as a sign not to mess with him because he only broke out the Camels when he was in the weeds. I walked up behind him as quietly as I could, toe-heel, toe-heel, like they taught us in the navy in a random drill about sentry removal (not that I spent a lot of time assassinating sentries – most of what I remember about the service was watching *8 Mile* over and over and trying to sleep despite the sound everywhere of guys jacking off).

I was actually pretty sure about what would go down and didn't expect to get too close to Marcus, but still, the speed of it surprised me. One second, I was up on tippy-toes, all sneaky behind him, and the next – so fast it felt like somebody had cut a few seconds out of a movie – I was on my face in the gravel with Marcus standing over me holding my palm between his thumb and index finger. He had twisted my arm into a precisely torturous angle that made any movement, even breathing, so painful that I briefly considered giving up on respiration. I looked up at him, and he was utterly bored, the cigarette held loosely between his lips, inflicting my agony with such one-handed ease he might have been flipping channels on a TV remote.

He let my arm unwind. 'Sorry, buddy,' he said. 'Startled me.'

'Don't mention it,' I said, playing down the red raging

soreness running from hand to shoulder. 'I think I figured out what I wanted to know.'

'Smart.'

I stood up. 'So what did you say you did before you joined Davies Group?'

'Trade adviser,' he said, completely deadpan, and dusted me off.

'Of course.'

So what do you get for the former CIA badass boss who has everything? I started getting my expenses in on time, that's for damn sure, and strictly by the book.

It was smart of Henry Davies to bring in old spooks and use their skills not to turn Soviets but to bring around pols. It sure explained a lot of the jargon Marcus used. There were plenty of intelligence guys around the navy, but I'd never met any of the operator types, the Special Warfare Group SEALs dudes, so it was pretty cool taking lessons from Marcus. I asked him one day, 'Are you ever going to teach me any . . . you know . . .'

'Monkey tricks? Killing people with an envelope? Shit like that?'

I guess that's what I meant.

'Nope,' he said. Instead he gave me a copy of a journal article: 'Adaptive and Maladaptive Narcissism among Politicians,' and a twelve-page psychology syllabus. Because all the sexy stuff was a distraction, party tricks. What the job required was a decent grasp of human nature and an iron-ass patience for both doing your homework and watching your prey.

Clearly, someone at Davies Group had done a good workup on Representative Walker. Before I met him, I knew him from the psych profile Marcus gave me: the gambling thing, the causes in Georgetown he 'supported', the crowd he ran with, a couple of hobbies.

Marcus asked me my plan for getting control of Walker.

'Waiting for another tip-off from the Hamburglar isn't going to cut it?'

'Nuh-uh,' Marcus said.

'Any suggestions?' I asked.

'Go make friends,' he said. He gave me fifteen hundred dollars out of petty cash and sent me out to get acquainted with Walker. It wasn't about dead drops or brush passes or whatever cool spy shit I wanted to learn. After all the psychology and jargon, it comes down to this: make him trust you, make him want to help you, make him your friend. That's the job. Hanging out with the bright young things. Tough life, huh?

The first time I really made any headway with Walker was at a preppy haunt on Wisconsin Ave. in Georgetown, a members-only bar. The crowd was mainly wealthy Southern ex-frat boys, guys named Trip and Reed with mop hair and year-round flip-flops. They were into shorts with blazers, driving around in open-top jeeps, and alpha-male-ing super-bitchy Fox News-looking blondes.

Politicians, and CEOs to a lesser extent, aren't like you and me. If you really want to understand how they think, go down to the leadership self-help section of the bookstore and you'll see a ten-foot shelf of books on how to fake a persona. Pols wear one mask for general consumption – TV and voters – and another for friends and acquaintances. There might be some real personality hidden down under all that, but I tend to believe that after all the years of polling and folksy anecdotes, they forget it themselves.

So far I'd known only Walker's professional guise: a charming Southern gentleman, Christian enough to get by but not Bible-thumping enough to alienate moderates. The file Marcus had given me on Walker was filled with psychological mumbo jumbo: early-life self-esteem issues, overcompensation, hypersexuality. It's not an uncommon profile among politicians. I'd heard similar rumors about him. Walker and I shut the bar down that night, and after a few hours drinking with the guy, I was starting to think maybe the hype about him being a skirt-chaser was a little overblown.

Then I noticed him eyeing a college girl across the room: twenty years old, tops. After last call, I asked him where he was heading. In that easy Mississippi drawl he told me, 'I'm fixing to get hip-deep in sticky,' then set out after her.

I didn't know, and didn't really want to know, what that meant, but I had a decent guess.

That was the first time he loosened up around me, and it got worse from there. I could barely understand the profane shock-jock creole of sex slang he deployed, which was probably for the better. I figured it was mostly talk. I had a bit of a short fuse when it came to ungallant behavior around women, the one good thing my dad passed down. Aside from going overboard on the locker-room chatter, he was a fun guy to hang out with and a welcome break from the bureaucrats' cocktail-party circuit.

Tonight, chez Chip, Walker was shape-shifting as per usual. After some gentle ragging on another rep about his party's chances in the midterms, he lowered his voice to a murmur, scanned the room, and asked me if I was going to get into any 'strange'. A fetching young woman arrived within earshot, and without missing a beat he turned the charm back on and engaged her in a perfectly chaste conversation about the relative merits of Yale versus Brown.

'I'll put in a good word for you,' he said, sent her along

with her tresses bouncing, and resumed the conversation on the finer points of a venereal subject I'm not even going to mention here. He thought he was being quieter than he was. I could see he was getting drunk, gulping down one glass in order to start a new one.

Marcus caught me on my way to the bathroom. 'Stick with Walker tonight, no matter what,' he said.

'Why?' I asked. 'What's going on?'

'It'd be best if you stayed close to him. Trust me.'

Typical sphinx bullshit from my higher-ups at Davies. I knew very little about what we wanted with Walker, only that he was on track to be a heavy and would be good to know. I had picked up some hints, stuff I maybe wasn't supposed to be aware of, and the few details I got from Marcus were like pulling teeth. We had a client, some dude from Bosnia or Kosovo – I could never keep those war-torn nineties' hellholes straight – who wanted a few amendments stuck in an upcoming foreign relations bill so that he could have cheaper exports or something. It was just another boring little loophole no one would notice. The trick was to wait until the House and Senate passed their different versions of the bill and the conference committee jammed them together. That's the real sausage-making on the Hill, and the closest thing you can find to the smoke-filled rooms of legend. Walker was likely to be a junior member in any upcoming conference on foreign relations, so it made sense to bring him in.

It was a perfectly typical case, the kind we did at Davies every week. What I couldn't figure out was why they were treating the whole thing like it was a state secret. I'd never seen anything so compartmentalized around the offices.

But I was just a soldier, so I'd keep my head down and keep at it with Walker. By now he had the tight look of concentration of a high-functioning drunk on a spree. I didn't like where this was going and would have beat it out of there if not for work. He was in flagrant violation of the first rule of Washington nightlife: never have fun at a party. He muttered something, looking hard at nothing in particular.

'What?' I asked.

'Are you okay, you know, with Tina?' he said.

I couldn't remember who Tina was – Walker's dance card was pretty crowded – but I wanted to keep him mellow. I certainly didn't have a *problem* with her, so I just nodded along. 'Sure,' I said and steered Walker to an empty living room. He was feeling in his pocket for his keys: bad news.

It wasn't quite a scene yet, though a few people were taking an interest, watching through the entryway. And I saw Marcus checking in, subtly, while talking to two lantern-jawed guys with goatees. I left Walker for a minute and stepped over to Marcus. I was hoping to get out of tonight's assignment: I just wanted to dump Walker in a cab and send him home, skip whatever adventure Marcus had planned for me.

'Michael Ford,' Marcus said. 'Let me introduce you to two dear friends of the Davies Group' – that was code. *Friends* alone meant C-list clients, *close friends* B-list, and *dear friends* A-list. These guys were priorities.

'This is Miroslav Guzina and Aleksandar Šrebov. They're with the Serbian trade mission.'

These trade advisers sure turned out to be an interesting bunch. Miroslav tore a piece of rare tenderloin on crostini in half with his teeth, then offered his hand.

'It's a pleasure,' I said. Aleksandar's handshake felt like palming a cinder block.

'May I borrow Marcus for a moment?' I asked.

Marcus excused himself and we stepped aside.

'What's the play here, with Walker?' I asked.

He gave me his dumb and innocent look, which I could only answer with a long sigh.

'Keep him happy,' he said. 'And remember: the Davies Group is always looking out for you.'

Damn it. These Balkans must be the guys who were bankrolling the seduction of Representative Walker, which put me in a tight spot. Walker was waving me over, antsy, ready to go. I walked back to him.

'You've got that new Cadillac CTS, right?'

'Oh yeah,' he said.

'You mind letting me get my hands on it?' I asked. I knew better than to get between a drunk with a Southern sense of honor and his keys, at least not without having a good cover.

'I don't know.'

'Come on.'

He shrugged a little bit, held the keys in his palm, and let me take them without a fight. That surprised me at first.

'Come on, man. Fuck this Girl Scout meeting. I know a place that'll take care of us.'

I didn't like the sound of that at all. To my ears it sounded a little bit like *whorehouse*. I realized he gave up his keys not because he thought it was the public-safety-minded thing to do but because he really wanted to get to wherever he was taking us next.

Normally, because Marcus and the Serbs scared the shit out of me and because I was a good little corporate kiss-ass, I would have just followed Marcus's orders and gone along with Walker.

But I was getting the distinct feeling that the Walker episode was not going to end well, and on top of that, tonight I had a very special problem on my hands. It was the enormous dude who was now watching Walker and me from the hallway, who had been keeping his eye on me all night and looked none too pleased that I was clearly about to paint the town with a reputed poonhound. And why should I care?

Because that particular dude was Lawrence Clark – forgive me, *Sir* Lawrence Clark, whom you may know as the chairman of PMG, a hedge fund that controls about thirty billion dollars in capital. More important, he was Annie Clark's father, and a former player for England's national rugby team. Annie was at my place right now, since that was easier for her than schlepping all the way back up to her house in Glover Park. And remember how the whole Annie thing seemed too easy, seemed like there must be a catch in it somewhere? Lawrence Clark was the first catch I discovered. I sure as hell didn't want him seeing me heading out to some cathouse with Walker. Clark had me pinned with a furious stare, Walker was begging to go, and Marcus was just standing there watching me squirm as I tried to decide between no good options.

Chapter Five

Before I met Sir Larry, I'd pretty much given up my class-resentment chip-on-the-shoulder bit. No matter how hard life has dicked you over, at a certain point (actually, I think it was when I bought a two-bedroom house for myself and maxed out my Roth), that attitude just starts to feel a little ridiculous. I decided to keep a few scraps of my checkered past around, strictly to add character, and let any bitterness go.

He lived in 'hunt country'. It's only about forty minutes from where I grew up in Northern Virginia. Yet I had no idea that a short drive from the pastures of my youth – where I spent so many idyllic summer days in the woods behind the strip mall making out to the flavor of Juicy Fruit, lighting things on fire, and playing with Rich Ianucci's father's pistol – was a paradise for Washington's wealthiest.

It's all green rolling hills between Middleburg and the foothills of the Blue Ridge. The land is parceled out into huge estates, dotted with quaint hyperexpensive towns where the economy depends on lunching ladies and cute bric-a-brac. The whole place is Anglophile in the extreme: social life revolves around the Saturday fox hunts and taverns with names like the Old Bull & Bush, where George Washington invariably did something or other. It's where Annie grew up. And after we'd been going out for a few months, she took me to her dad's estate.

If I may indulge in a little real estate pornography: twenty-five hundred acres overlooking the James River. An eight-bedroom 1790s Colonial mansion. Six-thousand-bottle wine cellar. Twenty-stall stable. Indoor *and* outdoor pools, *and* tennis courts, rugby field, pistol range, skeet and driving ranges, softball field with dugouts and a scoreboard and bleachers (because what's the point of a backyard game of ball unless you have seating for sixty spectators?). I could go on.

Annie's friend Jen from the office went out there for the weekend once, and she raved about it, so I was pretty excited. She'd gone on and on about Annie's cool dad, the incredible chef, getting drunk on *grands crus* and having the run of Sir Larry's private Xanadu.

The driveway was easily a half a mile long. In front of the house, Annie and I stepped out of my Jeep with the peeling paint and turned to see six black-and-tan Dobermans galloping toward us, covering the distance across the great lawn faster than seemed possible. Their mouths were moving as if they were barking, but there was no sound. It was scary, sure, but it was more eerie than anything else, seeing these sleek muscle torpedoes snapping their jaws but hearing nothing. It made me wonder if maybe I was just a little slow on the uptake, like maybe they'd gotten here already, and maybe I was already dead.

'Leave it,' a commanding voice said.

The dogs stopped immediately, five feet away, and sat. Their eyes remained fixed on me, and I pictured myself as a large, delicious spare rib. Lawrence Clark was a six-foot-four former fly half for England's national rugby team (he earned his knighthood via rugby wins and charity work) with sandy hair and a perpetual tan. Today he was wearing overalls that appeared to be made of movers' blankets and carrying what looked like a rolled-up piece of carpet remnant.

'Just doing a spot of training with the bitches,' he said. That's when I noticed he was also carrying a whip. He kissed Annie on the cheek, looked over at the Jeep, then extended his hand to me. He took my measure for a long, uncomfortable minute.

'Welcome,' he said, and cracked a practiced smile. The maid and butler helped us with our stuff and showed us to our bedrooms, first Annie's, and then, on the opposite end of a long wing, mine. 'Sir Lawrence said you'd be sleeping here,' the maid said.

Message received. Though I might have smugly pointed out it was a little late to lock that barn door, Sir Larry. Through my window I watched him on the lawn. He was wearing the rolled-up thing on his arm and screaming at and whipping the Dobermans as they gnashed and tore at it.

I couldn't wait to see what he had in mind for me.

I tried to strike up a conversation about wine at dinner, which consisted of the three of us at a table built for twenty. 'Wow,' I said, after my first sip. 'Seems '06 was a good year for Bordeaux?' I looked at the bottle of Mouton Rothschild on the table between us. I thought this was pretty passable fancy-people talk.

'I figured we'd go with something' – he looked me up and down – 'approachable'. A smile that didn't touch his eyes followed. Then the cauliflower on his plate suddenly demanded his attention.

I was starting to get an unmistakably frosty feeling from Sir Larry. This was not the guy Jen had described. Though I realized that it was probably a lot easier to have a 'corking good time' with the old limey if you weren't an arriviste who was banging his daughter. Maybe it was nothing; it's hard to say anything in a Brit accent as tony as Sir Lawrence's without its sounding condescending.

Annie didn't help matters when, after I'd gone to bed that night in my room – it featured red and green stripes, antique illustrations of bearbaiting, and seven shelves of creepy antique dolls – she came knocking on my door. We got into some boy-girl high jinks, fell asleep in each other's arms, and woke the same way.

I'm not complaining, of course, but it certainly made for an awkward situation come morning when we opened our drowsy eyes to find Sir Lawrence standing in the doorway, a Doberman and some other mean-looking beast at his feet.

'I wanted to let you know breakfast is ready,' he said.

'Oh, thanks, Daddy,' Annie said. She sat up and pulled the covers with her, revealing quite a bit of my naked legs. Any pajamas that had started the evening were in a pile on the floor.

Annie seemed oblivious to the fraught nature of the situation. 'Is Sundance tacked up?' (I gathered this had something to do with a horse.)

'Yes,' he said, all the while drilling holes in me with his stare.

We had a busy afternoon around the estate, a little shooting and some riding (I aced sporting clays and fell off the horse, so we'll call it a draw). Sir Lawrence and I had a moment alone just before Annie and I were about to leave for DC. She'd run back into the house to say good-bye to the maid.

Lawrence put his hand on my shoulder and, I guess just in case I was slow and hadn't picked up what he'd been laying down all weekend, said, 'I don't know what your game is, but I don't think you're good for her. She seems to enjoy you for the moment, however. So—' He grimaced, as if swallowing something extremely unappetizing.

'Now, if you hurt her,' he went on, 'even the slightest

mistake, rest assured that I'll track you down and I will crucify you.'

'All set!' Annie yelled. Clark's tone changed in an instant when she appeared on the front steps.

'Does that sound reasonable?' he asked me, putting on a cheery mug for Annie.

'A little overkill, actually, but I think I get the gist.'

We left him, and as my trusty Jeep trundled down the endless driveway, Annie turned to me and asked, 'What were you two talking about?'

I noticed one of the pooches off in a field lying on its belly and chewing contentedly on a scarecrow's head.

'Hunting,' I said.

'Oh, good,' she said, and put a reassuring hand on my thigh. 'He can be a little protective sometimes, but I think he's warming up to you.'

Chapter Six

However much I wanted to play nice with high society, there was still a little punk in me, and a little pride. So you know what I ultimately decided at the party at Chip's? To hell with Sir Lawrence Clark. He was a lost cause anyway. The guy had me pegged from the get-go, and I had a few ideas percolating on how to get him off my back. I gave him a big wink across the room and headed out of the party with Walker.

The only man I really owed anything to was Davies, and I owed him everything: the fresh start, the job, the house, the chance to meet Annie. I'd do whatever Davies Group asked of me. If I stepped carefully and watched myself, I could stick with Walker on his midnight monkey business without betraying Annie. It was work, after all, official duty. At least that's what I was telling myself as Walker murmured something ominous about Tina.

Should I wait up? Annie texted me.

Late night, hon. Work stuff. So sorry. Miss ya! I texted back. It was all technically true. Walker punched something into the Cadillac's navigation system, and I pulled out. We drove in silence, except for the occasional snap of Walker chewing his fingernails and the cheery female voice telling us to 'Continue. On. Wisconsin Avenue. For Two. Point. One Miles.'

I think we were in Maryland. We pulled off the highway near a strip of box stores and into a development called

Foxwood Chase. It was one of those bulldozed patches of woodlands where the contractors built so quickly there was not a tree or a bush left standing, only houses circling a retaining pond that looked like a gravel pit. I could see empty houses, and empty lots beyond them, not uncommon out in the exurbs of DC. A lot of developers had gone under, a lot of houses had been foreclosed. It gave the whole place the feel of a ghost town.

Our chirping navigator directed me into a gated driveway. Walker leaned over from the passenger seat and waved at the little video camera beside the fence. Open sesame. We pulled up to a mock villa McMansion: columns, three-story entryway, spiral shrubs, the whole nine.

A bodybuilder type – young, maybe about 280 pounds – opened the door. He had a baby face and dimples and wore a wife-beater and a white Cleveland Indians baseball cap set at a rakish angle. He gave Walker one of those bro-style handshakes where you clasp fists and pound each other's back. He gave me the hairy eyeball, at least until Walker said, 'It's cool, Squeak, I vouch.' Then the dimples were back in full effect as Squeak walked us inside.

I guess I, like many people, carry around a lot of preconceived notions about whorehouses. I'd pictured a Victorian mansion in New Orleans, an elegant, still-beautiful older madam, a lot of lace.

But the more I thought about it, the more this made sense: a four-thousand-square-foot white box of a house, unfurnished except for black leather couches and a sixty-inch plasma TV. I'd assumed there'd be a bar to hang out at, or maybe some kind of strip club setup where I could keep my eye on Walker without doing anything that would make me hate myself too much. This was VIP style, however, and there was nowhere to hide. Reluctantly, I took a spot on the couch.

A seatmate joined me, promptly entering my personal space and introducing herself: 'My name is Natasha. I am from Russia.'

'Very original.'

'I thank you.'

Where to begin with Natasha? She had a fake-diamond Monroe – a piercing in her upper lip meant to approximate Marilyn's beauty mark. She wore mostly glitter makeup and what I will generously call a dress. She started to get a little handsy, but I wasn't too worried about myself. I might have to make a scene or storm out, but there wasn't a chance in hell I was going to play moose-and-squirrel with this one. I didn't care what Marcus said. I had to draw the line somewhere.

Curled up next to Walker was a pigtailed Korean girl whose name I didn't catch. I began referring to her in my troubled internal monologue as Hello Kitty. Both girls were fresh off the boat; you could almost still smell the packaging. Kitty couldn't hold a candle to Natasha's trashiness; she was actually quite pretty and naive-looking. By luck I had gotten the girl who completely skeeved me out. No temptations.

I was playing good defense on Natasha as she walked two fingers of her left hand up my thigh, and I actually thought I might make it out of this with skin and soul intact. I could almost calm down.

Except for the kid in the kitchen. He was slight and young, maybe just college age, and paid no attention to what was happening in the living room (the house had one of those echoing open floor plans). Sitting on a stool at the kitchen island with a dead man's stare, utterly absorbed by his cell phone, he tapped the keys nonstop with his thumb, and with the other hand picked at acne scars on his cheeks. Every time I managed to ignore him, something diverting would come through the ether to his cell and he would explode with a girlish titter that filled the house and set my short hairs on end. The kid couldn't have weighed more than 110 pounds but somehow he scared me more than Squeak did.

Natasha seemed to have grown an octopus's worth of arms. The kid giggled again. Just when I thought things couldn't possibly get any creepier, Squeak walked over to the stereo and put in a CD. The strings swelled through giant speakers. It took me a moment to place the music: it was from *Dusty in Memphis*, 'Just a Little Lovin'.'

Somehow that gave the whole scene the quality of a nightmare. That was it. I was out. It wasn't worth losing my license to practice (I'd passed the Virginia bar in February) or betraying Annie. The question was whether I could escape without completely scotching all my work with Walker so far.

As I was rising to leave, some conversation-without-words eye contact took place between Walker and Squeak. Squeak nodded and reached for a lacquered box on the side table. I had a bad feeling about what lay inside.

And I guess it speaks to my unhappiness with the whole situation that I was relieved when he pulled out drug paraphernalia: a glass bowl.

I sat back down. I almost (*almost*) wanted to give Natasha a big hug. These weren't prostitutes! They were drug skanks. I nearly slapped my forehead. I hadn't smoked pot in years but I knew a bowl when I saw one. I wanted to explain the whole thing with a laugh to my new friends here at Foxwood Chase. I could even (maybe one day) tell Annie the whole story. She'd get a kick out of it: Representative Walker took me to his dealer's house to smoke a little weed and I got all freaked out thinking he'd dragged me to a brothel. Shit, I probably could have used a puff after I'd gotten myself worked up into such a lather.

'You want to throw a cloud?' Squeak asked me.

'No. Thank you,' I said. Squeak looked at me as though I were a narc but loaded the pipe nonetheless. I'd never heard 'throw a cloud' as slang but didn't think too much of it – I wasn't exactly in the scene – nor did I attach any particular significance to the butane torch Squeak pulled out, or the gentle tinkling noise as he packed the bowl.

No, it wasn't until he blazed the damn thing up and a sickly sweet vapor reminiscent of bathroom-cleaning chemicals wrinkled up my nose that I realized we weren't dealing with good old 'a little bit in college' American ganja.

I didn't want to set off Squeak, especially now that he had two lungs full of whatever that drug was, so I tried to inquire casually.

'Oh, is that . . .'

'Tina,' Walker said.

'Tina, right.'

'Ice,' Squeak added unhelpfully.

Crack? Was it crack? Was I in a fucking crack house?

'Oh, right,' I said. 'Coke.'

'No, Tina. Crystal.'

Natasha giggled at my language troubles, which I thought was pretty rich. So . . . crystal meth! Aha. I felt like I'd just won at Clue and infinitesimally better knowing that my new friends weren't smoking actual crack.

Here's what I did know about meth (from the navy, where a not-negligible number of snipes, the bilge-rat engine workers, were or had been tweakers). It makes your dick shrink as surely as a dip in the North Atlantic, and it makes you impossibly horny, a situation rife with paradox that leads to all types of trouble I certainly didn't want to find myself in the middle of.

Natasha let out a big puff of meth smoke and ran her eyes over me like I was a buffet dinner. Squeak, Kitty, and Walker beat it out of there (though I noticed both gents took some kind of pill first), leaving me alone with my Soviet love, who did a head feint and then successfully, finally, broke through my defenses for a proper grope. I managed to pull her hand away without her taking any important parts of my anatomy along with it.

She looked heartbroken, to be honest, but she was still almost shaking with energy from the drugs.

'Listen. I'm sorry. You're very nice. But I'm not this kind of guy. I've got to go.' I stood up.

And then, bless her heart, Natasha leaned back and gave me a sweet, saintly look.

'I understand you.'

'Good. Yes, it's nothing personal. I just need to go.'

'Yes. You are faggot. No problem. I fix.'

'No no no no,' I said.

She said something to the kid in the kitchen in a language that sounded more Polish than Russian, then shouted it a second time to get his attention. He looked put out, then sulked upstairs. I should have pegged that sketchball for a speed freak the minute I set eyes on him.

I checked my phone. From Annie: *Heavy lids, sweetie. G'night. Give me a hug when you come in.*

I'd been feeling like I was betraying her before, but that twisted the knife. I walked into the foyer, near the stairs. 'I just need to tell Eric I have to go,' I yelled up to the kid.

I waited there for a minute, rocking on my heels and occasionally, like an idiot, giving Natasha a nervous smile.

Finally the kid appeared at the top of the stairs and waved me up. The second-floor hallway was even more spare than the ground floor. He led me down a long corridor and into a small room with sliding doors on both sides, like the kind that separate hotel suites.

'Wait here,' he said, then disappeared.

One minute passed, then two. I thought of bolting, but to keep Marcus happy – he'd told me expressly to stick with Walker – I figured I had to at least tell the rep I was heading out. Finally Squeak, the baby-faced monster, came out in a bathrobe, his cheeks looking rather rosy. 'I just need to talk to Eric, or maybe you could tell him—'

Squeak gestured to the sliding doors with a flick of his head, then spread the doors wide.

'Hey, Eric,' I said as I recognized the congressman. Then speech failed me. He was tangled up in an orgy so elaborate it resembled a cheerleading pyramid. I looked away instantly, only to get a glimpse into another room where an older guy, who I didn't even know was in the house, was in a clinch with two ladies.

I stared at the wall next to me, momentarily paralyzed, summoning the muscular control required to book it the fuck out of there, when I heard Walker say, 'Mike! Come on in.'

Squeak shed his robe. Whatever pill he had taken more than made up for the side effects of the meth. 'Natasha said you wanted me,' he said.

I lunged for the door that would lead me away from all this. Squeak stepped between me and it.

'What's your problem?' he asked. I stared at the ceiling and gave him a wide berth as I sidestepped toward the exit. 'I mean, Eric already paid for everything.'

Squeak moved closer to me, as relentless as a zombie army. I hate to miss a party or a good deal, but by that point I started running as fast as I had ever run. For those of you keeping score at home, I was wrong when I thought it was just any old cathouse, and also when I thought it was some pot emporium. No, ladies and gentlemen, we had hit all the numbers: I was in a meth-fueled full-service bordello with the good gentleman from Mississippi.

I was in shock, trying to erase it all from my mind as I raced down the stairs, taking them three at a time, then stumbled on the landing and stood up to find that the cops had arrived.

For a half a second, I was almost glad. The cavalry would save me from the bad bad people and Squeak's giant dong. But as the cuffs closed around my wrists, I began to understand the enormity of the clusterfuck I now found myself in. This was no easy-to-beat trespassing rap, which was the worst thing that could have happened after I sneaked into the Met Club. Now I was looking at two or three felonies, and Virginia is packed with hanging judges.

But the only thing I could think about was my dad. The old bastard had told me so.

Chapter Seven

A thirty-foot-tall clown is the kind of thing you remember. This particular one, on a ratty stretch of Virginia highway, smiled maniacally in front of an abandoned store that had been called Circus Liquors. It gave me déjà vu and a serious sense of the creeps, but I couldn't remember exactly where I'd seen it before.

It's where my dad had told me to turn. His place was about a mile down the road. It was a gas station: two pumps, a garage, and a tiny box of a convenience store. I poked my head into one of the garage bays and found him working with a hog sander on the fender of a 1970s Cutlass, throwing out sparks. The garage was too cluttered for me to get into his field of vision, so I stepped a little closer and hoped he'd notice me. Nothing. Finally, I waited for him to pull the sander back and then gave him a little tap on the shoulder.

He flinched and turned, holding the sander up like he was about to take my head off with it. It took him a second to relax.

'Oh Jesus Christ, Mike.' He put it down, and gave me a hug. 'Might still be a little jumpy.'

Lesson: don't sneak up on someone who's been watching his ass for sixteen years.

It was March, ten months in at Davies Group, and a month before the cops picked me up at Representative Walker's meth house fiasco. My dad had been out of prison for about six weeks. I'd spent some time with him since, of course, but it was all welcome-home dinners and BBQs, the kind of thing where everybody puts his best face on and drinks too much and gushes and promises to keep in touch.

This was the first time it was just me and him, one-on-one, no celebrations, just the rut of the everyday. I could tell he was trying to get me back, fix up our father-son thing the way he'd Bondoed that Cutlass. I had been avoiding him.

I'd been through this already, with my brother. I hadn't seen him in years; last I heard he was living in Florida. He didn't show up for any of my dad's got-out-of-jail parties. Even though Jack was the one responsible for me nearly getting sent to prison when I was nineteen, I'd always tried to be the nice guy, the one who would call, the one who would turn the other cheek and keep the family together. Even after he left it to me to shoulder all the debts from my mother's treatments, however much I wanted to, I didn't shut him out. That was a mistake. He'd blow into my life every few years, resuscitate the good old times and keep me out at the bar until closing. It was always fun, at first – who doesn't want to hang out with his older brother? – but eventually I'd recognize that the grifter was closing the noose around me, scamming me for cash usually, or just a place for him to hide out with whatever crew of rejects he was currently tangled up with. Con men count on your decency, your kindness. They use it to get close and then use it to hurt you. After he'd done it to me half a dozen times, I cut him out of my life, ignored his calls, the appeals to family and pleas for help he had always used to worm his way back. And once he realized he couldn't get anything out of me, I never heard from him again.

With my dad, I wasn't that severe. The way I figured it, I'd more than done right by him by having Henry Davies pull the strings to get his parole. I was having a hard time with all the buddy-buddy shit. I wasn't going to just let him off the hook for what he had done to the family, but I wasn't going to torture him about abandoning us either. Think about whatever unpleasant chore you've been meaning to take care of but know you never will: cleaning out a basement or an overstuffed closet, throwing out old clothes. That was me and Dad. Mostly I just wanted to avoid the whole thing. But my father kept calling: tenacious but never pushy. Like me, he had will in spades.

'Let me get cleaned up,' he said. He led us out of the garage. In the woods behind the gas station there was a thirty-year-old trailer with a picnic table out front, along with a few camp chairs and a grill: his home.

The guy who owned the gas station, an old friend of my dad's named George Cartwright, was letting him stay there and manage the place. Since only two or three guys worked there, managing usually meant pumping gas and pulling dents.

The inside of the trailer was so neat it was a little disconcerting: everything stacked at right angles, the bed drum-tight. The desk was covered with accounting textbooks and double-entry ledgers. A dozen ramen packets lay on the counter.

He saw me looking. 'George has me doing the books now,' he said. He'd studied accounting in prison, even got a bachelor's despite every obstacle thrown in his way. Prisoners aren't allowed money, hardcovers, or the Internet. He'd tracked down a retired finance professor from a Quaker school through God knows how many letters and somehow managed to work his way through the credits. It sounded a little like my story, except a hundred times harder. The more I realized how similar we were, the angrier I got at him for being a fuckup. And at myself, I guess, for being too nice, for giving him a chance to work his way back into my life after all that had happened.

I studied him for a moment in the fluorescent light. He still had his hair the same way, a little long in the back, though not quite a mullet. It was gray now, but he looked healthy. He must have kept himself in shape while locked up. He still had the build of the sprinter he'd been in high school. A jagged scar ran from the corner of his mouth up his cheek. If you asked about it, he always said he cut himself shaving in prison, gave a nervous laugh, and changed the subject. The scratchy *Magnum, P.I.*, mustache I remembered from when I was a kid was still hanging on his lip, and he wore a lot of brightly colored zigzag Cosby sweaters. It looked like he'd just taken a time machine from 1994 to the present day, and for all intents and purposes he had.

Sixteen years is a long time in, and it showed. There was the ramen and the jumpiness. He didn't like being touched. He'd stand in front of a door for a half a second, then laugh at himself; he was used to having to wait for someone else to open it. And the first time we grabbed food – we went to Wendy's – he was completely overwhelmed by the menu, all the options. The guy had been told exactly what to eat and when to wake, sleep, walk, shit, and shower for sixteen years. He'd nearly forgotten how to make choices. You could tell he was in serious culture shock from the look on his face when somebody made a *Seinfeld* reference or told him to Google something or when he heard ringing noises coming from the pockets of people around him. He was usually the first to crack a joke about it, at least, and put everyone at ease.

He'd told me to meet him out here and then we'd go out for dinner, and he was a little cagey when I tried to find out where. I drove. He didn't have a car, so he was basically trapped at the gas station, though Cartwright had told him if he could get the Cutlass running he could use it.

He directed me along the way. It was about a half-hour drive, and I think I figured out where we were going before I let myself acknowledge it. He was trying to engage me with old stories about Mom. They were classics, but he had picked the absolute worst subject to try to warm me up with.

I guess I could have told him as we got closer to the spot, but I didn't have the heart. I pulled up to a block of red-brick buildings in Old Town, Fairfax.

It was gone: Sal's. It was a great Italian place. Or it might have been terrible, for all I know. I was ten the last time I went there. The food didn't really matter; more important, it was where we would go whenever the family had the money for a splurge. When my mother and father began dating, decades ago, they had often gone to Sal's. They would take me and my brother there when we were young, then get nostalgic for their courting days and stand up and take a dance or two by the bar and embarrass their kids.

Jack and I would plunder the garlic bread and they'd be in their own world, like teenagers, laughing, throwing in the occasional dip or twirl, but mostly just sticking close, my mom resting her head on my dad's shoulder.

It was our place. Once, anyway. Now it was a dog spa and a Starbucks.

My dad got out of the car and stood in front of where the restaurant had been. I stayed on the sidewalk nearby, and I thought he might break down. Just watching him, I felt a golf ball in my throat. I thought if I didn't get out of there, I was going to start the waterworks myself.

'You all right, Dad?'

No answer. I was going to put my arm around him, but I didn't want him to freak out again, so I just waited.

'Dad—'

'I'm fine, Mike.'

'Come on, I'll take you someplace. There's a decent steakhouse on Twenty-Nine.'

'No,' he said, his breath short and gravelly. He sounded like somebody had knocked the wind out of him.

'Please, I—'

'I don't have time, Mike. I've got to get back by ten.' He sighed and shook his head, then laughed a little. 'To make curfew, if you can believe that. It's part of the parole. I've got to call this computer thing from my home phone.'

'You've got to eat, Dad.'

He rubbed his five o'clock shadow for a minute.

'Fuck it,' he said. 'You want to go to Costco?'

Two minutes later we found ourselves at a metal table inside a giant floodlit warehouse. I'd thought I'd misheard him at first when he said this was where he wanted to eat, but all he wanted and had time for was a couple Italian sausages with peppers and onions, and a Coke. They were damn good. And there were only four things on the menu, which probably made it a little easier on him.

We took a stroll through the aisles, and I tried to figure out what the hell the old man was up to.

'This place . . .' my father said. He had the face – the awe-struck smile – of someone visiting the Grand Canyon for the first time.

It started to make sense. Prison jobs, if you can get a paying one, start at twelve cents an hour. A tube of toothpaste costs five bucks in the commissary, and to get it he'd have to fill out a little form and wait a week for it to come back. To him, Costco, with the glare and the screaming kids and the housewives' kamikaze carts, was heaven.

We talked a little as we rounded the frozen-foods corner.

He'd been working on getting a shot at the CPA exam. He consistently aced the practice tests, but anybody who'd been convicted of fraud was barred. It would take years to provide 'evidence of rehabilitation', and the examiners still might shaft him, but he didn't care. He was going to claw his way back up. He'd been trying to go to the library to get the phone books he needed to find the addresses and phone numbers of the state accounting boards so he could start sending letters and making calls, but going to a library meant missing a day of work, which was out. The guy's life was like a pile of pickup sticks, each little thing weighing down another and weighed down by the next, a solutionless mess.

'You can look them up online, Dad.'

He looked at me a little askance.

'With the computer?'

'Yeah. On the Internet.'

'And I attach the Internet to the computer?'

I grimaced. 'Kind of.' It was like explaining color to the blind, but I think I eventually got some of the basics across to him. I told him I had an old laptop he could have.

'You need anything else while we're here?' I asked. 'Stock up. Something besides ramen?' I figured that was part of why we came here, but I could see instantly I'd hurt his pride by implying he needed a handout. He swallowed it, though, just looked a little sad.

'No,' he said, 'I'm fine. You've done more than your share, Mike. But thank you.'

He checked my watch. 'I should get back,' he said. 'It's almost lights-out.'

Back at the trailer, he walked me inside and handed over an envelope. There was a thousand dollars in it, some twenties and tens, but mostly ratty-looking fives and singles.

'I'm going to make good,' he said. 'On the debts, for Mom. I fucked up, bringing those Crenshaw sharks in. That should never have come down on you.'

'Keep it,' I said, and held out the envelope. He didn't take it. 'It's paid off.'

'What?'

'The debt.'

'For how long?'

'Forever. It's paid off. All of it,' I said.

'But what about school? You should take care of that first.'

'Paid off. Save your money, Dad.' I put the envelope down on the peeling veneer of the countertop.

I didn't want to do this, to get angry, to deal with it all. I just wanted to put the past behind me. But the money, and hearing him talk about Mom being sick, and him thinking if he just repaid the debt, everything would be fine: it set me off.

Because every time he mentioned Mom, I would remember her, and I would try to picture her the way I liked to: making the sly face she always had when she was about to crack a joke. I'd fight to keep that in my mind, but her cheeks always hollowed out, and then the color disappeared from her skin. And I ended up thinking about her at the end, with this chilling rattle in her chest and her face all waxy and her mind gone on morphine, calling me by my father's name sometimes, and sometimes asking me who I was and what the hell I was doing in her room.

And it's poison, but you can't help tasting it: What if I had somehow been able to get enough money to send her to a really good hospital? What if she'd had a decent husband and insurance? What if? Would she still be around?

'You can't make good on what happened,' I said.

'Everything's paid off?' he said, still puzzled. And then he straightened up to his full height and tried to act fatherly, like he was about to ask me if I used condoms or something.

'Listen, George Cartwright told me you'd been asking about the trade.'

Oh, fuck. Not this. Not now. George was a bit of an expert in B and E and could get you any tool you'd ever need. When I was at my dad's first glad-you're-out-of-prison party, I asked Cartwright if there was any way to crack the Sargent and Greenleaf padlock that Gould had on his locker at the Met Club. Just out of curiosity. And so apparently my dad thought I had paid off everything by robbing the fucking Pentagon or something and now he was going to play scared straight with me.

'There's no free lunch, Mike. What are you into?'

'A good job. That I earned by being smart and busting my ass. Are you, *you*, going to tell me how to keep my nose clean?' I looked around the trailer, like it proved my point. 'Unbelievable.'

'I'm just saying, Mike. Don't get caught up being somebody's bagman. You try to play the game, run with the big-timers, you can get burned. You can only trust your own people.'

'Dad, please.' I was trying to keep calm, to watch what I said. It would have been easy to kick the guy when he was down, to point out how pathetic he was. The truth was brutal enough. 'Why don't you knock off this bullshit honor-among-thieves thing. You think because you kept your mouth shut and did your time you're some kind of fucking outlaw hero. You're not—'

'Mike, I couldn't—'

'Because you didn't know how to play the game, Dad. You could have talked. You didn't have to go in for twenty-four fucking years. To leave us high and dry. Who knows, maybe then Mom wouldn't have—'

I stopped. But the damage was done.

He was just standing there, eyes shut and nodding his head like he was saying yes. I was waiting for him to snap, start sobbing or come after me, but he just stood with his eyes closed, breathing fast and short.

'Maybe,' he said. He started rubbing his jaw. 'I did the best I knew how.' I thought he was going to cry, but he choked it back.

'I know I can't make things right, but just don't shut me out, okay?'

I didn't say anything.

'Please, Mike.'

I took a few deep breaths and steeled myself. 'I've got to go,' I said.

And that was it. I left.

That little Hallmark moment between me and my father had to do with, as you might have guessed, the crime – a burglary – that sent him away when I was twelve. Nothing about it made sense.

Most of his story I picked up from Cartwright and a few of my dad's other buddies. If you caught them late on a Sunday afternoon at Ted's Roadhouse, a windowless bar they inhabited, they'd be lubed up enough to tell the stories my father had kept from me. He'd turned to grifting young. For generations, his family had run an old foundry out near Falls Church. They'd made the stairs at the Smithsonian castle, the lamps on the Capitol grounds, and supposedly some of the twelve-pound cannons used at the Battle of Gettysburg. But manufacturing in America had long since crapped out by the time my father took over the business. His parents moved from Falls Church; he'd grown up in New Jersey, but he came back to Virginia in his early twenties to take over the business from his uncle. By then the ironworks was on hard times, reduced to a glorified machine shop. My dad didn't know much about business, and he was desperate for orders. Some guy named Accurso conned my father with a no-brainer invoice scam. A hundred-and-fifty-year-old business was dead, and Dad was out of luck. For his first con, my father learned the tricks that had been used against him, tracked Accurso down, did a false stock swap, and took him for everything he was worth.

As I understand it, my dad had done some petty crime growing up, but it was only after he started conning that he really flourished as a hustler. He was a natural, and he kept at it, trying as much as possible not to fuck over the little guys. It's always tempting to romanticize con men, but at the end of the day, he was a criminal, and the job ultimately came down to abusing people's trust. Still, he could sleep better at night than most of his peers.

He kept that part of his life from me, though occasionally he couldn't resist, and, broke and interested in showing his sons a good time, he would pull a cute street con, more for fun than anything else.

There was the fiddle game, where he'd bring us into a decent restaurant, posing as a respectable business traveler and his family. When the bill came, he'd say he forgot his wallet and give the mark something to hold for collateral while he went to grab his cash. This was usually some antique he 'couldn't bear to part with' (in the classic version, it's a fiddle) and that he'd say was worth a fortune. Next, he'd have a shill (an accomplice – it was Cartwright the time he did this with me) come by, see the antique, and offer to buy it for a small fortune. The shill would then leave, saying he would return shortly, and my dad would come back to pay the bill. The mark would offer to buy whatever it was from my dad for *half* a small fortune.

My dad, acting torn, would reluctantly sell it. Cartwright, of course, never returned to pay the better price, and my dad made off with half a small fortune and left the mark with a worthless piece of junk. Like all good cons, it took the mark's greed and willingness to screw someone and used those flaws to screw him first. That's how he sank Accurso, actually. Cartwright told me years later: it was a scaled-up version of the fiddle game using company valuations (my father had always been handy with ledgers, which explained why accounting came so naturally to him in prison).

He went to jail twice. The first time was a short sentence, when I was five or so, and the second was the twenty-four-year bid that started when I was twelve. That first time they caught him for bank and stock fraud. He was going after Accurso *again*, after he'd found Accurso working the same scam against other small businesses. Now, normally, whenever you lure a mark in, you use something illegal or embarrassing for bait, like a hot TV or a stuffed wallet with a name in it, so that if the mark gets scared or finally realizes he's been ripped off, he's shy about going to the cops. Accurso was so angry with my father from the first con that once he got wind of who was playing him the second time, he called the cops in anyway (which wasn't very sporting, I thought; at least he should have tried to turn the tables and re-scam my dad). They were both so dirty, though, the cops ended up hauling the pair of them in. I was so young I barely remember it. My dad was sent away for a year, and served six months. Accurso got two years.

After my father served that short sentence, supposedly he went clean. The crew at Ted's always talked about his retirement wistfully; they'd lost one of the best. He was working different legit jobs, or so I thought, at machine shops or whatever he could get, and my mom was working as a secretary. Then, when I was around twelve, things fell apart. One night, my dad said he was going to watch a minor league ball game – the Prince William Cannons – with some friends. I pulled on my jammies and hit the hay after *Home Improvement*, all pretty standard for a Tuesday night.

Then I remember waking up to the sound of my mother making a fuss. It was after midnight. I came downstairs and saw her on the phone, biting her nails and crying silently. She'd sort of slumped down, squatting against the wall under the telephone.

The police had caught my father breaking into a house in the Palisades, a wealthy enclave along the Potomac between DC and Bethesda.

I'd never been able to make sense of that night. The house they caught him in was empty, some well-connected DC guy's investment property. There was nothing to steal. My dad had never done any breaking and entering before. He liked the trust, the challenge, and the risk of the long con, the Robin Hood righteousness of fucking over people who deserved it. B and E – broken windows and snatched electronics – that was the sort of thing my idiot friends and I would get into later. A pro like my father would never go near it.

No one knew why he did it. He kept his mouth shut. Not a single word in all these years. I'd always assumed somebody had put him up to it. It just wasn't the kind of thing he'd put together himself. But he refused to cooperate with the DA, just faced him down in absolute silence, meeting after meeting. He never trusted anybody in power, anybody who even resembled a politician; he thought the whole justice system was just another type of con game, where he was the mark. I could understand why. The government had whittled his family business down to nothing through taxes, and as the foundry went under, the 'respectable' businessmen swooped in on it like vultures on a carcass. Or maybe it was from all those years of cons, of his passing himself off as the most decent, upstanding community pillar, all the while knowing he was on the hustle. Maybe he started seeing deceit behind everything that looked respectable.

Watching him refuse to make any sort of deal, and thinking about it all these years, I saw him as a small-minded neighborhood hustler. He didn't understand how to help the prosecutors help him, the give-and-take of politics, everything we trafficked in at Davies Group. No. For him it was simple: Never talk. Protect your people. Do your time. That code – honor among thieves – tore our family apart. I could never forgive him for choosing it over us, for abandoning my mother, my brother, and me.

I've spent half my life trying to figure out an answer to that question: Why rob an empty house? During the trial, through the thin wall between bedrooms, I'd overhear him and my mother crying and fighting, and I remember her begging him one night, 'Just tell them what happened. Tell them everything.'

I thought I'd learned from his mistakes, learned how to get with the program, how to play along with power. I sure showed him. Or so I thought, until my new job got me hauled off to the Montgomery County Jail in cuffs along with a crew of whores and meth addicts.

Chapter Eight

So my years of effort to get as far away from jail as possible had landed me back in it. That, of course, raises the important philosophical question: If you use the center-stage toilet in the holding cell and there's no one there to watch, is it still humiliating?

Yes. And tough on the quadriceps.

We were in a brand-new subprecinct near Poolesville, all primary colors and carpet. It looked more like an elementary school than a lockup. There weren't even bars, just metal doors with reinforced-glass windows. I was aware that my life was going down the lidless toilet, but somehow the whole thing seemed a lot less scary than the first time I'd been in jail, when I was nineteen. It probably helped that my partner in crime this time was a US representative and not my asshole brother.

Back at the McMansion, they'd put Walker and the old guy and me in an unmarked Crown Victoria, instead of the usual caged back-seat of a patrol car. Now we all had our own cells. It was the VIP package.

After I'd been stewing for a couple hours, a deputy came down the hallway. 'Let's go,' he said, then walked me to an open office, a little maze of desks.

'Can I make a couple calls?' I asked. 'I'd like to have a lawyer present during any questioning.'

'Well, you could, but—'

'I have a right to counsel.'

The deputy rolled his eyes and pushed the phone on his desk my way. I called Marcus first. That prick had gotten me into this mess, and he and Davies had damn sure better get me out. I wasn't holding my breath, though. I thought of another classic DC adage as I listened to the phone ring: the only scandal you can't recover from is getting caught in bed with a dead girl or a live boy. I'd never thought I'd find myself with either party, but hey, crazy night.

The phone rang three times, then I heard Marcus say hello.

'Listen. I got picked up. I—' I stopped. Something wasn't right. Marcus's voice was coming through the phone and—

I turned around and there he was, smiling, cell pressed to his ear.

'You mind?' Marcus said to the deputy. He left. Marcus took his seat.

'What the fuck is going on, Marcus?' I asked.

'Just take it easy.'

'Have the newspapers gotten hold of this yet? Does Davies know?'

'Mike, calm down.'

'How'd you get here so fast? Did they call you?'

'I told you, Mike,' Marcus said, 'that we'd be watching out for you. How's Tina doing, by the way?' He cracked a big smile.

I shut my eyes, gritted my teeth, and counted backward from five. All the while I reminded myself that if I tried to strangle Marcus right there and then, he'd probably kill me first, and even if I succeeded, I was in a police station, probably not the best locale for a murder.

'You knew what Walker was up to,' I said, finally. My gears turned for a minute. 'Was it a setup? Did you call in the cops?'

'No,' Marcus replied. 'Don't get ahead of yourself. We had a feeling, from watching Walker, that he might be getting himself into a prickly situation tonight. He's had some recent . . . I guess you could call them stresses. We also happened to learn that the police might be taking some action against' – he snapped his fingers, trying to remember – 'the big guy?'

'Squeak.'

'That's it. So we kept our eyes open, called in a couple favors, and made sure that if something happened to Walker, God forbid, we were in a position to help him out. Good old-fashioned back-scratching.'

'But why send me into that freak show? Why fuck me over? What happens now?'

Marcus dusted his hands off. 'It never happened. There's no record. Don't worry about Barney Fife.' He nodded toward the deputy. 'We've taken care of the locals. Everyone's free to go. You're going to go tell Walker that you called up your boss, and he managed to help you both out of a jam.'

Marcus smiled and shook his head. 'And the older gentleman who was caught at your little orgy: he's the head of the Family Values Coalition. A big fish. That's just gravy. Pure luck. Right place at the right time.'

'So now what?' I asked. 'We tell Walker we want the loopholes and earmarks for your Serbian buddies or we take him public? I thought you said we avoided straight coercion, that it had a tendency to blow up in your face.'

'It does. So you're going to go back to Walker and let him know that we did this little favor. And you know what you're going to ask for?'

'I give.'

'A decent tee time at Congressional Country Club.'

'What? You could have your assistant get that with a phone call.'

'Exactly. Start by asking him for the easy favor, the friend favor, so he knows that you're not trying to fuck him. You both got pinched, so you two are in this together. I'm sorry to have to put you through this, but that's why you had to be in the house. He won't suspect a thing. If we'd just shown up at the police station and offered him a deal, it'd be straight blackmail. If we tried to force anything out of him, it'd get antagonistic, and he'd turn around and bite us in the ass eventually.'

'So we ask for nothing, and ultimately he gives us everything.'

Marcus nodded. 'Gold star for Mike. We just keep doing him favor after favor, and slowly he'll start paying us back. He'll probably even volunteer it. You ask for a little more each time, and eventually you own him. And here's the best part: he doesn't even know it. He doesn't fight it. Because you never put the screws to him. You kill him with a thousand cuts. And once he crosses the line, even unwittingly, you own him. In the unlikely event he does try to squirm out, you point out that he sold his soul long ago, and you have the evidence to destroy him if he gets cagey. That's the long game, Mike. The big leagues.'

It's the game my father played, but never taught me.

'You could at least have given me a heads-up,' I said. 'Sort of an asshole move.'

'What'd I tell you about counterintelligence?'

'For Christ's sake, it's four in the morning and I've had a pretty unusual night. Can you spare me the quiz?'

He waited me out.

'Constantly test the reliability of your agents?' I said.

'Genius. We're all going to be working for you someday.'

'Bullshit. You weren't testing me, you were fucking with me for the sake of it.'

Marcus raised his palms: *I guess we'll never know*. The great sphinx of Kalorama had spoken.

The crew from the house – tweaker kid, Squeak, and Walker – were waiting sheepishly in the lobby of the police station. The girls and the old guy were gone. I'd already explained to Walker how Marcus had sprung us.

'Do you think . . . uhh . . . you could give us a ride back?' Walker asked.

'Sure thing,' Marcus said, as jolly as if we were at the end of a softball game instead of a vice sting. We all squeezed into Marcus's Mercedes-AMG and vroomed back to the meth house. Apparently I was making a habit of returning to the scenes of my crimes.

I've had my share of awkward car rides, but this was tops. Walker was still high, with purple circles under his eyes, trying not to grind his teeth and failing. Marcus turned the radio on. That helped things a bit, until about fifteen minutes in, when 'Son of a Preacher Man' came on. I killed Dusty, and we rode the rest of the way in silence.

After we dropped Walker off at his car, I could see that, for once, he was completely out of his trademark charm. He just looked defeated. 'I don't know what to say,' he said to me. 'Thank you. And if there's anything I can do to return the favor, just let me know.'

'Hmm . . .' I said. I saw him get ready, almost wincing as if about to get punched, probably expecting a shakedown. We had enough dirt, between the drugs and the boys and the whores, to destroy him four times over.

'Don't mention it,' I said. 'Just looking out for my friends. Tell you what, why don't you take me out for a round at Congressional and we'll call it even?'

He stared at me for a few seconds. I could see the relief

overtake him. He started beaming, took my hand and pumped it.

'Absolutely,' he said, then walked over to his car. He opened the door, and as I walked away, he added, 'Don't hesitate to let me know if there's anything I can do for you. I mean that. *Anything*.'

Marcus had watched the whole thing from the driver's seat. He gave me an encouraging clap on the shoulder as I sat back down in shotgun. Walker thought he'd just been sprung, but the trap was only beginning to close around him. The poor bastard thought he'd found a true friend in Washington.

As we drove home, I couldn't stop thinking about why Marcus hadn't even warned me about what would happen at the meth house. There were some possible explanations. Making Walker believe that he and I were in it together: that made sense. Testing me, hazing me: maybe. But my mind kept coming back to money, ideology, coercion, and ego, and how Marcus had been so cagey with me when I asked him about the C – compromise and coercion – about what he had on me. As a side benefit of the past night's follies, he now had some fairly potent dirt.

The whole thing left a bad taste in my mouth. When I took down Gould for his brown-bag bribes, it was strictly about catching someone up to no good, causing him to knock it off and pass some good policy in the process. But there was something troubling about how easily Marcus bent the law tonight (though, granted, I was glad he bent it to get me out of jail). It seemed like I'd been encouraged to stay out of the way, even to help Walker along toward self-destruction, so Marcus and Davies could swoop in and profit from it.

And Marcus's whole story was too convenient: that he knew Walker would go on a tear, that he knew the cops would go after Squeak, that it all happened to come together perfectly to suit the purposes of the Davies Group. I don't know if Marcus called the cops in, but it was one too many coincidences for me. I knew hardball was part of the job, that occasionally you had to hold your nose as you made a deal. But I was starting to wonder just how far my bosses would go to get what they wanted, and if perhaps there was a grain of truth in my father's warnings.

As I thanked Marcus for the lift home and headed back to the little dream house my job had won me, I put those worries aside. I was exhausted and my mind was still reeling from the whole fiasco. It just confirmed what everybody had been telling me about DC: if you want a friend, get a dog, and never have fun at a party, especially not with the Davies Group around.

Chapter Nine

After all that, I still wasn't off the hook; I'd stood up Annie. On the way back from Maryland, I watched the minutes on the clock count off like a ticking bomb's toward 6:30 a.m., when Annie's alarm would go off.

If I made it home before she woke, I could rinse off in the shower and jump in bed with no one the wiser. But that was looking increasingly unlikely. At six, I-270 heading back into the District began clotting with morning traffic. When I picked up my car in Georgetown, I started praying she'd slept in.

By six thirty, Connecticut Ave. was a parking lot. For me to get away with it, she'd have to be at least two snooze buttons in and still so deep asleep that she hadn't noticed I wasn't home.

I don't know why I even bothered worrying about it. I didn't get home until seven. All was lost. Annie would be halfway out the door. I switched over to damage control, but my brain was too fried to come up with a good excuse. I wouldn't lie, but I wouldn't tell her the whole truth: I'd say I had to entertain Walker because of work, and he kept me out all night. I'd own up to it and take my lumps. A few days of sulking from Annie would be nothing compared to the other punishments of the night. I'd be fine.

Except apparently I had more than Annie to worry about.

Sitting on my front porch, reading my newspaper in my rocking chair, was none other than Sir Lawrence Clark.

I said hello.

He didn't respond, just smiled. He had a good seat for the crucifixion.

'Mike?' I heard Annie say through the open window in the kitchen. She opened the door. 'Where were you?'

'Working,' I said. 'I'll tell you all about it later.'

I hoped she wouldn't notice Natasha's glitter shimmering on my thigh.

'Fine,' she said, looking pissed off but not like a lost cause. 'My father wanted to have breakfast. Do you have time?'

'Sure,' I said, still trying to get a bead on the situation. I at least wanted to be present to run interference on whatever Sir Larry was up to. Annie headed upstairs to finish getting ready.

Her father was still smiling, clearly enjoying himself. He must have had a good read on what I was up to last night. I knew the guy would hang me the first chance he got, so apparently this was his play: catch me red-handed slinking home – and then what? Probably call me out on it and try to blow up the relationship with Annie on the spot.

It was a pretty good play, maybe checkmate. He'd sure picked a good time to take a stab at me; after the night I'd had, I couldn't think straight. But I wasn't completely unprepared.

'I'm looking forward to this,' I said, and smiled right back at the old man. His grin disappeared. I guess that's when he started to realize he didn't have me as cornered as he'd thought.

'What are you planning on telling her?' I asked.

'I thought I'd let you start by explaining where you've been all night.'

'We could do that,' I said, and looked over the horizon, the clouds still stained orange by sunrise.

'Or,' I went on, 'maybe you could tell her about the fires in Barnsbury.'

Clark's jaw tightened. He stood and towered over me.

'What about Barnsbury?' he asked. Menace and a touch of a lower-class accent crept into his speech. I started to wonder if Sir Larry had despised me from the get-go because he saw himself in me: a guy who had faked his way into a respectable life. Barnsbury was a blue-collar neighborhood in North London where Sir Larry had made a good chunk of his early fortune in real estate. It was also how I was going to keep him off my back. I'd gotten to him, which is what I wanted. I hadn't been 100 percent sure whether I could threaten him with Barnsbury, but his reaction assured me I could.

After I'd spent almost a year at Davies, getting leverage on people was second nature to me. Clark was an interesting case because at first glance he was squeaky clean. But shafting him became a personal passion of mine. I took Henry's advice to heart: anyone can be gotten to if you find the right levers. Eventually, by going through old court cases from the UK, I came across a few lawsuits related to his earliest development deals in North London. They were all settled out of court, so there was nothing good on paper, but I called up a few attorneys who'd worked the other end of the cases. Their clients had been bought off, but the lawyers dished enough. Larry's first deals were wreathed in smoke: three extremely convenient fires had cleared his tenants as Barnsbury went from a blue-collar burg to a super-gentrified outpost of London's elite. Larry quintupled his investments and ultimately parlayed those riches into the billions he used to start up his hedge fund.

I guess Larry, like most people, assumed that if a sin got buried – no paper trail, only the memories of a few aging barristers – it never happened. All the better. I didn't mind the extra digging, and his false sense of security only made the dirt more potent when I dug it up.

'Let's not fool around, Mr Clark,' I said.

'What do you think you know?'

'More than enough.'

'You want money? Is that what this is about? That's why you're after my daughter? To get to me?'

His heated reaction told me I had him. But as any con man will tell you, a burned mark is a dangerous thing. He'll do anything for revenge. So now I had to cool him out. It's a lesson both my father and Marcus knew well.

'No,' I said. 'Never. I only mention it because I want you to know that I'm looking out for you, and I'm on your side, and I have only the best interests of your family in mind.'

I knew that Larry was extremely well connected in New York finance circles, but since he'd moved to DC, he'd been too busy chasing foxes around his estate to cultivate any real political juice. Which meant he was weak, and ill-informed, and maybe ripe for a bluff.

'If I know about Barnsbury, you can bet others do. I just want to tell you that I'll keep my eye out and make sure that no one – not the SEC, not the financial services committee – tries to tar you. Bankers aren't the most popular folks these days. This is a heads-up. A peace offering.'

The move was classic Davies: disguising extortion as protection.

'So what do you want from me in exchange? My daughter?'

'I don't want you to give me anything. I just want an honest chance to prove that I'm worthy of Annie.'

Annie opened the front door.

'Ready?' she asked.

'Absolutely,' I said.

Larry's expression eased from anger to caution. 'You know, Mike,' he said, 'if you have to be at work, we can do this another time.'

'I wouldn't think of it,' I said.

I could see that Clark was seriously thinking about what I'd said. I'd managed to get him off my case without leaving him so angry he'd stop at nothing to get back at me. A victory. And despite how exhausted I was, I wanted nothing more in the world than to sit down to an overpriced omelet with Sir Larry; for the free meal, of course, but more to watch the proud bastard squirm.

It was a good reminder, after all the bullshit my bosses had put me through last night, that there were some great perks that came with working at the Davies Group, like being able to wrap a billionaire around your finger before breakfast.

Chapter Ten

I liked Colombia. Apart from some guerrilla-controlled areas near Panama, it was pretty safe, a far cry from the shooting gallery it had been during the cartel days. The women were achingly beautiful, but I think my favorite part was the coffee. Colombians drink it all the time. Midnight in the dripping tropical heat, in some half-deserted town square, you could still find a guy walking around with a thermos offering *tinto* and finding takers. My kind of place.

I'd been there for four days. Henry and I were the guests of Radomir Dragović. He was the Serbian top dog who had bankrolled the seduction of Representative Walker. He had a nice little modernist house on the Caribbean coast of Colombia, near Parque Tayrona. On one side you have the Caribbean, a gentle blue rolling out to the horizon. On the other side mountains rise up eighteen thousand feet. Picture the Rockies beside the Pacific, like Big Sur only four times grander, and you start to get the idea.

People at work, Annie included, could only thinly disguise their jealousy that I had been tapped to jet down to paradise for some QT with Henry Davies.

I assumed we were here to hammer out the details with the Serbs about exactly what loopholes they wanted jammed into the upcoming foreign relations bill. Walker was turning out to be just as accommodating in that regard as Marcus had predicted. But so far the trip had been mostly R & R. We'd been staying in a guesthouse in an old fishing port that rich European expats had turned into more of a pleasure town.

The relaxation and free time felt almost eerie after nearly a year of working ninety-hour weeks at Davies. I figured two things: one, Henry was playing nice with me after the Walker imbroglio (cooling me out, as it were), and two, the fun wouldn't last.

The toughest part for me so far had been avoiding Rado's daughter, Irin. She'd shown up a day after I had, with four of her glamour-girl friends in tow. I'd actually met her once before, briefly, at the party at Chip's house with Walker, that crazy night when he took me to the meth house. She was the girl he'd been talking about colleges with. She was twenty or twenty-one. Apparently she'd done two years at Georgetown and was taking some time off to play Balkan Paris Hilton as she chose among Yale, Brown, and Stanford to finish her degree.

Brainy, sure. But the first thing you noticed about her and her crew was that they were party girls – big sunglasses, designer labels, smoking in that fuck-you way young people do. Irin clearly led the pack. I think *jailbait* was a fair label for her – she had a very sexy, curvy, dark-eyed Mediterranean-temptress thing going. She wasn't the most straight-beautiful girl I'd ever seen, but she absolutely nailed the trashy-troubled-use-me-up act. Most of her firepower came from her face, which was great-looking, of course – full lips and almond eyes – but more important, she had this look. Picture the expression a woman has at the end of a nice dinner, after a few glasses of wine: eyes that say *Get me out of here and take me to bed*. She had that look *all the time*. It was just her regular face. Very distracting.

One day at the beach, I found myself on the business end of it. She'd been asking me about what I did and about what business I had with her father. 'You work directly with Henry Davies?' she asked.

It seemed like she was feeling me out to see if I was a big-timer. She sat very close, in a bikini top and cutoff jeans, and every so often, she would lean over to shoo away a bug, brushing her breasts lightly against my shoulder. All in all, it was a very convincing performance. The girl was sharp, you could tell, and those eyes melted me like a mind-control ray. But I'd seen enough in my time at the Davies Group to beware of curious women bearing big boobs, so I did my best to shut her down. Indifference wasn't enough, however. She was working from the film noir guide to playing a hussy. After a few minutes of my giving her the runaround, she stared me in the eyes. 'You scared of bad girls?'

'Terrified,' I replied, and turned once more to my beach reading ('The Theory of Regulatory Capture', a real page-turner). She took a few steps back, still fixing me with that bedroom look, then pivoted and walked off, sure to find some trouble at the shady end of the beach.

It could almost have been comic, even endearing, to see the girl take delight in her newfound power: the way she could use sex like a crowbar against even the most self-possessed men. Except she didn't seem like some playful Lolita. She had the practiced confidence of a courtesan. And who was I to talk? I had to sit there on the seawall, reading and playing it nonchalant as I waited for my traitor hard-on to finally give up hope.

I had already met two of Rado's subordinates – Miroslav and Aleksandar – in DC. They were garden-variety Euro-trash goons, so I was pleasantly surprised to find that Rado was a class act. He always wore a beautifully tailored suit, seemed to lack sweat glands even down here in the tropics, and was always saying things like 'You'll forgive me if . . .' and 'whomsoever' with a little hint of an accent and totally making it work.

His house was about half a mile above the village where Henry and I were staying. One evening, Miroslav, Aleksandar, Rado, Henry, and I were drinking prosecco in Rado's garden and watching the sunset. Rado picked out a few herbs he would use in that night's dinner, explaining their subtleties as he bruised them gently with his fingertips and smelled the oils.

The whole house was open to the ocean breeze. He steered us back into the kitchen and laid out the finer points of steak tartare, namely: it was all about the freshness, of the eggs, sure, but mostly the meat.

He took his jacket off (the first time I'd seen him in shirtsleeves), rolled his cuffs up to his elbows, and had Miroslav bring a side of beef from the walk-in fridge downstairs.

'They killed Flor about two hours ago,' Rado said, and slapped the carcass lovingly. With a long knife of Damascus steel, he cut the tenderloin from the spine in one clean stroke, and set to work slicing off the fat and skin.

'I like to do my butchering myself,' he said with a smile.

I was itching to get down to business. Vacations make me anxious. I like to be busy, and after seeing Rado's knife skills I wasn't too keen on being in Irin's sights. She had come downstairs in a see-through wrap and was making eyes at me from across the table as she ate an apple. Henry's assistant, Margaret, had arrived as well.

Rado kept the chatter going more or less nonstop through the six-course dinner. However delicious the grub, after sitting through disquisitions on the most succulent grilled Mediterranean songbird (warbler), the most trenchant of Emir Kusturica's early films (*Underground*), and the best rye for a proper Sazerac (Van Winkle Family Reserve), I couldn't stop myself; I'd put my ass on the line to nail Walker for this guy and I just wanted to know what he wanted and how much he was willing to pay.

'So, Mr Dragović, how can we help you in Washington?' I asked. The little dinner party reacted like I'd just shit in the punch.

Henry saved me by changing the subject. 'So who's making the best absinthe these days?' he asked Rado, and our host, after giving me a patronizing smile, took up the new subject.

These fucking southern Europeans. They won't discuss business at the dinner table. So after four hours, dinner became dessert became coffee became drinks. Rado pulled out a bottle of some nasty-looking black liquor with Asian characters on the label and started pouring. I couldn't really tell you what it tasted like because after the tiniest sip, it was as if my whole mouth had been hit with a double shot of Novocain. I felt instantly unwell.

Finally, Rado suggested that we men take our drinks and adjourn to the library. What a relief. Brass tacks at last.

Rado refilled our glasses, and I thought I saw something floating in the bottle of Far East booze.

Henry laid out the terms of the arrangement. He was strictly no bullshit. No lawyers. No retainers. A simple handshake deal. You give us twenty million, we write your law into the books: official American statute, passed through both houses and signed by the president himself. It would be tacked onto a larger bill, but law was law. If Davies Group didn't deliver, Rado would owe us nothing.

Rado seemed content to draw this whole thing out.

'The more laws, the less justice,' he said, and took a sip of his drink.

Here we go . . . fucking Cicero quotes. I might as well make myself comfortable.

'This *soju* is from North Korea,' he said. 'Very rare. Aged seven years and reserved for the Party elite.'

He topped up our drinks once again, and yeah, there was no mistaking it: a dead black snake was floating in the bottle.

'An adder,' he said, noticing my gaze. 'The venom gives it a certain sweetness.'

Cheers.

'Twenty million American dollars,' he said, and started pacing, gazing off at a few lights bobbing on the Caribbean.

That's as far as he got. I guess it was part of some negotiating strategy, but on this occasion, it wasn't going to work. Someone knocked on the door.

A servant appeared with a note for Henry. He read it, consulted with Rado for a moment, and then the Serb said, 'Of course, send him up.'

Three minutes later Marcus appeared, all apologies, looking rumpled as hell and holding a digital recorder in his hand. He was supposed to have been on the trip, but something last-minute had kept him in DC. He whispered to Henry, and they both excused themselves.

When he was discussing something weighty or confidential, Marcus had a habit of putting on music. I guess it was some old fear of being bugged. Sure enough, soon an aria came streaming from a little side room where he and Henry had secreted themselves.

They returned about ten minutes later with dead-serious looks on their faces. Henry asked for a moment alone with Rado. I didn't know what was happening but I was fairly certain of one thing: Rado should have jumped at the twenty million, because it seemed like the price had just gone up.

Miroslav, Aleksandar, and I waited outside for twenty-five minutes as Henry and Rado consulted in the library. Despite the high-octane *soju*, I had been sobered up by the surprise appearance of Marcus. I wondered if they were pulling their own little con on Rado with some breaking news to jack the price up.

If they were, I wasn't in on it. When Henry and Rado emerged from the library, they didn't say a word about what had gone down, just kept whispering by themselves in the corner. Marcus gave the tape recorder to Henry's assistant, probably for transcription.

I waited as patiently as I could, then finally approached Henry and Marcus. 'What's happening?' I asked.

'We're going to have to keep this compartmentalized,' Marcus said. In other words: *Butt out*.

Fair enough. I didn't have to know everything, though the last time I went into a situation with incomplete information, I nearly got plowed by a 280-pound dude named Squeak and ended up in jail. At the very least I needed to know how this affected my end of the Walker-Rado deal.

'Okay,' I said. 'Just let me know what the next play is with Walker.'

Marcus and Henry exchanged a bad-news look for a moment. I guess Henry decided to take the bullet. He laid a hand on my shoulder and said, 'We're going to have to take you off this one, Mike.'

I was stunned. I blinked at the two of them like an idiot. 'What? I slip up with etiquette once at dinner and that's it, I'm gone?'

'That's not it at all,' Marcus said. 'You didn't do anything wrong.'

'This is no longer a simple matter of adding an amendment to a law,' Henry said. 'Things have changed. We're working an entirely different order of magnitude here. It would be too much too soon for you, Mike.'

I could have whined about being dragged to South America when I had work piling up in DC, about wasting a week, about how sick I was of them keeping me in the dark, but it wouldn't have done any good.

'I earned this,' I said. 'I took the risk. I hooked Walker. I'm ready for the responsibility. Bring me in. I won't let you down.'

'We're trying to protect you here. You're on track to be a player. Let this case go, for your own sake. It's the kind of thing where you make one wrong move and you're fucked. Irrevocably fucked.'

I mulled it over for a minute, then let it go. 'Message received,' I said. 'Thanks for being straight with me.'

I left them to their thing and took a stroll outside. I wondered if they'd bought it, my good-soldier routine. Because if they thought I could just drop this – turn off a lifetime of being a sneak as if I were throwing a switch and let them run me blind a second time – they knew a lot less about human behavior than they claimed to.

I had to find out what was happening with Rado's case and what was on that tape. Simple curiosity was at play, sure, and some of it was ego: I'd put the hard work in and I deserved a part in whatever play they were mapping out. There was more to it than that, however. I'd been wary of Davies and Marcus ever since they'd gotten me mixed up in the Walker shakedown. I was the point man on the Walker-Rado deal so far, and I had to make sure that if this new plan of theirs fell apart, I wouldn't be the one left holding the bag. If I happened to find some dirt, a little leverage to use against my bosses, insurance I could hide away in case of emergency, that wouldn't hurt either. I knew Henry had hired me in part because I'm a sneaky bastard, and I certainly didn't want to disappoint him.

* * *

Henry and Marcus were going to stick around the house for a while and map out a response to whatever big news had changed the game plan with Rado. Margaret, Henry's assistant, was heading back to our guesthouse in town with Marcus's digital recorder, presumably to get to work on transcribing the tape.

Of course I offered to walk her home. You never knew what unsavory characters might be lurking in a town like this.

I took her just slightly out of the way, a block or two over toward the boatyards and auto shops, which meant we would have to walk along the beach for a few minutes to get back to our hotel.

Henry's assistant carried the recorder in her hand. She'd been Henry's secretary for decades, both in and out of government. In her midfifties, hair always in a bun and wearing perfectly pressed clothes, she was the human equivalent of a safe. That tape was key to whatever big news Marcus and Henry had received, but she certainly wasn't just going to let me give it a little listen. I knew that once that tape got back to Washington, it was going directly into Henry's vault, and that was one formidable piece of hardware.

I'd seen him come out of it one day. It was concealed behind a false panel in his office. Henry's letting me get a glimpse might seem like a security misstep, but my knowing where that vault was didn't even matter, because it was a monster, another Sargent and Greenleaf. It would take an expert twenty undisturbed hours to crack it. If I wanted to listen to that tape, I had to get it in Colombia.

I kept up a patter as we walked, and soon enough we had company. Margaret glanced back over her shoulder, then took a second look. After that, she stared straight ahead and picked up the pace as her whole posture tightened up.

'Someone's following us,' she said.

'Okay,' I said. 'Just stay calm.' I looked back. A tall, wiry black-indigenous guy in his midforties was following us. He had unkempt hair and a beard streaked with gray.

A palm grove blocked the moon.

'It's too dark for me to check,' I said. 'Did you see what colors he was wearing back there in the light? It wasn't green and white, was it?'

Margaret hesitated for a moment as she thought about it. 'Yes. What does that mean?'

'Could be gang,' I said, and frowned. 'We'll probably be all right as long as we don't flash anything valuable.'

She showed me the digital recorder, shiny silver and $350 retail, in her palm. She was wearing a dress, so she had no pockets, and she had left her purse back in the guesthouse. 'Can you hide this?' she asked.

'I've got a money belt,' I said. She handed over the recorder. The guy following us sped up, and we tried to keep our distance. About fifty meters from the hotel, our new friend started mumbling something. Margaret nearly sprinted to the front door.

Sting accomplished. Now for the blow-off.

'Great,' I said, and pointed around the corner. 'I think I see some Ejército guys.' The Colombian army was all over the coast. Seeing sixteen-year-olds walking around with mortars on their vests and live Galil assault rifles can be a little disconcerting when you first get to Colombia, but you realize quickly they're only here to stop Yankees from getting kidnapped, and occasionally to shake down the locals.

'I'll tell them to keep an eye out,' I said. 'You head upstairs.'

'Are you sure?' she said.

'Yeah, I'll be fine.' Always the martyr, old Mike.

She went inside.

There were no soldiers around the corner. The dude in green and white was about fifteen feet away. He sidled up to me and whispered, 'Ganja. Coke. Ganja. Coke.'

'No, thanks, Ramón,' I said. I gave him about three dollars in pesos for his trouble, then went around to the rear stairwell of the guesthouse and up to my room.

I didn't feel great about conning Margaret. After all, it's almost too easy when you've had months to gain people's trust. But I needed to hear what was on that tape. You have to know your mark, and I knew that Margaret would follow Henry's orders more or less to the death. Her task that evening was simple: protect that tape. That made my job difficult. I probably could have wrestled it away from her, but that didn't really offer a graceful exit. I had to introduce some outside danger, something much scarier than me, so that for her to protect that tape she had to hand it over to the lesser threat: mild-mannered Mike.

Ramón was a local character, always prowling the beach in a ratty green-and-white soccer jersey. I made up the bit about those being gang colors to fool Margaret; they were actually for the Boyacá Chicó Fútbol Club. In the afternoons Ramón sold counterfeit Cuban cigars. After nightfall he peddled drugs and tried to get his hands on the backpacker girls. If you caught him late enough (and Ramón was usually in some sort of drug fugue by 2:00 p.m. anyway), he'd give you a hard beg about his starving kids. He was scary-looking, but harmless. Perfect for my purposes. I'd led us around to the beach to run into Ramón and scare Margaret into handing over the tape.

The memory card in the recorder was labeled SUBJECT 23: LANDLINE PHONE. It took thirty seconds to copy its contents onto my laptop, then I swung by Margaret's room. 'Don't forget this,' I said, and handed over the recorder with the card inside.

'Thank you, Mike,' she said. 'You couldn't imagine the trouble if I let this out of my sight.'

I waited until the other guests were asleep then plugged earbuds into my laptop and listened to the recording.

'I'm close to getting the information I need,' a voice said. 'I just hope I have enough time.'

The speaker was male, probably middle-aged, troubled now, but he also seemed confident, eloquent, used to speaking in public.

'Enough time?' the second speaker asked.

'They may know something about what I'm after. I don't know how much. I think they're watching me. Who knows what they're capable of. Others have disappeared when they got this close to the truth.'

The second speaker sighed. 'Who's this they?'

'You're the only one I trust, but I can't tell you everything. Too many bad things have happened. If I tell you, I would be putting you in the same danger. I can't put this burden on you.'

'Do you know how nuts you sound?'

'I do. I wish it were all paranoia. It's not. The man with the information: I think I found him. I have to get him before they do. They'd do anything for the evidence. If they had it, I know, I just know, it would be the end of me.'

'You need to report this to your security. You could get killed—'

'Not a word, you understand? You have no idea what's at stake.'

The second speaker hesitated, then finally said, 'Yes.'

The first speaker took a deep breath. 'If they come for me,' he said, 'I'll be ready.'

* * *

I was so wrapped up in the conversation on that tape, I didn't register the knocking on my door the first time. It came again, three loud raps, followed by Marcus's voice: 'You in there, Mike?'

I scrambled, put my laptop and earbuds on a set of shelves on the side of the room, then opened the door.

'How's it going?' I said, a bad attempt at playing it cool.

'I wanted to make sure you were okay with what happened back at Radomir's.'

'Yeah. I understand.' I could feel my pulse in my throat. I hoped he wouldn't notice.

'If you play your cards right, you're going to be a partner someday, a big office up on three with me and Henry. But this case has too many moving pieces. It's not right for a guy starting out. It's just too dangerous.'

'I get it. You're looking out for me.'

'Good.' He looked across the room at the laptop with the earbuds plugged in. The guy was a hawk.

'What are you listening to?'

'New Johnny Cash album,' I said.

'I thought he was dead.'

'Yeah, but they trot out some old recordings every year.'

'Like, uh, Tupac,' he said.

'Yeah,' I said. Marcus wasn't normally one for chitchat. Standing there with him watching me was excruciating. I couldn't tell if he was onto me or if this was just his usual spy weirdness, poring over every detail, dragging out the conversation to see if he could sniff out anything on me.

'All right,' he said finally. 'Change of plans. We're heading back to DC tomorrow. The car will be downstairs at ten. Don't be late.'

'Sure thing.'

He walked away, and I shut the door, threw the deadbolt,

and slumped down on the bed like a sack of sand.

After I calmed down, I played the tape a second and a third time. The questions grew with each listen. Who was this man, Subject 23? Would Henry and Marcus really go so far as to tap his phones? Of course. I'd just listened to the results.

But what was the evidence he was so close to finding? The secret dangerous enough to kill for? It must have had something to do with Radomir's case, with me being pulled off it and told it was too dangerous for a rookie.

As I turned it over in my mind, I wondered if Subject 23 was just worried that some of his sins would be discovered and that he would be another Davies blackmail victim. Or was his life truly in danger? Was he paranoid? Violent? Crazy enough to attack anyone who got close to the information he was hiding?

This went way past business as usual, past hardball. I had to find out who this man was, what he knew, and what my bosses wanted with him. Part of it was professional pride: this was my case and I'd earned my part in it the hard way. But there was also something deeper. Dirty tricks were one thing, but I didn't want blood on my hands.

Chapter Eleven

I love heist movies, especially the old stuff, anything with guys in turtlenecks, diamonds, Cary Grant. It's all so smooth, so classy, so inevitable that they'll get the goods, then wrap up each job with a little champagne on the French Riviera and a roll in the hay with Grace Kelly.

In reality, however, turtlenecks are a supremely bad idea; you wouldn't believe the amount of sweating that goes on when you're trying to steal something. And nothing ever goes your way. Usually you come out of a job with a smashed finger or two, a couple nice gashes from a screen or broken window, maybe some dog bites, and for all your efforts, half the time you head home with a grand total of twenty-seven bucks or a jar of quarters. You reek of terror sweat (even without the turtleneck), and the hourly wage, adjusted for prep and fencing and the number of times the whole thing falls apart, comes out to such a pitiful rate that you might as well work at McDonald's.

My attempts to find out what Marcus and Henry Davies wanted with that tape were similarly ill-fated. I didn't know what those two were up to, but they were doing it with such tight lips it might as well have been the Manhattan Project. Marcus was always out of the office for long lunches, and casual inquiries to his assistant – 'Hey, you know where Marcus is? I need him to take a look at a write-up' – never got me anywhere. Peeking into his office? Nope. The door was always locked, not that it mattered. Marcus kept up the old security habits from his government days. Every lunch and every night his desk was bare. He locked up every paper, and even pulled his hard drive and put it in the safe. Trash went in the shredder or the incinerator. And nothing of substance was ever discussed in the open where someone might have a chance to eavesdrop.

Some of that physical security stuff he'd taught me himself, like you should always vary your routine. He told me a story about a Marine, a lieutenant colonel, at an outpost in Helmand Province, Afghanistan. The guy never took the same route twice, standard practice in a war zone, and always varied his daily routines, except for one thing: he raised the colors every morning and lowered them every night, like clockwork. A sniper caught him one morning at dawn when the flag was halfway up the pole. Point taken. It seemed a little psycho in placid Washington, DC, but if you watched Marcus enough, you'd see it: him zigging and zagging on the way to sensitive meetings, taking long detours, and so on.

After a week or two, I was getting pretty frustrated trying to crack whatever they were working on. Marcus was out of the office more than he'd ever been. The amount of legwork he was putting in himself instead of delegating to humps like me confirmed it was a big-deal case. I couldn't get the voice from the wiretap, the talk of killing and fighting back, out of my head. I'd been involved in Radomir's case from the beginning, and I had to see where it was going, both to ease my conscience and to cover my ass.

The solution hit me when I heard Marcus talking in the break room about his kid's soccer game and then complaining about the cost of private school. He may have been a spy once, but now he was a salaryman and a cheap suburban dad. That meant I might have some levers to work with, because you could be damn sure that wherever he went and whatever he did, he was getting reimbursed down to the last cup of coffee. The corporate spy's motto: leave no trace, but save your receipts.

Expenses were due on the first and the fifteenth of the month. You reported them online, printed the report out, then put a hard copy of it with all of your receipts in an envelope and shipped it down to payroll on the first floor. Except I'd noticed that Marcus's assistant actually walked the expenses down herself. That made things a little trickier than simply intercepting his envelope while it lay in the interoffice mailbox waiting to be picked up.

It was the fifteenth. I knew Marcus was heading off somewhere. I'd tried to schedule a phone call with him, and his assistant said he was out of the office from eleven a.m. until two p.m. She headed down to the first floor at 9:30 a.m. as usual to drop off his expense report. I took the stairs down a moment after she left, and once she'd dropped off the envelope, I headed over to the desk of Peg, our payroll lady.

I carried with me a stack of manila envelopes and a couple interoffice envelopes for good measure. Peg had a wire basket on her cubicle wall where you could drop the reports. It was about half full, and, having watched Marcus's assistant leave, I knew his report was on top. The cubicles were jammed together, and the Davies Group had a ceiling-mounted black-dome security camera every twenty feet or so. I'd have to be sneaky.

There's a trick cardsharpers use called the bottom change. Without your mark noticing, you swap the bottom card of the deck with one you've palmed. Usually you do it so you can make the mark's card suddenly appear in your hand or jump out of the deck to oohs and aahs. It's good with boring uncles and socially challenged middleschoolers. More important for conning purposes, the bottom change is the reason the mark will never win at three-card monte. You know how the three-card-monte dealer will usually flip over the card the mark has chosen using another card? That's a variation on the bottom change called the Mexican turnover, and he's swapping in a losing card to take the guy's money.

The bottom change also happened to be how I was going to get Marcus's report. Misdirection is the key to getting away with anything. Peg was one of those aches-and-pains office-worker ladies. She had the footrest, the wrist pad, the RSI braces, the cat mug, and most conversations with her involved some sort of medical rundown on how she was doing (bad) and complaints about how long it was until Friday. I knew enough to get a patter going and keep her distracted.

And now, ladies and gentlemen, the amazing Michael Ford will attempt a bottom change with – dramatic pause – a stack of interoffice mail!

I approached her cubicle, readied my stack of envelopes, and asked Peg how she was doing. She took the bait and went on about how her floaters were back as I checked to make sure that the envelope from Marcus's assistant was on top. It was. So I asked her something extremely obscure about the next open-enrollment period for our group health-care plan.

'Great question. Let me check.'

As she turned to her computer and started clicking away, I brought my stack over to the wire basket. I pushed my expenses off the top of my stack with my thumb while I lifted the top envelope of the stack in the basket – Marcus's expenses – with my pinkie and ring fingers, adding them neatly and invisibly to the underside of my stack. A perfect bottom change.

Except as I glanced down during the change, I noticed that the envelope *under* Marcus's also had his assistant's handwriting. It was identical: *From: Carolyn Green. To: Expenses. First Floor*.

Shit. Did I grab the wrong envelope? Or not actually pick it up?

I looked away from the wire basket as Peg answered my question.

I needed another distraction. Time to scramble. 'And while I'm down here, can I ask you a second question? How does the annual fee for the Contrafund stack up against the Dow Jones index fund in the 401(k)? I'm worried they're eating me alive.'

This she knew off the top of her head. Shit. I pressed on. 'And the Diversified International?'

'Well, let's see,' she said, and started leafing through some files.

This time it wasn't as pretty, but I managed without being completely obvious to fish the second envelope from Marcus's assistant out from the wire basket. Peg turned back around just as I noticed a goddamned third envelope with the same exact handwriting. I was starting to feel like *I* was getting hustled at three-card monte.

For the life of me, I couldn't think of a question to get Peg to turn around one more time. I was just standing there like a dolt, acting odd, sticking out, attracting suspicion, everything I didn't want to do. I could tell she was losing patience. Finally, I looked at the mug and said, 'Oh, is that your cat?'

'Yes, Isabelle!' She reached for the mug and I grabbed for the third envelope. By this point I was palming a four-inch stack of paper and any attempts at subtlety were gone. My whole forearm was burning when we finally wrapped up our chat about Isabelle's hip problems. When I got back to my desk, I checked my stack, and there were three envelopes addressed identically by Carolyn. Maybe she handled some other people's expenses too. One report was for a guy named Richard Matthews, and another for Daniel Lucas, neither of whom I had ever heard of. Maybe they were contractors, I thought, and I put theirs aside. I unwound the red string on the third envelope, and there it was, Marcus's expenses, tracking him for the past two weeks better than a private eye. I scanned for restaurants, hotels, flights, names of the people he dined with, anything that would reveal what he'd been up to. The lunches drew my eye. It was what I expected from a cagey guy, no patterns, no routines, though he tended toward nicer places that required reservations. That might be handy.

Watching him closely for the past weeks I'd discovered a couple of his tells. On his long-lunch days, when it was impossible to track him down, he would sometimes just barrel out of the office, head down, like a man on a mission. He certainly wasn't the captain of the office pep squad normally, but the coolness was distinct.

Today had been one of those days, so I figured there was a decent chance he was off working on his and Davies's top secret case. And while he wasn't a regular anyplace, there were a couple restaurants he'd gone to twice. I sure as hell wasn't going to follow him anywhere. That was too much time and too much effort for an uncertain payoff, and frankly I was scared shitless of trying to out-tradecraft William Marcus.

But I could certainly ping a few of these restaurants and check to see if he had a reservation. My personal cell phone and I took a stroll, and I went down the list. 'Hello, yes. I just wanted to confirm a reservation for William Marcus. Oh, really. Is this Lebanese Taverna? I'm sorry, I must have called the wrong number.'

Try that one twenty times.

I came up empty-handed and returned to the office feeling a little silly; the whole thing was so Nancy Drew. I should have known; nothing is ever simple.

I went to my desk to take the reports back down to Peg before anybody noticed my stupid tricks and I got into real trouble. They would probably think I was stealing from the company and give me the boot. It was a crazy risk, and for nothing. But as soon as I sat down I had to take a look at the reports again. They had all been prepared by Marcus's assistant, and I'd been at the company long enough that I'd know if we had guys by those other names working here. I opened up the two other envelopes.

I stepped outside again and tried the office phone number listed for Daniel Lucas. Sure enough, Carolyn answered. 'Omnitek Consulting. Daniel Lucas's office.'

I hung up and thought about it for a minute. I'd just found Marcus's alias.

I considered the names again: Matthews and Lucas. They seemed familiar. It took me a few minutes to figure it out. There was a pattern to his aliases. The surnames were variations on the Gospels: Matthew becomes Matthews, Luke becomes Lucas, just like Mark could become Marcus.

I'd made a few missteps before I worked it all out, but I was still rather proud of myself. I copied the expense reports, dropped the originals back in interoffice mail, then took another walk and tried calling the restaurants that Marcus had been visiting and asking for him under his aliases. Nothing.

I had plenty of patience. I would just keep trying until I smoked him out.

* * *

I was asking to get caught, really. I'd been noticing her for at least fifteen seconds as she jogged ahead of me on Mount Pleasant Street while I walked back from work. Staring was unlike me, but this was a special case: a healthy female form of perfect proportions flying down the sidewalk, black ponytail swaying.

I turned a corner and broke away, glad she hadn't caught me gawking and called me on it. But as I walked on, I looked back and noticed that she stopped, then turned my way.

'Mike?' I heard her say. 'Mike Ford?'

And now, as she moved nearer, I recognized her: Irin Dragović, in black running tights.

'Don't let me slow you down,' I offered.

'I'm done,' she said, and leaned over and cupped her left knee.

'Tore my ACL playing soccer in school. It acts up in the cold.'

'That's a shame.'

'Which way are you going?' she asked.

I pointed up Mount Pleasant Street.

'Can I walk with you a bit?' she asked.

'Sure.'

We started back toward my house. The ingénue act from the beach in Colombia was gone. She apologized for it, actually, said her friends had put her up to it, that she used to be a shy girl and maybe went overboard as a result.

I told her not to worry.

'Where's the best place to get a cab around here?' she asked, and glanced back. We were a block from my house. My Jeep was parked across the way.

I had a feeling this run-in with Irin might not have been quite as accidental as she'd implied, but with the tramp act on pause, she was actually pretty charming: funny and down-to-earth.

Ever since I'd been pulled off Rado's case and found the tape, I had a lot of questions about the Serb's business. She had a privileged view into her father's affairs and the habit of shaking people down for information, which I'd witnessed firsthand when she tried it on me on the beach in Colombia. She seemed like a good person to chat with, to see what I could shake out of her.

And of course, it was the gentlemanly thing to do. I offered her a ride. We headed back to her place, in Georgetown.

I should have just dropped her off, but as I pulled up in front of the little daddy's-money Colonial (no roommates, of course), she finally slipped me a hint of what she was up to.

'My father's case,' she said. 'It's more complicated than wrangling a few loopholes for imports and exports.'

'Are you telling me or asking me?'

'Can I talk to you?'

'Of course,' I said.

She looked warily up and down the street.

'Inside?'

I looked from her upturned eyes to the house. Bad idea. There was Annie to think about – though with the hours we both pulled, I'd barely seen her for the past two weeks – and my bosses, who'd told me to keep my distance from the case. Keeping my hands off the daughter of Radomir, a semilegitimate businessman who was handy with a knife, seemed like good policy as well.

'Yeah,' I said. 'Let's go.'

I mean, why shut the girl out when she was just starting to give up info? Strictly business, I told myself. Though it sounded much less convincing with her shower on in the background after we'd gone inside and she excused herself to change.

I was half expecting her to come back out in a loosely tied kimono or a silk robe, some Mata Hari number. She did return in something 'a little more comfortable' – hospital scrubs on the bottom, and on top a Georgetown Basketball sweat-shirt with the neck cut wide enough to bare her shoulder. I could relax a little. She looked like any other everyday-PJs college girl.

The only thing to drink in the house was vodka – typical – so I had mine with tonic and she joined me. I noticed hers was all bubbles and mine barely any. It was an old trick; Lyndon Johnson would have reamed out his secretary if she'd ever given him an unwatered-down drink while he was putting the screws to some poor drunken mark in his office. I drank mine slowly, and twice switched our glasses while her attention was elsewhere.

I took a liking to the girl, apart from the obvious physical appeal. She had a decent sense of humor, with a spot-on impression of her father's overly refined manner ('Then it's simply not a Sazerac,' she intoned, with a dismissive hand) and a few nicely cutting jibes about Representative Walker's hypocrisies (apparently she knew him from his exploits among the women of Georgetown).

I steered the conversation back to her father, drawing out what she knew. I could almost forget that at the same time, she was probably trying to trap me into giving up anything I had learned.

Her angle in the whole thing, she said, was respect. Her father thought a woman's role was screwing and cooking. Irin had too much brains and ambition for that, and so she wanted to show him she was a worthy heir and maybe earn herself a role in the family business. She figured if she poked her nose in she could prove her value by helping her father out of the jam that had originally brought him to the Davies Group for help.

It didn't sound like the whole truth.

'All I know,' I said, 'is that he came to us to work out some boring import-export loophole.' That was basically a matter of public record, but Irin's eyes narrowed hungrily.

'It's more than that,' she said.

'What have you heard?'

'It's not just his business that's in trouble. It's him. He's worried about something with jurisdiction, extradition – some lawsuit or trial he needs to be protected against.'

Now I was starting to see Irin's real motives. Rumors trailed Radomir, suggesting he was connected to arms trafficking. Maybe Irin was interested in more than just overturning her father's narrow ideas of a woman's place. If he was brought to trial and proven to be a criminal, it would certainly make it a lot harder for her to keep up the charmed life of a darling American coed. The family would be ashamed, ruined, and the source of Irin's allowance would run dry.

I didn't say anything. That tends to draw people out better than any question. Most would rather say something they shouldn't say than sit in silence.

'It's out of Congress's hands too,' she went on. 'All I know is that there's a new person who's making the decision, someone powerful they need to convince.'

That sounded like it might have something to do with my man from the wiretap: Subject 23.

'And how did you learn that?' I asked.

'Deductive reasoning,' she said innocently.

I looked at her bra strap, the smooth olive skin of her shoulder. She had moved closer to me. I'd barely noticed. As we'd talked, the growing intimacy had felt as natural as curling up on the couch beside a longtime girlfriend. She noticed me taking in her body, my eyes lingering on the deep line of her cleavage showing through the widened neck of the sweatshirt.

'Pure logic, huh?' I asked.

'Well, I may have used some other gifts,' she said. She showed me a sly smile. 'It's good to have a full quiver.'

She leaned closer, rising slightly, her knees on the couch. Her scrubs hung loose on her hips, and I could trace from her belly down, lower, along the curve and shadows of her thighs: dangerous country.

'Does that make sense?' she said. 'There's one man who the whole thing rests on. A fulcrum?'

'Maybe,' I said. She didn't press, didn't puncture the illusion that this whole thing was more flirtation than interrogation. Her hand came to rest just above my knee, and then slid along my thigh. Those brown eyes moved closer to mine, then she turned slightly off to the side. Just a peck. Innocent almost. Her hand slid higher, and she pressed her breasts against me, her lips to my temple.

A desire, deeper and stronger than any willpower my mind could muster, drove me toward her.

And I'd like to think it was out of love for Annie. I'd like to think I was that good a guy. But I'm not sure. Maybe it was just basic self-preservation at work. The girl had tried the straight slut approach in Colombia, and when that didn't work, she sized me up and nailed my weak spot with this sweet girlfriend-material bit. I didn't know who she was working for, but she was dangerous. And now that I'd stolen the tape of that wiretap, I had some dangerous information of my own. However much I fancied myself a willful man who could keep his trap shut, I was sure that fucking her would, in one way or another, prove harmful to my health.

I couldn't believe it was happening. Like in a dream, I was watching it from outside my body: I took her shoulder and eased her back. She stared at me. I took a deep breath, then thanked her for the drinks and stood up.

'I'll see you around,' I said, and left.

Irin had handed me two hints – that her father was worried about extradition, and that his case involved a higher power than Congress – and I had given her none. I was glad to get away unscathed.

Meanwhile, I kept my eye on Marcus. Every time he left the office with his game face on, I rang up the restaurants he frequented and checked for reservations under his aliases. I began to think the whole thing was futile, but then, the next Tuesday, I hit.

'Yes, Mr Matthews. We have you for lunch for two at one thirty p.m. in the private room,' the host told me over the phone. He had a slight accent, Chinese maybe.

What I wanted to say was *Seriously! Are you fucking kidding me?* I'd almost given up hope in the exercise and was shocked that it worked. Now I knew where Marcus was heading on one of his cloak-and-dagger days.

I composed myself, said, 'Excellent. Thank you,' then headed out to the restaurant in Prince George's County to see exactly what the hell he was up to. PG County, as folks from DC call it and as PG County folks hate for it to be called, is terra incognita for most yuppies from Washington. The typical yuppie Washingtonian view is that PG is just an outgrowth into Maryland of the mostly poor and black southeastern quadrant of the District, so it's the last place on earth you'd expect to find a guy like William Marcus, which was exactly the point.

The restaurant was in a strip mall full of Korean grocery

stores. The restaurant's sign advertised karaoke nights. I'd actually heard about the place from Tuck, who was always searching out authentic grub on the outskirts of DC. The food was supposed to be amazing. I couldn't risk Marcus spotting me there, however. He would know something was up.

So I parked my car about three hundred feet down the road, then grabbed a spot at the window in the coffee shop across the street and waited him out. The coffee tasted burned and bitter, but the cup was bottomless. After fifty minutes I was bouncing on my stool and aching to pee, but I couldn't afford to miss him and his accomplice leaving the restaurant.

I was still a little wary about the whole thing. I felt like maybe I was chasing after shadows and taking needless chances. After the twelfth Korean guy in a suit exited the place, each one getting my hopes up and then dashing them, I decided to give up and hit the head. Then the door opened once more. It was Marcus. He held it open, and Irin Dragović, looking voluptuous as ever, stepped into the sunlight.

Now what the hell was going on?

Marcus got back in his Benz. Irin got into her white Porsche Cayenne. They both cruised away.

On the ride back to the District, I narrowed the swarm of bees in my head down to three possibilities.

One, Marcus was fucking Irin. But that was unlikely. The guy had set plenty of honeypots himself and should know better than to take orders from his dick.

Two, Irin was acting as liaison with the Davies Group for some family business. Possible, but Rado had plenty of lieutenants and clearly didn't want his daughter involved in his affairs.

And three, Marcus was using Irin as a honeypot to go after Subject 23. That seemed crazy. Why get the client's daughter involved in such a tricky situation? Who knows? Maybe Rado had offered her up, a sort of bring-your-own bait deal. Maybe she'd tried to seduce me because she'd been sent by my bosses to figure out what I knew and see whether I was getting out of line. That seemed a little self-centered, though, even paranoid. I was only a bit player in all this.

The more I thought about it, the more I focused on one possibility: Marcus had used me to lure in Walker, so why wouldn't he use Irin – so eager to prove her worth – to lure in the man on the tape?

Chapter Twelve

In the eleven months I'd been at Davies Group, I'd certainly gotten to know the seamy side of politics, but any jadedness I'd acquired fell away as soon as I heard my footsteps crack across the black and white tiles of the US Capitol. All the marble heroes and double-coffered gilt ceilings made me as excited as a civics geek on a class trip.

At least, I felt that way until I caught up with Walker in Statuary Hall. It's the old meeting place of the House of Representatives, and, except for the Capitol Dome, there's nothing grander.

I went to check in with Walker to see if I could get any more information about Irin and her father's business. Walker had some oversight on foreign relations, and given his extensive cocksmanship over in Georgetown, the odds were good he'd either run into Irin or at least heard a bit of background on her. And after our suburban adventure, the guy was just dying to do me a favor.

So in essence, I wanted to talk smut with Walker, and he invited me to Statuary Hall, America's closest thing to a sacred pantheon. The whole place was full of little kids and nuns. I was starting to feel worse and worse.

I caught sight of Walker standing near Andrew Jackson's feet and headed over.

'What the—' I edited myself as a kid toddled past. 'What's all this?'

'I'm not really sure. Tight schedule today; sorry about double-booking you. I think it's a memorial for a woman missionary. Maybe something about orphans. I'm just here for a couple photos. My pollster told me I need to soften my image among women. Charles knows.'

He pointed to the corpulent aide following about twelve feet behind us. Fun fact: senators and congressmen, the guys nominally running the country, typically have no idea what's going on. They spend all their time begging donors for money to get reelected, schmoozing, and flying back home to officiate at pig races at state fairs. Walking haircuts, they rely on their party bosses and an army of aides – socially challenged ex-debate-team nerds – to tell them what to think. Their lives are blocked out in ten-minute increments, and assistants constantly steer them like brain-injury victims from event to event.

'Can we keep this conversation between us?' I asked.

'Of course,' Walker said, and considering the dirt I had on him, I believed he actually would.

'Good. I wanted to ask if you know a girl named Irin Dragović.'

He repeated the name, then scrunched up his face in concentration. 'I may need a little more to work on.' Given Walker's volume, I had expected him to be iffy on ladies' names. I showed him Irin's Facebook profile photo: a lovely shot, about 40 per cent cleavage, of her drinking from a bottle of Moët & Chandon White Star.

'Oh, yeah,' Walker said. 'She's hard to forget.'

'What's her story?'

He thought for a moment. 'Comes on very strong. Knows what she wants. Gets off on the power thing big-time. She wanted to go for it in my hideaway' – those are little offices hidden in the hallways near the House chamber – 'no kid bullshit, either. No cling. No sentimentality. She's a pro. And . . .'

Walker looked around, checking to see if anyone was nearby. Charles was out of earshot. A pack of nuns was about fifteen feet away. Still, given Walker's typically dirty mouth, seeing him grow sheepish about saying something made me genuinely nervous about the bomb he was going to drop.

Daniel Webster's statue loomed behind us, glowering down. I felt like a heel wringing kiss-and-tell out of Walker under the judging eyes of the Great Expounder of the Constitution, but I had bigger problems to worry about.

'Give,' I said.

'Rough stuff,' Walker said. 'You remember that crazy chick I was telling you about?'

'Not particularly.' He had a lot of war stories, and I tended to zone out during them.

'At the Ritz?' he asked.

I shook my head.

'Well, I met her at that party at Chip's. You know, that night we went out to my friend's place and . . .'

'I remember,' I said. Getting arrested alongside whores and drug dealers tends to stick in your mind.

'She caught me alone in the library, came after me like a hungry whippet. We texted back and forth for a few days after that, then ended up meeting for a drink at the Sofitel. We got ourselves a room. One thing leads to another and I'm up to my ears in it and she asks me to give her a spank.

'I'm a gentleman, so I oblige. Again, and again. And then she asks me to smack her face, insists on it, actually. That's not my thing, but I give her a playful little touch on the cheek. And then she leans up on her elbow. She stops the whole show and she says to me, like she's my basketball coach or something, "Hey, listen. Give it to me real, across the face."'

Walker gave me a can-you-believe-that look.

'Well, that wasn't going to happen,' he went on. 'Who knows what this girl is after? And I am sure not going to be tussling with her like that, maybe leaving marks and all. We went on for a while, though I think by that point my heart wasn't in it.

'And God, we were going for it, and just as I was about ready to spit, she'd pull away. Just leave me hanging. She had me pinned and wriggling, boy, all the power in her hands. In the end she had me begging like a dog.'

I heard a gasp at that point in Walker's story; it sounded like it came from right next to us, which was weird, because we were off by ourselves. Fun fact no. 2: The half-dome shape of Statuary Hall affects the acoustics in the chamber, so if you stand at one spot (where John Quincy Adams's desk was, actually), you can hear conversations on the other side of the room as if they were a few feet away, and vice versa. Adams supposedly used it to spy on the loyal opposition. So too, apparently, had a sheet-faced Sister across the hall. I gathered she was the one who had gasped after picking up a few bars of our conversation.

I ushered Walker a few feet away.

'What was she trying to get out of you?'

'Access. Introductions. Whatever she wanted, really. I think she was using me as a stepping-stone to bigger things, more powerful men.' Walker shook his head. 'I'd rather not tangle with her again.'

'So you stopped calling her.'

'She'd already moved on. I heard she was going after some high-up at Treasury. That's the thing. It wasn't really about sex for her.'

He paused as we waited for a few representatives to pass.

'It was a power thing. You could see it in the game she played, letting you be the boss and then turning the tables, wringing out of you whatever she wanted. And she told me outright. "You're one of the most powerful men in the country," she said. "I'm a twenty-year-old girl. And I can make you grovel to fuck me." '

Walker laughed. 'She certainly was right about that. And with those eyes and that rack in this town, she might be running the country by the next election.'

'And her father?'

'He's the kind of man you never want to cross. I know just enough about him to not want to know more.'

'How's that?'

'I may have to do business with him at some point, so the less I know the better. Plausible deniability, that's the name of the game.'

'You know anything about legal troubles, some extradition issues?'

'No, and I don't want to.'

He was clearly in the dark on Rado, so I let it rest there. We walked on for a few feet, and I caught Walker giving me a look that pretty clearly meant *You sly dog*.

'And what's your interest in the lovely Irin Dragović?' he asked. 'Sparring partner, perhaps?'

'It's not what you're thinking.'

'I'm sure,' he said, and shook his head. 'Aww, sticky sticky.' Again with the sticky. And again, I didn't even want to think about what that meant.

An old schoolhouse-style clock buzzed five times in the corridor behind us. Near its top, between ten and two o'clock, it had eight lights. Five lit up white, and one red.

'I've got to go vote,' Walker said.

'Is that what those signals mean?'

'Fuck if I know,' he said, and lifted up his BlackBerry. 'I just got a text from Charles.'

He beckoned the aide over. 'You've got my cheat sheet for me?'

Charles handed over an index card.

'Yea. Yea. Nay. Yea,' Walker said as he read it. 'Easy peasy.'

'What's the vote on?' I asked.

Walker threw up his hands. 'Beats me. Ask Charles. I've got to run. Say, you have plans for tonight? Having a little party. Should be a real hoot.'

Walker and I had different ideas about what constituted a hoot. 'Rain check,' I said.

I fled the nuns as quickly as I could. I'd been hoping my suspicions were wrong. Everything would be so much easier if I could just let the whole matter rest. But no. Based on what Walker had told me, I was even more worried about where all this was going. Irin seemed like perfect bait for the man on the tape.

Chapter Thirteen

William Marcus was certainly a cagey operator, but I think after all his years in the field, the spy had finally met his match: Mrs Marcus. For every alias and out-of-the-way meet-up Marcus used to confound foes real and imaginary, there was Karen Marcus, Facebook fiend, posting *Is it wine time yet?* and *Can't wait to see you at the shower this weekend. xoxoxo.* She hadn't quite mastered the labyrinth of privacy settings, so it was almost as good as having a homing beacon up Marcus's ass.

Almost, but not quite, which is why I was skulking in the bushes outside his house in McLean, getting ready to plant a homing beacon on Marcus's ass. Well, actually, on the wheel well of his Mercedes. They were at her niece's baby shower up in the Brandywine Valley. The minivan was gone.

I'll be the first to admit that technology takes all the fun out of snooping on people, and I had tried to do it the old-fashioned honest way, with all the shoe leather that entailed. During the weeks I'd spent attempting to get a bead on Marcus's mysterious lunch dates, I'd dug into the literature on how to tail people. It's great stuff: leapfrogging, paralleling, the ABC technique. One night I was reading up on the best cars to use for a stakeout when I stepped back and asked myself what the hell I was thinking of doing.

The truth was, I'd grown very attached to my blissful

new yuppie life. I had a great crew of friends, the beautiful girlfriend, the backyard with the fire pit and the cold beer.

Annie and I, even though we were working crazy hours, were doing great. The week after my Irin run-in, Annie had to go to Paris for work (some Davies project that was being kept pretty quiet). I asked her if she could tack on a long weekend there and if I could come meet her (last-minute transatlantic trips were one of many luxuries afforded by the Davies Group that I could see myself getting used to). I'd been growing increasingly worried, even as we got more serious, that there was some conflict, some reservation, some hidden issue holding her back. It kept me from asking her to move in, or saying I love you. The latter I'd skirted around but always got the sense from her that it wasn't the time. It was strange, and I wondered if it had something to do with all her one-on-one work with Henry or with a wariness about my past or my family.

But after Paris, I felt settled, sure. On our last night there, we were standing on the balcony of our hotel room, with a clear view over the Tuileries from La Défense to Notre-Dame. The setting, coming at the end of a four-day romp where we'd barely left the hotel and Annie had surprised me with quite a bit of only-on-vacation new material, was romantic enough that she probably would have said 'I love you' to a pigeon, but I didn't care. She said it to me. I said it back. She was mine. It had all come true.

Maybe that's why I was letting these suspicions about my bosses drive me to take such risks: you get everything you want and all of a sudden you're bored and want to start fucking it all up. But I wasn't going to let that happen. Annie and I had reservations at the Inn at Little Washington coming up in two weeks. It's a super-deluxe country inn, the best on the East Coast, and I wasn't going to miss out on the meal of my life *and* vacation sex by getting myself killed playing spy versus spy against William Marcus.

Maybe I'd stumbled onto some wicked plot that endangered lives, but maybe I was just drawing lines between dots that didn't connect and getting myself worked up over nothing. It would have been easy enough to forget about what had happened, to lose myself in the countless hours I was putting in at Davies. But every time I tried to turn away from the case of Rado and Subject 23, some new reminder would appear, like when Tuck, my closest friend at work, quit.

One day, I was grabbing coffee in the break room, though *break room* doesn't do it justice. On the second floor, it was set up like an old-fashioned men's club, with beautifully worn leather couches, checkerboard marble floors, and food available at all hours. Tuck came up to me with a grim look on his face.

'I'm moving on, Mike,' he said. 'New job. Over at State. I wanted to tell you before you hear from somebody else.'

'Congratulations,' I said, though I wasn't quite sure if that was the right word. You could spend fifteen years climbing over bureaucratic deadwood at the State Department and still have less clout than a fifth-year associate at Davies Group. Tuck's father was the deputy secretary, though, so I was sure he'd have a little help on his way up.

'Why the shift?' I asked.

He looked along the paneled ceiling of the break room, and then said, 'Why don't we take a walk.' I glanced at the cameras hidden in the joinery overhead, then followed him out.

We walked outside, past the oddly juxtaposed compounds of Embassy Row: a Beaux Arts mansion beside a concrete box beside an Islamic complex crowned with minarets. Tuck went on about the dossier he'd be working on at State, about big opportunities and the family tradition of public service, but I could tell something else was on his mind.

'Why are you really leaving?' I interrupted.

He stopped walking and turned to face me. 'I talked to my grandfather' – he'd been CIA director in the 1960s – 'and he doesn't say much, as a rule, but he told me maybe I should try a few different posts. That maybe Davies Group wasn't the right fit for a man like me.'

'What does that mean?'

'That's all I can say. My grandfather knows just about everything that happens in DC, but he never tips his hand. You ever wonder how Davies does it, how he has the whole town wired?'

'Not by being a Boy Scout.'

Tuck raised his eyebrows. 'Maybe that's what my grandfather was getting at. You've had an amazing rise, Mike. Just be careful. I'd hate for it to be too good to be true.'

He started walking again, and as much as I tried, for the rest of our walk I couldn't pry any more information out of him. We circled around toward the office, and as we crested the hill on Twenty-Fourth Street, we could see the city laid out below us, tinted red by the setting sun.

'When trouble comes,' Tuck said, 'it's not the guys at the top who take the fall.'

Some of what Tuck told me I might have been able to dismiss as sour grapes; after all, he'd seen me, an outsider with no family connections, rise above him at Davies Group. But that sort of warning, however vague, from a guy as plugged in as Tuck's grandfather only rekindled my concerns.

I certainly wanted to keep an eye on Irin and Marcus, because if my worst fears came true – that there was something to the talk of killing on that tape I'd stolen – I could never forgive myself. And chances were that if something terrible did happen in the Rado–Subject 23 affair, I would end up taking the blame. I just wanted a little insurance, to keep my eye on what Marcus was up to.

I'd done lots of homework about how to tail people in the traditional shoe-leather style. But then I found out those methods were more or less obsolete. After extensive research (well, not quite; I got stuck on a plane for two hours on the tarmac at Reagan National and had nothing to read but the *SkyMall*), I found out that for a hundred and fifty bucks, you can buy yourself a little magnetic stick-on real-time GPS tracker. After you place it on your mark's car, you can kick back, sip your coffee, and track your prey on Google Maps, risk-free. Irin's tracker was already firmly adhered to the wheel well of her Porsche, but I was taking extra care planting Marcus's. That's why I was skulking outside his house. It would have been easiest to do it at work, but I didn't dare. The whole Davies Group building was lousy with cameras.

It took a quick dash from the bushes to clap the tracker in Marcus's wheel well. I heard a dog bark (well, *yap* would probably be more accurate) behind the fence and sped out of there. Mission accomplished. A little cash out of pocket, and now even an idiot like me had the drop on William Marcus, superspy. Don't you love technology?

I did. Maybe I geeked out a little too much. There were, as far as I could tell, no more Irin-Marcus meet-ups, but I was always peeking at their locations in a Web browser or on the little app for my phone. It was fun, like live Pac-Man in the city. And gradually, my concerns about Subject 23 receded.

Until six days later, when Marcus's assistant called me up to Marcus's office. Marcus was at his desk. He didn't stand, didn't offer me a chair. No greeting, no warm-up.

'You've been talking to Irin Dragović,' he said.

'I ran into her, yes.'

'I thought I told you to stay away from that case.'

'She was out running and hurt her knee. I happened to be walking by, pure chance, and gave her a lift home. That's all there was to it.'

He stared at me. 'You recall how dangerous I told you things would get for you if you meddle.'

When Marcus had talked to me about it in Colombia, his warning seemed more of a friendly I'm-looking-out-for-you message. This sounded distinctly like a threat.

'You understand me, I trust,' Marcus said.

I did. I had no idea how Marcus knew about what I'd been up to, and hopefully he only knew about my relatively innocent encounter with Irin and not my theft of his expense reports and tracking of his car. Whatever he knew, his point was unmistakable: back off or get hurt. Making excuses or pleading ignorance would only dig me in deeper.

'Absolutely,' I said. 'I'll steer clear, no matter the circumstances.'

Marcus looked over my shoulder, toward the open doorway of his office. I turned. Henry Davies stood behind me.

'Is everything clear, Mike?' Henry said. He obviously knew what this little check-in was about, and he'd stopped by to underscore the gravity of the situation.

'Yes,' I said.

'Then you can go.'

I left. As I rounded the columns that framed the entrance to the executive suites, I overheard Henry saying to Marcus, 'I have to head out. We'll talk about this more tonight.'

After Marcus's warning, I didn't get much work done. I was glued to the screen showing my GPS trackers all afternoon. Marcus's threat sounded like he was just keeping me in line, but if he and Henry were going to have a chat about my fate, I certainly wanted to know as much about it as I could.

Around six o'clock that evening, Marcus's tracker left the office and headed west along Reservoir Road. The proximity to Georgetown caught my attention. I was always watching for him to circle round to Irin's place. He drove straight over the Chain Bridge, however, to the Virginia side of the Potomac, near the CIA. That had my paranoia working overtime, until I remembered that Henry's house was in that neighborhood, perched over the Potomac Gorge. Marcus's car turned off onto a winding street that served the riverside mansions just north of the Chain Bridge. Most likely he was headed for Henry's.

That was enough for me to want to check it out. I cleared my desk, then headed downstairs and pulled my Jeep out of the garage. I had about two hours before I was supposed to meet Annie for dinner. I would just take a ride past, I told myself, to see if Marcus was really going to Henry's house. With traffic, it was a half-hour drive.

The long lane that led down to Henry's mansion had a formidable gate with video security. I drove on and stopped at a dead end near the river. I watched the white water break over the rocky course of the Potomac far below me.

The Virginia side of the Potomac is mostly parkland: all gorges, rock scrambles, and rope swings into the river. I bushwhacked down the steep hill and cut back on the far side of Henry's grounds. I still hadn't crossed onto private property. Seen from the road I had just left, his house was a well-hidden fortress. But vanity and river vistas trump security any time. Near the water, I had an unobstructed view of casa Henry: a manor house on a commanding spot high over the river. As I hoisted myself over and around the rocks and boulders, I made out two figures talking on the terrace, silhouetted by the warm yellow lights inside the house.

What I was thinking of doing next seemed crazy. But I was in danger. Marcus had more or less stated that outright. If I was being set up to take the fall in some matter of life and death I barely knew anything about, it seemed crazier to do nothing. I'd already gone too far. If they discovered what I had done – stealing the tape and the expenses, tracking Marcus's car – I was done for. I'd rather find the truth now and deal with what was coming with open eyes.

Henry's fence was high and so well hidden by hedges you could barely see the razor wire along the top. There was no chance I'd make it over, certainly not without ruining my dinner clothes and needing to stop by the hospital afterward.

I circled around to the side of the property and a utility area – a pair of Dumpsters and a lane for garbage trucks. There was a gate, electronic and accessed by an RFID – the kind you open by waving a key fob or access card. Picking the lock was beyond my skills. But high tech cuts both ways. Once people pay for the open-sesame stuff, they tend to want automatic exit on a motion sensor, doors that whoosh open like on *Star Trek* when you approach them from the inside. That's the trick: nothing but the key will open them from the outside, but anything will from within.

I found a nice knobbly stick, slotted it through the side of the gate, and waved it around at what I guessed was head height inside. I heard the telltale *thwock* of an electromagnetic bolt being drawn, then I opened the door and, wary of being seen, crawled through on my stomach.

Back by the Dumpsters, there'd been a single super-bright wallpack floodlight, there to lend a false sense of security. You'd be better off with motion sensors or nothing at all, the better to spot flashlights. Inside the fence was a different story. During a careful scan just inside the gate, I managed to pick out a half a dozen motion sensors – IR and ultrasonic, it looked like – mounted in the woods that led up to the house.

I'd spent many hours during my burgling years trying to learn how to defeat this sort of setup, and I'd heard all kinds of theories – wear a sheet over your head, walk the perfect pace, don a full-body wet suit – but the fact was I couldn't get within listening distance of that deck without getting caught.

So I would just get caught. The crying-wolf bit is an old trick, but it usually works.

I found a nice spot to hide: a hollow between the roots of a towering tree. I was still around the side of the house, out of view of the terrace where the two men stood. I stepped in front of the nearest motion sensor and waved my arms around like an idiot. That was plenty to set it off, but there were no lights, no sirens: bad news, hinting at some sort of central control and silent alarm. I walked about twenty feet the other way and did a few jumping jacks in front of another sensor. Then I hid in my hole.

It only took a few minutes for a grumpy guy with bowlegs, some kind of handyman, to come for me, swinging a flashlight. The beam of light passed over my tree two or three times. I was well hidden, though that wasn't very reassuring as I imagined the possible fates that awaited me if Henry Davies discovered me breaking into his sanctum.

The man walked away muttering curses and something about deer.

As soon as he got back to the house, I pulled my monkey act in front of the sensor again, then hid. After three rounds of this, the guy didn't even bother pointing a flashlight in my direction. I was safe to move.

I ran around the corner, then dragged myself on my stomach along a gully and, eventually, under the wooden deck where the two men were chatting. As I eased myself silently over the ground, I could hear my bosses' voices.

I lay awkwardly, with a rock in the small of my back, hearing their footsteps pass four feet over my head. I thought every breath would give me away. I could just barely keep it together a half an hour later when a charley horse twisted through my right leg. Their conversation ranged over office politics and a handful of cases that didn't interest me before they moved on to weightier matters.

'Was Ford on the level with you today?' Henry asked.

'I think so,' Marcus said. 'He hasn't been pestering us about what's happening with Radomir. I think he's let the case go. The girl did approach him, not the other way around. And we certainly put the fear of God into him today. He's a good kid.'

'Has Subject Twenty-Three moved any closer to finding the evidence?' Henry asked.

'We can't say,' Marcus said. 'He went silent on the tapped phones, very cagey all of a sudden.'

'Do you have a close enough watch to know whether he passed on anything incriminating?'

'Yes. We don't believe he did.'

'So it's safe to ease him out of the picture?'

'Most likely,' Marcus said. 'Say, eighty percent confidence.'

'Your thoughts?'

'He's close to that envelope. As much as we'd like him to lead us to it, if he gets it he can shut down our whole show. The prudent thing would be to take care of him sooner rather than later.'

'Can we catch him one-on-one? His wife died years ago, but are there any girlfriends? Is the daughter ever around?'

'He's not sleeping with anyone. Creature of habit, spends most weekends out in the country, with no security detail. The daughter's in boarding school, almost never visits during the school year.'

'Any other loose ends?'

'One. The Dragović girl won't stop meddling. I met with her last week to back her off.'

'How much does she know?'

'The particulars of her father's case: beating extradition, staying out of the courts.'

'Subject Twenty-Three?' Henry asked.

'She knows there's one linchpin, but she didn't let on that she knew who he was.'

'What does she want?'

'To help, apparently,' Marcus said. 'Save her father from extradition. She thinks her cunt is the ultimate weapon, that she can get anything by scratching the right itch. I gather that's how she learned what she knows about the case. I shut her down. Full stop.'

'If she's as stubborn as her father, we still have cause for concern.'

'Twenty-Three is jumpy enough. If she gets close to him with that clumsy seduction act, she's liable to get herself hurt, badly.'

Henry didn't respond.

'You think she could actually help find the evidence?' Marcus asked.

'Maybe. Twenty-Three is lonely. It doesn't matter, though. If she did get a look inside that envelope, her days would be numbered. It's dangerous intel, and then we'd have to take care of her ourselves to protect our end.' Henry exhaled in frustration. 'Anyway, we can't possibly use her. The whole thing gets so goddamn messy with Radomir, that psycho, and Twenty-Three on edge already. What a shit-show. We'll hold off for now, watch and wait. I'm still lining up clients. It's worth billions. If we pull this off, it'll be the last case we ever need.'

Rain began to drum on the deck.

'Keep your eye on the girl, very closely,' Henry went on. 'If she manages to get near Twenty-Three we'll have to move things up and take him immediately. Think through some options. It won't be quite so cut-and-dried, but there's always a way.'

'I will,' Marcus said.

'I'm freezing,' Henry said. 'Come on.'

I heard a door open, and then the bark of a dog getting louder and closer. Christ. All that good work to break in here, and then I'm sniffed out by Henry's wife's corgi.

I sprinted to the gate and then waded through underbrush back to my car. The rain pouring over me helped clear my head. Irin wasn't working for Marcus after all. She was a meddler like me, and apparently had made more progress than I had, though at least Davies and Marcus hadn't caught on that I was digging into Rado's case on my own. Irin and I were both playing catch-up in a game whose stakes we didn't understand. My bosses had spoken in vague terms only about what might happen to the man from the wiretap, to Irin. They could have been talking about buying someone off, or more blackmail, but it was getting harder and harder to ignore the possibility that crimes far worse were being contemplated.

Already twenty minutes late for dinner, I changed into some clothes I had in the Jeep that had been destined for the dry cleaner's. I still had a strong hint of terror sweat from breaking into Henry's place. When I showed up at the restaurant, I wasn't exactly looking my best.

Annie gave me a where-the-fuck-have-you-been face. Ever since I'd jetted down to Colombia with Davies, she'd been keenly interested in what exactly I was up to with the big boss. I'd catch her eyeing my open e-mail, glancing at my phone when it rang, idly chatting me up for hints about what I was working on. She'd been one of Henry's star pupils, and I imagined that behind her curiosity lay a touch of envy, maybe even a sense of being threatened by my rise at Davies Group. After all, only so many could make partner.

At least, I hoped that's why she was so curious – she was still close with Henry and sometimes I wondered if he ever used all that one-on-one time with her to draw her out and find out what I was up to. That seemed paranoid – the idea that maybe, intentionally or not, she was helping Davies keep tabs on me – but I certainly wasn't going to tell her I'd been spying on the bosses.

I blamed the Jeep for my lateness.

'You and that car,' she said.

We were at this really authentic Szechuan place; Tuck had insisted we try the *ma la*, which I was told translated roughly as 'numb tongue.' It wasn't just spicy. It tasted like pain and smelled like death. I did my best to appear to eat it as I fantasized about spaghetti and meatballs and checked in on the GPS trackers on my smartphone under the table.

Irin's car was parked as usual in the garage near her house on Prospect Street. Marcus cruised back through Georgetown that evening. Nothing too extraordinary. But now, at 8:30 p.m. on a school night, he was heading south of the Capitol.

Dinner was over. Annie was giving me her I'm-going-to-be-asleep-in-fifteen-minutes look, and I was dying to find out what was going down in Southeast DC, toward the Navy Yard, the last place you'd expect to find a guy like Marcus. The only problem was that we were right around the corner from my house, so it would be tough for me to blow off Annie.

I lifted up my phone. 'Oh God. I promised Eric Walker I'd stop by his house and play a few hands.'

'Maybe we should just curl up and watch a movie,' Annie said, which I knew by now meant her conking out after the opening credits.

'I would. But it's work stuff. Some freshman senators I should get to know. Why don't you come? It might be handy. A few of the guys oversee Homeland Security—'

Annie had a couple cases related to DHS, but I knew she was heading home for the night. It was a bluff.

'You go, hon. Should I head back to my place?'

'You can stay at mine.'

'Okay,' she said.

I walked her to the door and said I'd be back soon. The temperature had dropped. The rain had turned to sleet.

I'd been watching those trackers – two little bull's-eyes on my map – for so long, I had to see if they were up to something. Marcus had headed to the riverfront near the Navy Yard. The area had long been one of the seediest parts of DC, full of empty warehouses, grungy punk clubs, and bathhouses. They tore most of it down to make room for the new Nationals stadium and for condos. But the gentrification plan had tanked with the economy. Now it was a no-man's-land of vacant lots, empty parking garages, and massive decommissioned navy hangars with all the windows shattered. Not the kind of place you'd pick for a high-end business meeting. More of a concrete-shoes ambience.

The GPS said that Marcus's car was right on the waterfront. Maybe he'd cruised down here to watch the river go by, be alone with his thoughts, listen to 'Cat's in the Cradle'. But not likely. Hard by the 295 bridge and Buzzard Point, this was a better spot to get car-jacked than inspired.

A bitter April wind whipped curtains of frozen rain over the Potomac. I followed the tracker, growing more doubtful by the second. It led me along the river by the Navy Yard. I moved closer to the bull's-eye on my map and checked the surroundings, and it looked like Marcus was on the end of one of the docks. I scanned it, but saw nothing. Satellites don't lie, though, so, after looking around to make sure I wasn't being followed, I began walking down the dock, keeping to the shadows.

A little red light flashed faster and faster as I got closer to the bull's-eye. It's a handy feature, at least until you're skulking along in the dark on a deserted pier. Then that red eye, blinking faster and faster until it's almost glaring solid red, can start to feel a little sinister.

I stood on the bull's-eye, the end of the pier. It was freezing. Marcus's car sure as hell wasn't around. Did he find the tracker in the wheel well? Throw it in the Potomac, and have it wash up here? That didn't make sense based on the path it had taken.

A shadow moved at the far end of the dock. You could barely see it. Then it shifted again.

I had a second thought. This was the perfect place for Marcus to plant it himself, to find whoever was following him and trap him. So much for the digital future. If that was true, I'd cornered myself.

The movement was slow but unmistakable once I knew where to look. A silhouette cut across the yellow cones shining down from the sodium lights.

No exit. William Marcus bearing down on me like a Horseman of the Apocalypse. And there was no way I could lie my way out of this. I tried out a few stories in my head, but Marcus would see right through them. How could you possibly explain planting a tracking bug on your boss? Hiding outside his house? Stalking him?

No. It would be game-over for Mike Ford. At the least, the high times Davies Group had afforded would be gone. No medallions of Shenandoah veal with new potatoes at the Inn at Little Washington. And worse, my bosses had enough dirt to bury me for campaign-finance violations alone; they wouldn't even have to get into the meth-house business. Back to jail, the charade over, truly my father's son.

As I listened to the boards creak in the dark, closer and closer, I began to worry less and less about material things and more about Marcus's leathery hands. I mean, he wouldn't kill me, right? But what the fuck did I know about the habits of a guy who'd spent the 1980s strangling Sandinistas?

In any case, I couldn't risk getting caught. All of my options were bad. I didn't like the looks of the water either as it capped white ten feet below me. But I knew, however hellish the ride, I could make it to the next dock. One good thing about the navy: you learn to plunk yourself in all kinds of briny and haul ass without making too much noise.

A flashlight beam cut across the dock, and I jumped into the black. The main concern when you drop into icy water is that you'll gasp, breathe in a lungful, and go down like a fluke anchor. I managed to avoid that, though the cold shocked my body and I immediately started breathing all crazy and dropped about forty IQ points. If you don't kill yourself freaking out, you've got about fifteen minutes in arctic water far colder than this, so however much I felt like I was dying, I knew I had plenty of time. The light was scanning the water in long arcs, so I swam beneath the dock, a little cave of barnacles and foul-smelling green moss. I worked my way back under Marcus, cracking my head every now and then on a beam or a lag bolt.

I could hear him overhead. His light fanned through the cracks in the boards above me. As he came closer, I ducked under the surface, then swam beneath him.

I almost wished he'd been ranting and shouting threats.

That cold efficient silence scared me more than anything else.

I made it back to the bulkhead, where the dock began, and side-stroked, the sleet stinging my ear, to the next dock, about fifty meters. I hauled myself out and tried to sprint to my car, but the best I could manage was a numb stumble. His light flashed over me in the dark and lit me up, but by now it was far-off and faint.

A fence separated the two docks. That bought me a little time. Once I got to the Jeep, I headed out and brought it up to about fifty miles an hour on the surface roads, and I made it to 395. I had the heat blasting like an open oven. It was only twenty minutes to my house, but I didn't get back for forty, since I was constantly taking sharp detours and double-checking at every turn to make sure that Marcus wasn't following me.

I ran inside the house, threw my clothes into the washing machine in the laundry room, and went straight for a twenty-minute steaming-hot shower. My hands were still shaking so badly from the cold I could barely twist the knobs. The only thing keeping me going was the prospect of sliding under a thick comforter and lying next to Annie.

I slipped into the dark bedroom and eased into bed. When I put my hand out to feel her waist, I just hit mattress. She was gone.

I found her downstairs. Actually, she found me. She was sitting on the couch with a cup of tea, waiting. She had watched me as I came down the stairs. Her eyes hinted at tears earlier, but now she was strictly business.

'Are you fucking someone else?' she asked in an oddly calm voice.

My brain seized up. I'd been smiling at her, still just happy to see her after such a shitty night. But any relief quickly disappeared.

'What?' I said. 'No.'

She lifted one of the profile pictures of Irin I'd printed out.

'You're always late, making up excuses. You come home, get rid of your clothes, and head straight for the shower. You think I'm stupid? I know what that means.'

'It's for work,' I said. 'Her father is Rado Dragović.'

'Don't give me that. A twenty-year-old party girl is what, lobbying the Pentagon? I looked her up and a million searches came up on your laptop. Are you stalking this girl?'

'Hon, you know networking is part of the job. I'm checking up on her for a case, and I promised Walker I'd meet with him tonight—'

'Just shut up,' she said. 'Walker's at the House right now for the budget vote. Stop lying to me. It's disgusting.'

She stood and marched to the front door. I chased after her, stammering, wearing only my boxers. Once again I was freezing my ass off, but now I was half naked on my front porch. I realized that the truth would be much harder for her to believe than any bullshit I came up with, but I didn't want to lie to her again.

'Hon. I can explain. It was work; I lied because I didn't want to get you involved. It's about our bosses, about Davies. Please. Come back inside.'

'You want me to trust you?'

'Yes,' I said.

'Then trust me. You more than anyone know how this town works, Mike. You can't take without giving. Tell me what's going on.'

'I'll show you.' I walked her back into the hallway near the kitchen, and lifted my clothes out of the washing machine.

'That smells like a bilge,' she said, and wrinkled her nose. I guess she was expecting the odor of another woman's perfume or the scent of sex.

'I lied to you. I never should have. I'm sorry. Truly. I certainly wasn't fucking anybody reeking like that.'

'Just tell me what's happening.'

I chose my words carefully. Why trouble her if the whole thing was just me chasing shadows? And why involve her if there was real danger?

'I was worried that some unethical stuff was happening in a deal I was part of. So I had to double-check a few things. And, because I'm a moron, in the course of sneaking around I fell into some disgusting water and nearly froze to death.'

She considered this for a minute.

'That's too ridiculous an alibi to invent.' She scrutinized me for a second. 'You fell in the water?'

'Yeah. The Anacostia. It was freezing,' I said. 'I've had a really rough night. I'm so goddamned sorry.'

'Why didn't you just tell me?'

'I know I'm probably just being paranoid, and I didn't want to get you mixed up in it. It was stupid and I'm done.'

'Did you tell Marcus or Henry?'

'No. And please keep this between us. I was sort of doing this on my own and I could get in big trouble if they found out. All right?'

'You should tell them,' she said. 'They'll know what to do.'

Annie was a gunner, like me. Work was everything, and she was close with Davies. Hell, it was Davies who had thrown Annie and me together in the first place. I didn't want to think about what she would do if it came down to a choice between him and me.

'I know,' I said. 'But can we just keep this to ourselves? I checked it out, there was nothing to it, and I could get in trouble for going off the reservation. You won't mention it to anyone, will you?'

I could tell she was getting wary again.

'No,' she said, finally.

'You swear?'

'Yes.'

'Thank you. I'll never lie to you again. You have a right to be angry. Take your time. I can give you a ride home if you like, but I hope you can forgive me and stay.'

She stared me down and let me suffer for another minute.

'No,' she said. 'Let's just go to bed.'

At last, all I wanted: to pull the comforter up to my chin and curl up with Annie's little potbellied stove of a behind. It was heaven. She clicked off her light.

'And, hon,' she said.

'Yeah.'

'If you do ever fuck around on me, I will hunt you down and I will crucify you.'

Aww. Daddy's girl.

'As you should, sweetie,' I said. 'Love you.'

'You too.'

That was it, I told myself. To hell with Subject 23 and Irin. I was not giving up everything I'd earned just because I'd taken a few clues out of context and had a little fun playing detective.

Case closed, right? Except I couldn't stop thinking about Annie's reservations, about how her first instinct was to tell Marcus and Henry.

I tried to convince myself I hadn't told her the full story for her sake, but maybe it was for my own. As I tried and failed to fall asleep, I realized that my suspicions about the Davies Group were making me question everything connected to the company. The group was my whole world. The friends, the money, the house, and, in a way, even Annie: I owed it all to Henry. So who could I trust?

Chapter Fourteen

His head was shaved bald and he was built like a football center. The back of his neck had rolls like a pack of hot dogs. He sported tinted sunglasses, wraparound-baseball-player style. He walked stiffly, elbows out, like he either had a backed-up colon or thought he was in a Western. He wore a sack suit and a cheap tie. In other words: a cop.

With my family history, I get a little nervous around cops. Granted, now that I had the thick wallet and the cozy house in the city, I could see their appeal, but old habits die hard. Especially given my recent string of unorthodox activities, I was not at all happy when this palooka sat down next to me at a lunch counter and starting looking me over.

There are no decent diners in the neighborhood where I work. There's a spot called the Diner, but it's a retro/meta thing where a sandwich costs ten dollars. So I spend more lunches than I should at a restaurant called Luna's. It's one of those Berkeley-earth-mom places, the kind with a bathroom mural of Noam Chomsky and Harriet Tubman holding hands and sliding down a rainbow, but the burgers are good and cheap. If you tuck in at the counter and focus on the food and free coffee refills, you can hardly tell it from a regular greasy spoon.

But it certainly wasn't the kind of place I'd expect to find this red-faced peace officer.

'Michael Ford?' he asked.

'Do I know you?'

'Erik Rivera,' he said. 'I'm a detective with the Metropolitan Police Department, Special Investigations Division.'

'Okay.'

'This is a friendly visit,' Rivera said, which to my ears threatened an unfriendly future run-in. 'How's the cobbler?'

'It's good.'

'Good.' I guess this was how they taught cops to rapport-build at MPD summer camp. It left a little to be desired, but thankfully Rivera got down to business.

'I was hoping to get your help on a few questions we had about some goings-on at the Davies Group,' he said.

Goings-on? Was I on *Dragnet*? I took a deep breath and, in a perfect monotone, gave him my best lawyerese:

'I regret to inform you that we have confidentiality and nondisclosure agreements with all of our clients and I am legally bound to refrain from discussing, well, anything with you unless I am subpoenaed. Even under that circumstance, the obligation varies according to the relevant case law. I suggest you direct your queries to the general counsel at Davies Group. I would be more than happy to give you his contact information and see that this matter is addressed in a manner satisfactory to all parties involved.'

I turned back to my cobbler, scooped some ice cream on top, and took a bite.

'Fair enough,' he said, bringing himself up to his full tough-guy stature. 'I'll just let you know a few things, then, while you enjoy your dessert. What if I told you that the Davies Group was systematically corrupting the most powerful people in Washington?'

I considered responding, *Oh, you mean the Five Hundred*, or *No shit*. But I said nothing.

He sat down at the counter. 'And what if I told you that Radomir Dragović was under suspicion of committing crimes against humanity?'

Radomir was a bit long-winded, sure, but war crimes? Come on. That was just bigotry. Not every Serb was a genocidaire. Though that would explain his concerns about extradition.

'And what if I told you that you might be complicit in several felonies? I think you know enough about prison time and the importance of cooperation with law enforcement to make the right decision, Mr Ford.'

All right. Now I was actually a little angry. That was obviously a dig at my dad and a clear sign this guy had scoped me out. My impulse was to knock him off the bar stool and strip out his trachea with my dessert spoon, but a reaction was undoubtedly what he was after, so I bottled it up.

'You're not from DC,' I said. 'Is that a Long Island accent?'

Rivera was thrown a bit. 'Yeah,' he said. 'Bay Shore.'

'Then you should know,' I said, looking around under his stool.

'Know what?'

'When you go on a fishing trip, you ought to bring beer. Have a nice day.'

I don't know if the flatfoot got the joke, but he got the message.

'Suit yourself,' he said. 'I'll be seeing you.'

He left me his card. As I finished up my cobbler, I could finally let my nerves show. I shook my hands out and took a deep breath. What the fuck did the cops want with me? I wasn't doing too badly career-wise, but I was still a nobody at Davies. Certainly not an obvious target for the Special Investigations Division.

From a professional point of view, Rivera's play was clumsy at best. Starting out with threats, even tacit ones, never gets you very far. If he was trying to turn me into a mole, he'd already flubbed it. My bosses were likely to know if the police were sniffing around the firm, especially with Rivera being so brazen about coming up to me near work. Maybe that was the point, to cut me off from my bosses so he was my only friend. Or maybe I was overthinking it, and the guy was a total clod. Based on what I knew about your typical career law enforcement officer, the latter seemed a distinct possibility.

He hadn't really told me anything specific. Ten minutes of research on the Davies Group would give you enough straws to make a bluff like that at a fresh-faced young guy like me, maybe even scare him into blabbing. Shit, he might not even be with the police. Public corruption was typically an FBI matter, anyway. Something didn't make sense. I certainly had plenty of worries about my bosses, but my close calls with Marcus and Annie had made me wary about going too far with my extracurricular snooping. And I was still too much in the dark to even think about switching sides and working against Davies. The guy was unstoppable, and nothing happened in this town without his knowledge. I was certain of only one thing: My bosses would find out about this sooner or later. So I'd better go report back to them and earn some brownie points before they found out from someone else that the cops had approached me.

I headed to the cashier. 'Your friend already paid,' she said.

Motherfucker. I hated owing anyone anything. That's how people come to own you, drip by little drip.

Davies and Marcus had been impossible to find ever since Colombia. But as soon as I mentioned the Rivera run-in in an e-mail to Marcus, they were suddenly free and eager.

I sat between them at the conference table in Davies's office and related the story.

'That's all he said? No more specifics?'

'That was it,' I said. 'I hope I didn't say too much.'

'No. You did a great job. I'm sorry you had to deal with this. I imagine you're wondering if there's anything to it.' Davies seemed calm, eager to put me at ease.

'I believe in what we do here, though a little reassuring couldn't hurt.'

'Mike, you've been in Washington long enough to know that everybody is looking for an angle,' he said in a serious tone. 'The Metropolitan Police Department is the one exception.'

'Really?' I asked.

Davies laughed and dropped the deadpan. 'Of course not. You don't even need a high-school diploma to join. Crooks with badges. How often do the police or the FBI try something like this, Marcus?'

'Once, twice a year, at least,' Marcus said.

'Doesn't it seem strange, the way he approached you, a relatively junior employee here? And all on his own. Outside of any official setting or oversight?'

'It did.'

'There are no refs, Mike. No one is outside the game. It's a typical law enforcement stab at us. You know we're not Boy Scouts, but we are absolutely scrupulous. We never cross the line. I've been at this for forty years, Mike, and we are squeaky clean. Never one infraction. People throw a lot of shit at us, but nothing has ever stuck. The legit folks know that, and they leave us alone. But let's say you get someone, a detective, FBI, an inspector general, whoever. He figures if he can get some dirt on the most powerful firm in Washington, anything that will embarrass us or our clients, he can cash that in for some extremely valuable favors.'

'They're always looking for the same thing,' Marcus said. 'They want us to pull some strings to get them a raise or a plum assignment. Most of the time these guys are just looking for us to land them a job at a private company, a contractor, so they can make five times more than the government pays them.'

'Fortunately,' Henry added, 'it takes more than a slice of cobbler to buy off our best associate.'

He stood and clapped his hand on my shoulder. 'You did well, Mike. And we know it's been tough being in the dark on the Dragović-Walker case.'

'Can you fill me in on that yet?'

'Well, Mike, unfortunately, incidents like this Rivera business are part of the reason we have to compartmentalize. Marcus has people planting bugs on his car, for God's sake. Not everyone is a vault like you. And know that we don't take it lightly. You may have noticed that Marcus and I are working like first-year associates. Every so often things just come together – a piece of information falls into your hands, a once-in-a-lifetime deal lines up, and then you just have to go for it, flat-out. We do fine, of course, but when a chance comes to really bend the arc, to make a world-class firm something even greater, you have to seize it. One day we'll be able to explain it to you. You'll understand.'

I wondered if that deal had something to do with wiretaps, threats, and a man called Subject 23.

'We know that you're still clocking these ninety-hour weeks. It may look like we've disappeared, but we notice. Why don't you and Annie take the company bird down to the villa in St. Barth's? Whenever you like; just let us know. You'll get your own little place on the water, very secluded. And you can just relax. You've more than earned it.'

As far as buy-offs go, that topped pie.

'Annie and I would really appreciate that, Henry. Thank you.'

As I left, it made me feel better knowing that even pros like Marcus and Davies sometimes make mistakes, like mentioning the cobbler, which I hadn't talked about. Now I knew that they were watching me.

Chapter Fifteen

You take every important man in Washington. You narrow that group down to those with a possible say in matters of international jurisdiction, a daughter in boarding school, and a dead wife. You're left with 160 people. Expand your starting pool to include the national scene, and that number grows to 348. You spend a half an hour or so trying to track down some audio of each one – a conference recording, an interview on YouTube, whatever – and now you're talking two to three solid weeks of work. Never mind that for 40 per cent of the guys, you can't find the audio, so you put them on a maybe pile and wonder if Subject 23 is hiding somewhere in that stack while you dick around on the Internet listening to clips from the most recent TED conference. Normally I'd have a junior associate go through all this, but there was no way I could let the bosses catch wind of what I was doing. I'd been searching for Subject 23 for a week straight, every night since I'd eavesdropped on Davies and Marcus.

Doing all that on top of my usual work was murder. But my date with Detective Rivera had reawakened my concerns about Subject 23, the man my bosses had been wiretapping. I had to do something, and I was a little shy about getting back into any cloak-and-dagger high jinks after my run-in with Marcus.

So far I had squat, and I hadn't even had a chance to dig

into Radomir's past to see if there was anything to what Rivera said about war crimes.

It was eight o'clock on a Thursday. I wasn't normally one to whine, but I'd had a shitty week – frostbite-and-felony-accusations shitty. On top of all that I'd picked up a cold, probably from flooding my sinuses with the bacteria-ridden Anacostia River. I was hunched over a laptop at the kitchen table going through a list of potential candidates for my mystery man that never seemed to get any shorter.

I'd just about had it. I needed a break, maybe even to let myself enjoy this new life I'd won for a minute.

Annie stood in front of the open refrigerator in a pair of boxer shorts and one of my sweatshirts, acting acutely indecisive. She examined some take-out containers, then turned to find me staring at her.

'What?' she said, and aimed those blue eyes and curls my way.

'You,' I said.

'What's your problem, Ford?'

'Nothing,' I said. 'I love watching you.'

'That's sweet.'

'Forget this,' I said, and shut my laptop and stood.

'Come here.' I held her and swayed with her through the kitchen. She rested her head on my shoulder.

'Let me make you dinner.'

'What are you up to?' she asked.

'Nothing. Why so suspicious? A catch like you, you should be getting treated like this every day. How about dinner, a couple glasses of wine, then I'll take you to the Gibson. Whatever you want.'

The Gibson was a throwback bar on U Street, relaxed and classy, a speakeasy-style place I would have dismissed as pretentious if it weren't for the fact that the bartenders treated their spirits with an almost religious devotion. 'Dancing after?' she asked.

'We'll see.'

She smiled and headed toward the stairs. 'I'll get cleaned up before you come to your senses.'

I had some fresh New York strip in the fridge, and I started oil heating in a skillet. Annie disappeared upstairs to the bedroom and turned on the radio as I pulled out some salad. I could just barely hear it. She was always trying to catch up on the news.

Even in my own fridge I could never find stuff. I think it's a guy thing. I jogged up the stairs to ask Annie if she knew where the mustard was hiding.

But I stopped dead outside the bedroom.

There was no mistaking it. The voice of Subject 23 was coming from inside.

I pushed open the door.

It was him on the radio. When I'd listened to that voice on the tape, it had been freighted with violence, fear of what Henry might do to him, and threats to strike back, but now it was droning confidently; calm, technical, and dry.

'Before we get to extradition,' he said through the tinny speaker, 'don't we need to address the jurisdictional threshold of whether the alleged crimes violate the law of nations?'

'What is that?' I asked Annie.

'What?'

'On the radio?'

'I don't know. The news.' She turned away from her dresser. 'Some Supreme Court case.'

I listened as the reporter came on the air: 'That was Justice Malcolm Haskins in oral arguments last week, in a case that could have major repercussions for international human rights law. And now to Seattle, where . . .'

I ran downstairs to my laptop and tried to pull up audio of Justice Haskins. Everyone in Washington knew about Haskins; few, if any, knew him. He was a bit of a recluse and shied away from the usual parties and galas. In all my time schmoozing in DC, I'd seen him in person once, at the party at Chip's. Then I remembered: Irin had been at the same party.

An associate justice on the Supreme Court, he actually wielded far more power than the chief justice. He was a moderate, and so he was often the crucial fifth vote, the swing vote. In a way, he had more clout than anyone else in the capital: he had the job for life, he didn't have to fund-raise or cut deals, and his decisions couldn't be overturned.

And I knew his name was on my list.

I found a few clips from oral arguments the previous year, and I listened to his voice. Then I pulled up the tape of the wiretap of Subject 23 I had stolen from my bosses in Colombia:

'. . . I wish it were all paranoia. It's not. The man with the information: I think I found him. I have to get him before they do. They'd do anything for the evidence. If they had it, I know, I just know, it would be the end of me.'

I went back and forth between the two voices, one a pillar of the state, the other a cornered man, dangerous and afraid. I tried to calm myself, to not overreact. They were the same man: Malcolm Haskins.

'Mike!' I heard Annie yell. 'The stove.'

A grease fire jumped three feet off the range. I guess I should have turned the gas off before I dug into the wiretap. I stood, pulled a lid from a stockpot, and sealed it over the frying pan. The flames licked out the sides, then died.

I'd nearly torched myself, the house, and the girl of my dreams. But the scorch marks and stinging smoke crawling along the ceiling were the least of my problems.

Chapter Sixteen

After I connected Malcolm Haskins to the voice on Henry's wiretap, a lot of mysteries from the last few weeks started to make sense.

For instance, the oral arguments I'd heard on the radio. They came from a Supreme Court case that dealt with extradition and the alien tort statute. It's a law that goes back to the founding of the country. It says, in essence, that under certain conditions, a person can be brought to court in America for war crimes committed anywhere in the world.

If Rado had committed such crimes, as Rivera had suggested, he would be very interested in the outcome of that case. Maybe the loopholes I was going to have Walker put in the foreign relations bill weren't so innocent; maybe they were there to protect Rado from trial in the United States.

If my bosses discovered that they could get a Supreme Court justice in their pocket, the legislation wouldn't matter. That would explain why they took me off the case. They were all for getting me involved in low-grade hardball, but I guess it's a good bet to leave the rookie at home when you're talking about corrupting the highest court in the land.

I still couldn't quite bring myself to believe it. Trying to throw the Court just seemed nuts – but so did everything else that had happened since I met Henry, so why not?

The night I nearly burned down the kitchen, I figured out

that I had at least a little bit of breathing room before anything happened between Irin and Haskins. Henry had said he would hold off on going after Subject 23 – what exactly he meant by that I didn't know – but he would act immediately if Irin tangled with him herself.

I had a buddy who had clerked on the Court a couple years back. After that, he signed up with a corporate firm and got the half-million-dollar signing bonus that's standard for guys coming out of Supreme Court clerkships. He lasted a year, then bailed; now he just lived off the bonus and traveled.

You never knew where in the world he was going to be, but you knew he was going to be checking his e-mail. I asked him if he knew where Haskins lived or whether he was in town. He got back to me in two minutes: *Not a chance he's in DC. The guy's like fucking Thoreau. No oral args. or conference next week, so I can guarantee he skipped out to his place in Fauquier County to play hermit for the weekend.*

That same night I scanned the headlines from the past few weeks for Haskins's public appearances and checked them against the log from the GPS I had on Irin's car. Sure enough, at least twice she'd been to the same events Haskins had attended – one was a fund-raiser and the other a lecture at American University. She must have found out that it was Haskins who would decide her father's fate and was sizing up the justice herself. Maybe she'd already started working her magic on him.

I called Haskins's office the next day. I said I was from the school newspaper at Georgetown and asked if I could get some time with Haskins before his speech on campus.

'Well, son,' the press flack said, 'I'm afraid he's on vacation through next Friday. I don't have any record of a speaking engagement.'

'Oh my God,' I said. 'That's from last year. My bad. Have a

good one!' I'd probably gone a little overboard trying to sound college age, but I'd found out what I wanted. The tip from my buddy that Haskins was out of town checked out.

I could keep my eye on the tracker on Irin's car and make sure she stayed away from Haskins so that nothing would go down until I figured out what the hell to do. I was feeling a lot better, and when I checked in on Irin (who, like Marcus's wife, was another Internet oversharer), I found I had even more breathing room. *Have fun in Paris ;)* one of her friends wrote to her on Twitter. Great. The farther away from Haskins, the better.

I could head out to the Inn at Little Washington with Annie, clear my head, and figure out my next steps. I'd never needed a break so badly.

Saturday arrived at last, a beautiful spring day. Annie and I headed out of DC on 66, and soon enough the gentle folds of the Shenandoah mountains rose ahead of us.

Funny, though: I couldn't resist glancing at the tracker, and Irin's car had started moving when she was supposedly in Paris. Maybe a friend had borrowed it.

Funnier still, how the little bull's-eye of Irin's tracker seemed to be following me and Annie on our way out to the country. I didn't worry too much. Lots of people head into the country on nice weekends.

And not funny at all, after we arrived at the inn (and Annie jumped for joy when she found the champagne I'd asked to have waiting in the room, and I discovered a bathroom containing splendors I'd never thought possible), I noticed the bull's-eye turning right, off I-66, heading north into Fauquier County, where Haskins had his country place.

I suddenly lost my appetite for champagne and the six-course meal of a lifetime. I zoomed in and watched Irin get closer and closer to a little town about an hour away from us called Paris, Virginia. I'd never heard of it, but one of the many black-suited valets and concierges who were always hovering nearby and attending to our whims filled me in: it's a getaway town in Fauquier County for Washington's powerful, much like this burg. It seemed like a good spot for a crucial Supreme Court justice to get away from it all.

Henry and Marcus had said they would be watching Irin. And from what I overheard under Henry's deck, I knew that if Irin got close to Haskins and whatever evidence he was hiding tonight, her life, and maybe his, would be in danger. Based on the warnings from Tuck and Marcus, I suspected that if the whole thing came apart and people got hurt, Henry would set me up to take the fall.

Let this one go, I thought. I tried to convince myself it wasn't happening. I couldn't put my career on the line. And if I fucked up again with Annie, I could lose everything I'd built with the kind of girl who if you're lucky comes along once in a lifetime. I could barely believe what I was doing – it was like I was watching myself in a dream – when I told Annie I had to go, and I would do everything I could to be back by dinner.

'Tell me you're kidding.'

'I wish.'

We went around in circles for twenty minutes. I couldn't believe I was arguing against her when everything she was saying – to stay here, away from trouble – made so much sense. How could I abandon all this? Risk everything I'd earned?

I could see she was getting suspicious again, thinking about the other night, the lies, the photo of Irin.

'I would think you were cheating on me, but you're not dumb enough to do it this clumsily,' she said. 'So that's reassuring. I just . . . just tell me what's going on.'

'You can't tell anyone.'

'I won't.'

'Swear to me.'

'I swear.'

'It's a case from work that got out of control. I need to drive about an hour from here and stop something from happening. Stop someone from getting hurt bad, or worse. I won't lie to you, but I can't tell you everything because it's a dangerous situation, and I could never forgive myself if you got pulled into it. I'm sorry.'

'Fine,' she said. 'I'm coming with you.'

'I'm sorry, Annie. I can't let you.'

'Call the police, then.'

'I will. I won't let myself get hurt.'

'Then go. It's fine. Just go.'

I knew I couldn't call the police. I'd already seen Henry and Marcus put local cops in their pocket, and what could I say without sounding like a nutjob? No. This was strictly damage control: find a way to stop Irin from approaching Haskins without putting my neck on the line.

I just hoped I could do it without the whole affair blowing up. There were so many ways it could go wrong, bringing in my bosses, the press, the law; I couldn't begin to imagine the wreckage.

The tracker on Irin's car had stopped moving halfway between Upperville and Paris. The bull's-eye sat in the middle of the highway. As I drove to the spot, I saw nothing: no cars and no homes, only woods and a pothole that nearly swallowed my Jeep. Maybe it had knocked the GPS unit off Irin's car. Or it was another ambush. Either way I sped past it toward Paris.

It wasn't really even a town, just a dozen or so Colonial houses scattered in a hollow running up to the Blue Ridge: that augured well for my odds of spotting Irin and Haskins.

I cruised the area looking for Irin's Porsche but found nothing. After half an hour, I pulled into the Red Barn Country Store. I was starving. Tonight's special was a bitter cup of coffee and a Snickers. Not quite the inn. I was getting a little cranky and angry at myself as I batted away doubts. I mean, what the hell was my plan here? Maybe I'd just gone nuts with paranoia.

But I didn't have a chance to fret for very long. The long coil spring creaked as the screen door opened and slammed shut. Malcolm Haskins walked in, wearing loose-fitting jeans and a Yale Law sweatshirt. I watched his reflection in the glass doors of the refrigerators as he did his shopping: a box of shotgun shells, some trash bags, and a folding saw, the kind you use to prune trees. He could have just been provisioning for a good old country weekend – spring turkeys were in season – but his shopping list sure didn't set my mind at ease.

As he reached for his wallet to pay, his sweatshirt drew against his waist. I could make out the outlines of an inside-the-waistband holster, sized for a hefty pistol, maybe a .40.

Bad news.

It was easy enough to follow him. There were few lights near the town, and the streets were mostly empty. I parked on a fire road hidden from the highway about four hundred yards from his house. There was no sign of Irin or her Porsche. Haskins's cottage sat in a meadow at the foot of the hills.

I walked through sparse woods behind his house, parallel to the main road. Hiding between two trees, I could see glimpses of the interior. It seemed the appropriately stealthy thing to do, at least until I saw a white Porsche pull up in front of the house. If I had been on the road, maybe I could have spooked her somehow, or just tipped my hand and, damn the consequences, warned her.

I started toward the house, but I was too late. Irin disappeared through the front door.

Storming in and announcing that the whole thing was a setup seemed, well, rash. I'd just calmly explain to Haskins that I'd been stalking him, but only because my dear colleagues were trying to shake him down, corrupt the highest court in America, and maybe kill him. I was doing him a favor, really. That'd go over like gang-busters. And then I'd only have to deal with the consequences of having betrayed my bosses and thrown myself in front of whatever they had had planned for Haskins. Piece of cake.

No. I was not going to put my ass on the line. There had to be another way. If I could just break up the party before my bosses had a chance to find out what was going on. They'd said they'd be keeping their eyes on Irin. I couldn't spot anyone else around, but I suspected Marcus must be close.

I figured if Irin was playing out her seduction act, both she and Haskins would be pretty jumpy and easy to scare off. So I picked up a handful of gravel and threw a piece at the house. It bounced off the shingles of the little two-story cabin. The next plinked off a window. I waited for a sign, but no lights came on downstairs, no exterior floods lit up.

Well, I'd done my part. I'd tried, at least. I could tell myself that. No sense in missing dinner. It wasn't like I was responsible for what might happen. What else could I do? Just waltz in and announce my bit part in Henry's conspiracy? No. The only option was to walk away and let what would happen happen.

We all make compromises to get what we want. Would I give up my happy little life – veal Shenandoah, heated bathroom floors, the girlfriend who looked like I'd mail-ordered her straight from J. Crew – to fuck myself trying to do the right thing?

Not a chance. I wasn't some martyr; I was just taking care of myself and . . .

Wait. What was this? I didn't even remember making the decision. In fact, I thought I'd decided *not* to go up to the house. But there I was, heading in. I just sort of smacked my forehead mentally – *Fuck me* – as I noticed my feet moving and the branches thwapping against my legs as I neared the house.

Either I was a more decent guy than I'd thought or I wanted to ride in like the fucking sheriff because I knew my soul was half in hock to Davies. Either way, my better angels were going to get me killed, and I was none too happy about it.

But all wasn't lost, not yet. I knocked on the back door, three times, and then three times again, harder. We called it ding-dong-ditch growing up. You rang the bell and booked it out of there.

No response.

I stepped off the porch, then heard Haskins barking something at Irin. I caught a glimpse of him peering nervously out an upstairs window, shotgun in hand. He didn't see me. My worst fears from Marcus and Henry's conversation about the danger Irin had stumbled into were confirmed.

There weren't many windows in the back of the house, but there were enough to get in. The problem, burglary-wise, is that while it's tempting to take the glass to gain entry, you inevitably end up slicing open your arm or leg while you rush around nervous as hell.

I saw a handle sticking out from behind a stack of firewood. It was a maul for splitting wood. That'd do. The easiest way to get inside a house isn't battering away at the door – that usually takes at least five minutes or so unless you have the right pry bar. It's pulling the lock.

I tried to let all these little technical details of B and E fill up my mind to get away from the basic lunacy of what I was doing: the fallout that would come from breaking into the house, from inevitably exposing myself.

I set the tip of the maul behind the face of the door lock and gave it two taps with my palm to seat it. I twisted the handle hard with both fists, and popped the cylinder neatly into the dirt beside the porch. Then it was just a matter of reaching in and pulling the bolt back.

I'd been quick, maybe ten seconds from the first tap until I was through the door. I thought I'd have a chance to surprise him, maybe talk some sense into him. No such luck. He was waiting with an over/under shotgun pointed directly at my face.

Irin sat on the couch, eyes red from crying and her face half hidden by her hands, as Haskins stood on the plank floors aiming the gun at my head with a very competent-looking stance.

He put the barrel of the gun under my jaw and frisked me for weapons.

'I came to help you,' I said. 'Don't do this. She's not part of the setup. They know everything. They're coming. They'll use it against you.'

'What do you think you know?'

He backed up. The two barrels kept staring me down.

'She's not working for Henry Davies. She's just a dumb kid trying to help her father. If you hurt her, they'll own you. You'll play right into their hands. They're probably on their way right now. Don't do this. They'll blackmail you with it.'

'Who are you?' he asked. I saw his knuckles go white, his grip tighten on the stock of the shotgun.

'I found out what was happening. That they were trying to set you up. I came here to help.'

'You work for Davies.'

'They didn't send me here. I'm just trying to stop them from getting anyone hurt.'

I was trying to sweet-talk a Supreme Court justice into putting down his Beretta. The only thing keeping me going was that the whole situation was so surreal I couldn't fully believe it was happening. Otherwise I probably would have frozen up.

'So that's a yes,' he said. Then he started chuckling half-heartedly and shaking his head. 'It's too late,' he said. 'There's not enough time.'

He sat down on the couch, the gun still leveled at me. I had a feeling the guy had lost it.

'Have a seat,' he said, and gestured with the gun toward a rocking chair.

I sat. For someone supposedly so paranoid, the justice seemed pretty calm.

'What's your name?'

'Michael Ford.'

'You really came here to head off this mess?'

'Yes,' I said. 'It's not too late.'

He laughed again. It didn't sound crazy. It sounded like he'd just been let in on a great joke.

'Well, that's all very noble, Galahad. But you've just thrust yourself headfirst into an extremely fraught situation for no reason. I don't think this is going to end well for any of us.'

Maybe he was so calm because he'd already resolved to take us out.

'Don't do this.'

'For the love of God,' he said. 'Stop saying that. You really have no idea what's going on, do you?'

He had a point there.

'I don't think he'll believe it coming from me,' he said to Irin. 'Would you tell him?'

'You don't have to stop him, Mike,' she said, staring at the ground. 'He wasn't going to hurt me.'

I looked from her back to Haskins.

'I could never. I have a daughter,' he said. 'What did you hear from Davies? That I was some psychopath willing to protect my dirty secret by any means? That I'd kill this girl if she got too close?

'No,' he said, and shook his head. 'They're coming for me tonight, aren't they?'

'They've been watching the girl,' I said. 'They said if she got too close to you, to the evidence, then they were going to take you.'

'And now I know for a fact they're after me. It's not dirt on me they want, Michael. It's dirt on Henry. They want it back. They want to make it disappear once and for all. I have it. They're not going to blackmail me. They've tried every enticement, every bit of leverage against me already, and failed. They're going to kill me. The girl knows too much now, so I imagine they'll kill her too.'

'You're not going to hurt her?' I asked.

Haskins sighed with frustration. 'As I said before, no.'

'So you were just trying to protect yourself?'

'Yes.'

'And I was just trying to do the right thing.'

'In your completely misguided way, maybe. If you really had come here on Davies's orders, you wouldn't be chatting with me unarmed, you'd have come in ready to kill.'

'Then I don't understand. Why don't we all just walk away from this? Why does it have to end badly?'

'Because we're too late,' Haskins said, and looked out the window at the shadows outside.

He moved closer to me and lowered his voice. 'How long have you known Henry Davies?'

'About a year,' I said.

'I've known him for more than three decades, since college. We were roommates freshman year. I imagine you've heard him give his talk about how any man can be corrupted?'

'Yes,' I said. I'd heard a slightly different version, of course, that any man can be controlled if you find his levers. But I could no longer pretend there was a distinction between control and corruption.

'He's built his entire world on that belief,' Haskins said. 'All the money, all the power. And the tragedy is that he's right. I've watched him for years. Slowly but surely he's picked them all up: senators, congressmen; he's even had presidents in his pocket. He's a collector, of sorts. One by one he's proved that he can buy or manipulate every powerful person in the capital. He nearly had them all.'

'Except you, right? He never got to you. You proved him wrong.'

'It doesn't matter. Every man has his price. Every man can be corrupted. Those are the rules in Henry Davies's world. An incorruptible man doesn't exist, so if one shows up, well, you have to take him out of the picture.'

Haskins stood and turned the lights out. It was pitch-black for a moment, then gradually I began to make out the gray contours of the room.

'What are you talking about?' I asked.

He lifted the shotgun again and stared out the window.

'I made the mistake of trying to stop him with the law,' he said. 'The institution to which I've dedicated my life. The honest way. It wasn't enough, and now it's too late. He never loses. Has he told you that one?'

'Yes. But he lost tonight. We're fine. Let's just go.'

'No. They'd been hoping I would lead them to the evidence. I haven't. And I know too much. That leaves him only one option. If I can't be corrupted, I'll be killed. Davies's rules.'

'That's crazy,' I said. But now the rustling was unmistakable: someone, maybe several someones, was outside, and getting closer.

'I once would have thought so too. This is beyond the usual full-contact Washington give-and-take, Michael. It's beyond entrapment and blackmail. It's murder. And this isn't the first time.'

'Henry has killed people?'

'Yes. And ordered their deaths. He prefers to make it look like the usual quiet salaryman exits: a stroke, a heart attack. Nothing too suspicious.'

Haskins sidestepped me to peer out another window, and he eased the rack on his pistol back a half an inch to double-check he had a round chambered. 'I won't go so quietly. I'm going to make this thing as hard for him to cover up as I can.'

I looked at my phone but I had no reception. 'Do you have a land-line? Can we call the police?'

'The line's out, probably cut. I told you. It's too late. I don't have time.'

'Too late for what? What are you talking about?'

'Henry's after me for more than just the Supreme Court. I've watched him for years, and I've always suspected him. I've been piecing together the details of his empire, the way he's gone after the Five Hundred. I believed I could do it through the law. But as you probably know, he owns the law. I should have passed on the evidence.'

He leaned over to glance through the window again. 'I thought I had more time. But now we all know too much. This is a goddamned mess. And Henry hates a mess.'

Footsteps creaked along the front porch. Haskins led us to the back door.

'What evidence?' I asked.

'No one learns without making mistakes. And as far as I know, Henry made only one, a long time ago. He started out as a political operative, in the sixties, dirty tricks and rat-fucking. He made Watergate look like a summer-camp prank. An investigative reporter, a man named Hal Pearson, was looking into Henry. Henry killed him. I know that the evidence that would prove Henry did it still exists. I should have told someone where to look, as insurance. But now it's too late.'

'Why are you telling me?'

'They know that she and I are in the house. Not you. Here,' he said. He took a legal pad from a side table, wrote something down, tore the page off, and handed it to me. 'This is how to find it.'

For a moment, there was only the sound of our quickening breath and the men on the porch. I saw a figure move through the backyard. Henry's men. Thank God I'd hid my Jeep on that fire road.

Haskins looked me over. 'You're thinking of making a deal?' he said.

The thought had crossed my mind. If everything he said was true, Haskins had handed me a very powerful bargaining chip with that piece of paper. If Henry's men trapped me, and they really were bent on killing, I could trade the evidence Haskins had just handed over to save my own ass.

'No,' I said. 'But why trust me with this?'

'Think it through,' Haskins said as he moved to the stairs. 'This is the one thing in the world Henry Davies is afraid of. The evidence of his one mistake. He'll stop at nothing to get it. So yes, it's valuable. But do you really think he'll let anyone who knows about it walk away? Live a long and happy life?'

Haskins laughed.

I didn't know. This was all too much.

'You'll see. I haven't helped you, Michael. Knowing what I told you is a death sentence. It's the only lever on Henry Davies, and that man won't let himself be controlled. He'll never let anyone who knows it survive. That's why I've never shared it. Believe me or not, it doesn't matter. You'll see soon enough.'

'So, what? What am I supposed to do?'

'Hide. Survive. Your only choice if you make it out of this is to find the evidence and take Henry Davies down. Because if he sees that you have it – and somehow, God help me, he sees everything – it'll be simple: either you or he will have to fall.'

He was laying on the *Lord of the Rings* shit a little thick, but as black silhouettes surrounded the house, I couldn't really argue with him.

He told Irin and me to hide. I refused. If they were really coming for us, I wanted to help fight back.

'No chance,' Haskins said. 'They don't know you're here. That's our one hope. You have to stay hidden and get away. Get upstairs, or I'll shoot you myself.'

He directed Irin, who seemed to be in shock, to an upstairs bedroom. She glanced back over her shoulder just before the door shut.

'I'm scared, Mike,' she said.

'You'll be fine. Just keep your head down.'

I looked for a way out from the second floor. Every time I put my face near a window, a shaft of white light would flash on me from the backyard. I was trapped. I guess they were covering the back and sweeping up from the front. Very tidy.

So what happened? Fuck if I know. As they closed in on the house, I did what the guy with the shotgun told me to (always a good bet) and hid in an upstairs bedroom, sweating my ass off and trying to figure out how to get out of there. I heard someone force the front door a lot less gently than I had the back. Then someone was barking orders. It was hard to tell for sure, but the voice sounded a lot like Marcus's. Then a shotgun blast boomed through the house, and there were screams.

Someone was banging around down there. It was quiet for a minute, and then I heard the sound that chilled me most: two loud cracks from a handgun or rifle half a second apart, and then a third shot. It's a standard military drill: body-body-then-head, the distinctive pattern of a good marksman making a kill.

I heard footsteps on the stairs, and the squeal of a door opening at the far end of the hallway. The house was old and creaky and kept no secrets. They were searching for others. I lifted my head and peeked through the window, then pulled back just in time to avoid the scanning flashlight beam.

The last thing I wanted to do was just sit there, but if the searchers didn't know I was in the house, there was a chance I could hide until it blew over.

I heard another door open, and footsteps drawing closer. I could barely keep it together. I guess Irin couldn't. Someone started running, crashing into things upstairs. I figured she'd freaked out and made a run for it.

Then I heard it again, gunshots: *crack-crack . . . crack.*

I checked the inside of the closet by the faint glow of my cell phone. If I was going to be executed, I didn't want it to happen while I was cowering among old photo albums and mothballs. I was going to cross it off as an option, but then I saw the contours of a little recessed square in the top of the closet, over a shelf. It was just barely enough to get my shoulders through: access to the attic. Maybe I could get out onto the roof, away from the spotters out back.

I swung the door shut behind me, hoisted myself up onto the top shelf of the closet, then pushed away the wooden square and shimmied into the attic. It was all open framing with no floors, just pink fiberglass insulation on top of the drywall that made up the ceilings below. The joists groaned with every move I made.

I replaced the square piece of wood that covered the access from the closet. Some planks lay across the top of the joists and fiberglass, for walking around the attic. I lifted one up, set the wood against the access panel I'd come through, and then wedged the other end against a ceiling joist. It was a pretty rudimentary version of the police lock that every thief fears: a metal bar set into the back of a door and then angled down and anchored in the floor. It makes an entry almost impossible to force. Burglars learn to look for the telltale bolts in the center of a metal door and move along when they see them.

I could hear the men in the bedroom I had just left, shouting out to the spotters in the backyard. They must have known I was in the house. I looked for an easy out, any kind of vent on the roof or gable I could get through. But there was nothing wider than a pipe. God, it was hot up there.

A fist banged on the access panel. I stepped away, balancing on the joists. I'd learned the hard way to keep my footing in attics. Once, during one of those Murphy's law nights, Luis and I had broken into a house in Falls Church. We'd gotten into the attic, and the kid stepped wrong. His left leg went right through the insulation, and his right leg hung up on a joist and tore a ligament in his groin.

The joists in this attic flexed and pulled at their nails as I moved: an unmistakable creak. Just then, the air cracked with two gunshots. Shafts of light poured through the holes in the attic floor six feet to my left. The shafts looked almost solid from all the dust swirling through.

The men below were pounding on the access panel now, and I could hear the wood start to splinter and give. I moved farther away.

Crack-crack: two more shots, two more shafts of light shining up through the holes, closer now. Any time I moved they could fix my position. I waited for them to break through the access panel. I heard the wood splinter and give. The plank I'd used to secure it fell through. My plan, if you could even call it that, was to wait as long as I could before my next move so as to get as many of them into the attic as possible.

I saw hands come through the access panel.

I waited.

And just as the head appeared, I took what I'd learned from my old accomplice Luis and jumped off the joists, aiming for the front of the house, over the two-story foyer, praying I'd hit only insulation and drywall.

I remember a weightless feeling in my stomach as I fell. Everything was going smoothly until my chin got hung up on the drywall or some wiring and sent me spinning backward. I was still moving forward, though, so I hit the wall just above the front door with my hip, adding to the spin, and landed, mostly on my shoulder and the side of my head, on the hardwood floor.

That rang my bell. I stood, took a stagger-step, and straightened up. If there was anyone alive on the ground floor, I didn't see him. Irin lay sprawled on the stairs, shot in the upper torso and the eye socket. Haskins was in the living room, lying on his back with gunshots to the chest and forehead. I'd never seen a dead person other than in a funeral home, all cleaned up and with the hands crossed. I guess I was almost lucky to be dazed by the fall, because the whole thing seemed unreal, bodies as fake as you see in a cheap amusement-park haunted house.

The gunmen were coming back downstairs, so I ran out the door.

I pulled the porch flag down and shoved the pole through the door handle to buy myself a little more time. There was no one out front. I guessed I'd made it behind the men sweeping the house. I ran about twenty-five yards until the shock wore off enough for me to notice the limp, and then the tear in my pants. I looked down to see that a long, half-inch-wide sliver of white-painted molding had slid deep into my thigh.

With the injury, I didn't think I had a chance, even if the front door held, of beating them to my car. There was a single streetlight on the road in front of the house, about twenty feet down, in the direction opposite where my car was parked. I ran close to it and then tore back my pant leg. I eased the chunk of wood to the side, let the blood pool in my hand until I had enough that I was sure Marcus would see it. I splashed it glimmering on the ground and ran the other way.

The fire road certainly made for interesting driving with my headlights off, but it put me back on the valley byway heading away from Paris. The leg wound needed only eight stitches at the little urgent care-storefront in Front Royal. Instead of veal Shenandoah, I had a chicken sandwich in the Arby's parking lot, then unfolded the piece of yellow paper Haskins had given me: my death sentence and my only hope.

Chapter Seventeen

Annie was still awake when I returned to the inn. I went straight into the bathroom and showered, washing the dried blood off my leg. When I came back into the room I told her I was fine, tired but okay, and that all would be explained in the morning. It was dark, and the stitches were hidden under a bandage. She pressed me on what happened, of course, but showed mercy when I told her all I needed was sleep.

Breakfast, where we were surrounded by the ever-helpful, ever-present inn staff, was obviously not the place to discuss confidential matters. It gave me a short reprieve before I had to explain what had happened.

The minute we sat down in the car, I turned the radio up. Annie watched me, waiting for me to talk as I stared straight ahead and drove. After fifteen minutes, she twisted the volume knob and switched off the music.

'Mike. You have to tell me what happened. Your leg – are you okay? Did anyone get hurt?'

'I'm fine,' I said. 'I . . .' My voice trailed off. I'd hoped that my old gift for extemporaneous bullshit would provide me with a way out of this. It didn't. The past night's events still had the unreal quality of a dream, and trying to find a way to react to them, to go on, paralyzed my thoughts.

'I need some time,' I said. 'To think. It's . . .'

I watched the white lines blink past on the highway, and shook my head.

'Can I talk to you about it later?' I asked.

She nodded her head yes, then took my hand as we curved through the long valleys of the Shenandoah. I was surprised it worked, frankly. She was as persistent as I was. It wasn't until I looked in the mirror that I understood why she'd let it drop. It was my first real glimpse in the sunlight of what I looked like after last night: circles under my eyes dark enough to be bruises, flat unfeeling gaze, an unhealthy pallor. I looked like a dying man.

I didn't sleep at all Sunday night, just stared at the ceiling, listening to Annie breathe, taking small comfort every time I glanced over and saw the little pout she made as she slept.

From time to time I sat up on the edge of my bed in the darkness and fingered the corner of the business card that Detective Rivera had left me. Was this all too much for me to handle on my own? Should I talk to the cops, commit the one sin that can't be forgiven in a family of thieves? Was there really any way I could escape Henry, let alone outmaneuver him?

'Geez, you look like shit,' the guy with the office across from mine said when I showed up on Monday morning. 'Good weekend, huh?'

'Great,' I said.

I guess the disastrous situation I'd stumbled into was showing in my face, which was bad. Routine and cool play were the only ways to make it through this, to stall Marcus and Davies until I could figure out what to do.

Two dead, and the papers had nothing to say about it on Sunday or Monday. Maybe only the killers and I knew. That wouldn't last.

I'd never found an Outlook inbox more soothing, and I dug into the banal routine of my day. I could almost pretend the weekend hadn't happened.

Almost.

Through the glass around my office door, I saw William Marcus turn the corner by the stairs and start down the hallway toward me. He was looking typically untroubled, a mug of coffee in one hand and a blueberry muffin in the other.

I heard his muffled steps on the carpet.

He walked right by my office.

I was safe catching up on my e-mail for now. After a few minutes, I turned around and ventured a peek down the hall, and didn't see him. I turned back to the computer.

'Mike. Davies's office. Now.' It was Marcus's voice, behind me. Like a gunshot had gone off nearby, my whole body tightened instantly, and my fists drew up to my chest. Then I stretched out my fingers, and forced myself to take a long, slow breath.

'Sure,' I said.

We walked upstairs, and my heart bucked in my chest like an unbalanced dryer. I tried every plausible run-of-the-mill scenario for a call-up like this, and found none. The only explanation was that they knew I was in the house when Haskins and Irin were killed. Still, I followed him meekly, knowing but not quite believing I was walking right into the killers' hands.

Davies sat at his desk, peering through reading glasses as he pecked out an e-mail. 'Just a moment,' he said without looking up. 'Sit down.' I sat. Marcus remained standing.

'Did you have a nice weekend?' Marcus asked me.

'Yes,' I said. 'Annie and I headed out to the Inn at Little Washington.'

I spoke calmly despite the pulse pounding in my throat and temples. Marcus and Davies exchanged a look, then Davies nodded.

'Did you try the veal?' Davies asked.

'Yes. Superb. I really need to find a good butcher around here—'

Marcus moved closer to me. 'Empty your pockets,' he whispered in my ear, and he held out a plastic desk tray. I pulled out my cell phone, keys, wallet.

He ran his hand along my jacket pocket, felt a pen, and gestured for me to drop it and my watch in the tray.

'Well, good,' Davies said. 'So nothing out of the ordinary?'

Marcus gestured for me to stand. I obliged.

'The inn was a special treat,' I said. 'But besides that, no.'

Marcus, still silent, patted around my belt, then ran two fingers along my sternum. They felt like a head of a hammer against the bone.

'Lovely,' Davies said. 'Marcus, you have a good meat man, don't you?'

Marcus was poking through the tray, examining my belongings.

'Yeah. Eastern Market,' he said. He finally appeared satisfied, and gave Davies the okay sign.

I'd done my share of warm-up chitchat in these meetings. It was standard. But I'd never done it while getting frisked.

'So nothing out of the ordinary?' Davies asked me again.

'No.'

He looked at Marcus, who shrugged.

Davies smiled wide. 'Well, fantastic,' he said.

'Great,' Marcus chimed in.

Maybe I'd misjudged. The pat-down was odd, but everybody seemed to be having a good time. I relaxed a hair, even grinned a little myself.

'Terrific,' I said.

'Ha,' Davies said. 'Well, just keep that story going and we won't have a problem. You and the rest of the world will first hear—' He looked to Marcus.

Marcus checked his watch. 'Probably around eleven thirty.'

'—in a few hours the first hints about the unfortunate deaths in Fauquier County. The full story will leak slowly over the next few days.'

They watched me, assaying my response. I simply nodded. In a gesture, the whole arrangement was laid out. They wanted me to keep up my story, to play along with the murders.

'You understand?'

'Yes,' I said.

Henry looked from me to Marcus. 'See? Apt pupil. That will save us a lot of breath, and a lot of unpleasantness.'

'You don't need to worry about your involvement,' Marcus said. 'We've taken care of that. You'll be fine. The police arrived later that evening, and discovered a murder-suicide.'

Henry cleared his throat. 'You should know that we regret what happened out there as much as anyone. We were growing concerned about the justice's involvement with this young woman, his increasingly erratic behavior, his paranoia. We can never be sure exactly what happened between them. We tried to stop him. We were too late. I'm not sure what you know or think you know, but you can rest easy. We are not the bad guys here, Mike.'

'We're not exactly the good guys,' Marcus said, 'but we aren't cold-blooded killers. It's bad for business.'

'That's what happened,' Henry went on. 'I don't need to tell you that the situation is dangerous for all of us. Your hands aren't clean, Mike. There will be an extraordinary amount of attention. A circus like we haven't seen since, I don't know . . . Chappaquiddick? The Mary Meyer murder?

The work you've done with Walker, with Radomir, would not look good under scrutiny.'

'I was in the dark on both of those cases.'

'Or you didn't want to know. Money tends to dull one's ethical curiosity. It's only natural. You know well from your work with Marcus that he and I don't do threats. I will tell you that, while every person thinks he's the guy in the white hat, few individuals are. People think they're honest, but that is only because they are never tested, never forced to pay the true price of honesty. I tell you this because I enjoy you. I see myself in you. And I can save you from a lot of pain.

'I knew about your history from the beginning, Mike. You were born to live in the gray. That's why I took you in. I know more about your past than you do. Marcus and I would have preferred to continue taking our time grooming you, slowly introducing you to all the complexities of our work here, but I'm afraid things have accelerated. You've always been precocious. You can be great. You can be me one day. It's your choice.'

He stood and moved closer to me.

'Now, tell me. In the house, did you talk to Haskins? Did he tell you anything? Did he give you anything?'

I felt Marcus's eyes at work on me, taking in every blink, every tic, every drop of sweat. Even if I lied, my turncoat body would tell the truth.

'No,' I said.

Marcus kept up the stare.

'All right,' he said finally. I guess I passed.

'And we're all on the same page about the weekend? Is that correct?'

Their play was good, but I wouldn't expect anything less from Davies. He'd given me a cover story – they'd been trying to stop it and failed – just plausible enough to ease my conscience. No one is a villain in his own mind. I could see myself misremembering, replaying the evening in my head until what Henry said was true.

He made the yes sound so easy, just one more baby step like all the others I'd taken here at Davies Group. Each was so small that you barely noticed it. Then one day you turn around and can't believe it, can't do a thing about it: you've pawned your soul. His questions sounded like he was double-checking on dinner plans, not covering up a double murder and the corruption of the Supreme Court. It was so easy: just a yes. All eyes were on me once again.

'Yes,' I said. 'Absolutely.'

'Excellent, Mike. And I'm sure you realize we reward loyalty here at Davies. Marcus, who's the youngest to ever make partner here?'

'Collins. He was thirty-six.'

'You're at the front of the line, Mike.'

'Thank you,' I said.

'Now, take your time with this. Discretion is key, of course, but this needn't be the last conversation we have.'

Davies gave me another twenty-five minutes or so, feeling me out. I played along as a good soldier, not showing the fear, though every word he spoke tightened my stomach until it pained me to talk.

'So we're fine,' he said, finally.

'Yes.'

He passed me the tray. I gathered my things, and then he led me to the exit. Just before I left, Davies turned me around to face him with a hand on my shoulder.

'And if there's anything you maybe forgot to mention, you should tell me now. I'm glad you've been here long enough to appreciate, without my having to underscore the point, the gravity of the situation. There will be an extraordinary amount of attention, and pressure. Come speak to us. Because if you decide to talk out of school, I'm sure you realize that we'll know about it before you do.'

'Absolutely.'

They waited a decent interval for the payoff so it wouldn't look like a quid pro quo. It was a quarterly bonus and a merit-based pay raise: all in all, it came to an additional $200,000 over the next year. Marcus let me know that there was a bit of a slowdown in cases. If I wanted to take any time off, I could have as much as I liked.

Chapter Eighteen

Just take the money and keep your mouth shut. If I had done that, things would have been so much easier. But despite my best judgment, I couldn't sell my soul to Henry just yet. I wasn't an evil corporate goon (though soon enough I was a wanted man, a notorious double murderer). Saying yes to Davies and Marcus was really the only way to handle the conversation. If I was going to run to Rivera or to the Feds, or if I planned, in a fit of suicidal pique, to find the evidence from Haskins and take down Henry myself, I had to pretend to play along with my bosses to buy time. What else could I do? Give Davies and Marcus a from-the-heart Jimmy Stewart–style stem-winder and then hold their hands while they confessed to the police? Not a chance. I could only play along or pretend to. I knew it, and I was fairly certain that Davies and Marcus knew it too and would be watching my every move.

A voicemail came from my cousin Doreen. She invited me out to her son's first-communion party the next Sunday. I was about to delete it – I hadn't heard from her in five or six years – but then she nailed me: she was making my mom's beef stew.

As I said, the key to a successful con is to use the mark's greed against him, and I missed that stew. The whole invitation reeked of a setup. I knew that a couple days before the event, she'd call me up to mention my dad might be there too and check to see if that was okay. I wouldn't be able to say no without being the bad guy. My father was probably orchestrating the whole thing. Well, at the very least it was good to know the guy hadn't lost his touch for setting people up.

I'd let him have this one. The fact was, I needed some time with the old crook. Right now I had the unsavory choice between, on the one hand, playing along with Henry and keeping my dream life, and, on the other, snitching to the police and facing down William 'I Know Nine Ways to Kill a Guy with an Envelope' Marcus. It was either honor among thieves or, like my mom had once begged my dad, just tell them everything. Now that my ass was on the line, the answer didn't seem so clear-cut.

So I skipped over Doreen, called my father myself, and asked him to meet me.

'Great,' he said. 'I'll pick you up.' I'd thought I was throwing him a bone, but he didn't sound like he needed much sympathy.

When he arrived, I saw that he'd gotten the Cutlass up and running and then some. At traffic lights, it felt like a plane taking off.

'I had to hone the cylinders,' he said.

'Add some volume?'

'Maybe,' he said with a guilty smile.

I gave him a look.

'I figured while I was in there, you know? It's about four-sixty now and I managed to scrounge a five-fifty top-end kit.'

And off we zoomed. He'd straightened out Cartwright's books and credit and saved the station about six thousand dollars a month. His jumpiness was gone, as was the cornered-rat look he'd been sporting right after his release.

I took him to the steak house I'd mentioned the first time we'd met up. He'd become rather chummy with a fellow on the Virginia Board of Accountancy.

'I Googled him,' my dad said.

Not bad. The upshot was that he might have a chance to take the exam if he kept his record clean for two years after probation. He'd aced his last sample test.

I didn't give him a hard time about the usual shit. I mean, who was I to judge? I'd just gotten myself into a jam that made his burglary look like a jaywalking ticket. It took me a while to bring up what I really wanted to ask him, mostly because I kept hoping the whole awful situation would go away. But right after the coffee came, he got there first.

'What's on your mind, Mike?'

'You can tell?'

He nodded. 'You're chewing your nails. It was one of your tells when you were a kid. I'm not going to . . . I mean, we can talk about whatever you want. I'm sorry things got so heated last time. I'm a little rusty. There aren't a lot of heart-to-hearts down in Allenwood.'

'I wasn't trying to break into any Sargent and Greenleafs, but you were right about the free lunch. I got myself into some trouble.'

His pocket started ringing.

'Shit, sorry. That's me,' he said, and reached in to silence it. 'Alarm. I've got to get home for my parole call.'

The guy had really caught up with the times.

We went back past the big former-liquor-store clown to his trailer behind the gas station, and he phoned in to the parole system. When he turned around, he found me looking over some construction plans he had tacked up on the trailer wall. Old and tattered, they showed a three-bedroom Craftsman-style house. They looked awfully familiar.

He watched me for a while as it sank in. I remembered where I'd seen those plans, and now I knew why that clown gave me the heebiejeebies. My dad had taken me out to this spot in the woods before, when I was a kid, before there was a gas station. He'd had the plans back then, and he was showing me the land where he was going to build a house for me and my mom. It was right before he got sent away for the twenty-four years.

'You sold the lot to Cartwright?'

'Yeah,' he said. 'We needed the money.'

'Did he chisel you?'

'About sixty percent of what it was worth. But I didn't have much choice. I had to get it settled before I went in.'

The guy was pumping gas where he'd hoped to put up his little Mayberry.

'I'm sorry,' I said.

'It's not worth worrying about now.'

'I fucked up, Dad.'

He leaned against the counter next to me.

'That's my area of expertise,' he said.

I remembered what Haskins had told me about how dangerous it was to know dirt about Henry Davies. By getting himself killed, the justice had only underscored the point. I didn't want to involve anyone any more than was necessary, especially a parolee trying to get his life straight. So I gave my dad the radio edit of what had happened.

'My work. They want me to keep my mouth shut about some stuff they're up to.'

'Bad stuff?'

I nodded.

'How bad?'

I looked over at the newspaper on his kitchen table. The stories about the missing Supreme Court justice had finally made their way onto the front page. The newsprint folks were way behind the curve, however. The online chatter had raced ahead to the most salacious possibilities, yet those rumors still had nothing on the sordid truth.

'The worst. I can't say much more than that.'

He grimaced, then ran his hand back through his hair.

'Talk,' he said after a minute. 'Like a magpie. Tell them everything. It's the only way.'

Like most people, I tend to seek the advice I want to hear. I guess that's why I was so hot to talk to my dad, a guy who was a living example of keeping your mouth shut. And then he went and encouraged this really troublesome do-the-right-thing habit I'd been trying to kick. My honesty was really starting to mess with my seeming respectability, my career at Davies.

Now this. What good's a bad influence if he tells you to do the right thing?

'But you never talked,' I said.

'No, I didn't.'

I sighed in frustration.

'Why do you think I kept my mouth shut all these years?' he asked.

'You know,' I said. 'Don't turn over. Protect your friends. It's like . . . a code. Honor among thieves.'

'God, Mike.' He shook his head. 'I wouldn't have kept myself away from you kids, and your mother, for that. That's what I was trying to get at last time we talked. My biggest mistake wasn't trusting some crooks from the neighborhood; it was trusting the honest men.'

'What happened?'

'That doesn't matter. It wasn't about talking or not talking in the end. It was about doing the right thing. I didn't go to prison to protect my accomplices. I went to protect the family. I had no other choice. Just trust me. These things never end well. Talk. Get out while you can.'

The full Haskins story broke early the next morning. A dozen TV reporters stood on platforms across the street from the Supreme Court so each could get a clean shot with the building in the background. Lined up under the floodlights, they looked like carnival barkers. News crews and trucks practically shut down the five blocks around the Capitol, completing the ambience.

It was the kind of circus only Washington could muster: pure tawdriness, but with a thin veneer of public importance so even the most respectable outlets could indulge in the peep show. The press had a squatters' camp out in Paris, near the scene of the crime. The major networks preempted the prime-time schedule with updates, and the big four all broadcast the president's statement on Haskins's death.

By the next day, the news had become a standard conversational opener among strangers, constant background noise on the street: *I heard he killed her during. I heard before. Drudge says it was suffocation. No, bullets.*

All that week, it was like nothing else in the world mattered except those deaths. I watched Davies's cover-up slowly begin to establish itself as reality in the minds of millions, in the mouth of the president himself. All the early findings pointed to a murder-suicide. Henry must have taken care of every bit of evidence that contradicted his fiction, must have somehow gotten to whoever it was that the Supreme Court justice had been talking to on the wiretap. I couldn't begin to imagine the sort of pull, the scope of backroom deals and whispered threats such an undertaking would require.

And I was going to take down the man behind it all? Not a chance.

The lies about who killed Malcolm Haskins and Irin Dragović were everywhere, inescapable, pressing in on me like deep water. I managed a passing similarity to my usual routine as the pressure built up, but finally I just wanted to stand in front of the White House with a piece of poster board and a Sharpie like every other maniac and start screaming the truth until the cops dragged me away.

Annie could tell something was wrong. She asked me to take a walk the night after I spoke to my father, to get me away from the thousand excuses – work, e-mail, phone calls – that I'd been using to avoid talking about what was on my mind. We passed through Adams Morgan then turned down Calvert St. and stopped on Duke Ellington Bridge, a ribbon of limestone stretching over Rock Creek Park.

'What really happened on Saturday, Mike?'

I guess the ghostly look I had after the murders was enough to keep her from prying then. But I'd known that wouldn't last.

'Someone got hurt,' I said. 'I tried to stop it but I couldn't.'

She watched the clouds slide over a fingernail moon.

'Haskins.'

I didn't say anything.

'You're not alone in this, Mike. Tell me what I can do to help you.'

'I just need you around. That's enough.'

I listened to the creek rush over the boulders below, and I gripped the railing. Annie's eyes stayed on me.

'Something very wrong happened. Part of it's on me. And

I'm going to make it right. I'm going to get the truth out there. Even if that means going against Henry Davies.'

She stood close to me and rubbed my back.

'Listen,' I said. 'I'm going to ask you a dumb question, because I don't know how this is all going to work out. I'm . . . I'm worried. Because I may mess things up with Davies, with the job, and that could put everything at risk: the job, the house, maybe me and you. You'll still be here, right? Without all that stuff, if I end up on my ass with nothing left?'

She was glaring at me, her arms folded across her chest. I hadn't wanted to make her choose between me and Davies, because I wasn't sure that was a contest I could win. She might have been interested in me only because I was Davies's new rising star. For all I knew, Davies had arranged the whole relationship – the offices so close, the same assignments. She spent all that time one-on-one with him in his office. Was it crazy to think he'd set his right-hand girl up with me so he could keep his eye on me? Maybe. But given what I'd seen Davies pull, it wasn't all that far-fetched. No. I pushed the thought out of mind. The pressure, the fear, was getting to me. 'Forget I asked,' I said.

'That's a silly question, Mike. Because you know I will.'

She unfolded her arms and put them around me.

It was a dumb question, not because the truth was obvious but because her answer didn't tell me anything. It was the same as when Marcus and Davies asked me if I was going to play along with their cover-up. There was really only one thing Annie could say, whether she was going to stick with me or not.

The truth or a lie, I didn't care. It felt good to hear her say it.

I was going to talk to the police, but not because I was certain it was the right move. In fact, I was pretty sure I was running headlong into a world of pain. I possessed dangerous information. No secret stayed safe from Henry for long, and I'd rather go after him than wait for him to come after me.

Chapter Nineteen

Henry had hinted he would be watching me, and losing any tails, real or imagined, turned out to be the easiest part. The area around Nineteenth and L Street Northwest is built like a multilevel labyrinth: generic glass office buildings, back alleys, one-way streets, and underground garages with four exits each. I nearly lost myself.

The hard part was finding a working pay phone. I finally came upon a greasy one outside a Greek deli. I made a call to the Metro Police main number and asked them to put me through to the extension for Detective Rivera, just to make sure he was who he said.

No answer. I left a voicemail. I told him I wanted to talk, in a safe place, provided he could prove his identity and good faith. I left him a Hotmail e-mail address and a password. I'd leave any messages for him in the drafts folder, without sending them, and he could do the same to get in touch with me. I'd read an article about terrorists using that to communicate, so I figured if it worked for the Taliban, it ought to give me a decent chance of avoiding Henry's electronic sniffers.

Once I called Rivera, the creeping nausea of the last few weeks lifted almost instantly. The dread was all in the anticipation. However lunatic the plan, now that I was moving against Henry Davies, I felt relieved, almost manic.

I could barely stomach watching as the lies about the murder spread through the news, but that day, the story changed. I watched with growing satisfaction as Henry's neat narrative of the murder – an obsessed Haskins killing Irin and then himself – unraveled on the front page.

With all the scrutiny that came with a case like this – the FBI had been called in to investigate the deaths in Fauquier County – surely even he couldn't conceal the fact that both had been murdered. CNN had sources saying it might be more than a murder-suicide. Other rumors suggested the police were searching for a gunman still at large.

The updates only bolstered my confidence. Part of Henry's strength was that image he projected of being all-powerful and everywhere, of being able to lever anyone he wanted, no matter how influential, and remake the world as he saw fit. But that image was starting to crack. Marcus's and Davies's neat narrative of the murder was getting a whole lot messier, and I could relax a little, knowing that even their power had limits. Sure, they could buy off a few local cops, but the whole FBI? Come on. I'd made the right call.

I kept up appearances at Davies Group. Around seven forty-five that night, I was still working, down in the law library on the first floor. I was reading, digging in on Rado Dragović and the alien tort statute. Normally the building would be almost empty at that time, but I heard a commotion.

I took the stairs up, following the noise. When I opened the stairway door on the third floor, I saw a few detectives walking away from me, down the hallway and toward the executive suite – to Marcus's and Davies's offices.

I swallowed a smile. So much for omnipotence. Had the cops figured out Henry's role in the murders that quickly? I was almost disappointed. I'd expected a bit more sport.

Soon enough, Henry Davies came striding down the

hallway, leading the detectives. I ducked back into the stairwell before they could see me. Henry sure didn't look like a man in the early stages of a perp walk.

When I poked my head out on the second level, where my office was, I started to understand what was happening. Through the windows, I could see the festive flashing reds and blues of a large assembly of police cruisers. I took a rear corridor and glimpsed Henry leading the detectives to my office. Another cop took a post near the main stairwell. More clustered around my office door.

I checked the news on my BlackBerry. I didn't have to look very long. There were banner headlines on every site. I'd just entered the center ring of the circus.

They hadn't published my name, but according to various officials close to the investigation, the police were closing in on a person of interest in the murders of Justice Malcolm Haskins and Irin Dragović. Henry had told me he'd know my next move even before I did. He must have known somehow that I was working against him. Had he set me up as the killer?

Sneaking away from cops happened to be one of my specialties, though I was a bit rusty. One former burgling buddy of mine, a guy everybody called Smiles, had quit the residential-break-in game to be an 'office creeper'. He tripled what he'd been making. You'd be amazed at the tunnel vision people acquire at the workplace. Smiles would just pick a building and waltz in wearing halfway decent clothes, and no questions were asked. He'd take a couple laptops, maybe a cup of coffee from the commissary, then head out with a wave to the security guard.

The cops hadn't fully mobbed the Davies Group mansion yet. I hoped, per my buddy's experience with office creeping, that no one would notice the well-dressed young murder suspect dragging himself by his elbows along the carpet between the lesser-used cubicles.

I slunk fifty feet, past an occupied office and a fellow listening to headphones and bopping slightly in his chair, then hauled myself past one of the executive assistants' desks. My vantage brought me eyeball to eyeball with a small collection of heels that Jen, another senior associate, kept under her desk. She wore sneakers on the Metro and changed when she arrived at work.

More cops were moving in by the second, and when I noticed them posted by the men's john and the main stairwells, I was pretty sure they'd have the exits covered. Something occurred to me then. It would probably be too generous to call it a plan, but it's all I had, so I went with it.

By crawling through a little-used conference room, I made my way past the two cops acting as sentries and into the women's room. There were only three female senior associates – Davies Group was a bit of a boys' club – and it looked like they'd left, so I had a good chance of having the place to myself. The cops were all men too. I figured, with the nice pair of Jimmy Choo sling-backs I'd grabbed from under Jen's desk, I could wait them out in the ladies' room.

It certainly was a lot less badass than drop-kicking my way through the thin blue line, but man, that women's room was something else. It had flowers, and a couch, and magazines. I was starting to feel positively discriminated against as I grabbed a *Martha Stewart Living* and camped out in the far stall.

It seemed to be working. I sat undisturbed for an hour as the police made their sweep. Then I guess one of the cops worked up the courage to check the ladies' room. I'd been hoping it wouldn't come to this, but I went ahead and crammed my feet into the heels against the creaking protests of the leather, tearing a few stitches in the process.

I was glad I had the shoes, because the cop started trying the doors one by one. If I'd just squatted on top of the toilet, he'd have found me as soon as he came to a locked door with no feet behind it.

When he got to my stall, I gave my daintiest throat-clear.

'Excuse me,' the cop said. I heard the footsteps get closer, then a little groan, probably the guy leaning over to check out the feet. I stretched my dress pants a little forward to cover most of my feet, and I guess I gave a fair impression of the fairer sex from the ankle down.

I listened to him walk away and finally let myself breathe once the door opened. *The Shawshank Redemption* it wasn't, but it had worked.

Then I heard talking in the hallway. The door opened again, and I heard footsteps on the bathroom tiles. Bad news.

An hour is a long time to be stuck in a toilet stall, and during my stay I realized a couple things. First, from reading Martha, that I really needed to deal with my junk drawers, and second, and more important, that being framed for two murders by Henry Davies wasn't all bad. Sure, they still have the death penalty out in Virginia, where I'd be brought to trial, and they use it. But I try to be a glass-half-full guy, and the fact was that now I really had nothing to lose. In good white-collar-speak, the marginal cost of any further crimes was zero. I could go to town, indulge every criminal impulse I'd been bottling up for the last ten years, and still be no more fucked than I was now, because with Marcus and Davies gunning for me, I was *completely* fucked.

And so, when the cop came back to the stall a second time, my pulse picked up: a little fear, sure, but mostly I felt liberated. No more hiding and waiting. When he stuck his head under the door, I could see in his face the face of the cop who had slammed my adolescent nose into the patrol-car door's frame and then shoved me, cuffed, into its backseat as he chuckled and said, 'Oops'; I could see the face of the flattopped piece of shit who showed up one morning when I was twelve and took my dad away forever; I could see the face of the corrections officer with the huge gut in the visiting room at Allenwood who, when my mother, bone-thin with cancer, reached for my father's hand, barked, 'No touching.'

The cop looked up from under the bathroom door, smiled, and said, 'Nice pumps, asshole.'

I stomped his temple before he could get to his holster. His head slammed into the marble tile and his body flopped like a quilt onto the floor. A lifetime of resentment uncorked, or maybe I was just sensitive about my shoes.

I cuffed him to the bottom of the stall and checked out the hallway. Fortunately, the KO'd cop in the women's room had been the one watching the rear stairwell. I double-timed it downstairs to the underground parking garage without being seen.

I guess the bathroom cop's reconnoitering was a last-ditch effort. There were still a couple patrol cars out front, and a loose perimeter of police around the building, but not nearly as many as before.

A few cops probably saw the cleaning service's truck pull away, but they must have missed when it slowed at the stop sign and a shadow jumped from the back of the truck and booked it toward Rock Creek Park. That was me.

I'd gotten away, but every cop in DC would be looking for me.

Fortunately, Rock Creek Park threads its fingers through Northwest Washington, connecting to parks that run through Georgetown and the surrounding neighborhoods.

I'd spent a lot of time running in it, and I knew it well. It's twice as big as Central Park, and much more wooded, full of hidden homeless encampments and God knows what else. I figured if Chandra Levy's body went undiscovered for a year in there, I had at least a few days' freedom. I was sure whoever was looking for me had gotten to my apartment by now, but maybe not Annie's.

I picked my way along the trails toward the Naval Observatory and then across Wisconsin Ave. to Glover-Archbold Park. Every rustling branch or startled raccoon made me jump, but the dark kept my mind occupied with old, simple fears, a relief from the real dangers waiting for me in the city.

I took a roundabout route through Annie's neighborhood, watching for signs of surveillance and finding none. She had a second-floor apartment in a converted townhouse. Taking no chances of being seen from the street, I clambered up the wood-frame decks in the rear and hauled myself over the railing.

She sat on the couch, in an oversize sweatshirt and flannel pajama bottoms, drinking tea and reading. I could have watched her for hours.

I tried to get her attention without scaring her, so I tapped gently on the window with my knuckle and said, 'Hey, Annie. It's me.'

She didn't spook, just laid her book down on the arm of the couch, walked into the kitchen, and pulled out the fourteen-inch Wüsthof chef's knife I'd gotten her for Christmas. She held it in a hammer grip and, unafraid, sidled toward the door.

God, I loved that girl.

'Mike?' she said.

'Yes, it's me.'

'Oh Jesus,' she said, and slid open the door. 'I nearly killed you.'

'It's been that kind of day.'

She laid the knife on the table, then pulled me in and hugged me.

'What the hell is going on?' she asked. 'Have you seen the news? Are they talking about you? Are you a suspect?'

She had CNN on mute. The irresistible news-bait of the country-house murders had only grown juicier. Now they were reporting that the incident had stemmed from a love triangle. The killer was believed to be Irin's jealous stalker, a double murderer now on the run. I was amazed that they didn't yet have my picture plastered over every channel.

'Don't believe any of it,' I said.

'Are you okay?'

'Yeah.'

'What's happening?'

'Remember that I told you I was going to try to make things right? That what happened had something to do with Haskins? Well, Davies was behind the murders. I knew about it, and I was going to tell the police. Davies warned me I should play along, that I didn't understand the price I would pay. This is what he meant. He framed me. Everything you see on TV is a lie. He's behind it all.'

'But how could he orchestrate all that? There are so many people involved.'

'He owns this town, Annie. Blackmail, extortion; he's gotten every player in DC, one by one, into his pocket. Haskins was the grail: the Supreme Court.'

As I heard myself say it, I knew it sounded like the ravings of a conspiracy wack. She stepped back and crossed her arms.

'They said something happened at Davies Group. That a police officer was assaulted.'

'I had to get away, Annie. Henry owns the cops. I've seen it myself.'

I was losing her, I knew. What would I have thought if the roles were reversed, if she'd been spouting this sort of madness and stomping on cops' heads? I was just a crook's son once more, out of my league, the con slowly unraveling because I'd stayed too long and gotten too greedy.

'You're only making it look worse by running, Mike. What are people going to think?'

'I can't turn myself in, Annie. Henry can get to anyone.'

Lights flared in the front window of the apartment. I stepped over to look. It was Marcus's Mercedes-Benz. He and Henry Davies stepped out.

Henry can get to anyone. I looked from the window back to Annie.

'Did you tell them what we talked about last night, that I was going to try to stop them?'

'No, Mike.' She stepped away. Her eyes widened. I could see she was afraid.

The whole romance with Annie had been so easy. As I thought back, I saw Henry's hand in it: setting me up near her on the second floor, talking me up to her at the company Christmas party. God knows what other tricks he'd used, with or without her knowing, to throw us together.

Framing me for the murders must have taken some time, had probably started well before I called Rivera that morning. I'd told Annie that I was going to talk the night before. No one knew as much as she did; she knew that I was going to the authorities, that I knew the truth about Haskins's death. She must have told Henry and Marcus. Was our whole relationship a setup? Annie another honeypot? All of it engineered from the beginning so Henry could spy on me, keep me under his thumb? Is that what he'd meant when he said he'd know before I did that I was going to talk?

I'd stayed in control all that week but I could feel my grip starting to loosen. I felt the same pull, the thrill of action without concern for consequence I'd felt right before I crossed out that cop in the bathroom.

Annie saw it in me. She glanced over at the knife on the table. And that's when I knew, whether she'd told Henry or not, whether this whole relationship had been a sham or not, that I'd lost her.

'Stop running, Mike,' she said.

Henry and Marcus were at the front door.

'I'm innocent. It's the truth.'

'Then turn yourself in.'

'No. The truth doesn't matter anymore.'

I opened the door to her deck and vaulted onto the soft spring grass twelve feet down. A few stitches tore in the wound in my thigh as I landed and started sprinting toward the dark woods.

Chapter Twenty

Annie ratting me out to Marcus and Davies destroyed me, of course, but in a way it also eased my mind. Davies had framed me after he learned I was going to talk to the police. If Annie was the one who had told him, then the leak didn't come from Rivera. And right now I needed to trust Rivera.

Ever since the murders last Saturday, I'd been digging into the evidence that Justice Haskins had given me before he was killed. He'd pointed me toward a man named Karl Langford and provided his address. Langford was the only person who knew how to find the evidence that would link Henry Davies to the murder of the journalist, Hal Pearson, forty years ago. The only reason Langford was still alive was that Henry didn't know Langford knew.

Justice Haskins had tried for years, through legal means, to coerce Langford into cooperating, into producing the evidence against Henry. He failed, but I didn't have to worry about niceties like the law anymore. I'd done a bit of homework and knew Langford was in Sarasota. He wouldn't be too difficult to chase down, because – and here's where things get tricky – he was dead: a stroke in 1996.

So, getting the evidence from this guy and nailing Henry on my own was a dead end. I needed Rivera. Maybe he could help me reopen the case or piece together what Langford had known. I certainly couldn't do it with no help and every cop on the East Coast looking for me. I didn't even have a change of clothes.

Detective Rivera had left a message for me through my Hotmail account. The Friday after the murders, I called him from a prepaid cell phone I'd bought. He told me that I was the prime suspect in the Paris killings, and that my identity and photo had gone out over the wire to all law enforcement agencies.

The first thing I wanted to know was why a DC cop would be mixed up in a political corruption case.

'Davies does plenty of dirty work in the District,' Rivera told me. 'He has sources everywhere, from paid-off concierges and maître d's, all the way up to madams and purveyors of every other form of high-end vice. That's what first got me interested in him. I'd have kicked it upstairs to the Feds a long time ago, but I learned he has even more people on the take at the top of the heap than on the street. I have people I trust I can get this to, but first I need to know how strong is the evidence you have against him.'

Rivera kept pressing me on what I had on Henry, on the details of the murder. I was still wary, of course. But when the law is convinced you're a homicidal maniac who likes to wear ladies' shoes, it's hard to overstate how nice it is to hear someone say, 'Mike, I know you're innocent. I can help get you out of this. I've been talking to a few folks at the FBI, people I'm sure of. They want to bring you in as a witness against Henry.'

I taped him saying that and discussing his suspicions about Henry Davies, and I told him I'd keep it as insurance. I was sure the press would gobble it up in the frenzy around Haskins's death and my escape.

* * *

Never do what they expect. It's the first rule of running. I told Rivera to meet me the next day at the coat check in the West Building of the National Gallery of Art. That's the classical half of the museum, a Roman Pantheon-inspired building, all great halls, columns, and domes, designed by the man who later did the Jefferson Memorial. It's a place they'd expect from a guy like me, all excited about my first date with the boys in blue.

Rivera and I were supposed to meet at 3:30 p.m., which was why at 3:30 p.m. I was in the East Building – all hard angles and contemporary art – on the upper floor. From there you can look over the atrium with a clean view of all the exits. Both buildings had metal detectors, so any uninvited guests – whether the cops or Marcus – would, I hoped, be unarmed.

I pulled out the prepaid cell and called over to the coat check in the West Building. After hearing my lost-tourist story, the sweet lady who'd answered the phone asked around for Rivera. He was there, right on time.

I heard her tell him, 'Your son is in the East Building, at the Flavin installation. It's the top floor. Look for a lot of lightbulbs.'

She was right about that. Behind me there was a tunnel made of fluorescent tubes in every color of the spectrum. Walking through it felt like a Willy Wonka acid trip.

I waited and watched. If Rivera was going to trap me, I would have a better chance of spotting the ambush now, when he and any accomplices hustled across the courtyard from the West to the East Building.

The National Gallery was a requisite stop on the tourist death march, and among the class-trippers, bored teens, and snap-happy Asian tour groups, I spotted Rivera. He didn't look like he had company, though that may have simply meant that they were skilled enough to avoid being spotted.

'What the fuck happened to you?' Rivera asked once he found me at the end of the art installation. I was wearing a bandage over my nose, and sunglasses.

'Nothing.'

'Not a bad idea,' he said.

I couldn't go around DC wearing a ski mask to avoid being recognized by the police, but the bandage did the trick. My face was mostly hidden, and people figured I'd broken my nose or had some work done.

'So what do you have on Davies?' he asked.

'I witnessed his lieutenant William Marcus kill two people.'

'You said you had evidence.'

'I need immunity,' I said. 'A deal with the Feds. Assurances that the murder allegations against me will go away.'

'It's not looking good for you, Mike. There was a store owner who spotted you in Paris. He said you followed Haskins out on the night of the murder. Your buddy Eric Walker says you had a thing for the Irin girl, were asking about her sex habits. The stalker profile fits with some purchases you made, specifically these GPS trackers. One that you purchased was found a few miles from the crime scene. And the whole putting on heels and tying up a cop in a ladies' room . . .' He clicked his tongue. It didn't look good.

'Now, I know enough about how Davies works to know that there's a good chance he's behind all this somehow. But dumb cops like me prefer simple cases. It's an uphill battle clearing you, and I'm not about to make a martyr of myself. What do you have? The tighter the evidence and the less it's just your word against his, the better.'

'Like what?' I said.

I knew from Haskins that Langford had hidden away some open-and-shut evidence implicating Henry Davies in the reporter's murder. But I held off on mentioning that to Rivera.

There was something about his manner I didn't like, beyond my usual distaste for police. He was sweating, lightly, but the lurid red and purple glow of the fluorescents made it more visible. I wanted to tease him out some more.

'Did Haskins tell you anything?' Rivera asked. 'Give you anything?'

I concentrated on his question, keeping silent. I wanted him to talk, to say more than he should.

'Any evidence we can use against Henry?'

I'm sure he was a good cop – pigheaded and uncurious – but he was a bad con man. The rub at the center of most swindles is this: you have to not want what you desperately want. You have to hide any greed, even go so far as to refuse at first when the mark offers you the item you're trying to steal, keep going until you make the mark practically force it on you. The minute you ask about the object in question – a watch, a wallet, whatever – the minute you want, the minute greed comes to town, it botches everything. People smell it, then it's game over. And Rivera was all greed right now.

'No,' I said. 'Nothing.'

I took a step away and considered my exits.

Rivera lifted his hand and ran his finger along his right eyebrow. The guy was a brick shithouse, the opposite of twitchy. It was a bad signal for him to use, because it didn't seem natural. To make things worse, he looked toward the gesture's recipient as he tipped it – just a glance, but it was there.

Without a word, I started walking fast in the opposite direction. 'I have to go check something,' I said. 'I'll meet you back here.'

'What?' Rivera started after me.

During the whole conversation, Rivera had focused on the one thing Henry would want: the evidence Haskins had pointed me to. The details of the double murder – what should have been Rivera's priority – he'd more or less skipped over. He also seemed sure not only that I was in the house but that I'd had time alone with Haskins. I'd never said so. Maybe I was paranoid, but everything about his performance smelled. I was out.

I thought I had decent radar for undercovers, but apparently not today. As I moved out, Rivera's backup materialized. Where one minute there was a student, a retired guy, and a tourist, the next there were several men, clearly working with Rivera and watching me, who looked like they knew how to handle themselves. Switching buildings may have bought me a little time, knocked them off their game, but now they were closing in quickly.

Most of my fighting experience has come while drunk, very drunk. Funny coincidence. As a result, the lessons learned are a little hazy. Nonetheless, I picked up two moves in the service that have, for the most part, helped me avoid getting the shit beaten out of me too badly.

Thing one: As I raced away from Rivera, a guy in shorts and a ball cap came around the corner and tried to collar me. I peeled his hand off, grabbed his wrist, and twisted his right arm back across his body. I know from firsthand experience (open bar, military police) that this hurts like a motherfucker, especially when you get the elbow going in the opposite direction, twisting the ligaments in the shoulder like a dishrag. Like most of the other goons coming at me, the guy had a fifty-pound advantage, so this sneaky-bastard stuff was my only hope. Once he was off balance I leaned my hip in near his center of gravity and threw him over my shoulder.

I would like to take this opportunity to sincerely apologize to Mr Flavin for the damage to his tubes. I really didn't mean to send my man that way, though I'll admit that the shower of shards and sparks as the twenty-foot wall of lights came down was pretty spectacular.

By the time I made it to the atrium floor, I could see I was trapped. The exits were all covered. Something about these men, a lethal competence, convinced me that they were Marcus's agents, not cops. I was probably only making things harder on myself by fighting back, pissing them off without any possibility of getting out of there. But after the week I'd had – seven days since the murders – there really was nothing more satisfying than unrestrained violence.

As I skidded around a Richard Serra sculpture – massive steel plates leaning at impossible angles – I encountered Marcus himself. He appeared beside me out of nowhere and grabbed my hand with a much more effective wristlock than I'd managed on his pal. A Taser threw off a little lightning bolt in his hand. He told me to come along and save myself the pain.

Since I'd already used one of my two moves, this was a no-brainer. My shoe had a hard edge to the sole. I scraped it down Marcus's shin, ending with a hard stomp that wrenched his ankle to the side with a popping noise that made *me* wince.

His grip eased for a split second, and I managed to get a half a step away before he seized my wrist again and twisted it up in front of me. To keep my shoulder ligaments from tearing, I spun, but my back slammed into the cold steel of the Serra sculpture. Marcus, now facing me, kept up the pressure. I felt something give in my shoulder. His other hand stabbed the Taser at my face, arcing blue an inch from my eye. I wrestled it back with my free arm. The hold he had on my wrist positioned him so that his weapon hand was at an awkward angle to my body. I couldn't get away, but I could keep him from lighting me up: a stalemate.

After a few seconds, Marcus tilted his head slightly and looked at the sculpture. He couldn't get to my body, sure, but he didn't need to. He had an eight-foot-high metal plate pressed against my back that would do the trick nicely. I had already used both my moves, so I was out of luck. He let go of me as he shoved the Taser against the steel, and shot small blue arcs of lightning into it.

I screamed without pause every obscenity I knew. He kept me cooking on the plate for four seconds before I slumped, and he Tased me for another five on the ground. Everything started getting hazy by the time I hit the floor, though I distinctly remember feeling every muscle contract with the current, trying to tear itself off the bone, and then seeing Rivera holding his badge up and saying, 'Metro Police, please clear this area, make way,' as Marcus hauled me out a rear door and threw me in the backseat of a sedan.

Chapter Twenty-One

Laid out in the backseat, I could see only trees whipping by through the car windows. I had barely regained my senses when we turned off the road and approached a concrete tunnel set in a hillside. A steel rolling door opened slowly, and swallowed the car.

We stopped. Marcus wrenched my cuffed wrists high behind my back and marched me through an underground garage and then up to a heavy door. He stopped twenty feet down the corridor and looked up at the black dome of a camera set up in the ceiling. A second later, the door opened.

'I need the Clark tape,' Marcus said to the man inside. The guy stood six six and was a soft three hundred fifty pounds. He took a gulp from a twenty-four-ounce bottle of Mountain Dew, then waved us in. It took me a second to recognize him. It was Gerald, the lead IT guy from Davies Group. He led us into a room lit only by the gray-blue glare of a dozen computer monitors covering an entire wall.

Some monitors showed what you'd expect from a security office: hallways, offices, exits. Other footage unsettled me: a woman folding laundry in a family room as toddlers played around her; a man's face in close-up, staring blankly just to the right of the camera.

Gerald handed Marcus a disc. We started back through the hallway, then went up three flights of concrete steps. We turned and passed the gray door of a Sargent and Greenleaf vault with a biometric-entry system. Marcus pressed on a door at the end of the hallway. Sunlight flooded in, blinding me for a moment. When my eyes adjusted, I saw Henry Davies, wearing a broad smile.

'Welcome back,' he said. Marcus and I stepped into his corner office through the door hidden in the wood-paneled wall behind his desk. We were at the top of the Davies Group mansion. Everything I'd just seen must have been a secret annex extending into the hill behind it.

'Maggie,' Henry said through the open doors of his suite. His assistant – the woman I had lifted the tape from in Colombia – stuck her head in.

'Would anyone like anything?' Henry asked. 'Coffee? A soda?'

She looked around the room, at Marcus, at Davies, and finally at me. My hands were cuffed behind my back. I had a ridiculous bandage hanging off my nose and a growing red welt on my neck where Marcus had cooked me with the Taser. Henry had several assistants, but Margaret had been his secretary for decades. She must have been in on it; she didn't seem any more put off by my condition than if I had been wearing mismatched socks.

'Water,' I said.

'I'll have an RC Cola,' Henry said.

'Nothing for me, thanks,' Marcus chimed in.

She returned a minute later with the orders and set a tall glass of ice water in front of me on Henry's conference table. Just your typical business meeting/hostage situation.

'Why don't you take off those cuffs,' Henry said to Marcus. He unbound my hands. Henry indicated that I should sit at the table. It was where he always conducted meetings. I took a chair.

'What do you want from me?' I asked.

'Simple.' He patted my hand on the table. 'I want you back. Of course you tried to play the hero. It's understandable. I told you already: most people think they're honest until they learn, as you are starting to learn, the real price of honesty.

'I can't blame you for coming after me. I tried the same thing when I was your age – pushing my bosses out of the way, taking the top spot for myself.

'I, however, succeeded,' he added. 'I see a lot of myself in you, Mike. Whenever anyone – and there are only a few around here in the know – initially grasps the scope of our endeavor, the first reaction is either to run away or to try to stop us. People think it's their fine moral fiber at work, but really, it's fear, hesitation, lack of will.'

'And what are you up to, exactly, in this endeavor?' I asked.

'You're a smart boy. I'm sure you already know. I own the capital,' Henry said. 'I've collected every powerful man and woman in it like baseball cards. Everything used to be so easy. You could own a man if you caught him cheating on his wife or taking a ten-thousand-dollar bribe. But nothing shocks anymore. A senator will bounce back from infidelity with a press conference and a month of church. It's a shame, really. We live in a debased time. I don't particularly like the rough stuff. But since so little horrifies people today, we've had to raise the stakes, the circumstances in which we ensnare our targets.

'And now, for all intents and purposes, I am the government, all the power without all the bullshit that comes with actually running it. Who has time for details?' He waved them away, and went on.

'I've pursued that vision for a long time, and Haskins was going to be the last piece. Things didn't go quite as I had planned, but I am certain that his replacement on the Court will be more amenable. As an employee here, you have enjoyed the fruits of that vision. You never seemed that curious about where all the money came from. You can't pick and choose, Mike. It's time you pitched in on the dirty work.'

'And if I say no?'

Henry chuckled. 'I see you're still a little confused. No isn't a possibility. It's not a question of yes or no. At some point you'll beg to be taken back.

'Everyone breaks,' he said, and glanced at Marcus. Marcus looked at his own feet. I could only wonder what decades-old hold Henry had on him. 'The only question,' Henry went on, 'is how much leverage we'll need to apply.'

'Like killing me?'

Henry seemed disappointed. 'That's always what people think of first. It shows a lack of creative spark. On the continuum of fears, death is pretty easy to beat. Most people won't admit it, but they'd choose death any day over betrayal, over embarrassment, over pain to the ones they love. Probably over public speaking. It's just a question of slowly applying those . . . we'll call them inducements, in order of increasing severity and sitting back and waiting to see how long your subject holds out. It's fascinating work, really.'

'So how far along am I?'

'Well, we started small. Take away a man's work, his esteem, his reputation. If his worst fear is being a criminal, next we make the world revile him as just that: a pervert, a murderer. Then we take away what he loves most. Annie, for instance.'

'Not quite,' I said. 'If Rivera sold me out to you, then Annie didn't. She knows me. She won't buy this garbage you've been feeding to the cops.'

'What aren't you understanding here, Mike? It's not either-or, Rivera or Annie. Anyone can be bought. As for Rivera, I gave you fair warning that he would hand you over for the right price, I just didn't mention that we'd be the buyers. Do you know why he turned you over? To get friendly with us, of course, but the money he needed for granite countertops. As for Annie . . . well.' He turned to Marcus. 'Play the tape.'

Marcus put the disc Gerald had given him into the side of the laptop and turned it to face me. He started a video: Annie, sitting where I was sitting now.

From the perspective, the camera must have been on the bookshelves. I looked. 'You won't see it,' Davies said.

A sickening realization came to me as I thought back to the surveillance footage I'd seen down in Gerald's lair.

'You're watching through all of our laptops and cell phones too,' I said.

Davies smiled. He could tap into the cameras on all the company-issued equipment. I'd seen Gerald lumbering through the hallways, leering, his head turning as women walked by, Annie especially. I shuddered when I thought what he might have seen of my private life.

Henry nodded toward the laptop on the table as the video played on. In the footage, he was wearing the same clothes he had on now.

'It's from this morning,' he said. 'She came to us.'

'I thought about what you said last night,' Annie said to Henry and Marcus in the film. 'I want to help. When Mike came to my apartment, he had this look. I was terrified. I'm scared he's going to try to hurt me. Is it true what they say? Is he dangerous?'

'Very,' Henry said.

She stared at the table for a long moment, then looked back to Davies. 'What can I do to help you stop him?' she asked.

My fists tightened on the arms of my chair. 'This is bullshit,' I said.

Marcus shushed me. 'This is the best part.'

Annie went on. 'Mike told me certain things about the work you and Marcus do. Perhaps I haven't yet had a chance to appreciate the full scope of the group's undertakings. I want to help you find him, and I hope that you'll consider me for opportunities in the more sensitive, and lucrative, areas of the enterprise.'

Henry stood behind her in the video and put his hands on her shoulders.

'I'll do anything,' she said.

'You motherfucker.' I jumped at Davies. Marcus grabbed my biceps and, curling his fingertips inside the arm, pinched a nerve against the bone. Pain knifed up to my shoulder.

I dropped back. He watched me warily as I cooled down.

'You can see how this will go, Mike. Step by step, we'll ratchet up the pain. We're just getting started. At a certain point you'll swallow your pride and give in. If you do that right now, I'll give it all back to you: the money, the job, respectability, freedom, the life you've always wanted. Save yourself and the people you love. Work with me. Tell me what Haskins told you in that house. Where's the evidence?'

I smiled. It threw Henry.

'I know something you don't. It kills you.'

'It may kill you, Mike. Don't get smug.'

'Is it true?' I asked. 'You killed the reporter?'

'Pearson?' Henry ran his fingers along his throat, the scar along his neck I'd first noticed back at Harvard. I could hear gravel in his soft voice. 'I lost something that day. I want it back. You're playing a game whose dangers you don't understand. Just talk, Mike. It all gets so ugly if you don't.'

'You're going to torture me,' I said.

'In so many ways,' he replied. 'You probably have some silly picture in your mind. What, the rack?'

'I was actually imagining Marcus with a car battery hooked up to my nuts,' I said.

Henry sighed. 'You shouldn't be afraid of the police, Mike. Life or lethal injection would be the path of least resistance. If I wanted exotic bloodshed, I would turn you over to Radomir.'

'Dragović?'

'Yes. I guess you've been too busy to grasp that angle. You killed the Butcher of Bosnia's daughter.'

'So he is a war criminal.'

'He's *the* war criminal. But once the war ended, he took the warlord thing private, started taking extension classes at Harvard Business School. He grew very enamored of what we call best practices, and he applied that concept to intimidation. He read in the *Economist* about some nineteen-year-old warlord in Liberia who liked to snack on his opponents' hearts. He thought it made him invisible or invincible or something. Radomir saw synergies between those tactics and his burgeoning human-trafficking syndicate. He invited all but one of his rivals to dinner, and in front of them ate the heart of the missing rival, formerly his main competitor.'

'Sous vide,' Marcus added.

'A bit theatrical, in my opinion,' Henry said, 'but it got the job done. Dragović wrote the case study on psychopathic violence. Torquemada, Wu Zetian, Saddam Hussein: he took all the best-ofs. Now he's in the United States looking for the man who killed his daughter, looking for you. What suffering he has in mind beggars the imagination.'

'But the extradition,' I said. 'He wouldn't risk coming to the US. He could be tried. That's why you dragged me to Colombia.'

'I thought you'd put that together. You're right. Only a madman would risk his empire to avenge a daughter he considered a whore. Dragović is an interesting case, though.

Marcus and I are good American *Homo economicus*. However ugly it gets, we always pursue our best interests. Dragović is trickier. He lives by blood and honor. Irrational, and frankly a pain in the ass when it comes to my usual calculations. He can't really be bargained with. He'll risk every penny he's earned, he'll risk his life, he'll risk anything to get you. The only way he can buy his honor back is with your dead body.'

'Threats won't work,' I said. 'Haskins didn't tell me anything.'

'It's so easy to act tough, Mike. Dragović uses an ax. We prefer a scalpel. Are you really willing to risk the people you love?'

'Annie's gone. My mom's dead. Who's left?'

'Sixty-two fifty-one Dominion Drive,' Henry said. My father's address.

'The guy who abandoned my family. What happened to doing your homework? I couldn't care less what you do to him.' I'd softened on my dad since his release, but Henry didn't know that.

'I've owned you your whole life, Mike. You're just finding out about it now. That's why I plucked you out of Harvard. Tell me, why would a competent financial swindler like your father suddenly take an interest in burglaries? Why would he rob an empty house?'

I sat up straight in my chair. I'd been asking myself that question my whole life.

'I'm not the only one who's done some killing,' Henry said.

'What are you talking about?'

'Perry, James Perry,' Henry said. That was the name of my mother's old boss. 'He was an acquaintance of mine, a good political hack, the party chairman out in Virginia.'

Henry loomed over me and looked me in the eye. 'Your father murdered him.'

'That's impossible,' I said. My father had one rule: no violence. He'd pounded that into everyone he ever worked with. No one gets hurt.

'It wasn't a burglary, Mike. Your father was in the house to cover his tracks. All these years with that big brain, and you never put that together?'

'Why?' I sneered at Henry.

'He was probably trying to protect his family,' Henry said. My father, in his cryptic explanation of that night, had said the same thing.

'After all, Perry was fucking your mother,' Henry said. 'And who could blame him?'

I lunged across the table at Henry, and Marcus grabbed at my belt. I kicked him hard in the face. My heel connected with his eyebrow. As I was looking back at Marcus, I saw a blur out of the corner of my eye. The edge of Henry's hand came down on my throat like a steel bar.

I hadn't expected it, hadn't figured him to get his hands dirty. The blow choked me instantly. Marcus dragged me back, wrenched my shoulders up, and threw me in a chair.

The pain in my throat wasn't too bad at first, but something felt off, loose. Like he'd popped some of the cartilage around my windpipe. I could feel it swelling.

'I guess you and I both know there's no statute of limitations on murder,' Henry said, standing over me.

'I'm not telling you a goddamned thing,' I said. A wheeze started creeping into my voice. The slow, silent swelling of my throat was the worst part. It was as if Henry, without lifting a finger, were choking me tighter and tighter.

'That's going to close up your trachea, Mike.'

'Compromise and coercion,' I croaked, and smiled. 'It's not going to work, Henry. Blowback. It always returns to bite you in the ass. I'm going to get you.'

Henry laughed to Marcus. 'Everything you know, we taught you, Mike. We've been saving one lesson. It's true that coercion – blackmail, extortion, whatever you want to call it – gets a bad reputation.'

I felt my windpipe narrowing down to a pinhole, felt the lightness creep through my brain.

'But that's only because so few people really have the necessary resolve,' he said. 'You have to be willing to take it all the way, to violence, to killing.'

The room seemed to slip away. I was starting to black out.

'Your father had it, Mike. I just don't think you do.'

Henry dumped the ice from my glass into his handkerchief, pulled my head back by the hair, and pressed the freezing bundle on my throat. I wavered on the edge of unconsciousness, half suffocated. After a moment that felt like forever, I finally pulled air into my desperate lungs.

'Take him downstairs,' Henry said. 'Then tell Maggie to send in my five o'clock.'

They locked me in an empty office with an ice pack for the swelling. I lay on the ground, trying not to move, hoping my throat would get better before it got worse. It did. After an hour, I could take small breaths without too much trouble.

A guard was posted outside the door, and I knew that Gerald was on the other side of the ceiling-mounted camera, watching me.

As I surveyed the office, I pressed my hand against the wall and felt the slightest give. Most of the Davies Group mansion was lath and plaster and brick. For my purposes, it might as well have been reinforced concrete. When they chopped the building into interior offices, however, they must have used the usual shoddy modern construction: drywall over steel studs. A shame, architecturally, but good for me. I used to see this all the time, especially in commercial break-ins. Somebody would spend two thousand dollars on a security door and lock, then mount it in a wall you could punch through.

It took me a few minutes to size up the wall, looking over the doorways and switches to determine what lay inside. I had done some carpentry during college, framing houses under the brutal Florida sun.

I was buying time, waiting for the swelling in my throat to go down. There was no point in running if I was going to pass out as soon as I started breathing hard.

Finally, I put my back to the wall beside the door frame and broke through the drywall with my elbow. I was a few inches off, but still close enough to yank the Romex out of the junction box. I wanted the black wire; black's always hot. I shoved it into the keyhole of the door handle. I didn't need the other wire for a ground, because I was going to use the guard outside.

The noise must have gotten the guard's attention, which had been my goal, and hopefully had made him sweat a little. That would increase the current through his body. The door handle jiggled, then a scream came from the hallway outside.

I knocked away the black wire, then shouldered through the door, knocking the guard's still-shaking body to the ground. I considered it fair payback for when Marcus had zapped me at the museum. I held the guard's arms behind him and searched his pockets, coming up with flex-cuffs and a set of keys. I cinched his wrists up and pulled the baton from his belt.

It sounded like a stampede was coming down the hall. The corridor, lined with empty, windowless offices, was a dead end. I slammed shut every office door and holed up in the last one on the right. I picked it because behind the walls I could hear the faint throb of a generator, which gave me a rough sense of where I was.

Sure, I was trapped, but I've never been one to let a floor plan stand in my way. I stabbed the tip of the baton through the office wallboard and levered it down, tearing a three-foot-tall hole. I ran a second down, in parallel, a foot away, then stomped through, breaking a small passage through the wall. It was a firefighter's trick.

I crawled through it into the hallway that Marcus had dragged me along when I first arrived, then raced through the door, back into the underground garage. After running for a minute, I could barely get enough air through the crumpled straw of my throat. I clicked the unlock button on the guard's keys and followed the chirp to a late-model Volvo wagon. Not bad for a goon. Henry clearly paid for the best when it came to security.

The rolling steel door blocked the exit, but I had more pressing problems. Marcus and his men would be here any second. I threw the car into reverse and sped backward, hitting a railing beside the door I had just exited. I rammed it with the rear bumper a second and third time, until it was finally mangled enough for my purposes. Faces appeared in the glass window of the security door, but with the railing jammed against it, they couldn't get out.

Glass tinkled. I saw the barrel of a gun slide through the window in the door.

I looked at the steel door. The fundamentals of breaking out are the same as for breaking in. There are real-life jewel thieves running around; one group in particular, called the Pink Panthers, has made off with loot worth more than five hundred million dollars from stores in twenty countries. They don't fire grappling hooks, slink through AC ducts, or crack safes, however. They prefer to drive high-powered cars through the doors of luxury malls and crash them into jewelers' windows. Ugly, but effective.

My rolling door looked formidable. I didn't like what I was planning, but really, how fucked up can you get in a Volvo?

I floored it and got up to forty-five miles an hour before I crashed. It felt like my stomach was going to tear through the front of my torso and like I'd been smacked in the face with a board. A cloud of dust filled the car. It smelled awful. I fell coughing from the car and crawled along the concrete. My nose was bleeding, and the friction with the air bag had burned the skin on my face.

The steel door had fared a lot better. So much for my easy escape. Bullets skipped off the car not far from my head. A shaft of sunlight lit up the dust. I had succeeded in wrenching the rolling door back far enough to clear a foot-high space along the ground under the car's buckled fender. I crawled through it, dragging my flank along a jagged piece of steel.

Adams Morgan was only a couple blocks away, and, as always, full of Ethiopian cabbies. I looked like hell on a holiday, but a second twenty-dollar bill was enough to convince the driver to get me as far from Davies as fast as he could.

Chapter Twenty-Two

Henry had nearly broken me back at his office: Annie betrayed me, Rivera sold me out, my mother was unfaithful, and my father a murderer. He'd also done me a favor in a way, proving beyond any doubt that my dream of a legit life was dead. I could now let that dream go without a second thought. Haskins was right: Henry owned the law, so I would just have to go outside it. Being a born criminal helped.

My first stop was home. There is a certain perverse thrill to robbing your own house, especially with a cop car parked out front. I had Henry Davies trying to torture me back into the fold with his creepy father-figure act and Rado Dragović hankering to eat my heart; the police were the least of my worries.

Like most untrustworthy people, I had a hard time trusting the banks, so I kept about six thousand dollars in hundreds interleaved in my old red-and-gold criminal-law casebook. After I escaped from Henry, I grabbed the money, a change of clothes, a suit, and my beat-to-shit pre-Davies Group laptop from my house and made it out without getting pinched.

I knew that using any of my credit cards or bank accounts would lead Henry and the police to me. I would have to steal to get by. It was a practical matter, sure, but there was more to it than that. I felt the sweet relief only someone who's been on the wagon for twelve years can feel as I dove back into crime.

My favorite approach to boosting cars was to just cruise past a valet box. Those guys were always sprinting off to fetch another car. I'd pull a set from a nice marque, then take a leisurely stroll, blipping the keyless entry and looking for my new ride. People who used valets tended to have pretty upscale wheels; I made off with a V8 Infiniti from outside the Arts Club of Washington.

DC is now riddled with red-light cameras and new police cruisers that scan every license plate they pass. Both can spot stolen cars, so I had to ditch the Infiniti as soon as possible. I needed a clean car, a clean cell phone, a clean gun, and a few other essentials. Basically, I needed a Walmart for bad guys, and I knew just where to go.

I drove forty minutes out to a swampy section of Manassas near the Occoquan Reservoir. I parked around the corner from an aluminum Quonset hut set back in a ratty patch of woods, checked for police, and then, finding none, headed for a rear door secured by a Yale bump-proof padlock. I knew that lock well, though it still took me about two minutes to get it open.

Inside was a thieves' paradise. Hanging neatly on the walls was every burglary tool imaginable – cylinder pulls, pick sets, even hydraulic shears and gas-powered circular saws that could cut a hole through a concrete wall in under a minute. In the cabinets I found a half a dozen prepaid cell phones, and took two.

Opening the locked gun safe, about as big as a closet, took me longer than I would have liked. But given the inventory of tools I had to choose from in that warehouse, it was only a matter of time before I got it open. There were a dozen long guns inside, even two AR-15 assault rifles with the sears swapped out for full auto; a little too Charles Bronson for my taste. I grabbed a pair of nine-millimeter Berettas like the ones I'd trained on in the navy.

'Why don't you take one of those forty-five HKs too,' said a voice behind me. 'The nine doesn't really get the job done.'

I turned, gun by my thigh and hand tight on the grip. And there was Cartwright, smiling. He pointed to the far corner of the garage: a motion detector and camera, well hidden, that I'd missed.

'Silent alarm,' he said. 'It wasn't here the last time you pulled this.'

'Sorry. I was worried they'd be watching you, watching my father.'

'They're watching him. Not me. Is that your car out back?' he asked.

'Yeah. Well, not mine, exactly.'

'I can swap you a ten-year-old Honda Civic with clean plates.'

'Thanks,' I said. It wasn't much of a trade, but I was desperate. Cartwright was always there when you needed him and always exploited the situation to the hilt.

The whole scene was eerily similar to the first time I had faced down Cartwright. This was the second time he'd caught me breaking into this garage; the first, I was sixteen. For my brother and his delinquent friends back then, Cartwright's garage was a mythical place, like Aladdin's cave. One day, my brother asked me about the lock securing the garage – the Yale bump-proof. I said that, given enough time, I could probably pick it. My brother dared me to do it. Of course I said yes. He and his friends, Cartwright's son Charlie included, drove me over and egged me on. The lock took only a minute.

They all peeled away when Cartwright showed up, leaving me alone inside the garage. The first thing Cartwright did when he caught me was slap me, hard, across the face. No one knew how Cartwright made his money, but everyone knew not to cross him. And there I was, trapped in his storehouse of sharp things and guns and very much on his bad side.

'Do you know what it would do to your father to see you taking stupid risks like this, running around with these fucking morons?' he asked me that day.

I just looked down and shook my head, embarrassed.

'How'd you get in here?' he asked.

I held out the lock, open and undamaged. 'I didn't break it. I didn't take anything. I just wanted to see if I could.'

'You picked this?' he asked. After a moment, he seemed less angry, even a little impressed. 'Who showed you how?'

'Nobody. I just like taking them apart. For fun,' I said.

He knew, between my father being in jail, my sick mother working two jobs, and my fuckup brother and his friends serving as my main role models, that I'd probably end up dead or in prison soon enough. There was no way he was going to stop me, though; I needed the money to help pay the medical bills. He made a deal with me that day: he'd teach me the trade – locks and picks to start – if I stopped pulling stupid bush-league juvenile-delinquent stuff with my brother's crew. He must have felt bad for me. Maybe he knew he couldn't keep me out of trouble, so he at least wanted to teach me not to get caught. Maybe he just recognized a precocious talent that he could exploit. Whatever it was, he showed me how to work like a professional, and taught me everything I knew. I did jobs for him and stayed away from tempting fate with the older kids for the most part. Though I could never say no to my brother, and ultimately that was my downfall.

Now, twelve years later, after I'd sworn off that life, I was back in his garage, caught red-handed once more.

'You okay?' he asked.

I nodded.

'What else do you need?'

I looked over to the wall, the racks of burglary tools, and then pointed high, to a steel bar that ended in a claw. I hadn't touched one in years, not since the night I got arrested, the last break-in I'd pulled.

It's called a Halligan, a fireman's tool, essentially a hopped-up crowbar. It has a thick, slightly offset forked wedge on one end that you can ram between any door and jamb and pry easily. There's a pick and adze at the other. The New York Fire Department designed it, but the basic idea they stole from thieves. The story goes that some firefighters in the 1920s or 1930s were sorting through the ash and rubble of a bank in Lower Manhattan that had just been robbed and then torched to hide the evidence. The thieves had left behind a custom-forged pry bar with a claw. The smoke eaters copied it, passed it around to different firehouses, and over the decades improved on it to the point where it could gain entry against almost any door in less than a minute.

Then thieves like me, true to form, stole it back.

Cartwright passed it down. God, it felt good in my hands.

He looked me over. 'It's nice to have you back, Mike.'

'Tell my dad that I'm okay.'

'Sure,' he said. 'And don't worry. You can pay me for the guns later.'

After I left Cartwright, I stopped by the local Greyhound station to plant some red herrings. I bought a ticket to Florida on my corporate AmEx and one to San Francisco on my personal card.

Then I walked through the station like Robin Hood, handing my credit and debit cards out to the folks in the waiting room – a dreadlocked white dude wearing patchwork pants, a shell-shocked-looking teenage couple, and a guy with one arm who was sipping on a bottle of grape Robitussin – after which they scattered to the four corners.

Now that I'd given up on help from the police, the murder evidence against Henry that Haskins had pointed me toward was my only hope. I had to assume that Haskins wouldn't have died trying to tip me off to this guy Langford if Langford were really dead.

I needed to dig into Langford's affairs, and after five hours at the Reston Regional Library (looking and smelling about on par with the other bums who populated the place; I hadn't had time to change), I pieced together a few glimmers of hope.

Langford's lawyer was a man named Lawrence Catena. Catena appeared to be working out of his house in Great Falls, Virginia, another high-end suburb of DC, and he specialized in living trusts and Delaware corporations. Delaware allows people (even if they're from out of state) to incorporate there anonymously, without listing the names of any of the owners or managers of the company, and so it attracts a lot of shell corporations and the bottom-feeding lawyers who specialize in them. Trusts and Delaware LLCs are perfect for hiding assets, ducking taxes, and so on. A corporation has the legal rights of a person, and some rights that people don't. Against a well-paid money-hider like Catena, I had no chance of prying into Langford's affairs – *unless* some local clerk made a mistake, as clerks sometimes do, and put down some information on the articles of incorporation or a chain of title that linked the dummy companies to the people they were shielding.

Enter my iron ass. I was nearly blind from reading small type on my computer, but just before they shut the library down and sent me back onto the streets I found it: a transfer of a vacation property in St Augustine from Langford to an inter vivos trust.

It could have been simply that Langford knew his health was going downhill in the years before he died and wanted to keep Uncle Sam from fleecing the inheritance. But I was starting to get a distinct feeling (probably fueled by the fact that it was my one lead and I was supremely desperate) that Langford was among the walking dead. Most people think plane crashes or staged suicides are good ways to fake your way out of this life. Too many questions, though, as I'm sure a good lawyer like Catena could tell you. No, better to go down quietly in Florida and have a simple cremation as Langford did.

All of this cogitation had me feeling pretty smug, but it didn't do me any good. No close relatives had survived Langford, and part of the reason you pay the Catenas of the world five hundred bucks an hour is that they keep their mouths shut. It's impossible to pry secrets out of their attorney-client-privileged hands.

It's almost impossible *legally*, that is, which Haskins had realized too late in his quest to find the evidence against Henry Davies that Langford was holding on to. I didn't have to bother with such niceties and had just picked up from Cartwright tools with which I could pry open pretty much anything. Those were my backup plan, though. I didn't have time to break into and sift through Catena's office. I was hoping this would be more of a finesse job.

I tailed Catena leaving his office and followed him to a house down in Georgetown near Dumbarton Oaks. There were valets out front, and clear signs of a high-toned party going on within. I waited for him to go inside, then drove past and parked in a dark spot around the corner where I had a decent view into the kitchen and living room of the house.

I called Catena's cell and watched him through the window.

'Larry Catena,' he said.

'Mr Catena. Hello,' I said. 'Sorry to bother you so late. This is Terrence Dalton at the office of the chief medical examiner. We have a body here, and according to the identification we found it's a . . .' I pretended to read. 'Karl Langford. Date of birth is March fifteenth, 1943. We were looking for next of kin and saw that you were his lawyer.'

'I'm afraid you're mistaken. Karl Langford is dead.'

'Yeah,' I said, sounding annoyed. 'I know. This is the morgue. That's why we're calling.'

'You found Karl Langford's license on a body in the District?' he asked. Concern crept into his voice.

'Yes, and some credit cards, a few other things. Can you come down tomorrow and identify the body?'

'I'll be there,' he said.

I gave him a time and a phony number and let him go. I don't know if Catena really bought my story, but that hardly mattered. It was an old con man's trick to get information out of people. You'd call someone and inform him that, according to some ID you'd found on the corpse, you had his wife or daughter on ice at the morgue. After you had the person in hysterics, you'd cool him off by describing a body that didn't match the loved one – a play normally known as the dead black female. The one-two punch of horror and relief would usually knock a person loose enough for him to give you whatever information you needed – typically a Social Security number or name and address – and that you claimed was necessary to straighten the matter out. I knew that Catena wouldn't just hand over Langford's current address, but that didn't matter. I only needed him to contact Langford, and I figured killing someone's dead client is a sure way to find out if he or she is still kicking.

I watched Catena step outside and make another call. Perfect.

By now, I'd changed into a clean suit. I'd spent enough time hanging around Washington high-society types that I could waltz into any party and fake it just fine. If only I'd known how easy it was when I was younger. Instead of prying open doors and falling off roofs, I could have just walked right into any given house party, said, 'Oh, I'm a friend of John's from work,' helped myself to the bourbon, talked about *NYPD Blue* or some stale political gossip, then sneaked into the bedroom to pocket the jewelry at my leisure.

That's more or less how I entered the house. It was a beautiful Colonial Revival with a columned porch. They were using the caterer who did the Davies Group Christmas parties, a good sign. I had a couple lamb chops and scanned the crowd for Catena. Polite folks all, the partygoers carefully avoided staring at the guy with the bandage on his nose.

I spotted Catena, looking ill at ease, by the base of the stairs, and set a pick. When he rounded the corner, I backed into him, then apologized profusely.

'It's fine,' he said. I set my drink down and got the hell out of there. I'd worried that my pickpocketing skills would be a little rusty, and they were. I'd practically felt him up trying to get his phone, but he didn't seem to notice. Perhaps he was preoccupied by the recent news about Langford's corpse showing up at the DC morgue.

A little Googling will tell you the backdoor key sequence to get around a password on an iPhone. All I needed was a glance through his recent calls to find what I wanted. Right after I'd done my morgue bit, Catena had called someone listed only as MT, with an eastern Maryland area code. I didn't even have to bother with a reverse directory. The address was in the phone's contact list: an assisted-living facility on the Eastern Shore called Clover Hills. I looked it up on his phone's Web browser: it seemed like a nice place, and even had a golf course.

That's how I found myself standing, that same night, in a deep bunker guarding the green of the seventeenth hole at Clover Hills. I peered through binoculars in a drizzling rain. The old burgling duds, a hooded sweatshirt and canvas jeans, felt good as I cased the house. Looking through the bedroom window, I could make out Langford, the man Justice Haskins had told me held the key to the evidence against Henry. Langford looked awful, with tubes running from his chest, but still pretty good for a dead guy.

With the Halligan, I did a neat job pulling the lock on the sliding doors next to his patio, and barely disturbed him when I broke in. By the time he woke up, his arms were bound neatly to the rails of his bed with duct tape. Having my old tools in my hands made me feel calm, however precarious my position: I was dressed like a thug and standing over a terrified old man hooked up to what I guessed was a dialysis machine.

The apparatus pumped slowly. A small wheel squeezed blood through a tube that ran through a host of different plastic bottles before it snaked back to Langford's bed, across his torso, then tucked neatly through the wall of his chest. It looked like it went right into his heart.

'Henry Davies sent you,' he said.

I wasn't sure if Langford's fear of Henry or his hatred of Henry – cooperation or spite – would be a better pry, so I left him guessing on that point.

'I need to know about Hal Pearson,' I said.

Langford licked his dry lips and looked at the ceiling. 'Henry murdered him. You kill me and the evidence goes public. Now would you please take this goddamned tape off my wrists and let me get some sleep. It's hard enough being hooked up to this fucking vampire without people wasting my time with stupid questions.'

'What evidence do you have?'

'Enough.'

'What exactly?'

'Fuck your mother.'

Maybe that was his default tell-off, but he'd sure picked the wrong man and the wrong time to use it. The topic of my mother was still a little raw with me after my run-in with Henry.

I watched the pump turn, the red fluid go around. Small clamps, nothing more, held together the tubing his blood ran through. I checked to see if the monitor was hooked up to anything – a phone line, an Ethernet cable – that might let a nurse know that Langford was having trouble. It wasn't. I'd already moved his phone to a chair far out of reach.

I stepped a little closer to the machine. A few twists and a pinch and I would hold Langford's life between my two fingers. I could bleed him slowly, splashing him out over the brown wall-to-wall carpet.

No violence. It was the only law my father respected, the only one I'd never second-guessed. Until today. Now I wasn't sure what I believed. Apparently my dad was a killer too.

These bloody impulses suited my recent mood. Ever since I'd seen Henry twist my life into a lie, setting me up for the murders, I'd been enjoying my time back on the dark side – a theft here, roughing up a cop there. What did I have to lose? I could show Henry he'd misjudged me. I had what it takes to apply the last lesson, to use it against him. I had the will to take coercion to its absolute, to the worst kinds of violence.

I watched the wet grow in Langford's eyes, watched him stare as I touched my knuckle to the center of the pump, felt the throb of the machine, the cool plastic slide against my skin.

Then I let my hand fall.

That wasn't me. *This whole thing is impossible,* I thought.

Henry could get me by hunting me down, by using my father as bait, by turning Annie against me, by hooking my nuts up to a car battery, by feeding me to Rado.

Or he could sit back and enjoy watching me corrupt myself, torturing geriatrics, becoming exactly the black-hearted little soldier he had always wanted. If I drained this poor old fuck Langford, how long before I'd be back in Henry's party?

I stepped away from the machine.

Langford considered me for a long while.

'So you're trying to stop him,' Langford said finally, then made a noise between a wheeze and a laugh. 'I've always had a soft spot for dimwits. What do you need to know?'

I cocked my head.

'If you were working for Henry,' he said, 'I'd be a sticky puddle around your shoes right now.'

This threw me. I wasn't sure where decency fit in among money, ideology, coercion, and ego. Everything I'd learned about Langford hinted that he was just as crooked as the rest of Washington. But my better self, by not killing the guy, had just gotten me somewhere. I wasn't about to let it slip away.

'Where's the evidence?' I asked.

He looked more closely at my face.

'Are you the guy who did in the Supreme Court justice and the girl?'

'So they tell me, but I imagine you can guess who's really behind that.'

He looked down at my feet. 'What happened to your pumps?'

I guess the press had really eaten up that detail of my escape from Davies Group. 'They were slowing me down. What have you got on Henry?'

'You know the meat of it. He killed a reporter in 1972.'

'Why?'

'Pearson was onto Henry's dirty tricks. You know about G. Gordon Liddy? John Mitchell?'

'Of course.'

'Operation Gemstone?'

'I've heard of it.'

'Watergate was just the tip of the iceberg. Liddy was mapping out some truly off-the-deep-end stuff: firebombing the Brookings Institution, feeding LSD to Ellsberg, kidnapping activists and shipping them to Mexico.'

'But he never got the green light.'

'*Liddy* didn't get the green light. The attorney general, Mitchell, told him thanks but no thanks, and by the way, burn those flip charts with all that crazy shit outlined on them. Liddy was a wannabe-big-dick chicken hawk, a moron, which is why you've heard of him. He got caught. You haven't heard of Henry Davies's part in the same conspiracies, because, as I'm sure you know, Henry Davies is ruthless, supremely competent, and more of a better-to-ask-forgiveness-than-ask-permission type. What Davies pulled off made the wing-nut shit Liddy proposed look as innocent as tearing down campaign signs. I'm sure you can imagine what he's capable of.

'Davies was a comer. In two years he'd gone from answering phones to being the number one rat-fuck artist on the Committee to Reelect the President. It was unreal. People were starting to hitch themselves to his coattails. They figured he'd find his way into Congress soon enough, and after that, who knew? The guy was a rocket. But then Hal Pearson started sniffing around Davies, started to piece together his role in the dirty tricks. Pearson threatened Davies's rise. He threatened the whole campaign. Woodward and Bernstein were a couple JV metro reporters who got lucky. They scratched the surface. Pearson would have taken the whole capital down.

'Davies found out that Pearson was investigating him and went to his apartment, up in Mount Pleasant. I guess Pearson was expecting the usual hardball, a browbeating, maybe some threats. He wasn't expecting Henry Davies. I don't know what Davies said to Pearson, but the guy was a big drinker with a big temper and I imagine he didn't take it well. It got physical, and Pearson turned up dead, strangled, his throat a purple mess, the next day.'

'Henry left evidence?' I asked.

'Yes,' Langford said. 'The police pulled part of his earlobe out of Pearson's throat.'

That explained the scar along Henry's neck.

'Pearson sure as fuck wasn't nibbling his ear. He nearly killed Davies, crushed his voice box, must have been choking him right back. That's where he got that creepy whisper.'

'So how did Davies get away with it?'

'He was damaged goods. His bosses wanted to bury him, to get him out of Washington as quickly as possible. They gave him some bullshit defense attaché position in Luxembourg, gave him time to get his ear fixed up. He was out of the States for six months, maybe a year.

'For anyone else, that would've been the end of the road, but not for Davies. His higher-ups destroyed his career in government, sure, but Davies had always been the paranoid type. He was a collector, of sorts. Most young guns like him were happy taking orders, rubbing shoulders with the bosses, glad to even get a chance to chat with an attorney general. But Davies was always planning, so that when the time came, he had knives to draw.'

Langford nodded toward the duct tape. 'I think I earned my way out of this, huh?'

I pulled it off.

'Thanks,' he said. He took a shaky breath, then continued.

'Henry had kept evidence, documentation of every order he received from his higher-ups, every dirty trick they were complicit in. When his bosses tried to throw him under the bus, he was ready. Bad things started happening to them. He used the secrets he'd collected like a scalpel. One by one he cut them out. It was unbelievable. In exile, he dismantled anyone who tried to cross him. A massacre. He came out unscathed. Well, mostly unscathed; he returned as a pretty dark character after his time in the wilderness. I think that's when he learned that he could be more powerful out of sight, working the strings.

'He'd been going along to get along, trying to please the bosses. He was dirt-poor, just wanted the big office and the big house. It corrupted him, cost him his career in government. And ever since then it seems like he's dedicated his life to proving that every honest man, as well as the whole capital, can be corrupted, that they're no better than he is.

'He made coin while he was at it too. Piece by piece, he built it into an empire. He started by getting into the vetting for campaigns: vice presidential searches, cabinet secretaries, whatever. He would go deeper than was needed for the jobs, and if those candidates ever crossed him, they'd find their skeletons on the front page of the Post. At some point he cracked the Federal Investigative Service. They do all the background checks for the government, the guys who ask CIA applicants if they want to fuck their brothers and all that. It was a gold mine. Next he got his fingers in the prayer groups. That started in the eighties. All of a sudden every heavyweight in DC was confessing his deepest secrets once a week before breakfast. Those were supposed to be sacred, strictly off-the-record, but Henry made damn sure he always had someone listening.'

'But what about the evidence?' I asked. 'The blood? They

found a chunk of his ear in the dead man's throat, right? It doesn't get any more open-and-shut than that.'

'You're right. But the politicos bigfooted the local cops. The evidence file with the police report and the chunk of ear disappeared. The official story went out: Pearson was killed by a burglar. Someone must have thought they could buy that file off the cops and use it to rein Henry in. They thought wrong.

'At first, the file commanded a pretty high price. After all, leverage on Henry was looking to be increasingly precious. The evidence had disappeared while Henry was overseas, and at first he didn't know it existed, and then he didn't know who had it. As he grew stronger, and the men who tried to cross him fell, holding on to the one thing Henry would kill to obtain started to seem less and less a good idea. The price dropped. Eventually a friend of mine, James Perry, the party chair in Virginia, got his hands on it. And he was either cowardly enough or sensible enough to hide it. He couldn't destroy it, just in case Henry came knocking, so he buried it.'

I took a deep breath. James Perry was the man who Henry Davies had claimed was sleeping with my mother, the man my father had supposedly murdered. My mother had been Perry's secretary. This whole mess was closing in on me, on my family and my past. I steeled myself. Above all, I needed to get that evidence against Henry. Whatever connection my father had to Henry Davies would have to wait.

'Where is it now?' I asked.

Langford let out a bitter laugh. 'That's the best part. Perry had a contracting company on the side, construction and renovations. His cronies steered him a lot of government work. He had keys to half the federal buildings in Washington. So he hid it in plain sight in one of these massive file warehouses the Feds have everywhere, just miles of shelves in an archive gathering dust. If you didn't know the name he put on the file, you'd never find it in there.'

'Where's the archive?'

'Nine hundred fifty Pennsylvania Ave.'

'Wait . . .'

'You got it.'

'The Department of Justice?'

'So good luck with that.'

'He never told you the name?'

'No. He never told anyone anything. What I just told you he let slip in a blackout while we were drunk on a golf junket in Myrtle Beach. Not that my ignorance would help if Davies found me. I'm sure he'd have a real time of it, sipping an RC Cola while Marcus went snipping off postage-stamp patches of my skin until I gave up a name I didn't have or bled out. Only Perry knew the name on that file. And he's been dead for sixteen years.'

'Who killed him?' I asked. Henry had just told me my father was the murderer.

'A mugging was the official story. DC can be a very dangerous place for knowledgeable people. I always thought Davies must have been behind it somehow.'

'Did you ever hear Perry mention a woman named Ellen Ford?'

'You think she killed him?' Langford smiled, then considered it. 'Maybe from blue balls.

'Not that I could blame him,' he added.

'You knew her?'

'Just from what Perry told me. Said she was a good-looking woman. Some fuckup ex-con for a husband. Perry figured she was working for him trying to butter him up so he'd help get her husband's prison record cleaned up, help out with his parole. Perry, class act to the end, was just stringing her along while he tried to drag her out to the Palisades. His friend had a house out there Perry used for a fuck pad. Why do you ask about her?'

'She was my mother,' I said.

Langford sucked in air through his teeth and winced. 'If it's any consolation, I never heard about her going along with it. Perry liked girls who took a hard sell, and he couldn't keep his mouth shut. I'd probably have heard.'

I didn't say anything.

'Give-and-take,' Langford said. 'I imagine you know that game. Now, how did you find me?'

'Malcolm Haskins.'

'And how did he find out I knew about the evidence against Henry?'

'He never told me,' I said. 'We didn't really have a lot of time to chat before Henry killed him. Is Haskins the reason you disappeared?'

Langford nodded. 'He started bugging me, asking me questions about all this. I stonewalled him. But when a Supreme Court justice sets his mind to making you testify, dying is one of your more palatable options. And if Haskins knew, then I was sure that eventually Henry would find out and then we'd be back to the RC Cola-and-skinning scenario. So I ran, tried to hide. This thing with Henry, it's personal for you?'

'Yes. More and more with everything I learn.'

'He offered you some kind of deal?'

I nodded. 'It was strange; he wanted me back. He seemed more interested in my obedience, in being able to watch me suffer under him, than anything else.'

'You said no.'

'I kicked Marcus in the face and tried to strangle Henry.'

'Good,' he said, then corrected himself. 'Well, survival-wise it was pretty dumb. You should have taken the deal; it was the reasonable thing to do. I said good because I like seeing those guys hurt, and the only thing you have going for you is that Henry has trouble dealing with unreasonable men. Somehow, though, no matter who he's working on, he always manages to find a compelling enough reason to get the guy to do his will.'

'Is that why you're talking to me? You think I can get out of this?'

'No. You should have said yes to Henry. You're going to be a corpse, or worse, before the week is out. I'm talking to you because if you can find me, he can. I'm as good as dead. And it's nice to go down making a move instead of waiting for Tuesday lasagna.'

He looked around at the furnished room, the same nailed-to-the-wall landscapes that who knows how many people had seen from the same bed as they died slowly. I got the feeling he'd taken a deal, a long time ago, and it had left him here, at the end, nameless and alone.

Chapter Twenty-Three

Sending the message through Cartwright, I told my father to find me where he'd lost me once. The Cutlass growled along the dirt road and parked beside the baseball diamond. I was taking a risk, for both of us, by meeting him, but I needed to make sure he was okay and warn him that Henry was coming for him.

I rested the Halligan bar against the chain-link fence of the backstop. When I was ten, my father left me at this field, thinking my mother had taken me home after the game. As night fell, I found some local kids and we had a ball playing manhunt then taking turns shooting one another with a little one-pump BB gun. I'd never seen my father scared, but he was white as a ghost that spring night as he came stalking through the fields looking for his son.

He looked just as worried now.

'You okay?' he asked me. His eyes took inventory of my bad week: the friction burns on my face, a mottled black bruise across my throat (which still wasn't working quite right), and a marked limp from crashing the car into the wall. The gash in my thigh from Haskins's country place had finally scabbed over. It itched like a motherfucker, which was good, a sign of healing.

'Yeah,' I said.

'Been better?'

I nodded. He hugged me.

'Anybody follow you?' I asked.

'No. Haven't given someone the blow-off in a long time. I sorta miss it. Were you the one who killed those two on the news?'

'No,' I said. My name still hadn't gone public as the main suspect in the murders. I imagine Henry had something to do with that, keeping my identity out of this so he could lure me back, dangle the promise of making it all go away if I gave in to him. Just one more piece of leverage.

'Stomp the cop?'

'Yes, but just to get away. The rest is a frame-up.'

He seemed unsurprised.

'They're watching you?' I asked.

He nodded. 'The cops occasionally and some guys I took to be private muscle are parked across from the trailer. I called them in as peepers, whack-off artists, and sneaked out the back when the local PD came to check them out. Your friends Marcus and Henry paid me a visit too.'

'They threaten you?'

'In a real classy way. They said if you cooperated with them, they'd make all your troubles go away. They wanted me to help.'

'What'd you say?'

'I told them I hadn't talked to you, but I would see what I could do. It's better to keep them on the hook while I get my bearings in the situation than to tell them to fuck off straightaway. Keep them interested in case we want to make a play at them.'

'Did you kill James Perry?'

'Yes,' he said, without hesitation. 'They mentioned that to me too. Are they trying to lever you with it?'

'Yeah. They want me to help cover up that they killed the Supreme Court justice and the girl.'

'Give me up then,' he said. 'I've got the hang of prison.'

I looked at the scar on his cheek. Someone on the inside had slit open the side of his mouth, with what kind of nasty shiv I couldn't imagine. No. He wasn't taking any hits for me. He'd done his time.

'I got myself into this, Dad. If there's a fall, I'm taking it. Why'd you kill Perry? Were you working for Davies?'

'No. I never met Davies before this week.'

'Then why?'

'I didn't want to,' he said. 'You remember Perry? You may have met him when you were a kid.'

'Vaguely,' I said, thinking back to a hazy recollection of a company picnic, something like that. 'Fat guy? Thin hair?'

'That's him. He was a real glad-hander, always chortling right in your face. I don't know how your mother met him, maybe around the courthouse, but he was a big deal politically. After I got out the first time, she thought he'd be a good friend to have. He offered her a job as a secretary. She took it.

'She never told me about it, but I guess he was . . . hot for her. And, as with most of those respectable folks, his kindness turned out to be a scam. He was holding my parole over her, breaking his word, trying to get her . . .'

He scratched the infield dirt with his toe.

'. . . you see?'

I got it.

'I didn't know any of this. Maybe I hadn't been looking hard enough. She called me at home one night. She'd been out working late. She and Perry had been driving back from a meeting. He said he had to sign some papers, out in the Palisades, some house. He got her inside, and he started getting a little pushy, I guess.

'She distracted him somehow, called me. She didn't want to bring the cops in. Understandable. I showed up in a rare mood. Perry was drunk, obnoxious. He came at me. I shoved him, kept him back. He stumbled, tripped over a step, and fell. He landed on his temple on the corner of the hearth. It was a lot of blood. Just gushing. I sent your mother home to take care of you, and I cleaned up Perry.

'I dropped the body down in Southeast, fixed it so it looked like a mugging. That went over, eventually; it took a few days for anyone to find the body. I went back to the house that same night with some bleach and hydrogen peroxide. It was a fucking mess. Hours. When I was done, with the trash down at the dump, just taking a last look at the place, the sirens came. Somebody must have called them. I was in and out all night in a beater that didn't fit the neighborhood. I was stuck. I smashed a lock and played it like a badly planned B and E. The rest I think you know.'

He'd told most of the story in a calm voice, looking over the woods surrounding the fields. Then he turned to me.

'I don't want you thinking I'm a killer, Mike.'

As a con man, he'd made a living making people believe him, and I believed the gist of his story, believed that he was protecting my mother, that he wasn't a cold-blooded murderer. Yet something about his account was off, something I couldn't place.

I didn't say anything. What can you say when you find out that the defining facts of your life are false, that you've hated your father, tortured him for sixteen years, because you didn't have the story straight, had it exactly backward, in fact? He wasn't covering up for anyone. There was no sordid thieves' honor at play. He'd stayed silent to protect my mother, to protect me, to save himself from a life sentence, maybe worse, for killing a powerful man.

I didn't need to ask him why he'd never told me. He blamed himself for that night and didn't want to get me involved. What would he have said? *I was a fuckup, and when your mom tried to help me out, my bad decisions – the past crimes, the parole – made her vulnerable to scum like Perry?* To scum like me? I mean, after all, Perry was an extortion artist the same as I was when I worked for Davies.

There was nothing to say.

Not that it mattered, because we didn't have time to talk. Flashlights scanned the park. I don't know how they had found us. Far off I could hear cars doors slamming shut and the clanks of chains: dogs. They were a few hundred yards away, near where I'd parked the Civic. There were a lot of them, and they didn't look like police. A shaft of light turned. My father and I were already in the woods, sprinting, but I had made out faces: Marcus was here.

I ran with my father until fire coursed through my legs and lungs. We hauled each other back up when we stumbled, racing blind through the woods. A half a mile in, my father led us splashing down a freezing creek, then cut a ninety-degree turn. I hoped we'd lose them. We had a decent lead.

Then I heard it, a rustling behind us, then panting, now and then a clinking of chain. Closer and closer, the noise came fast. I knew it was the dogs. But I didn't hear any barking. The pack materialized out of the dark, a dozen gleaming eyes circling us on the wet leaves, mouths snapping, teeth like razors, yet all so strangely silent. Their vocal cords had been cut.

Sir Larry Clark, ever helpful, must have loaned Henry his dogs.

I'd seen them take a kill order once before, the weekend I met Larry. They'd cornered a rabbit at his house. Larry gave the command. They hadn't seemed like dogs anymore, just a blur of muscle and sharp white teeth. When they finished, slinking away with bloodstained faces, it looked like someone had thrown the rabbit in a blender.

There was a strange moment of calm. They kept a circle. When the first moved, the rest would join. I had the Halligan bar and could probably fend them off for a minute or two, but by then we'd be found. I held it with two hands, the sharp point of the pick ready to strike.

A Doberman started toward me.

'Leave it,' I heard a voice say behind me. The dogs eased back.

I turned. Annie stood above me on a downed tree. Apparently she was part of the posse.

'Who the fuck is she?' my dad asked.

'My girlfriend.'

'Pretty.'

'Thanks.'

'How's that going, by the way?'

'Not too great.'

I could handle Annie selling me out and stealing my job, could probably even put up with getting eaten by a pack of Dobermans, but having my ex-girlfriend supervise and savor the butchery? All right, life, you win. You got me. I mean, how fucked up was this whole thing going to get?

Annie stepped through the circle of dogs and moved closer to me. I guess I should have taken a swing at her, but she was just too sweet-looking to KO with the Halligan.

She threw herself into my arms, then leaned her head back and kissed me.

'You're okay!'

Actually, more confused than okay.

'They'll be here any second,' she said. She held my hand.

'But what about the tape Henry showed me, of you in his office? Aren't you working for him?'

'Mike, no!' she said. She stepped back, took me by the shoulders, and looked into my eyes. 'I only went along with Henry to find out if what you were telling me was true.'

'And?'

'I've been watching him. I believe you now, Mike. I had to see for myself. It was all so fucking crazy. You can't expect me to buy that whole story – the murders, the framing – without double-checking. You're a great guy, but come on, there are a lot of nuts out there.'

I couldn't blame her.

'I joined the search so that I could find you before they could hurt you. I'm inside, Mike. I can help you stop them.'

'There's evidence against Henry,' I said. 'I know where it is. It's a file, but we need the name on that file to find it and stop him. Without that name, we've got no chance.'

My father scanned the shadows. 'Annie, very nice to meet you. You seem like a lovely woman, but I'm afraid we need to get going.'

Annie looked back through the woods. I took her hand.

'I can't let you go back to him,' I said. 'He's a monster.'

'You can't take him without someone on the inside,' she said. 'That's your only chance.'

'Annie . . .' I looked from her to my father. It was the truth. And if she ran with us, with no one to mislead Henry, he'd catch us all. I told her to get a prepaid phone, to call when she was safe, that I'd find her.

'Head toward the highway,' she said. It was a faint yellow glow in the distance. 'I'll lead the dogs the other way.'

She kissed me again, started back, then stopped.

'Wait!' she said. 'They won't believe that you just miraculously escaped.'

A look passed among the three of us.

'Hit me,' she said.

'What?'

'Either one of you. Mark me up a little. Or else you got away too easy. They'll know. Then we're all screwed.'

I could see from my father's face that he was in awe of this girl's wiles.

She looked to me.

'Annie, I can't.'

'Oh, fuck it,' she said; she shut her eyes and brought her fist up hard into her upper lip and nose.

'God!' I stepped to help her.

'How's it look?'

Blood trickled between her front teeth and beaded in her nostril.

'Awful.'

'Great.'

'Are you okay?' I asked.

'Uh-huh,' she said. 'Now go.'

My father pulled me away. We sprinted for the highway.

'Marry that girl,' he said as we ran.

'No shit.'

A half a mile on, we jumped into a culvert, then scrambled into the far back corner of a half-empty strip-mall parking lot.

'You know how to steal cars?' my dad asked.

'The light touch.' I swung the Halligan into the passenger side window of a VW sedan. I set the bar's pick in the groove around the glove box and pried it open. Then I leafed through the manual. Nothing. I smashed the window of an Audi and repeated the process.

'It's in the manual?' he asked doubtfully. I detected that distinct fatherly note of I-don't-think-you're-doing-this-right.

'Yes,' I said, and pulled the valet key from the back page of the car's manual. When you buy the car, it's glued in there, and people always forget to take it out. Really, who reads the instructions for a car?

I unlocked the doors. 'Get in,' I said.

We tore out of the parking lot and raced down back roads toward farm country. We were both still breathing fast, pulses racing, high from the chase.

'It's weird. I almost miss the thrill,' my father said.

'Me too.'

'Though I am sorry everyone's trying to kill you.'

'I appreciate that. Thanks for telling me what happened, with Perry. I'm sorry. For everything.'

'I'm glad you know why I never talked. It killed me not to tell you.'

Finally understanding each other, we set to work like old accomplices.

Chapter Twenty-Four

My father and I hauled a box of supplies and a Coleman propane stove into the cabin. Rambling, lunatic graffiti covered the walls. *I never tried to hurt mother. They put handcuffs on me. They tore my skin.*

'Who's your decorator?' I asked Cartwright.

He looked at the walls. 'Oh. Some junkie squatted here last year.'

It was a three-room house in the hills outside Leesburg that Cartwright, who had more black-market sidelines than I could count, kept for whenever he needed some serious privacy. 'And the smell?' I asked. It was a potpourri of BO and socks.

'I had like nineteen Salvadorans holed up here last week.'

I didn't ask.

'Do you have everything?' I said.

He pulled six cans from the bag – I was going to make chili – and then an envelope. Inside was a heavy gold badge with an eagle across the top. The Bureau of Alcohol, Tobacco, and Firearms seal filled the center, with DEPARTMENT OF JUSTICE above and SPECIAL AGENT underneath.

I glanced at my watch. Annie was supposed to have been here two hours ago. I hadn't seen her since our encounter in the park last night. I was sure that Marcus and Henry had figured out her double cross, that she was dead or worse. God knows what they would do.

My father had been poring over the DOJ blueprints for hours. Based on what Langford told me, we were able to pick out the areas in the basement big enough for the warehoused files. That's where our evidence against Henry was hiding.

Headlights appeared on the fire road below. Cartwright blacked out the cabin. We took our spots: my father on the shotgun at the front door, Cartwright and I on a pair of AR-15 rifles at the windows.

If they had gotten to her, she'd lead them to us.

The car stopped. A door opened and shut in the distance. With no moon, it was impossible to see who was coming.

'Plastics!' Annie shouted.

The password. I'd been trying to keep things light, so I went with *The Graduate*. The guns fell. I ran out and held her, then led her inside.

'Charming,' she said as she stepped into the flophouse and tossed her jacket on a chair.

'Jeffrey Billings,' she said.

My father and I exchanged a glance.

'The name on the file?' I asked.

'Yes,' she replied. We had everything we needed to go after Henry. I lifted her up and spun her. She winced in pain.

'Are you okay?' I asked.

'I'm fine.'

There was something off, though. Red rimmed her eyes, like she'd been crying. Gently, I pulled back her sleeve to look at her forearm where I had held her during the lift. A blue bruise circled her wrist.

'Henry. Did he find out? Is that why you were late? Did he hurt you?'

'No,' she said, then laughed a little, covering up the pain. 'Not Henry. When Henry saw my face back at the fields, he thought you'd tried to kill me. He doesn't suspect a thing.

They lowered their guard. That's how I heard them talking about the name on the file.

'This,' she said, pointing to her wrist, 'was Dragović.'

'Radomir? He's in the country?'

'He's in DC. I was leaving the office tonight when these two men who work for him came up beside me, took my arms, forced me into a car. They brought me to some nightclub, through the back door.'

The White Eagle. It was an old Beaux Arts mansion where Aleksandar and Miroslav held court, a magnet for Arab and Eastern European new money.

'They took me into a back room. When I ran, they grabbed me' – she pulled her sleeve back down – 'dragged me back. Dragović was there, eating dinner.'

'What did he want?'

'You,' Annie said. 'I told him that you had disappeared, that we were all on the same side in this, that I was working with Henry, and Henry was working with the police to hunt you down. He didn't seem to care.

'I tried to back him off. I said Henry wouldn't stand for me being treated this way, talked about how powerful Davies was. None of that concerned him, he said. He said he would go through Henry, go through any man, pay any price for honor.

'He stood behind me, very close. I could feel his breath on my neck. "I loved my daughter," he said. "Mr Ford loves you. Mr Ford killed my daughter, and so . . ."' She trailed off for a moment. 'He didn't finish the sentence. He just sat down, buttered a roll, and swirled some wine.' She looked at the floor, reluctant to speak.

'What did he say, Annie?'

'The deadline is eight o'clock tomorrow. If he doesn't have you by then, he'll take me.'

'For what?'

She pressed her lips together and shut her eyes. 'Nothing good.'

I took her in my arms. She was shaking.

'He didn't hurt you.'

'No. Just pushed me around a little.'

I looked from her to my father. They were all I had left. And I was going to get them both killed for my mistakes, for this crusade against Henry Davies. Davies wanted me back. He was right about me not knowing the full cost of honesty. Maybe he'd finally found my price.

Rado had Henry beat when it came to sheer psychotic meanness, but Henry had enough clout to keep Rado at bay. If I gave myself up to Henry, maybe he'd keep Rado away from Annie. Sure, it'd mean hocking my soul, but half of Washington seemed to have made that deal. They survived it. So would I.

'Listen,' I said. 'I can't let you two suffer for me. I can go to Henry. I—'

Annie and my father looked at each other.

My father rolled his eyes.

Annie said, 'Pfff.'

'Not a fucking chance, Mike,' he said. 'He's the most fearsome man in the capital, and for once, he's afraid. There are a lot of people out there who are looking to get out from under Henry's thumb. He says everyone has a lever. We've got his. You can't let that go.'

'So how do we do it?' Annie asked.

I walked her over to the blueprints.

'This is the Justice Department,' I said.

It was a level 4-security federal building, on par with the FBI. The only targets more hardened were the CIA and the Pentagon. That meant smart-chip IDs checked against a central database, visitor escorts at all times, intrusion detection, CCTV cameras monitored centrally, x-ray and magnetometer at every entrance, and group 2 locks (yup, the old Sargent and Greenleaf).

The building housed the FBI, the marshal services, the attorney general, the DEA, and the Bureau of Prisons: a criminal's most feared enemies all gathered in one convenient spot.

'I'm going to break in and steal the file,' I said.

'And then?' she asked.

'I go haggle with the devil.'

There were four guards in the DOJ entrance, all armed. For good measure, the two Federal Protective Service officers near the front door carried HK MP-5 submachine guns. Bags and briefcases went through the x-ray. People went through one of four metal detectors with curved doors, which held each one for a five-second scan before allowing the person to proceed.

It was the middle of a holiday weekend, so the place was almost empty. I'd have preferred the distracted bustle of rush hour, but we didn't have much time. Annie had overheard Henry and Marcus talking about the Eastern Shore when they mentioned the name on the evidence. I don't know how they'd found out – maybe the lawyer's stolen phone – but they would find Langford soon, if they hadn't already. They'd have no hesitation about forcing it out of him. Once they knew where the file was, I would have company here at DOJ.

Annie had cut and dyed my hair at the safe house, and Cartwright added a little bump to my nose. It was just a sliver of latex, but with it I could barely recognize myself.

All the confidence I'd felt in my disguise drained as I stepped up to the guards.

My father had busted my chops when I showed him the printouts at the safe house. 'They tell you how to break into the DOJ on the Internet?'

Actually, they did. Congress's watchdog, the Government Accountability Office, ran stings every five years or so to see if they could sneak past the guards at the CIA, FBI, DOJ, federal courts, and so on. They'd usually try ten sites or so and had never been turned away or caught at any of them. Then they were nice enough to write up how and where they'd done it and publish it where enterprising young crooks like me could find it. Your tax dollars at work. There was even a nice little paragraph at the end explaining how, due to funding issues, these faults aren't likely to be fixed any time soon.

I sure hoped not. The guard glared at me.

See, if you pay attention in Washington you start to realize that, as in most bureaucracies, 90 per cent of the effort is dedicated to the appearance of getting something done. In security, that number was probably even higher. More guards, more guns, more barriers. Trillions of dollars spent to prove that trillions of dollars were being spent, to have the exteriors of every building bristling with armed men, to reassure the public and the higher-ups with a great show of force that something was happening.

Maybe it helped, but there were still ways to slip through, and that hard exterior may have even backfired because it was a false mask on vulnerability. A good thing for me. From a con man's point of view, it was an easy belief to exploit. If the people you want to put one past have absolute faith in the law and the gun, you simply make yourself the law.

I showed the guard my badge.

'How you doing?' I said, moving with my best high-noon cop walk. 'I need to drop off some data at the DAG's office.'

I lifted my valise. He looked from it to my badge, then sucked his teeth.

'Go on,' he said. A flat pry bar was hidden in the side of the case, to avoid the metal detectors, but he just waved me past them. I could have had a claymore mine in there.

A claymore actually would have come in handy, because he beckoned over a hard-looking young woman, fresh from college, in a power pantsuit. I'd expected an escort, but it made things trickier. In most level 4 buildings, unless you have a security clearance and a hard pass, you get a nanny at all times. A friend of mine worked at State for six months waiting for his clearance to come through. Every time he wanted to take a piss he had to ask for permission and bring a chaperone.

I'd planned for it, though. As we walked I pulled my phone out and started tapping (in Washington, you'd stand out if you weren't staring at your BlackBerry like a zombie at all times). Call it in, I wrote, and hit Send.

It was a ten-minute stroll to the office of the deputy attorney general, DAG for short. She pulled up in front of his door. 'Here you are.'

'DAOG,' I said.

'The officer downstairs said you wanted the deputy.'

'Debt Accounting Operations Group.'

She let an angry little puff of air come out of her nose, then forced a smile. 'Okay then.'

I was playing for time. I guess I could have hit her with the pry bar and dragged her into the bathroom, but this was more fun.

We were halfway to our destination when the strobes started flashing and a pleasant female voice came over the public address. 'Emergency evacuation. This is not a drill. Please proceed calmly to the nearest exit. Please do not panic. This is not a test. We repeat. This is not a test.'

'We need to go,' she said, looking distinctly alarmed. She beelined for the front of the building. Near the exit, I peeled off in the commotion and headed for the stairwell.

My father had been waiting for my signal – the text message – to call in the bomb threat. He'd done his time, and then some, so I wouldn't let him near the actual dirty work, the break-in. That was all mine.

Now the place was completely empty. I popped two doors with the pry bar to get into the subbasement where Langford had suggested the evidence against Henry was hidden.

It looked like nothing had been touched since the 1970s. The walls were concrete. Dusty bankers' boxes were piled four feet high on industrial shelves. Metal cages cut the room into grids. Utility pipes hung low overhead.

Hidden somewhere in this labyrinth was the only way to save my ass, as well as my dad's and Annie's: a file labeled JEFFREY BILLINGS. I entered the first cage and started flicking through papers. Some were alphabetical, some not. I scanned the sides of the boxes for the names, for any legend that might suggest their contents. It was all pretty random. Some had dates, some names, some codes. I tore through anything that hinted at having the files starting with *B* in it. I didn't find Billings.

I could hear the sirens outside. I didn't have much time before the bomb squad would sweep the building. I stepped back, tried to think calmly, systematically. The file should have blood and tissue samples and the police write-up. It would have to be thick. I stood in the middle of the room and shook out my hands.

A door creaked somewhere off to my left. I wasn't alone. I ducked behind a pallet of boxes and scanned the room. Footsteps, now straight ahead. I stalked in parallel, trying to glimpse the source of the noise through the boxes and wire mesh of the cages.

Then I saw his face. You're never lonely when William Marcus is hunting you.

I circled the room away from him. I had to find the file before he could find it, or find me. I had the pry bar. He had a pistol. I was fairly sure that he hadn't seen me yet, or else he would have already closed in.

He was making a slow circuit of the room. Crouching, I cut straight across the storage area, then tucked myself behind a few boxes along his path. I waited, pry bar cocked, for him to pass. I had one shot. With him out of the way, I could focus, find the evidence.

I concentrated, slowing my breath so he wouldn't hear me. He must have rounded the corner by now. Any second. I tightened my grip on the bar, felt the sweat cool against the metal.

Five seconds passed; ten; twenty.

He didn't come.

I heard a clanging from the corner, and turned my head to look. I could see the corridor, the exit.

Marcus was gone.

I waited a moment. Was he trapping me? Had he already found the evidence? I turned the corner, then smelled it, a smell I knew well, because it had permeated my childhood: the stale cabbage funk of leaking natural gas.

Marcus had smashed open the valve on a gas line overhead, about fifty feet away. Through the overpowering fumes, I could pick up something else: burning paper. Flames licked at the base of a pile of boxes on the opposite side of the basement.

He hadn't found the evidence, or missed me. He simply was going to take care of both his problems with one tidy inferno. I turned on my heel and moved away from the flames.

I was inside one of the cages, so I would have to double back through the fire to reach the exit.

I heard a roar. The gas ignited. Heat and pressure boomed past me. The flames would come right behind. I'd never make it out. Standing empty against the metal fencing ahead was an open safe – about four feet square and three deep. I didn't think, just threw myself inside and slammed the door shut behind me.

The curtain of fire roared past like a jet engine. It lasted for a few seconds. The metal walls felt warm, and were getting warmer. I could still hear the fire roiling, but it sounded quieter now. I pressed on the safe door. Nothing.

Huh. I'd locked the safe. This was a new one. I was the loot, and I'd have to steal myself.

I could taste the fire in the thinning air. I tucked into a ball to get away from the scalding walls of the safe.

The beauty, of course, is that a government safe typically takes about twenty hours to crack, but that's supposing you're cracking it from the outside. In the blackness inside the safe, I ran my fingers over the lock assembly, a box about the size of my hand behind the dial. Two Phillips-head screws attached it to the vault door. I backed them out with the pry bar and groped around inside the lock.

My head was swimming from the smoke. Sweat soaked my shirt and ran stinging into my eyes.

It was a typical group 2, with four wheels. All combination locks, whether cheap Master padlocks or the boxes on vaults, keep their secrets with what's called a wheel pack: three or four discs, each of which has a notch in the side. The dial connects to the rearmost disc, and there are little tabs sticking out from each one. The tabs are arranged so that when you spin the lock four times to clear it, you're actually picking up all four wheels by their tabs. As you move to a number, then turn back, you're leaving a disc with its notch under a bar called the fence. If you rotate it back and forth in the right order, the four notches line up, the fence drops, and the bolt pulls.

I could smell my hair burning as I jammed my pinkie into the mechanism to feel for the notches in the wheels. It was awkward, painful work as I gasped and wrenched my finger.

I set the forward wheel, then the second. The air was hot enough to burn my skin. The safe, first a buffer against the fire, was now an oven. I twisted wheel three into place, then four, then prayed the fire had gone down enough so that I wouldn't get torched as soon as I opened the door.

The room was black as I opened the safe. Flames danced past. I crawled along the floor, pulled my shirt over my mouth, and moistened it with what spit I had left.

The fire singed my skin, and the heat burned my lungs with every half breath, but I made it to the exit door, slammed it behind me, and stumbled up the steps.

Through the glass pane I could see the room was solid with black smoke and fire. The papers burned. Henry's secret burned with them. As I mounted the stairs, the pressure built, the glass windows blew, and the greedy flames gulped all the air they needed to reduce everything to ash. The evidence, the only leverage against Henry, his only mistake and my only chance, was gone.

I crawled up the stairs, away from the heat, finally managing a few breaths. The dull red smear of an exit sign appeared in the smoke overhead and sharpened as I moved closer. I pressed the bar of a heavy door and stumbled out a rear exit, raising my face up toward a sun that a minute ago I'd thought I'd never see again.

Freedom. At least until I looked down and saw the legion of police, firefighters, EMS, SWAT, and FBI swarming toward me. Everyone in the national capital region with a pair of cargo pants, a crew cut, a bad mustache, or a flashing light had laid siege to this one block of Pennsylvania Avenue, and now they were all storming at me.

If I had a recurring nightmare, this would be it: a flatfoot zombie army. The first guy took me by the arm. It was all over. I was a wanted man and I'd been caught by cops who I was sure Henry could buy off if he hadn't already. I'd just watched my only bargaining chip burn. I put my hands in the air, surrendering.

'Are you okay, buddy?' he asked, then shouted, 'Give me some room here! Get the EMTs. We found him, everybody. We found him!'

Apparently there had been some concern about the missing ATF agent, aka me. They helped me walk outside the riot fence they had up around the DOJ as a blast barrier.

Having this many law enforcement types staring at me made me slightly more uncomfortable than my scalded skin. Putting my hand over my mouth, I gestured for air. They brought an oxygen tank and laid me out on a gurney. I hoped the mask, and the burned hair and soot covering my face, would buy me some time before I was recognized. I felt for it, but the bump on my nose had fallen off or melted.

The EMTs threw ice packs on me. A half a dozen other victims were receiving medical attention, some sitting on the curb, some laid out.

There was another fence, about a hundred feet away, to hold the crowds back. The media had descended and the riot gates bristled with camera lenses. The evacuees were penned in another area. I could see them getting questioned by police and then walking out through a single gap in the fence. That was the only way in or out.

And there was William Marcus, chatting away with one of

the cops as he scrutinized every person leaving the scene. A plainclothes gave him a nod and pulled the fence back for him. He started walking toward the ambulances, toward me.

My ATF ruse may have been enough to get me past the cops but not past Marcus. I was hoping some turn for the worse – shock, cardiac arrest, anything – would have them throw me in the ambulance and get me out of there, but I couldn't will a medical catastrophe or fake my vitals.

Marcus looked into the faces of the police, of the other victims, as he approached. I tried to sit up, to get off the gurney, and the EMT – a guy with a ponytail and hands like vises – clamped me back down.

Marcus was walking directly to me. I stared straight up, and prayed he'd pass. But he never even arrived.

When I looked back he was gone. I turned and saw him walking toward the fence. Henry Davies was beckoning him away. They talked for a moment, then started across Pennsylvania, to a man standing beside a black sedan.

He stepped into the car with them, then the car drove away. It was my father.

Chapter Twenty-Five

The medic brought me to George Washington University Hospital. The triage area for the ER was overcrowded and chaotic, and I was able to slip away while waiting for the EKG tech to show up. After returning to the scene of the crime (apparently my new specialty) I picked up my car near the DOJ and set out to determine what the hell my father had gotten himself into.

He and I had made a deal before I set out that morning: I would do all the heavy lifting, and he would stay back.

But I guess I should have known: never trust a grifter's word. Granted, he'd saved my ass, but now I wasn't sure if I could save his.

I drove to the Davies Group mansion, and cruised past, peering up at Henry's windows. When he'd had me tied up in there, the blinds had been drawn. Now they were wide open. The office was empty.

So what exactly is the plan here, Mike? Raid the castle, take Henry's head, and rescue Dad like some shining knight? Not likely. I was doing a number on my fingernails, chewing away, running through the angles when my phone rang.

'Mike,' the voice said.

It was my dad.

'Where are you?' I asked. 'You okay?'

'The Bel-Air Motel on New York Avenue. Been better, but at least I got away. Got a car?'

'I'm on my way. Any heat?'

'Not that I can see,' he said. 'Sooner the better.'

I knew the guy was a stoic, so the distress in his voice, the uneasy strain, had me worried.

I hauled ass over to New York Ave. I knew that area. The front door to DC along the Baltimore-Washington Parkway, it was about as nasty as it comes, all druggie hotels and empty industrial buildings

The Bel-Air was a world-class dive: whores working out in the open, sheets across the windows, crackheads begging or selling stolen shit – it always seemed to be packs of socks – to the cars stuck in traffic.

But, hey, free HBO. Some drug dealers mean-mugged me as I walked across the parking lot to the room where my dad had said he was holing up. The door was open, the lock forced.

I found him inside, aiming a gun at me. He dropped it as soon as my face showed. He lay on the bed on his left side. A wad of napkins, soaked red, stuck to his right shoulder.

The smell of coffee filled the room. Like father, like son. 'Want some?' he asked. 'Made a pot while I waited. Fixed me right up.'

I helped him sit up. A drop of blood ran from his ear.

'Henry did this?'

He nodded.

'Is he around?'

'Maybe. They had me in one of the warehouses. I got away.'

'Can you walk?'

'I ran when I needed to, but I'm feeling a little shaky now. Maybe you want to help me down the stairs.'

I draped his arm over my shoulders and we walked along the back of the motel to my car. His shirt lifted up. I saw red welts along his back, over his kidneys.

'I'll get you to a hospital.'

'I think I'm good, Mike,' he said between short breaths. 'Cartwright has this doctor, well, more of a veterinarian – good surgeon, bad gambler – who owes him. He'll take care of me.'

I eased him into the front seat of my car. There was no sign of Henry or Marcus. We pulled off New York Ave. onto the surface streets, heading to the reservoir and Washington Hospital Center.

'You'll get picked up if you go into a hospital, Mike. There's always cops. I'm doing better than I look. Don't worry about it.'

I kept driving to the hospital. I wasn't going to argue with him.

'What happened?' I asked.

'I saw they were going for you, so I stepped in. I told them you already had the evidence.'

'I lost it, Dad,' I said, shaking my head with shame. 'Marcus burned it.'

'That's fine,' he said. He didn't seem fazed at all. 'I just said that to get him clear of the scene, to get you a little breathing room. Henry has the same weakness we all do. He'll believe what he wants to believe: that everyone has a price, everyone wants to make a deal. We can use that against him. So I told him we wanted to bargain.'

'What deal?'

'Nothing. Once we were clear of DOJ, I shut him down. He was' – my dad made a flapping lips gesture with his hand – 'about sending me to prison, lethal injection, going down for the Perry murder.

'I didn't bite. I wasn't going to let him use me to lever you. So they brought me over to some old shipping warehouse, and Marcus went to work.'

He grimaced, twisting in his seat. 'He's a real artist, that guy.'

'What were they going to do?'

'They said they'd kill me if I didn't bring you back to them, to strike a deal for the evidence. I said they could go right ahead. That pissed him off something proper. Thin skin.'

'I don't think Henry is used to hearing no.'

'I could tell Marcus wanted to take it easy, but Henry just kept barking at him. "More! More!" I was half blacked out, so . . .' He shrugged. 'Not so bad. I think Henry stepped in himself at the end.'

He groaned. 'Oh, fuck.'

'What is it?'

'Back here and here.' He pointed just above his butt and down toward his groin. 'Kills. Just drop me at the hospital and go. Give Cartwright a call. Tell him we don't need the vet and you just leave me out in front of the ER.'

His face was white. He couldn't stop shivering.

'We're almost there, Dad. Hang on.'

'I beat it out of there,' he said, his eyes shut now. 'The way I figured it, I was the only leverage he had on you, so with me off the table, you could take him down, no deal. I ran. Either I would get away or I would die trying. Same difference in the big picture.'

'Not to me. How'd you get out?'

He reached into his pocket and handed me a tooth, a canine flecked with red. I looked at his mouth. It wasn't his.

'Still got a few tricks left,' he said. 'The good news is, Mike, he's scared of that envelope. I guess there are plenty of people out there looking to get back at him, but no one has the goods.'

'Neither do I, Dad. It burned. I fucked it all up. I've got nothing.'

He waved that away. 'That doesn't matter. Henry thinks you got it.' The beating he took to keep quiet assured him of that.

I pulled the car up to the hospital, then shouted to the nurses by the emergency room doors. One look at my father and they rushed him in on a stretcher. I followed alongside.

'Dad. You shouldn't have done it.' He'd put himself in Henry's hands to get me out.

'Fiddle game,' he said and smiled: swap something worthless for something prized.

'No, Dad. Not at all. You shouldn't have given yourself up. This is too much.'

'It's what you do for your family,' he said.

He kept his hand on mine as they admitted him. His words and the ringing telephones inside the ER reminded me, but I think I'd already known it. He sacrificed himself for me, the same way he'd sacrificed himself for my mother.

The night he was arrested for breaking into that house in the Palisades was so clear in my memory. I'd relived every detail a thousand times, trying to make sense of it. And I knew that there hadn't been a phone call taking my dad away. I remember from the trial there wasn't even a phone in the house he broke into. My mother had come back at least an hour before my dad left, 'for a baseball game,' he'd told me.

No. Perry was dead before he got there. My mother was a fighter, and when Perry had tried to force her, she'd knocked him onto that hearth. She'd killed him. Everything my father had done – never saying a word in his defense during that long trial, leaving his family for sixteen years, surviving in that hell – he'd done for her, taken the fall to protect her, the same way he'd sacrificed himself to Henry Davies for me.

I could never sneak anything past my father when I was a kid; you try putting one over on a con man. And as he looked up at me and saw that holy-shit look of comprehension on my face, I knew he knew.

'Thank you, Dad. I love you.'

'You too,' he said. 'But don't get all sappy. I'll be back out of here in an hour, good as new.'

His hand was cold. A doctor picked up a phone and ordered a crash something and eight units of O positive.

'I lost the evidence. I let you down, Dad. I'm sorry.'

'It doesn't matter, Mike. We've got him scared. Pig in a poke. Play the man, not what's in your hand.'

I probably said a couple more sappy things. He humored me. Then they wheeled him up to surgery.

One of the cops working the waiting area would not stop strolling by and checking me out. He walked over to a colleague for a little parley. I wasn't going anywhere, though, until I knew what was happening with my dad.

Cartwright showed up a half an hour later. 'How is he?' he asked.

'In surgery. I don't know.'

'This place is crawling with police,' he said. He nodded toward the far doors at the end of the corridor. I took the long way around and checked that hallway. Sure enough, there was my friend Detective Rivera, the cop who had betrayed me. God knows how many other goons Henry and Marcus had descending on this place.

I circled back to find Cartwright. 'You need to get out of here,' he said.

'I'm not leaving him.'

'There's no point in you handing yourself over to the police, Mike.'

'I won't go.'

'I'll take care of him,' he said. 'Your father and I go way back. I'll get him through this.'

I heard the door open at the far end of the hall, and Rivera led a pack of what looked like plainclothes cops toward us. We ducked around the corner.

Cartwright grabbed my shoulder. 'Get the hell out of here. I'll take care of your dad. You get whoever did this to him.'

I'd lost my only means of taking Henry down, but that didn't matter. I had to find another way to stop him.

The police moved closer. I held on, refusing to run. Cartwright grabbed my shoulder again. 'Go!'

I started off and just missed the cops by darting through a service door. They'd swarmed over the hospital. It took a half an hour of sneaking around corners and hiding in empty rooms to end-run around them as they swept the surgery wing.

But I couldn't leave yet. I had to see my father again, to know he would make it. I found a call room, cracked the door, and stole some sleeping resident's coat and stethoscope off the hook inside. I headed back to my father's wing, my face down, buried in some papers I'd pulled from the coat pocket.

I came through an inner hallway into the surgery wing, striding past two cops who were scrutinizing all civilians but seemed blind to anyone in white. I walked to an empty nurses' station. An older nurse with a grim look approached and asked, 'Can I help you?'

'I need the chart on Robert Ford.'

Apparently the stethoscope did the trick. She didn't question me, just rifled through the hanging files on the counter. 'It's probably with the body over in pathology by now,' she said.

Impossible.

'Could you double-check?' I asked, and nodded toward the computer. She typed his name in. I stepped beside her and read over her shoulder. The screen flickered, the text black on green. I couldn't believe the words as I scanned his record. The last line read: *Transferred – morgue – cold storage.*

'Oh,' she said. 'He's down in the fridge.'

Chapter Twenty-Six

Because of my mistakes, my father was dead, and I had three hours until Rado would come after Annie and get to work on third-world-inspired violations I refused to imagine. My only weapon, the evidence against Henry, was ash.

I had to make a choice. Lose my soul to Henry or lose what I love to Rado. Even if Annie and I managed to duck the Balkan psycho, sooner or later Henry would find out that Annie was still on my side and would use her as leverage against me. There were no secrets from Henry Davies.

Two men wanted me dead, or suffering so badly I'd wish I were. My father had the luxury of not choosing, of taking the honorable death, a martyr to the end. But if I tried that, not only would I suffer, so would Annie, and she was all I had left.

It was an impossible choice. I saw one way out, and I would pursue it with a cold, unfeeling resolve. If the honest men were all criminals, then maybe only the criminals were honest. I had to make a deal. My father may have been gone, but he'd left me the answer. I would deliver myself to my killers and hope I could con my way back out.

After I escaped the hospital, my first stop was the White Eagle, the club where Aleksandar and Miroslav regularly held court.

Black Mercedes sedans lined the two blocks around the building, a beautiful former embassy. I walked up the curving steps to the front door. Thick men in slim suits stopped me cold.

'Tell Miroslav and Aleksandar that Michael Ford is here. Tell Radomir too, if he's around. He'll want to know.'

One goon pressed on his earpiece. A wire trailed from it into his suit. Pretty heavy security for a 'fraternal society'. They frisked me, thoroughly, then dragged me through the salons – the place was full of Euro trash and beautiful whores – to a cozy little room in the basement with a fireplace, a chandelier, and two banquette couches.

Miro and Alex appeared and bound my hands behind my back, then knocked me onto the floor, my face on the carpet. Miro stepped on my bound wrists, pinning me to the ground. He held me like that while they talked about something – I got the sense it was soccer – in a language I didn't understand. They were extremely casual about the whole thing.

Rado arrived a half an hour later, suggesting a freedom of movement pretty bold for someone hiding from a war-crimes tribunal. After some snapping of fingers and barking in what I took to be Serbian, Alex lifted me up to my feet.

'It's very brave what you've done,' Rado said. 'To come here and take your punishment like a man. I'm almost sad to not be able to enjoy the little black-haired one, but this is honorable what you're doing.'

'You want revenge?' I asked.

'This is clear, isn't it?' He smirked, raised his palms, and looked to his accomplices. They nodded.

'I'll help you get it,' I said.

'I have been to this dance before,' Rado said, and smiled, pleased with the Americanism. 'Allow me to hazard a guess.

I've' – he put on a sort of cop-movie tone – 'got the wrong guy.'

'That's the only reason I'd walk in here defenseless. Think about it.'

He stepped very close to me, almost kissing distance, and put his hand gently on the side of my head. He looked into my eyes, and then, with an alarming, sudden strength, snapped my head sideways into what I can only guess was the mantelpiece because I was instantly unconscious.

I wish I had stayed that way. When I came to my wrists were still bound behind my back, but now the ropes around them ran up to a hook on the ceiling behind me. The blow to my head gave everything a swimmy, underwater quality. That made it especially hard to balance. I was standing on a small crate, on the tips of my toes. Any lower, and the ropes tightened, yanking back my shoulders. One was already pretty bad off from my run-in with Marcus at the museum. Whenever I lost my balance, the ropes jerked my arms back, wrenching the sockets.

Alex held the other end of the rope and would periodically, even when I managed to keep my balance, give it a yank.

'A Palestinian hanging,' Rado informed me, ever helpful. 'Known as the *strappado* to Machiavelli, when he received it for conspiring against the Medicis, and the ropes at the Hanoi Hilton. I believe it is how the North Vietnamese deprived Senator McCain of the full use of his arms.'

The only thing worse than torture is torture at the hands of a bore. Whenever I managed to slip into half-consciousness or retreat to my happy place – sleeping in on a cool Sunday with Annie's warm bottom beside me – Rado would break in yammering with another fun fact. Fortunately, they had given me some high-octane painkillers at the hospital for my burns. I'd swiped some more on my way out. Without them, I probably would have just fessed up to the murders I didn't commit and let Rado kill me. Instead, the pain was merely excruciating as I felt the tendons and muscles in my shoulders tear, the bones grind out of place.

'Done well, it leaves no marks,' Rado said. 'And yet it can quite easily paralyze, permanently destroy the feeling in both arms.'

I was almost relieved when he stopped talking and walked behind me.

'It's Henry you want,' I said. 'And Henry wants me.'

Rado came back with a fillet knife, thin and sharp as a razor. One by one, with a few quick cuts, he removed the buttons on my shirt, then spread the fabric, exposing my chest.

'What you are saying does make sense. But as you know, it will need to be corroborated. Trust isn't one of my strong suits.'

He touched the cold tip of the knife a few inches above my belly button and pricked the skin.

'You've heard about the heart thing?' he asked casually.

'Yes,' I said.

'It takes far too much effort to go through the breastbone.' He thumped mine with his fist like it was a hollow door.

'You can keep your victim conscious for more of the experience if you go under the sternum, what's called a subxiphoid incision.'

'I'm offering you a deal,' I said. 'We can help each other.'

'We'll see,' Rado said and pressed the knife against my skin. As he tightened the flesh with two fingers of his other hand, my skin opened cleanly under the knife.

It was a long night with Rado. And that was just my first stop.

The next day, a blue spring morning, Rado and a handful of his favorite goons gave me a lift up to Kalorama, to the

Davies Group mansion, for an appointment with Henry. I believe this is about when you first came into the story. My heart was intact, for the moment.

As they dropped me off, Alex flashed me his Sig Sauer. As if the gun weren't enough, in the backseat Rado lifted a napkin to his lips, still hungering for my heart, to underscore what was at stake.

They waited around the corner while I shuffled my injured body toward the office. Davies Group had shut down for the holiday weekend, leaving only Henry and his war cabinet: the security team who toiled away in parts of the mansion the respectable folks never saw.

Marcus greeted me at the door. I could see the gap where my dad had knocked out his tooth. I hid a smile. As he brought me through security, I could tell his interest was piqued by the metal detector's beeping at my chest. They frisked me, then stripped me, looking for weapons and wires. Henry was too smart to fall for any sting, any electronic surveillance.

Marcus searched my pockets and came out with two sets of fake credentials and something I didn't know I'd been carrying: blueprints for a house, carefully folded, which my father, sleight-of-hand man to the end, must have slipped in my pocket at the hospital.

Even Marcus winced as my shirt came off. The cut was about four inches long, and the skin puckered around the metal. Rado hadn't gone too deep with the fillet knife back at the White Eagle, and the bleeding stopped not long after he picked up what he had at hand – a dependable Swingline stapler – and clamped the wound shut.

It had been a long and strange week, easy enough to catalog from head to toe as I put my clothes back on: the hand burns from the DOJ fire, the facial cuts from the car crash, the two-pronged welt on my neck from the Taser. The hanging had almost dislocated my shoulder. Rado's fresh handiwork stood garish on my chest. The healing puncture wound on my thigh from the night – it felt like a year ago – I'd listened as Marcus executed Haskins and Irin. And my swollen knee, something was definitely off in there, either from one of the falls or from barreling the Volvo through the door.

After I suited up, Marcus pointed to the weathered envelope I was carrying and said, 'Envelope.' He wanted to search it.

'Not until we have a deal,' I said. 'This will go wide if I disappear.'

Marcus escorted me through the concrete corridors of the secure areas, past where Gerald worked his surveillance magic, to Henry's office. Marcus led me in, then stood guard outside.

Davies was at his window, taking in the view. Washington lay at our feet. I knew the bargain he wanted.

He would give me the kingdoms of the world in all their glory for my soul. It would be so simple. Just give in to him, let him corrupt me, and the whole nightmare would be over. No worries about Rado and his fillet knife, or about Annie's safety.

He wanted a deal. He wanted to feel like he owned me again. And I was afraid, not of all the physical threats laid out against me, but of not being strong enough to resist Henry's promises, his practiced manipulations that had slowly, insidiously consumed this town. I feared that he would turn me, that I would do anything he said, that, now that I understood the price of honesty – my father's life, Annie's pain – like all men I would happily choose corruption.

I couldn't let that happen. I had to beat him at his own game.

Henry sat me at the far end of his conference table and leaned over me. 'Just say it and all this is over. Come back to us, Mike. It only takes one word: yes.'

Henry wanted me as a protégé, as a son. And I knew he wouldn't let me give up easily. To be worthy I couldn't simply accept his terms, roll over, and beg to be taken back. Henry would only accept a man as cagey as he had been in his young, hungry days, someone playing hard to get.

I placed the sealed envelope on the table. For Henry, it was the one piece of leverage that could take him down: the torn-off lobe of his ear along with the police report that laid out his role in Pearson's death. I had two things he wanted: that envelope, and myself.

'This is the only real trust, Mike,' he said. 'When two people know each other's secrets. When they have each other cornered. Mutually assured destruction. Anything else is bullshit sentimentality. I'm proud of you. It's the same play I made when I was starting out.'

Only I knew who really killed Haskins and Irin. With that and the envelope, I was very dangerous indeed.

My dad was dead, and Henry for now believed that Annie had betrayed me. He had nothing to lever me with. For once, Davies didn't have the overpowering advantage he was used to. It was time for me to get greedy.

'You and Marcus killing Haskins and Irin, owning the Supreme Court. That move was for more than just Radomir's case. That's a long-term investment. How much will it bring in over time?'

Henry smiled, a proud father. He saw where I was going. It's exactly what he would have done.

'Enough.'

'I'm curious,' I said.

'I had a dozen clients with interests in Supreme Court decisions lined up, just to start. Over the next decade, we're talking ten, maybe eleven figures.'

Billions, or tens of billions.

'See, Mike. This was to be my last work for clients. Soft-minded people always ask, How much is enough? How many houses do you need? It shows how limited their vision is, how narrow their wants. The money, the houses, the women a third my age: it's all very nice. But that's never been what it's about.

'After the Haskins job, I would finally have enough. Enough to not have to rely on clients. Sure, I own this town. But I have to finance it by doing others' bidding. Not anymore. No more bowing to others' wishes. With the money that will come in now, I can finally seek my own ends, financed from my own coffers, executed through my own power. This swamp along the Potomac will be my empire, and I will answer to no one. I have only a few loose ends to tie up. That envelope, for one, and the recent regrettable unpleasantness between me and my star senior associate.'

'Partner,' I said.

'We could talk about that.'

'What does a partner bring in? Last year, say?'

Henry tented his fingers. 'We use modified lockstep compensation. I could probably bump you up the ladder a bit, given your contributions. At that point, five to seven million a year. With the money from the Court coming in, next year will be a very good year. Figure four or five times that.'

I thought for a moment. 'I will give you this evidence,' I said, tapping my finger on the envelope, 'and guarantee that you will never have to worry about it again. In exchange, Rado goes away. The police leave me alone. I get my life back. And I become a full partner.'

'And from now on, you're mine,' Henry said. 'A full partner in the wet work too. When we find Rado, you'll slit his throat.'

I nodded.

'Then we're agreed,' Henry said. The devil held his hand out.

I shook it, and handed over my soul with the envelope.

Plink-plink. The noise came from below. It had started a moment before, but now, in the silent room, it was impossible not to notice.

Henry stepped to the window, then circled around to the window on the other side of his office. Rado's Range Rover, and another for his men, was parked outside the hillside entrance to the secure area of the mansion.

'Marcus,' Henry yelled. 'Get in here.'

Marcus arrived, gun drawn and held beside his thigh, but my broken-down ass was the last thing he needed to worry about. The *plink-plinks* now sounded a lot more like the crack of gunfire.

Rado and his men were inside.

Henry pointed to me. 'Tie him up,' he said.

Marcus swept me over his hip and slammed me onto my neck and shoulder blades on the ground before I realized what was happening. He hiked my arms behind my back and handcuffed the right wrist tightly. He ran the cuffs through the handle of Henry's filing cabinets before clamping the other cuff on my left. I was stuck, arms behind me, sitting on the floor.

It could have been worse. After Rado's rope work, I'd made it something of a personal rule never to walk into a likely hostage/torture scenario without swallowing a few pain pills first. It dulled the sharp edges of the encounter nicely. Add to that the numbness, the complete indifference to my fate I'd felt since my dad died, and it made getting tossed around a bit more, the repeat wrenching of an already busted shoulder, seem like no big deal.

Henry and Marcus were too smart to fall for me wearing

a wire, but Henry, as a good former soldier for Nixon, should have known not to wire himself. He glanced up at the bookshelves, where the hidden camera I'm sure he'd used to blackmail dozens of politicians had finally captured him. I guess he'd never had to worry because he controlled it.

He pressed a button on his phone. 'Gerald!' he barked into the speaker. But Gerald, I'm afraid, was unavailable.

Annie, when she'd first heard about my plan for today, was as pesky as a little sister about helping. I wasn't going to let her risk her life. But after she'd said she would simply show up at this little office party, uninvited and uninformed about the dangers, the greater risk would have been keeping her in the dark.

After her performance in the woods with my father and me, taking a punch while chasing me down, she was very much in Henry's good graces. As part of the crew searching for me, and a budding Davies dirty trickster, there would be nothing too extraordinary about her strolling into the secure areas of the mansion.

When I first told her about how Gerald had an omnipresent eye on the private lives of the Davies Group, Annie couldn't place the name.

'Big guy, lots of Star Wars figurines.'

She replied with a nauseated look.

'Sorry.'

She had also noticed Gerald's creepy attention around the office, and today all she had to do was play a little damsel in distress to get him to open the door to the room where he monitored the cameras around the mansion. The 100,000-volt stun gun I'd given her took care of the rest. She cuffed up Gerald (two pairs, double locked, just in case), then, via an off-the-shelf wireless intercom, piped the audio/video from Henry's office to Rado in his car.

Sure, once I said yes and shook Henry's hand, he finally owned me. But once he acknowledged killing Irin and Haskins when he thought I was just haggling over my price, I owned him. Rado was listening, and that's all it took to redirect his vengeance to the proper target: Davies.

The gunshots picked up, closer now, answered by the distinct *rat-a-tat* of an assault rifle going full auto.

I certainly wasn't a fan of Rado the war criminal. I'd told Annie to get out of the building as soon as Henry said the magic words that revealed to Rado that he'd killed Irin. Rado's men advanced through the hidden stairs and corridors of the mansion, and I really didn't have a dog in this fight. I wanted to make sure Henry's men were wiped out, so I'd given Rado the basic layout, but not too easily, so I'd kept a few things from him. Mostly, to borrow a line from Kissinger, I was hoping both sides would lose: Henry and Rado. I wanted casualties more than anything else.

Henry wasn't happy about the armed invasion. He walked over to the table, glowering at the envelope. I was sure he was angry at getting taken, but there was more to it than that, a sense of betrayal as well.

Behind all the posturing and power, he was a lonely guy. His wife he'd more or less purchased. No kids. Nothing in his life but work. Instead of friendships he had complicities, and the only trust he knew was the uneasy suicide pact that came when two men had the goods on each other. He wanted a protégé, a son, but I sure as fuck wasn't going to join him in that hell.

He lifted the evidence.

The pig in a poke is one of the oldest and simplest cons. You sell someone a pig and give them a bag (known way back when as a poke) with something else inside.

It's a risky play, typically a stupid move. But I had a few

things going for me. My dad had held out under a fatal beating to protect the evidence, so Henry would assume I had something.

But that was only part of it. Henry was blindingly obvious about what he believed. We swindlers don't believe in anything, really. But we can clue in pretty quickly to what someone else does. And if some mark believes unfailingly in one truth, you can bet your ass we're going to find a way to use that truth against him. Henry wasn't shy about trumpeting his one true maxim: everyone can be gotten to, everyone has a price. He had faith in one thing: treachery. It was his strength, sure, but I was going to make it his weakness. There was no such thing as honesty in Henry's world. He had to believe he could own me, that I, like every other man, could be corrupted. So I let him. The envelope didn't matter. I wasn't playing my hand, I was playing Henry.

Now, as Marcus ducked through the false panel into the corridor that led to Henry's vault, Davies picked up the envelope. He opened it and emptied it onto the table.

A slice of dried apricot slid out, and behind it, floating down, came a menu from the White Eagle. (Radomir, God bless him, had offered me an actual human ear to make the whole ruse more realistic. 'It's really no problem at all,' he'd said. I declined.)

'There is no evidence, Henry,' I said. 'Marcus burned it at the DOJ.'

The gunfire was close now. A bullet exploded through the molding of the panel. Plaster dust and splinters sprayed through the room.

'Radomir heard everything.' I looked up toward the camera hidden in the bookshelves. 'He knows you killed his daughter.'

I'd seen Rado's old-world style on display in Colombia, of course. But it had been Henry who tipped me off to just how dangerous a man who lives only by blood and honor can be in Henry's world of calculated greed and fear.

Back at the White Eagle, I stuck to my story even after Rado opened up my skin. I guess that was enough to convince him I wasn't lying, and he was game to listen to my plan. If I could back up my claim that Henry had killed his daughter, if I could get Henry to admit to the crime, I could just let Rado's charming brand of psychotic violence do the rest.

He may have been a war criminal, but he at least had a code, a thief's honor, that in its way made him more honest than the seemingly respectable men Henry whored out every day.

Henry had fucked with Rado's daughter, the same way Henry had fucked with my dad, and Henry was about to realize that the one truth that defined his world was false. Certain things were priceless. Certain men couldn't be bargained with.

'You ingrate fuck,' Henry said. 'I offered you everything. I offered you this city on a platter. And when you come at me, you don't even have the decency to do it like a man. You hide behind Rado?'

I was still bound to the cabinet. He stood over me, seething.

'That cunt Annie.' He smiled. 'I see. The two of you, still together. Now it all makes sense.'

He looked toward the door.

'I'll be back in a few minutes. She'll suffer first. You'll watch. And then it's your turn. You think you've found a way out, Mike? Think I can't get to you? No. You've only made it worse. You'll beg me, plead for it to stop. You'll give me everything I want and more.'

He kicked me hard in the face with his wingtip. The room briefly fuzzed out like an old TV, but I stayed conscious. By now gunfire and screams surrounded Henry's suite.

Davies pulled a pistol from a drawer in his sideboard and stepped through the false panel in his wall into the corridor by the vault. I spit some blood out, trying for a nice long arc but succeeding only in dribbling it down my shirt.

The painkiller was wearing off. To keep a clear head, I'd taken only one. So I had better be quick about it. The handcuffs hit right above the bones of my hand. They were too tight, double-locked, with the keyhole facing away from my fingers, so I wouldn't have been able to jimmy it even if Marcus hadn't already taken everything off me I could have used as a pick.

The shots came louder now. Practically in the room. I heard a groan. The handcuffs weren't getting any wider. My hand would just have to get smaller. I pried my left thumb back with my right hand, felt the pressure build, the bone flex, just barely. I let go. I was going to make myself pass out. It felt so creepy and wrong. The Band-Aid approach, then.

I jerked back my thumb. The bone cracked like kindling. The room went all wavy once more, and I squeezed the hand through, raking the cuff over the broken bones. I retched, tried not to throw up from the pain. My hand was free. I stood. The cuff dangled from my right wrist.

Searching the desk, I found that Henry had taken the only gun. I sidestepped to the open panel that led to his vault. The area immediately in front of the door was empty. I heard only labored breathing, no more gunshots.

I moved in deeper and glanced around a corner. There were four or five bodies: Marcus was down, and Rado. Henry had been right. Rado would defend his honor no matter what the cost. It's what I'd been counting on, but Rado hadn't gone far enough. Henry, with the pistol drawn in front of him, stepped over Marcus's corpse, checking the far door for more gunmen. He'd survived massacres before. I couldn't let him survive this. I would have to get behind him and get one of the guns off the bodies. The few pistols I could see, on the floor or in dead men's hands, had their racks slid back, chambers open: out of bullets.

I didn't even see the body stir; Rado played a good corpse. Only his hand moved as he lifted his gun and shot Henry twice through the back of his left shoulder. The old man turned around, grimacing, stumbled back into a trash bin, then sat straight down all the way to the floor, the way a toddler does. He slumped back against the door and, groaning through clenched teeth, emptied a nine-round clip into Rado's prone body.

Nothing angered him so much as a man like Rado, a man he couldn't control. I think the Serb was at least halfway dead before Henry shot him up, which meant he was good and dead now. As I moved past the bodies, Henry realized his anger had gotten the best of him. His gun was empty. He didn't have a second clip.

Davies seemed to suffer with every breath. Rado's round had opened a fist-size hole in his chest. I moved toward him slowly, stepped on his gun hand, and kicked his weapon away. I watched him for a moment.

'I knew you didn't have the stomach for this, Mike,' Henry said in a gruff whisper. It sounded like blood was in his lungs. 'Hiding away, hoping someone else will clean up your mess: your dad, or Rado, even Annie. You think you're some good guy, so moral. But it's cowardice, Mike. You can't kill me.'

He lifted his right hand, beckoning me to help him. 'The cavalry isn't coming, Mike. Nice try, but they're dead. Give me a hand. I'll teach you. Behind that door' – he nodded his head toward the vault – 'is every secret in Washington. It's worth billions. You ran a nice play against me. Help me up. I'll cut you in. Full partners.'

I took his hand and lifted him away from the door.

He smiled. 'That's it, Mike.'

I pulled the thick plastic trash bag out of the bin to my right. Henry looked at it, puzzled. He tried a new gambit.

'You can't kill me in cold blood, Mike. Then you'll be as bad as I am. Corrupt. A murderer. Part of my team in the end. You can't win. Just help me up and we'll run Washington together.'

Henry had a point. I recalled the flood of anger I'd felt when I'd stomped the cop, when I'd thought that Annie had betrayed me, when I'd watched Langford's blood spin through that dialysis machine. I just wanted to give in, to let the rage run unchecked, to destroy everyone in my way. God, it would feel so good.

But now I knew that my father had been telling me the truth when he said he wasn't a killer. No violence. We may have been thieves, but we weren't murderers.

Henry watched me waver. I saw relief in his eyes.

I snapped the bag over his head, knocked him onto his stomach on the ground, and sat on his back while I tightened it over his face with my one good hand. As long as Henry was alive to work the strings, the corruption would never end. I'd never be free.

He clawed at the bag, at me, kicked against the tiles, the bodies beside him: a full three minutes of him moaning and writhing under the plastic. The whole thing was a lot nastier and more exhausting than I'd expected.

I'm sure I could have found a gun with a few rounds left or a clip among the downed men. There were more bodies in the outer corridors. But I needed Henry's eyes. I held on for a long time after his feet made their last feeble kicks against the ground.

'Mike,' I heard someone say, back near the office. I snapped my head around. It was Annie.

I pulled the bag off Henry's head, then threw all the weapons in it. I flipped over Marcus and searched his sticky clothes until I found what I wanted: the papers he had taken off me during the search, the plans for the house my father had dreamed of for his family, but never built.

I took Henry's right arm and dragged him along the floor to the door of the vault. Annie looked in through the false panel.

'Are you okay?' I asked.

She nodded, staring at the bodies, eyes wide.

'Good,' I said. 'I just need a sec.'

She shrank back into the office.

I looked over the vault door: palm print and eye scan. Fancy stuff. I lifted Henry's limp arm and pressed it to the screen. The red light went green. I reached under his armpit, and, though it was a nightmare with my busted hand and shoulder, managed to muscle his limp body up with my knee and good arm. His eyes were wide open, staring, creepy. I nudged his head forward, and got his eye next to the retinal scan. The bolts of his vault retracted with a low mechanical whine.

I let his body drop and opened the door. Files, videotapes, old reel-to-reels lay on the shelves, carefully stacked and indexed. Every secret Henry had collected to build his empire, decades of blackmail and extortion, were there for the taking.

Henry was right. They were all I would need to be everything he was, to control Washington. As I stepped over the man I'd just killed and entered his sanctum, I certainly wasn't feeling like one of the good guys.

Now I had an even better deal. The kingdoms of the world in all their glory, and I wouldn't even have to knuckle under to Henry. All for me. Maybe he was right. Maybe everyone did have a price. Maybe this was mine.

'Mike,' Annie said. She stood outside the vault and looked in terror from one injury to the next on my bruised body.

'Are you okay?'

'Never better,' I said. 'You sure you're all right, hon?'

'Yeah. A little shaken up, that's all.'

'Good.'

I limped over. The best I could manage hug-wise, given my limb situation, was to sort of lean against her. She ran her fingers through my hair.

'What's in there?' she asked, looking at the vault.

'Keys to the kingdom.'

'What are you going to do with them?'

I looked at the bodies, the blood pooling, clotting on the floor. I had an awful mess to deal with, here and at the DOJ, and there was that whole double-murder rap and a handful of other crimes I'd committed while on the run. It would take a whole lot of convincing, a lot of leverage, to get out of this bind with what was left of my skin intact. I stepped back into the vault and started leafing through files. This one was a senator, this one a committee chairman, and here was a police chief.

I'd been running from my father's, from my crooked past, for years, gunning for that respectable life. The crooks turned out to be, in their own ways, honest, and the honest men crooks. Now I had to choose. Should I shut that door and walk away? Let the police chase me down like a criminal and be the only one to know I'd done the honorable thing? Or should I take Henry's throne? Choose corruption, live like a king, and buy all the respect I needed?

I looked around the vault. Washington's secrets now ran through me. I chose neither. I was born crooked, sure, but like my father, I was an honest thief.

I would take them, use what I needed to get out of this, and then I would destroy them.

Annie's cell began to ring. She looked to me, raised the phone. It was Cartwright's number. I answered it.

'He's alive, Mike,' he said.

'What?'

'Your father.'

'What happened?'

'No time. You're at the Davies Group?'

'Yes.'

'You okay?'

'Fine. Annie too.'

'You need backup?'

'Just a way out of here,' I said. 'Everyone else is dead, and this place is about to be swarming with law. Where are you?'

'Turning off Connecticut, toward you, hauling ass. Are the cops there already?'

I checked the far windows. There were two patrol cars out front.

'There's a second entrance,' I said, and steered him to the underground garage Henry and Marcus had dragged me through after they'd picked me up at the museum.

I grabbed trash bags and emptied what I needed from Henry's vault. The two sides – Henry's men and Rado's men – had torn each other apart. We picked through the mess, met Cartwright downstairs, and sped away just as the police arrived to cordon off the Davies Group mansion.

Cartwright filled me in on what had happened at the hospital. The beating had left my father with a retroperitoneal bleed, a hemorrhage in a hard-to-find part of the abdomen. They had had to give him two transfusions before the surgeon could find it and close it. My father was fine, medically, but by then Henry's men had surrounded the hospital. Cartwright realized the only way to get him out was to kill him.

He switched my father's wristband and chart with those

from a guy who had come in after a motorcycle crash and died in the emergency department. A variation on the morgue con, I guess. With Henry's men thinking my dad was dead, Cartwright had enough time to get him to his veterinarian friend. It certainly wouldn't have been my first choice of doctor, but when I finally got to see my father, in the back of a storefront office out near Ashburn, surrounded by barking Pomeranians and squeaking parrots, he seemed okay – white as a sheet, but okay.

'I think you stole something of mine,' my father said, and he put his arm around me.

'Is that how it happened?' I asked, and handed him back the bloodstained plans for the house.

'How'd you get Henry?' he asked me.

'Pig in a poke.'

He nodded. 'Good boy.'

We got to work on building that house. There'd been a healthy bale of cash in Henry's vault. I considered it hazard pay; part of it went toward Quikrete and 2 x 12s, and my father's home took shape.

Any really unforgivable crimes that surfaced in the files from Henry's safe found their way into prosecutors' hands. Where Henry had bent the law, I used the dirt that he'd collected to apply enough pressure to straighten it out once again. That let me sort out some of my own recent misunderstandings with the police and see that Detective Rivera of the Metropolitan Police Department never got his granite countertops.

In the end, we found a good use for all the blackmail material I'd taken from Henry's office. The first bit of construction we did on my dad's new place was a stone fire pit in the back. Once he'd healed up, my father, Annie, and I brought some lawn chairs out in the backyard and got a nice fire going. I brought out all the files and tapes from Henry's safe. We sat around, grilling, drinking a few beers. It was all just right, like my memories of when I was a kid creaking away on the swing set, my parents laughing in the summer night, before my father got sent away. Now we were once more just your typical happy family, except we happened to be burning evidence.

Annie and I had plenty of money left to head someplace warm for a while, then start over somewhere new. It would take a while to get my father fully back on his feet, though, and he and I had a lot to catch up on.

So while I was stuck in DC, I figured I'd make the best of it. I was honest, sure, but I could never fully kick those sneaky habits. And I didn't want to. I'd learned that much. The honest men had gotten me into this mess, and those criminal ways I'd never kicked, the ones I'd inherited from my father, got me out. I could barely remember it now, but there was a time, only a year ago, when I'd busted my ass – two Harvard degrees and a full-time job – with the hope that one day I could get some good done in this brothel of a town.

Everything from Henry's vault was gone. I'd guarded those secrets with my life and seen that every last shred disappeared in the flames. They lived on only in me. Even without the files, the mere knowledge of all those dark histories was plenty potent.

I had to wonder if there was a way to make something good out of all the evil Henry had stirred up. It's an interesting question: How do you go honest in a city run by crooks?

As that house rose up, strange things started happening in the capital. There was less partisan squabbling, less posturing for the next election, less kicking back to special interests. Good bills somehow passed with votes on both sides of the aisle. It was the most productive session Washington had seen in a long time, almost as if each of the most powerful men in town suddenly found himself with a conscience, or maybe a gun to his back.

No one knew who or what was behind it all. And I made damn sure it stayed that way.

Acknowledgments

My wife, Heather, kept me going throughout this risky proposition with her constant encouragement, humor, and patience. My parents, Ellen and Greg, and brothers, Michael and Peter, served as sounding boards and narrative-knot untanglers at every step. Allen Appel was an incredibly generous guide to the genre and the business. Sommer Mathis, Miranda Mouillot, and Kevin Rubino pitched in as readers and plot doctors.

Dr Evan Macosko patiently answered all of my loopy medical questions about faked deaths and the like. Gary Cohen shared his experiences in the world of corporate espionage. Alexander Horowitz helped with background on prisons, as did Elaine Bartlett's memoir *Life on the Outside*. Joe Flood's *The Fires* introduced me to the Halligan bar, which led me to the New York Fire Department's manuals on how to break into anything.

David Bradley gave me my first job at the *Atlantic*, when I was twenty-one, and with it a chance to peek behind the curtains of official Washington. My thanks to him and everyone I worked with at the magazine, especially Josh Green, Jim Fallows, Cullen Murphy, Scott Stossel, Joy de Menil, Ross Douthat, Jennie Rothenberg, Abby Cutler, Terrence Henry, Robert Messenger, and Ben Schwarz. I'm indebted to all the amazing reporters and editors I've met and traded stories with in DC.

My agent, Shawn Coyne, took a gamble on me and helped hash out the idea for *The 500*. I'm extraordinarily grateful for his help and unerring guidance. He and the rest of the team – Justin Manask and Peter Nichols – worked magic to get Mike Ford off the page and into the world.

Reagan Arthur is a writer's dream of an editor. My deepest thanks go to her and Michael Pietsch and everyone at Little, Brown for trusting a first-time author and making this book possible. Copyeditors Tracy Roe and Peggy Freudenthal did a beautiful job tightening up the text and saved me from many errors. I'm indebted to Marlena Bittner, Heather Fain, Miriam Parker, Amanda Tobier, and Tracy Williams for their enthusiasm in spreading the word about *The 500*.

About the Author

Matthew Quirk studied history and literature at Harvard College. After graduation, he spent five years at *The Atlantic*, reporting on crime, private military contractors, the opium trade, terrorism prosecutions, and international gangs. He lives in Washington, DC.